A TENT
FOR THE
SUN

A Story of Extraordinary Love

To Lisa, with Gratitude —
Best wishes!
Enjoy the book!
Mary Ellen Feron

MARY ELLEN FERON

A TENT FOR THE SUN
Copyright © 2013 by Mary Ellen Feron
All Rights Reserved

Cover Design: Jessica Schmelzinger
Interior Formatting: Ellen C. Maze, The Author's Mentor,
    www.theauthorsmentor.com
Author Website: www.maryferonzablocki.com

ISBN-13: 978-1482318005
ISBN-10: 1482318008
Also available in eBook publication

PRINTED IN THE UNITED STATES OF AMERICA

Note to the reader:

A Tent for the Sun is the first of three books in the trilogy based on the author's family history in 19th Century Ireland. In *A Tent for the Sun* we first meet Tom Phalen and Meg Wynn, characters based on the author's third great-grandparents, Michael Maloney and Margaret Webb.

The year is 1835. The place is Glynmor Castle in the valley of Clydagh Glyn, County Mayo, Ireland. The story is one of star-crossed lovers caught up in the class and religious struggles that set the stage for the near destruction of a way of life. The Wynns and the Phalens co-exist peacefully within their designated classes until Meg and Tom fall in love. The lovers' illicit liaison explodes the false serenity of their lives and Meg's father, Lord Jeffrey Wynn, responds swiftly and violently, plunging the lovers into exile. Their life together is threatened from the beginning by a political system that reaches its long tentacles into the very heart of both castle and cottage.

A Tent for the Sun could be any family's story. The characters of Tom and Meg embody their land, their class cultures and their history. Tom, strong and handsome, is a man of quiet depth and fierce loyalty. Lovely Meg is the fine, graceful child of privilege. Filled with passion and adventure, their story takes the reader into the towns and kitchens of Western Ireland where Tom and Meg, each sustained by different faiths, take us on a spiritual journey as they face their uncertain future.

In the second book of the trilogy, *My Tears, My Only Bread*, the devastation of the Great Potato Famine descends like a shroud upon the Phalens and their young family. *My Tears, My Only Bread* builds on the themes of love and sacrifice as the reader follows Tom and Meg into the pit of starvation and despair even to the brink of death.

In the third book, *White Dawn Rising*, the themes of rebellion and oppression in a remote land filled with rich, complex characters sweep the reader into the universal struggles of human existence as Tom and Meg find their love tested in life's crucible. Facing starvation every day, barely living on the charity of friends, Meg is torn between her love for Tom and her need for food and shelter for her children. Danger and intrigue plunge the Phalens beyond the brink in the final culmination of their story. The love so strong in *A Tent for the Sun*, stretched to the breaking point in *My Tears, My Only Bread* is put to its final test as *White Dawn Rising* brings both Tom and Meg to a place of heart-wrenching choices and unlikely redemption.

A Tent for the Sun will be followed by:
My Tears, My Only Bread (expected February 2013)
White Dawn Rising (expected March 2013)

Dedication

Helen Casey Zimmer, my Grammie;
from beginning to end, this is for you.

Acknowledgements:

I wish, with a full heart, to acknowledge all those who made this book possible.

First, and without a doubt, foremost, my beloved husband and long-standing supporter, Ed. Without you, I would never have been able to write a single word. Ever since you put my very first essay in the mail, when I was too shy to do so myself, I have trusted your advice and relied on your support. Thank you. I love you.

Secondly, my sons, Francis and Paul whose personalities and traits, experiences and journeys are infused into some of my characters in ways so intimate and complex that only I, as your mother, can tell. You both are so very precious to me.

I need to say thank you to many friends, who over the years of writing, listened and supported my work. Thank you to the first reader of my first chapter, Meg Stoll; my colleagues in the Labor and Delivery Unit at Sisters of Charity Hospital, who allowed me to read a chapter to them one slow evening and offered some of the most solid encouragement I ever received and didn't take: the suggestion that I quit nursing and just write. I cannot number the times I remembered that advice during the course of this creation. Even before that, I thank my fellow nursing students at Sisters of Charity School of Nursing for appointing me editor of our senior yearbook and giving me the opportunity to hone my skills. I want to thank Tim Denesha, dear Old Bud that he is, forever so gently nudging me throughout the years, sharing his own wonderful stories and poetry, always turning me forward; always believing.

I must credit the leaders of the many writers groups I worked with: Tom O'Malley of Canisius College in Buffalo, New York; Kathryn Radeff of the Just Buffalo literary group; my dear friends and fellow writers, Diane Riordan, Patty McClain and the late Grace McMeneme. I learned so much, writing with you. Diane, you have been beyond supportive and I am so grateful.

I chose certain individuals to read my manuscript with the clear goal of editing and winnowing, correcting and critiquing. I thank my friend, Ann Szumski for starting me off on the right path; Karol Morton, a writer herself, who read the book with a red pen. I thank her for her honesty and holding me to the integrity of the story; Bev Malona and my mother, Joan Feron read the manuscript before it was finished and lovingly badgered me to keep writing once they had reached the end of the pages; my friends Lynne Dulak and Elise Seggau, former editor of "The Cord" at St. Bonaventure University; my sisters, especially Kate who many times kept me from burning my computer my nieces; my cousin Kathy and my daughters-in-law who read the first printed draft and offered such positive response that I persevered in the final push to publish. I particularly wish to thank my male readers, especially my uncle, David Zimmer, whose suggestion to publish the book as a trilogy was the advice that provided the missing piece to the publishing puzzle.

There are many others to thank. Many of these are people I know only slightly or have never met. Thanks go to Allen Abel for his wonderful article in Sports Illustrated which gave me Dan Donnelly's arm and Lane Stewart whose photographs for that article haunted my dreams. It was a high point in my research to speak with Irish writer and former editor at the Evening Herald in Dublin, Patrick Myler who was interviewed for the SI article. His article on Dan Donnelly (The Ring, May, 1998) was kindly sent to me by the author himself to help me include old Dan in my novel. Dan's arm can be found in the third book of the trilogy as a bit of comic distraction in the midst of the potato famine.

I have been writing since I was a child. There is one person without whom the dream would have died on the vine. She deserves a special acknowledgement. When I first began to test my wings and seriously put pen to paper, Sr. Mary Matthias SSJ, now known as Sr. Joan Wagner, believed in me when no one else did. She took a dejected Freshman and calmly, sweetly planted the seed of confidence that has finally bloomed in this work. Sr. Joan, I thank you from the bottom of my heart. You taught me to believe in myself and never let go of the dream. Rich lessons indeed.

Day unto day takes up the story
And night unto night makes known the message

No speech, no word, no voice is heard
Yet their span extends through all the earth,
Their words to the utmost bounds of the world.

There he has placed a tent for the sun.
Psalm 19

CUSHING FAMILY TREE

Lord Bentley Cushing b.1768 d. 1820
1787 m.
Lady Eleanor Mcintosh b. 1769 d. 1835

Beverly b. 1788   Robert b. 1793
1806 m.   1815 m.
Jeffrey Wynn   Adelaide Dubois b.1799, d.1820

Madellaine b. 1820, d.1820

WYNN FAMILY TREE

Lord Henry Wynn b. 1735, d.1820
1767 m.
Lady Rose Carver b. 1750, d. 1815

John b. 1768. Willard b. 1770, Gerald b. 1781 d.1781, Jeffrey b. 1784
1806 m.
Beverly Cushing

Margaret b.1808

MEAHRA FAMILY TREE

Seamus Meahra b. 1743 d.1808,
1765 m.
Monica Shea b.1748, d.1795

Sean b. 1767 d. 1808, Daniel b.1768 d.1809, Terrence b. 1772 d.1834

Clare b.1774 d.1808,
1792 m.
Thomas Phalen

PHALEN FAMILY TREE

Thomas Phalen b.1772
1792 m.
Clare Maehra

David b. 1794   Paul b. 1796   Thomas b. 1796 Francis b.1808, d.1808
1811m.   1816 m.   1835 m.
Molly Quinn   Anna Dunleavy Margaret Wynn

Chapter One

The thin veneer of ice cracked and splintered as the big man stirred his hand in the nearby water. Moments before he had knelt in deathlike silence, staring at his reflection in the shallow pond, as if he searched its depths for a beloved lost treasure. A pair of beautiful gray-blue eyes with long, dark lashes reflected back at him from the clear water but he did not see himself. His gaze fell deep beyond the ice, below the depths to the murky place far beyond the smooth mossy rocks at the bottom of the pond where dwelt images too frightening to form. His broad, handsome face, framed with thick black curls, wore an expression of hopeless pain. Like a thundercloud, his anger shrouded his eyes and rested on the high cheekbones and square jaw. Pregnant with the coming storm, his mouth worked against tears, so ready, so close behind his brow.

With lightning swiftness he struck the smooth water, almost drawing back with the shock of the cold, determined to erase any sensation, any memory of her from his fingertips. He splashed violently, his hand like the body of a drowning man flailing and fighting the water until spent, it carelessly waved and stirred, causing gentle ripples to lap around his aching wrist.

Satisfied that he could no longer feel the warm softness of her neck, sure that the wicked cold had banished forever the sweet fragrance of her hair, he played his fingers gently along the thin misty edge where the icy skin rested lightly on the water. He watched absently as the thin brittle crystals flaked and drifted into nothing, lost somewhere between the death of ice and the birth of water, neither one nor the other.

It was then that he saw himself.

As the water ceased its dance, he caught the look of desperate agony in the eyes that looked up from the depths at him and startled, drew away, scattering tiny flecks of icy foam as he turned.

The cold wind echoed the harsh terrible voices in his head playing and replaying her goodbye. The hard ground beneath his knees hurt him and his hand throbbed with the return of warmth, beating out a dolorous pulse,

"She's gone, she's gone."

He knelt motionless, plunged so deeply into his heart that the world around him receded into a vague hollowness, all sound save his ragged breathing, all feeling but the burning of his blood gone and with it all knowledge and all thought. He was dying and felt dull gratitude for it. Pulse after pulse, breath after breath he willed it to be his last, to die in this glade and to slip oblivious into the water which, pray God, would mercifully cover him with ice.

He felt his death upon him but he did not die. His heart died, shattered like the water's icy coating, but still, he could not die. He knelt still and frozen at the edge of the pond trying desperately to die, losing this battle just as he had lost the battle to have her. Finally, weighing far more than he could remember, he hauled himself up from the ground and began trudging home.

The biting wind quickened his step as he followed the well-worn path away from the pond. He plodded along the bank of the creek listening absently to the steady babble that brought the fresh scent of Derryhick Lough to his father's kitchen door.

This was the creek that flowed anonymously through the years of his life. This was the unnamed eddy in which his mother had bathed him, the pool tucked deep within the rock face untouched by the sun till the day was long. Somewhere sounded the clear cascade of a narrow waterfall carved into the rock of his homeland by the cold hard water of Lough Cullin to the north. For centuries, these waters had coursed through the green countryside around Clydagh Glyn guiding the traveler along the borders of his existence. This day he found himself the stranger, cast into the depths, tortured and lost.

He trod upon a thousand, thousand footprints, all seeking the water of life. He himself had placed both bare sole and brogue along this path for almost forty years. In this twilight, he had found himself here again hammered by a frigid wind as he had sought meaning and refuge, refreshment and harsh catharsis countless times before. He was unaware he even sought, so grave was his pain. He hastened, unfeeling of the drafty chill howling around the ancient sycamore. The boughs of the giant yews seemed to seek him, bending and reaching in futile embraces. He would not be drawn into their shelter. He braced against the wind that caused their graceful gathering. Suddenly freezing, he hugged himself tightly, realizing vaguely that he had no coat. Hot tears began to sting his eyes when he remembered that he had left it at Meg's.

A queer sense of lightness pervaded his body when he realized that he would have to go there to retrieve it and he felt a sudden urgency to get home.

Old Thomas Phalen hardly stirred in his chair when his son entered the cottage. His eyesight was poor but he knew it was Tom who had come in and sighed a prayer of thanksgiving. He also knew by the sound of the heavy brogues on the threshold that things did not go well. Old Thomas simply waited, his face toward the waning fire. He knew Tom would tell him everything in his own time.

Thomas had been waiting for Tom to come in since a man on horseback had galloped up to the door and thrown his coat onto the stoop hollering an epithet, which he did not make out. He had hung the coat on the third hook in from the door, the second hook being his own and the first hook always reserved for the unexpected guest. Then he had poured the last drop of last fall's whiskey, picked up his pipe and sat down. He dared not look in the direction of the empty coat on the hook for fear that the fairies would fill the sleeves with a scourging itch. He knew they were about and up to no good this day and he prayed for the safe return of his boyo.

When Young Tom approached the hearth his father turned and squinted to make out the familiar form.

" 'Tis a turrible thing when yer own boyo don't come home 'a time to put a log upon th'fire and yer bones that sore and tired that ye can't lift th'bugger out o' the box yerself. And then t'have t'go to th'door and be pickin' up his coat off th'stoop, 'tis a turrible thing indeed. So, where was ye all this time Tommy me lad, it was that worried I was that I had to take me last drop o' the craithur with me pipe."

Young Tom dropped, shivering, onto his knees before the low amber glow, and put another brick of turf on the fire. His father, in an effort to ease the reality of their poverty, always referred to the turf bricks as 'logs', his whole life denying the truth that there had never been a real log on his hearth, not even on Christmas Day.

"So, what did he say?"

In response, Tom merely shook his head, and his father, intuitive and patient, quietly waited for him to begin. The smoke from the new peat filtered out into the room long before the warmth reached Tom's frozen feet and hands. After a long time of poking and prodding the fire, he shifted to face his father and with his head in his hands, his fingers wrapped tightly in his hair, began to tell his story.

"The answer is no. He wouldn't even consider it. I'm lucky he didn't kill me."

Old Thomas pulled on his pipe, drawing in the sweet pungent sponc smoke and absently puffing little rings over Tom's lowered head.

"Did ye see the girl, then?

"Yes I saw her! I saw how her face was bruised and how he had beaten her. I saw how she cried and how her mother held her in her chair so she couldn't come t'me. Oh, Da! I thought I'd kill 'em both if I'd had a gun."

His breath came in loud gulping sobs, like an abandoned child, for despite the sympathetic arm of his father wrapped tightly around his shaking shoulders, he felt abandoned and cried as if he'd never stop, while Thomas, still pulling on his pipe, stared dry eyed into the hearth.

After what seemed like hours, Thomas became aware of a chill in the room, and rousing Tom from his reverie, he inched his way out of his chair and labored to his feet.

"'Tis a curse this damp weather. I don't remember when it was this cold this late in th'season. Put another log on the fire, there's a good lad."

Placing his clay pipe on the mantel as delicately as he would a rose, he turned to Tom, who had not moved from his place on the floor, and said, "I'll not be havin' ye set there and die this very night, and me with an empty stomach. Come on now, boyo we'll eat well if nothing else tonight."

Tom, beginning to realize how hungry he was stood up and stretched his arms over his head. The name "Young Tom" which he had been given at birth, being the son of a Thomas and the grandson of another, was hardly appropriate now. At thirty-eight years and standing over six feet in his bare feet, Tom was one of the biggest men in Clydagh Glynn. He had long since outgrown the diminutives of "Lad" and" Boyo" but his father knew nothing else to call him.

"What is there to eat?" asked Tom rummaging around for another peat brick.

"Oh, we have a feast tonight. Paulie was here this mornin' with Philip. He's on his way into Clydagh Glynn t'pick up his post. Millie O'Boyle sent word that yer sister-in-law, Anna, had a parcel from her sister. He plans t'stop here tomorrow and take me fer a visit up th'lough t'see the children. "By some miracle of clever hordin' Anna found enough to make a shepherds pie, no meat in it of course, but plenty of tatties, and not them awful lumpers either, mind you, and the turnips still left from her own little garden."

Hesitating, he added, "And Philip brought a beautiful trout. By all the saints, that boy has a magical way with fish."

Tom scowled. He did not like Philip, his brother's adopted son. Paulie and Anna had a houseful of wonderful children and they treated Philip like one of their own. He was a good lad, and Tom did not really know why he disliked him, but he had never been able to warm up to the boy.

"That he does, but I don't like th'way he's been behavin' around little Julie."

"Now, Tom,"

His father set brown bread on the low bench that served as a table.

"She's only a child of nine and Philip is just a boyeen."

Tom began to speak, but his father cut him off.

"We have had this speech of yers b'fore."

"And with good reason!"

Tom shouted, scattering ashes and embers across the hearthstone.

"Don't I know what he's thinkin' when he looks at her with her pretty little red head and blue eyes? Don't I know how he's loved her since th'day she was born and him the only one there t' help Anna birth her? Who better than I t'see the danger? Good Christ bless us, Da! Am I not dyin' on me own cross because I loved a girl and wasted me whole life waitin' fer her t' become a woman? I tell ye! 'Twas a mistake th' day me brother brought him into his house, as kind a man as he was t'do it. He'll rue th'day when Philip comes t'him like I came t'you, a father with no right t'be called one, full o'regret and no hope of ever marryin' the mother of me own babe!"

"But Tom, ye know it's a different story entirely. Ye niver stood a chance of marryin' Lady Meg Wynn. Ye led, God bless ye, with yer heart all these years and she was niver fer ye, Boyo! Oh, Tom we've had this talk in spring and in fall, over and over since ye were twenty-four years old and she a child of thirteen!

6

Me old heart is broken fer ye both and now the wee bastard. Mother of God bless ye. I can't help ye now."

Tom approached his father, a look of such black rage on his face that the old man caught his breath. His voice an ominous whisper, Tom hissed at the older man.

"Don't ever call me babe a bastard or so help me God, I'll niver darken yer door again."

With this he slammed across the tiny room, yanking the thin sheet that passed for a door between the living quarters and sleeping cubby in their drafty little cabin. Alone he lay on his back, and looked at his ceiling and began to torture himself remembering the first afternoon he had spent in this room with Meg.

She had been home only a month from an extended stay in London. Tom had just finished loading her mother's stallion, Bay Rum into the wagon that would carry him to Lord Robert Cushing's stables in Killarney. This horse was Lady Wynn's prize and she was taking him to breed with Morning Glory, her brother Robert's beautiful chestnut mare. Lord Robert Cushing had always held the beauty of his horses over his sister's head while she had always argued that the breeding of hers was far superior to any Robert had in his stable. Together they had created three beautiful steeplechase winners over the years. Despite his strength and speed, Lady Wynn would never expect her beautiful animal to trot alongside the big Double Brougham that would carry her and her husband Jeffrey to Cushing House.

Tom had met Lady Meg inside the stable. It was early February and very cold. The sky promised a storm in the afternoon. Lady Beverly Wynn had been very harsh with him that morning, particular to the point of obsession, that Bay Rum's grooming and feeding be perfect, and his shoes be examined still one more time.

Tom had been impudent that day, remarking about Bay Rum's undeniable endowments. Lady Beverly was generally frank and unabashed when discussing horseflesh with other breeders, but never failed to be embarrassed when the handsome Irish groom overstepped her invisible lines of propriety. Already irritable due to her husband's plan to join her on this trip, Lady Wynn was not in the least amused. There was something knowing in Tom's wide open smile that forced her to look away and it irked her that this insolent peasant could affect her so.

Still chuckling at his humorous little jibe Tom watched his mistress stalk across the wide yard and slam the kitchen door. He muttered that she would surely tickle a Chinaman's head if she hit the dirt with her umbrella any harder. A shuffle and a stifled giggle brought him around to face Lady Meg, who had witnessed the little exchange between her mother and the groom with great amusement.

"That, good sir is not the way to keep this job you so badly need," she said with an impish smile.

He smiled back, flushing a deep shade of crimson. Silently cursing his shyness, he walked away from her, tripping and stumbling on a rake in his haste.

"Divil!"

He rubbed the place on his forehead where the rake had struck him and feeling the warm stickiness of his blood he cursed again, this time bringing her to his side.

"Here! Oh, my! You're hurt. Let me see it, here take my hankie."

She took his face in her hand and dabbed at his left brow where blood flowed out of an ugly gash.

Throwing off her hands, he took a large rag out of his pocket and wrapped it around his head, hands trembling, struggling to control the effect of her touch.

"I'll thank ye not t'trouble yerself with me no more m'Lady," he said, his back turned to her.

"Tis enough trouble we've had fer one mornin. Please m'Lady, go on inside, it's not right fer ye te be wanderin' around th'stables dressed as ye are in yer nice things."

He was babbling and could feel his face hot beneath the rag. Were there a door in the floor of the stable he would have happily dropped through it.

"Nonsense, these are not my nice things! These are my riding clothes and you know it. Now, if you are so anxious to rid yourself of me then saddle up Jewel and I will be gone."

Head throbbing and face burning, Tom led the gelding out of the stall and put the bit in his mouth. His embarrassment was childish, he knew, and it only compounded his misery to acknowledge it. He had been in love with Lady Meg since he had first come here as a stable hand in the spring of 1821 when Lady Meg was only thirteen. Fourteen years had passed as he watched her grow up before his eyes. The time had only increased his pain and strengthened his resolve that she would never know how he felt about her.

The last four years she had been in England where she had cared for her grandmother, Lady Eleanor Cushing, widow of Lord Bentley Cushing, long regarded as one of England's foremost authorities on racehorses. Lady Cushing had died on New Year's Day, and Lady Meg had returned home to carry on the tradition of her mother's family, with a new interest in horses, displeasing her mother and amusing her father, Lord Jeffrey.

Tom had missed Meg terribly during those years, the memory of her loveliness burning in his mind day and night. When he finally believed himself beyond the regrets and the fantasy of what might have been, she returned, older and more beautiful than ever. Since her return, she had been in the stables every day, underfoot and filled with an enthusiasm and expertise he found admirable in Lady Beverly but disconcerting in Meg. She was full of questions and seemed intent on engaging him in endless conversations about every aspect of raising horses. He privately cherished their brief meetings in the morning when she rode and in the afternoon when he and old Ben took their break, she always found time to quiz them on some matter of great interest to her.

Naturally a shy man, Tom found each encounter with Lady Meg both pleasurable and uncomfortable. Despite his air of indifference, and Ben's constant silent presence, he feared he would somehow slip and reveal how he really felt about her. He loved her deeply and knowing how impossible and hopeless this was, his days were a torment, a constant battle of will over desire. But his days were nothing to compare with his nights.

At night he was tortured as he thrashed and tore at his meager bedclothes at once hot and cold, sweat soaked and chilled, in an agony of longing so powerful it brought him to his feet more than once and sent him out into the night in vain search of release.

He knew that he could wait no longer and both the thought of leaving her and the fantasy of having her were intolerable, leaving him to drag on in a state of half death, gray and exhausted, eating little, sleeping less, finding solace only in the evening visit to McPhinney's for a pint. It was on the slow walk home from McPhinney's that he would share some of his pain with his father, unable to resist the gentle enquiries of that good and kind man.

But this day he would end it. This cold blustery day in February 1835 he would either have her or die, because his life was over either way and he could stand no more.

As he took the horse out into the light the pain in his forehead began to throb anew, and he said, in a voice rasping with emotion,

"M'Lady, I thank ye for treating me so kindly. I believe me head will recover, but if ye ever lay yer hands on me again I can't promise I'll be behavin' like a gentleman toward ye ever again. Before ye came home, there was no place fer me but these stables, so well do I love yer mother's horses, but, I'm a fool and I've lost me heart to ye m'Lady."

He took a deep breath and continued quickly, before he lost his nerve.

"I've loved ye since th'day I met ye but I'm not fool enough t'think ye'll have me so there's nothing to it but fer me t'go."

Breathing began to be painful and he could feel the blood rushing to his head as he hastened to finish what he had rehearsed a thousand times in the dark of night.

"So, I'll not be here after this day. When ye return from yer ride I 'll take Jewel inside and rub him down but after yer mother and father leave fer Lord Cushing's, I'll be packin' me things and leavin' th'job to old Ben."

A faint nervous smile began to spread across Meg's face as she mounted Jewel and took the reins from Tom's outstretched hand. Without a word she turned and rode off at a full gallop toward the path leading into the woods.

As he watched her round the curved hedge and disappear from sight he felt a weight on his chest as heavy as a boulder and barely breathing walked in the other direction to wash his wound in the frigid waters of the pond.

Meg rode hard for a long distance and then reined in her horse with a start. Sitting perfectly still in the middle of the bridle path she drew in one deep shuddering breath and dismounted. Taking Jewel by the bridle she began to walk slowly through the towering yews, the soft footfall of her horse the only sound. The morning was gray and frosty, the birds remarkably quiet. As she wandered through the woods, the path curved toward the creek. Jewel's breath steaming warm against her ear, she began to relax and her heart slowed its pounding in her temples.

What had he said? What were his exact words? She groped through all of the words he had spoken in the yard sorting them each carefully and putting them in order so as to mistake no inuendo, misinterpret no double entendre. She knew that without this position in her father's stables, Tom Phalen and his father would starve. She tried to ignore the implication of his words, the raw passion in his voice as he said them. But there was no mistaking what he had said. He was not one of the lecherous old men who felt it their privilege to dally with her at one of her father's soirees, nor was he one of the many young dandies who had played the gallant gentleman while she had made the obligatory social calls with her grandmother.

This was a real man who spoke his piece and left it lying at her feet to take or leave as she willed. Here was a man who would risk the wrath of her father by speaking to her so. He was poor, even with his steady work in the stables. How dared he risk punishment, banishment even gaol by blurting out his feelings like that in the stable yard? Only a man overcome by passion, undaunted by danger would expose himself the way Tom Phalen had just done. This was indeed a man of substance.

She had thought it all along and she had been right. How was it that a man of such low birth and such a meager existence could ever become so brave, so forthright, so reckless? She marveled at this new Tom Phalen, and yet she believed his profession of love, for hadn't she seen him grow in stature right before her very eyes right there in the windswept yard of her father's house?

She was sure he had no idea how she felt about him. She had never encouraged him but she had almost lost her resolve many times and thinking distance would rid her of her fierce attraction to him, had begged her mother to send her to London when her grandmother became ill.

How she had wept on the journey! How she had regretted her decision when she realized how long she would be away from him. The time, the men Lady Cushing had foisted upon her, the long rainy days and cold restless nights had only increased her desire a hundredfold. She had studied and learned everything she could about horses and prayed that he would still be there when she returned.

When she thought she could stand it no longer, Lady Cushing had suffered a stroke and Meg thought she would soon be set free from her terrible bondage.

It was then that the worst trial began. It was then that she had been forced to stay at her grandmother's bedside hour after interminable hour, enduring her frantic cloying and garbled demands. The servants resented Meg's ministrations and her grandmother would have no other caretaker. Exhausted, with almost no help, Meg had lost weight and fallen into a deep silent void where all light was filtered through gauze curtains and all sound was hushed.

She had hated the doorway the most, for it lied to her of escape. She shuddered even now as she remembered the nausea she had felt as she leaned into the doorframe of the sickroom, desperate to run from the smell of death and the crushing boredom of her endless repetitive tasks.

She stopped in her tracks as faint nausea returned, and her knees weakened as she recalled in vivid detail the image of herself alone, terribly lonely, imprisoned in that windowed tomb, with no exit and no relief.

She had loved her grandmother, but this shrewish pointed face was not the face she had kissed and laughed with. Meg had always enjoyed her grandma's company, and had often thought herself like her, but now she buried her face in Jewel's neck to rid herself of the memory. She could see the withered finger darting out of the ruffled peignoir, piercing, demanding, tapping out its vile code on the nightstand. Meg had wept with guilt that she could hate with such venom this broken, pitiful woman she had once loved.

One year and three days this sentence had been imposed upon her. The day of Grandmother Cushing's funeral was the first day of Meg's new life but when the black buggy finally did come to rescue her, Meg knew it was a hansom cab. Instead of Tom, the driver would be a hired coachman. The only passengers were her mother and Reina, her mother's maid.

Lady Beverly, who had never been fond of either her mother or her daughter, took charge of all the arrangements, indifferent to the wishes Lady Cushing had expressed to Meg before she became incapacitated.

Meg's mother cared only that she be back in Ireland soon enough to breed her prize stallion and had never once indicated that she had missed Meg or regretted the terrible length of her exile.

Lord Robert Cushing, Lady Beverly's brother and only kin, had been abroad and sent word that he would not be able to return for several days. This upset both Meg and Beverly, because Robert had genuinely loved his mother and would have lent some measure of dignity to the old lady's memory, as well as taking charge of the details of the funeral and the legal papers. The fact that her father did not even come for the funeral had not surprised Meg. Over the years, Lord Jeffrey had become increasingly estranged from the lives of his wife and daughter.

Meg shook off a chill as she realized how far her thoughts had wandered. She did not want to remember that terrible time. It was Tom she wanted to think of, his words to her that morning, the sight of his face so filled with feeling. She caught her breath as the image of his handsome, rugged face formed in her mind. She had never seen his eyes so blue, his mouth so hard as when he boldly looked at her and declared himself. Recalling the feel of his grip on her arm as he threw off her attempt to wipe the blood off his brow, she felt a weakness flood her lower body and a warmth burn beneath her petticoats as she imagined what it would be like to be held by those big rough hands and kissed by that wonderful full mouth.

She tried to shake off the sensation that he still held her wrist and clear her head of the piercing image of those moonstone eyes as she padded along the path. She breathed deeply of the woods, cherishing the familiar scent, caressing the thick cushion of needles with the soles of her boots. She realized with a sigh how she had taken this freedom for granted. She vowed never to leave these woods again, to always have trees around her, to breathe daily the sweet fragrance of this beloved place.

As she walked along the path near the pond halfway between the manor house and Thomas Phalen's cottage, she caught sight of Tom.

He was bending over the icy water, dipping his ragged kerchief in and washing the wound on his forehead. She could see that it had stopped bleeding and that a small swelling had formed around it.

Unaware of her presence, he washed and dried it carefully, rinsing the cloth and ringing it out in the freezing water. He turned slightly and laid the cold cloth across his eyes, and as he did so, she could see that he had been crying. The sight of his swollen red face made her gasp and he turned to face her with a start.

Without a word she went to him, but he was too quick for her. He turned away and walked around the ancient sycamore putting the huge tree between them and standing stone still. How he thought this would stop her she could not know, but she left Jewel on the path and in two steps was behind him.

Neither of them spoke a word. For several breathless moments they stood there, Tom, rigid as death, Meg so close to his back that she could feel the heat of his body in the chill of the February morning.

She could not touch him. To do so would break the spell of his closeness and risk his disappearance into the phantasm where she had always kept him.

No, she dared not disturb this captive silence for in this frozen moment lived her whole past and her future. Time seemed to have stopped altogether. Had her life ended right there among the rocks and frozen shamrocks, Meg would have had no regret at its passing. She might have willed it but she knew in some murky hollow deep within her that if she died now, so close to him but not touching him, she would exist forever in hellish torment.

Still he did not move. She could feel his suffering, so close to his unyielding back, the warmth radiating from his tense and rigid shoulders. With her hand almost upon his collar, she checked the impulse to touch his neck, to curl his hair around her finger, to break the spell of this dreadful silence.

Finally turning away from the brook, but still not facing her, Tom began to walk toward his father's house. He paused and turned back to the path, taking Jewel by the reins and led him along, still in the direction of Thomas's house. Meg said nothing, and followed him, her heart pounding in her ears.

"We can get a bit of food at the house. Me Da's off to me brother Paulie's fer a few days. I can take care of Jewel there too, he's that sweated up. Ye must be careful to keep 'em warm in this kind of weather. Ye know that I'm sure."

He paused, still not facing her.

"Yer mother and father got off to yer Uncle Robert's all right, just so ye know."

Meg sensed resolution in Tom's voice. Trailing behind him like a child, she became aware of a new purposefulness about him, as though a decision had been made at the brook side that had fundamentally changed the course of both their lives.

They walked on in silence until they came to the meadow behind the Phalen house and then he turned to her. His expression was clear and calm as he held her locked in his gaze.

There they stood, captives of each other's eyes with only the pale thin rays of the sun and an occasional bare twig dropping between them.

He probed her soul with unwavering gentleness. Meg, her own green eyes unblinking, her long blond lashes lying still upon her cheek, arched her neck in the instinctive language of surrender. In his eyes Meg saw his heart and joined it to her through her own. Silently he raised her hand to his lips, and with his gaze never yielding, fused their souls.

His handsome features were serene and relaxed, his voice like water lapping deep within a cavern as he whispered,

"This is where ye can turn back, Meg. I have placed me heart upon th'ground before ye, and there it lies. If ye want me I'm yers but if ye can't come th'whole way with me then turn back now. I am only a man and if ye follow me into me house, I'll be havin' ye fer me own, and that's the all of it."

With this she finally dropped her gaze, and slipping her thin gloved hand deep into his big worn palm she followed him wordlessly through the field to the faded blue kitchen door.

Tom carefully tied Jewel to a thin sapling and while Meg watched his every movement, memorizing each step to the creek, the filling of the feedbag, the brush strokes on Jewel's back, she felt as if she watched him through a veil of gold and each motion was slowed down to an unnatural pace.

She felt as though she was wandering in a dream, watching herself watch him. Her regular breathing and her still hands belied the terrible restlessness inside her. She thought he would never finish and take her in his arms. She could not even permit herself to imagine what would happen after that. Flushed and faint, starving for him to touch her she was queasy with the thrilling knowledge that he intended to do much more.

When he was finally through with Jewel, he turned to her and with a diffident smile, led her into the rude cabin, his hand gently pressed against the small of her back. They wasted no time with awkward conversation, and as she looked around the neat little room, so masculine and austere, her heart burst with love for this man for his habits and the details of his life.

They reached for each other at the same time with a great groan of release, their enforced loneliness finally at an end.

Meg was twenty-seven years old, a spinster by anyone's standards and Tom, by no means a young man, was as new to this experience as a schoolboy. But the desire and intensity of their lovemaking was no youthful rush. They had burned out their fever during long anguished nights alone and now time sped up in tandem with their pounding hearts. Fighting the urge to strip away their years apart and shed the fierce continence that had kept them from this moment, they took each other slowly, drinking in every flavor, every fragrance. Finally, no longer able to hold back the tide, they succumbed totally, each to the other in the glorious deliverance of complete surrender.

It was the surrender Tom remembered now, lying on the straw mat where he had given all of himself to her, and taken all of her into himself. A wave of penetrating shame washed over him as he smelled the stale dank air of the tiny cubicle and realized how much Meg had overlooked the pitiful surroundings of her first experience of love.

A woman like Meg, used to the finest linens and laces, the sweetest fragrances and lotions, how could he have brought her so low as to bed her in this place, this awful stifling hole of a back room, not even a room at all. What could he have been thinking of, laying her down on straw, on a few boards set upon four piles of flat rocks, stealing her virginity when he had nothing to give her in return?

Where was his brain? Could he not see that it was impossible, that even a woman as passionate and strong as Meg was no match for the sacrifice he was asking of her and now they had made a child. He was such a fool to think it could go on, meeting in the meadow, sneaking into the ruins of the old abbey.

They had never returned to this room after that first time. Was it lack of opportunity or had she been so repulsed that she found new and better places to enjoy their love? Was the chilly stone floor of the mossy overgrown Abbey of St. Anselm really better? Or was it shame, embarrassment for the way he lived that turned her away from his door? He had never thought of the reason, he was so blind with desire that he cared little where they met as long as he could have her. She never complained. She never asked for more than he could give her but then she never invited him in either, not even when her parents were away.

He had never thought of the reasons why they always met at the abbey or in the shelter of the overhanging rocks near the pond between their homes when it rained. He never even realized until now that they had always met somewhere between her life and his, never really entering one or the other since that first time right here in this sunken dark pit of a place not fit for the devil himself, much less his lady.

His Lady! Aye that was the truth. She had been and always would be his Lady. She was not of his ilk; she was far superior to him by birth and destiny. Like a queen, she lived on a plane above him, and only when he lay her down beneath him and covered her with his body and filled her with his passion were they the same. Only when he heard her cry out his name did he feel a man in any real sense. Only when she clasped herself to him and begged him never to stop were they equals, both naked, both human, like Adam and his Eve, lying in the chilly breeze, no rags or silken threads to separate them, no manners or pretenses to shield the raw desire in their hearts.

Hot tears stung Tom's eyes as he realized what a fool he was. Sharp knives of pain burned in his chest as he saw and knew that love and desire and even the hard coupling of soft flesh could never erase the barrier between them. By the fates he was born a cursed laborer and she a lady. And now lying on his bed of straw, he contemplated the death of his dreams even as he recalled every sensation of that first time, when it mattered not at all what they lay on, and even less whom their parents were.

He pressed his palms into his eyes, willing them to dry themselves. He strained to remember the feel of her ivory buttons as he had unfastened them one by one, kissing her sweet skin between each one and he thought the musty room filled again with the scent of her talcum, as in his mind's eye he untied her chemise, unthreading tiny pink ribbons through delicate handmade loops of silk lace and finally, burying his face in the rough straw to stifle the cry rising in his throat, he felt with agonizing clarity the surprising softness of her full breasts against his lips.

How could he live without her? How could he ever survive the end of this love that had poured over them both like a tidal wave, drowning them both and leaving them desiring nothing but to drown again and again? How could he leave her to have his child alone and unloved in that terrible prison of a house? His big heart breaking, he could almost hear her voice in his own mouth pleading with him to take her away from there.

There was no way he could approach her father again. Lord Jeffrey had made that clear enough but as he lay on his bed, in a voice trembling with angry resolve, Tom willed Meg to hear him as he promised on his very life to take her and their baby out of Lord Jeffrey's house and away from the iron fists that had blackened her beautiful green eyes.

When Tom emerged from his room, it was with a set jaw and a clear gaze.

Old Thomas glanced up from his plate and said thickly,

"Come and sit down Tommy, the fish is nice and tender and Anna's pie really is a good one."

Tom pulled a three legged creepie up to the bench and sat down. After scrutinizing his father carefully, he leaned across the makeshift table, his face inches from the old man's.

"And?"

"And what?" asked Thomas without looking up.

"And what else is it ye want t'say that ye're bitin' on so hard?"

Old Thomas took a deep breath and spoke hastily.

"I was that afraid ye were havin' tears. 'Tisn't a wise thing fer a man t'weep. It gets to be a habit, and weakens a man."

"There will be no tears, Da. Me heart's set on action not cryin'."

With that promise Tom dug in and ate heartily of the pie and downed several cups of fresh water. After wiping the plates and pitching the water out the kitchen door, he turned to his father and taking his coat off the third hook, he said,

"I'll not be goin' to McPhinney's with ye tonight Da. 'Tis off to talk to old Ben I am. I'll maybe join ye later fer a pint or two, I can't say."

Chapter Two

Lord Jeffrey Wynn stood perfectly still in his drawing room looking out on the formal garden of his home. The spring had been a profound disappointment with late freezes and rainy weather right through March and well into April. There had even been hoar frost on the lawn this morning when he had taken his ride. This was disgraceful for the first week of May!

His gardens, usually sweet and renewed by now were a dismal gray mess of tangled brambles and half sprouted buds, and his gardeners were becoming fat and lazy wiling away the rainy days in the greenhouse when they should have been busy hoeing and bending their backs over his roses.

But the concern foremost in his mind this evening was not the state of his roses or the habits of his gardeners. Lord Jeffrey had just expelled from his drawing room a piece of Irish filth who had the nerve to ask for his daughter's hand in marriage.

The thought would have amused him, even brought a laugh to his throat if the circumstances were not so vile, so sordid. He smiled in dry amusement at the memory of Tom Phalen being heaved out his front door by Stiller and his boys. It took three men to boot that big ox out onto the steps, and then he'd had the temerity to leave his filthy rag of a jacket behind. Well, let the fool freeze. He had told George to take the bloody thing and burn it.

Why was it the Irish were so damn much trouble? Why couldn't they be satisfied with their little plots and their foolish church and their round willing women? They were always wanting more, and this was what brought them so much trouble.

He drew a shallow draft of a fresh cigar and thought about the Irish women, girls really, that he had known since coming to this godforsaken farm of Beverly's.

The last had been only a week ago, a cheeky little she devil from the kitchen by the name of Mary. Of course they were all named Mary. He chuckled to himself to think how few of these "Marys" were virgins like their beloved namesake.

Ah, yes Mary. A pretty little thing, though a bit young. It seemed the older he got the younger he liked them. She gave him a good fight for a little one, but he'd had her in the end, right there on the pantry table, spilling turnips and potatoes everywhere, eyes as big as saucers when he opened his pants. How he loved to see their petticoats fly up and feel them struggle and fight beneath him. There was nothing like putting a brassy little colleen through the paces to make him hungry for more. The thought made him think of his regular girl and he promised himself a visit later tonight to treat himself after the wretched business of today.

He heard his wife call to Stiller in the foyer and turned to listen as she instructed the old butler that she and Lord Jeffrey were not at home to guests tonight.

Beverly.

What a waste of a good-looking woman. It was no wonder he warmed the skirts of the serving girls when his wife would rather watch horses mating than partake of that part of their marriage. He had long despaired of ever bringing her back to his bed and since had found the local Irish girls more than enough to compensate.

"I locked her in her room, as you insisted though I think it's silly to bother now that the damage is done."

Beverly's mewling voice intruded on his pleasant reverie.

"Are you listening, Jeffrey?" she whined, approaching him with the air of a disgruntled nursemaid who had just reported the naughty doings of her charge.

"Jeffrey, I said that I thought…"

"I heard what you said and I do not care what you think!" He thundered.

"You are vile," Beverly spat as she turned away from him to pour herself a class of sherry.

"And you drink too much," he countered.

"You didn't have to hurt her Jeffrey. And I will not permit you to keep her locked up in her room till this wretched child is born."

Beverly sipped her sherry and swept her gown around her knees as she sat down.

"She is your daughter after all."

"I will decide what you will permit me to do with this daughter. She is a slut, Beverly, a pig that ruts in the bed of a filthy, lying Irish bastard who spawned a filthy bastard like himself. This 'daughter' you refer to is no daughter of mine. Today she is no daughter of this house, and I forbid you to speak of her or appeal to me on her behalf."

"We are not speaking of an errant child, dear wife, not that it would make any difference if she were thirteen or thirty, an Irish bastard is still an Irish bastard, and I will have no daughter before I'll have this one who has betrayed my good name."

"What will you do Jeffrey? If you keep her locked in her room, she says she will starve herself. If you let her starve herself, you will have an uprising on your hands. Tom Phalen is no sniveling boy, Jeffrey. He is an extremely well liked man and his family has a large circle of political friends who would be delighted to avenge the death of his sweetheart."

"You speak as if you know him well, my little wife. Could it be that you and your daughter like the same kind of jig beneath the sheets?"

Lord Jeffrey laughed and threw his whiskey down in one swallow, turning hard on his heel and gripping Beverly by the arm, bringing her to her feet.

"I don't care what you think my cold little bitch, and I don't care if your daughter and her bastard die tonight and rot till hell freezes. You may leave her in her room and allow her no visitors. You may have her meals served three times a day by a maid who leaves the tray outside her room and knocks on the door. You may allow her to bathe as often as needed. And you may allow her to know that today's taste of my crop was not the last she'll have. I will be back to remind her whose house she lives in and whose food she eats and whose rules she will obey. Do I make myself clear, Lady Beverly?"

"Perfectly, My Lord, perfectly."

Beverly's arm throbbed in his viselike grip. She was chilled by the venom of his words and the beady hardness of his eyes. Anxious to rid herself of him, she would have agreed to anything he demanded.

"Good. Now, where is my supper? These little discussions leave me with a ravenous appetite."

Meg lay barely conscious on her bed, her left arm out straight across the counterpane and her right arm tucked tightly against her side. She lay very still to keep the searing pain in check. She had soaked her pillow with hot tears that slid out of her swollen eyes when she did not even know she was crying. Now her tears had dried and she felt arid and shrunken. Seeing Tom had torn her heart open and watching him manhandled and thrown from her father's house had filled her with a sorrow deeper than the pain of the slap that had stifled her as she called after him.

She had been shocked to feel her father's hand across her face for the second time in one day but more than shock or pain she felt defeat. She realized then in the drawing room of her own house that she had never been more than a tenant in Lord Jeffrey's building, no more than a vague figure on the periphery of his vision.

Never had she been so stunned as she had when her father took his riding crop to her. She had known this man all her life and had never seen him show any interest in her nor any emotion. When she told him that Tom Phalen would be coming over and why, she had been totally unprepared for the rage that had come over him.

It was shortly after dawn when she had heard him leaving for an early morning ride. She had followed him into the hallway that connected the east wing to the servant's quarters and called softly to him. He turned and gave her a puzzled look and seemed to breathe a sigh of relief when he saw it was Meg. She had motioned him into an empty guestroom and asked him for a few minutes of his time.

At first amused by the urgency of this unusual encounter, he had followed her into the bedroom leaving the door open. Quickly she spilled out her story, her love for Tom and her desire to marry him, her lonely years in London, and in a rush to finish before he could stop her she told him of the child she carried.

He had listened with icy indifference to her confession, but when she revealed her pregnancy his face became that of a stranger.

Never had she seen her father in such a rage. His eyes became like black beads in his pale face and his neck mottled with ugly purple hives. He lunged at her and tearing her robe off in one wrenching motion, he raised his riding crop over her and began to lash at her, flailing and cursing as he brought the crop down again and again, shredding the thin muslin gown and raising horrid red welts across her back and buttocks.

When she tried to break away from him he grasped at her gown and stripping her, continued to beat her, oblivious to her screams until exhausted and trembling, he stood looking down at her heaving, crumpled body. Without a word, he dragged her to her feet and with one fierce wallop across the face he sent her sprawling against the foot of the bed.

Turning on his heel, he left her to the servants, who had come running in terror while he had administered the most savage beating any of them had ever witnessed.

Chapter Three

Tom was chilled almost as soon as he closed the kitchen door behind him. He cursed the creaking hinges, the drafty splits and cracks in the old wood. His rage mounted to fury as he yanked at the worn latch, slamming the door harder than he intended, sending a shower of feathers and bird dander from the nest in the thatch above.

The moon hung low in a sky streaked and soft as a mourning dove. The stars could not be seen yet, though the clear night promised to bring them out in their usual glorious array. Tom often took his pipe slowly as he allowed his thoughts to drift through the long spring twilight. Sometimes he used this time to pray though he was not a man of deep faith. Most of the time he came out to the yard to think, to draw peace and strength from the closing of the day.

But tonight he could not allow his thoughts to ponder the eternal truths of peace and holiness. His heart had sunk to the bottom of his soul, and his prayers had been crushed beneath it. A blinding white pain replaced his thoughts and the softness of the gentle pink sky was lost on him as he struggled to corral his mind, knowing he needed to be exceedingly clear in his plan for Meg's removal from GlynMor Castle.

Ideas careened around his head, reckless, fearless, frightening in their desperation. He could not calm himself. The harder he tried to concentrate on a plan, the greater panic descended on him.

He felt himself suffocating, his gorge rising up in his throat, as though he had been poisoned and could not rid himself of the asphyxiating mass in his breast. His wool muffler stifled him like a garrote about his neck. Tearing and clawing at it, he gasped and dragged the damp night air into his lungs.

The revolting scene in the Wynn's drawing room coursed around and around in his mind while his footfalls resounded with her name. With each step chilling nausea assaulted him anew.

Stopping against the low stone wall of his father's rented pigsty, he pressed his big hands hard against his forehead as if to take into his own face the pain he saw in Meg's as he was expelled from her father's house and ordered never to return.

God in heaven, poor Meg! Wordless prayers escaped from beneath the boulder in his chest and teeth bared against the descending night, he willed them heavenward. He could not feel his heart for Meg was his heart. He could not see the descending night for his days and nights were Meg's. Unable to find his own voice, he shuddered as the sound of a single piercing wail roiled and seared through his mind. Her voice echoed like that of a snared animal in a crescendo of agony; one word, one elongated, tortured utterance.

His name.

Never had the sound of a slap been so crisp. Never had the moan of a woman ripped through him like the shuddering sob that followed Meg's outcry. It took three powerful menservants and the murderous steel in her father's voice to keep Tom from racing back into the room and crushing Lord Jeffrey's throat with his bare hands.

The last sound he had heard before the massive oak door crashed behind him was the spitting hiss of Lord Jeffrey's voice, filled with hatred, carrying the terrible threat of another whipping if Meg so much as breathed Tom Phalen's filthy Irish name again in that house. The door had loomed behind him as he staggered to his feet. As tears of helplessness burned his eyes, he had realized, looking at the impenetrable oak that she was as lost to him as if the door had been the iron gate of Old Bailey Prison slamming closed.

He groaned now, flinging himself against the ancient wall, hammering the cold unyielding stone, yearning to crush Lord Jeffrey and all the gentry with him who would call his name filthy. He pummeled and mashed the jagged boulders that made up the gatepost, finding some perverse fulfillment in the pain.

Tom continued blindly to grind and twist the stones until, finally, the warm trickle of his blood brought him out of his rage. He halted, his hands around a large stone, his mind's eye seeing the face of Lord Jeffrey between his fingers. The fury of his actions left him damp with perspiration despite the cold wind that was beginning to blow down from Derryhick Lough. He forced himself to breathe in the wind, taking strength from it as it howled around the old cabin. He shivered as he thought of the banshee wailing across the bog and the shiver took the last of his anger leaving him ready to think.

Taking a rag from his coat pocket he bound up his raw knuckles. His breathing came more evenly and he actually felt stronger for having beaten already senseless rock into oblivious submission. He afforded himself a small, bitter smile as he reached for his pipe. Lighting up a smoke always brought him comfort, the sweet aroma of sponc, the poor man's tobacco made from coltsfoot and wild rose petals, always put him in a reflective frame of mind. With a pipe to clench in his teeth he could think.

He needed to approach Old Ben in just the right manner. He'd known Ben for years and knew he had been with Lord Wynn's father since he was a mere boy. Ben had owed Lord Henry Wynn his life but Tom knew there was no love in the stableman's shriveled old heart for Lord Jeffrey. As long as he had worked with Ben, he had kept his counsel about his feelings. Tom really wasn't sure Ben would help him if it meant going against the family that had taken him in as an orphan all those decades past.

Ben spoke like a native though he was born a French Jew.

He had not the passion of the Irish though Tom had heard him speak of the persecution that stole his dear *Maman* from him when he was only a lad. Tom needed an ally and Ben was the only one he had. Ben might help or he might prove an obstacle to rescuing Meg. Tom needed to talk to him tonight about the plan forming in his mind. He could risk no balking on Ben's part and he would know before he slept where the older man stood.

Tom had nothing to bribe him with and to be sure he doubted the old man would be bribed when all was said and done. He needed to appeal to Old Ben's sense of justice and whatever manly outrage he could extract from his heart. Ben had lived so long with animals, Tom wasn't sure he had any feeling for humans at all.

Tom was still in his father's yard when he turned back and almost reconsidered visiting the stable, thinking perhaps it would be better to find a more forceful accomplice, perhaps even a group to storm the big house. Leaning his tired shoulders against the cold damp stone of the pigsty wall, Tom lit his pipe, drawing the smoke in short shallow puffs. He silently cursed himself for the stupidity of that idea. He could no more storm that fortress than Buckingham Palace.

He listened with disgust to the contented grunting of the sow behind the mossy stone wall and heard his father close the front door as he left for his evening libation. He could have loved this farm. The land was poor but beautiful with its rugged windswept vista. It was home to him since birth and deep inside Tom's soul burned the Irishman's love of the land.

But this land was owned by Lord Jeffrey Wynn and had been owned by a despicable, thieving race since long before Tom was born. This shabby plot, this dirty broken hut reminded him of all that was contemptible about both the English and the Irish. He spit upon the English cur who would lord it over good honest people like his father, reducing them to sniveling beasts, no more than slaves begging and groveling for a piece of land and a hearth. And he cursed the ineffectual sentiment that kept them coming back for more of the bitter slop tossed their way by "His Lordship".

His rage threatened to overpower him again as he caught sight of the blackened chimney of his grandfather's burned out old cottage and recalled the strong and noble lads who had died right here in Clydagh Glyn the summer he was twelve and his grandfather had refused to obey the eviction order of the landlord, then Lady Beverly's father, Lord Bentley Cushing.

It was too much to ask! It had to be inhuman, his grandfather had pleaded with the bailiff. His daughter, Tom's mother, was laboring in childbirth inside his house, while the bailiff and his men were threatening the roof with torches ablaze.

In the end, his Granda Meahra's house was torched; his mother and the unborn baby trapped inside while his grandfather and father along with his three uncles were arrested. Young Tom would remember till the day he died, the sight of his father and his Uncle Dan breaking free and disappearing into the burning house while his mother screamed in both pain and terror and his grandfather, held down by the ropes of the bailiff cried out for the life of his Clare.

He remembered too, the sight of his father and his Uncle Terrence barely able to walk themselves, carrying Uncle Dan home from the village square where they all had been flogged for menacing a government agent and threatening the king, and where his grandfather and Uncle Sean had died screaming epithets against the whole royal family. No one had expected Uncle Dan to survive both the burning and the beating, but he did, long enough to wish he had not.

Tom's mother survived the blaze, only to succumb to pneumonia a week later from the smoke. His new brother Francis, born on the bog with no one but his mother and a few brave women from the village, had to his dying day never been quite right in the head. Uncle Dan was never able to work the land again from the burns on his hands and the crushing blow of a shillelagh had ruined his handsome face.

He died a year later of a shot to the head at the age of forty-two, leaving a widow and six children.

When the priest came to give him absolution for his terrible sin against God and himself, he had cursed his scarred hands for missing his shot and cried that he could no longer bear to frighten his children with "the withered homeliness" of his disfigured face. The priest had forgiven him in the name of Father, Son and Holy Ghost, and Daniel Shea Meahra died in a state of grace, one hour to the minute after putting a bullet in his own head. Upon leaving his bedside, the priest gathered the men of the village to plan a confrontation. It was this foolishness that had led to the death of three more village lads and the imprisonment of Father Shanahan himself.

It was the futility of the angry proclamations, the bellowed threats in the safety of McPhinney's, the sad heads shaking in the cemetery behind the church that caused the fierce anger to well up in Tom's chest. Calm rational thought was really the answer to the outrageous oppression by the English but the anger of the Irish was a killing force, choking off the mind and driving the men to act purely from their hearts. It was this anger so easily churned up which threatened to cloud his thinking now and delay the planning of Meg's rescue.

Exhausted by the events of the day, eyes burning dry in his head, Tom was tempted to follow his father's fading footsteps as they fell in regular rhythm toward the welcoming, yellow pool of McPhinney's window. Instead he continued drawing on his pipe, mulling and brooding until satisfied that he had at least a rudimentary plan made.

Shivering both from the chilly night air and the hatred in his heart, he turned into the lowering darkness and carefully picked his way across the uneven slope toward the old stableman's shabby quarters.

Chapter Four

"M'lady? M'lady. Lady Meg, can ye hear me now?" Maureen's voice came in gentle waves, ebbing and flowing over Meg's consciousness like pond water against rock. In fact Meg could hear the sound of the water both rushing and lapping, as she weaved her way through the gauzy stupor of sleep. Meg did not want to be conscious, but somehow she knew that it was in that place that she would find Tom, and not in the half light of this swirling red dream. As she relinquished her dreamy world, Meg's body, as though thawing from a great freeze, slowly began to feel itself, and the pain caused her to moan aloud.

"Lady Meg, it's me Maureen. Now don't ye be tryin' to open yer eyes. 'Tis that swollen they are ye'll never do it. Can ye hear me? Can ye say anythin'?"

Meg ran her tongue across her lips, wincing at their thickness and the metallic taste of old blood. Without speaking, she tried to raise her right hand to her eyes, finding it would not move. Fear gripped her when she felt the scalding pain across her shoulders as she tried to turn her head to touch her eyes with her other hand.

She was lying prone on her bed, and as the maid softly murmured her name, Meg began to remember the day's happenings, the whipping in the early morning, the horrible scene in the drawing room. She felt tears ooze from her battered eyes though she did not think she was crying. Her voice hardly a whisper, she spoke.

"Maureen. My arm. Why can I not move it?"

"M'lady, I have it wrapped in a gauze. 'Tis badly bruised and Lady Wynn insisted it be bound t'you. We aren't even sure 'tisn't broken, but Lord Wynn refused to allow Herself, I mean Lady Wynn, to have Dr. Simmons in t'have a look."

"Are both of my eyes swollen shut? I feel as though I could open the right one if I could move my head to the other side."

"Oh, M'lady, sure and Lady B. would be havin' me sacked if I let ye move too much. But I can try t'help ye if ye like. Ye see, ye have a turrible big thrashin' welt across yer shoulders, that wants to keep bleedin' and 'tis that afraid I am t'move ye."

"Well, I suppose I can wait. It is very painful to move. But I am so very hungry, how can I eat?"

The serving girl took the soft muslin rag and wrang it out carefully. Dabbing it in a jar of ointment provided by Mrs. Carrey, the cook, Maureen began to slather a fresh layer of the soothing unguent on Meg's back.

"M'lady, let me finish dressin' these stripes and perhaps we can spoon in a little broth."

Meg nodded her assent, bringing a fresh wave of flame across her shoulders and down her arms. Meanwhile, the housemaid recited a mantra of Aves, hoping they would ease the suffering of Her Ladyship. Within minutes, Meg had drifted off again, spiraling downward into the dark velvet comfort of a drug induced sleep.

Maureen, whose room Lord Jeffrey had been leaving when Meg had called him aside that morning, had witnessed the whole spectacle from the beginning. She had been the first of the servants to arrive at the scene of this mornings "turrible occurrence", as Meg's beating had been referred to in hushed whispers in the back stairwells and linen cupboards of the house. Lord Jeffrey had threatened like punishment to anyone who was caught mentioning what had taken place, and Maureen had felt his eyes bore into her as he spoke. He had taken Maureen by the collar of her dressing gown and ordered her to look after Lady

Meg. Maureen, who had flushed with shame at his touch, prayed that her obedience would keep him away from her bed.

Mrs. Carrey, and the other servants gathered in the hall, had stood in dumb silence until they heard the great front door slam and His Lordship's horse gallop off into the misty dawn. Then they all descended upon Meg, one trying to outdo the other in kindness and solicitation, until Mrs. Carrey had swept them all away and personally lifted Meg up from the floor covering her with her own dressing gown.

Meg had promptly fainted and Mrs. Carrey was forced to summon two of the menservants to carry her to her bedchamber. There they gently laid her face down on a fresh linen sheet draped across the counterpane.

Mrs. Carrey had held Maureen in disdain ever since she had shattered a crystal candlestick her first week on the job. But as she noted the girl's scarlet face and trembling hands, she felt pity for her. Though she could not say for sure that His Lordship fancied Maureen, Mrs. Carrey had an idea of how Lord Jeffrey exacted the submission of the maids and thanked Holy Mother Mary she had been spared such disgrace when she was young.

After dismissing all but Maureen, Mrs. Carrey ordered her niece, Sharon to fetch her medicine bag, and Lady Beverly in that order. She was just beginning to dress some of the slashes on Meg's back when Lady Beverly swept in, fastening her velvet pelisse and demanding to know immediately what was going on. Gasping at the sight of her daughter lying naked to the waist, bleeding and bruised, Lady Beverly grew suddenly weak and clutched the dressing gown high around her throat.

She grabbed the back of a slipper chair and steadied herself by running her hands over and over the silk brocade of the upholstery. Her eyes were riveted on Meg's slender frame, pale and limp, marked by vicious lines of red and crimson. Heat flushed upward from the pit of her belly as she caught sight of her daughter's thick blonde curls tangled on her pillow. Lady Beverly had never had much feeling for Meg, had even been jealous of her beautiful green eyes and rosy complexion, but now, seeing her laid out like this, looking so small and vulnerable brought whatever meager maternal response Beverly's cold heart could muster.

Before she could repeat her demand to know what happened, Meg began to stir and Lady Beverly went immediately to her side.

"Who did this to you Meg?"

Her mother spoke close to Meg's ear, glaring over her damp brow at Sharon and the other maids still lurking in the doorway, scanning faces for guilt. Her eyes rested upon Mrs. Carrey whose face was a study of grief and fear mingled with a peculiar knowing satisfaction that Lady Beverly found alarmingly revealing.

"You tell me, Mrs. Carrey. Which of the brutes in this house did this to my daughter? Was it Cory? One of the drivers?"

Cory was an apprentice gardener and Sharon's brother. A stifled gasp from Sharon made Lady Beverly spin around to confront the frightened girl. Mrs. Carrey was about to defend both her niece and nephew when Meg herself whispered,

"Father".

In her misunderstanding, Lady Beverly turned to Meg and taking her hand in a rare show of affection, bent down to reassure her that certainly her father would hear about this immediately and ferret out the guilty party for the severest of punishments.

Meg was only able to shake her head before lapsing into merciful unconsciousness once again.

As if she were just waking up to realize how sordid this all was, Lady Beverly quickly released Meg's hand and probed Mrs. Carrey's face for an explanation. As the two women locked eyes across the bed, neither speaking, neither daring to break the spell by looking down at Meg, Lady Beverly's expression changed like the sunrise. At first cold, filled with scorn at her rude and untidy awakening, the pinched white cheeks gave way to high color as shades of rose and crimson crept upward from her neck over her brow, stopping just short of her own blonde hair and giving her light blue eyes a sheen like well-polished pewter. As her eyes held Mrs. Carrey's deep azure gaze, and the impact of Meg's single utterance made itself known, Lady Beverly's color again paled, and she found herself snapping shut her mouth which had gone slack with shock.

When Lady Beverly finally found her voice, she could still not utter her true suspicions. Fumbling around in her mind for something to say, someone to accuse, she could only stare, and Mrs. Carrey, fear having struck her dumb, was not about to speak first.

Collecting herself in some semblance of decorum, Lady Beverly broke the silence by addressing the maids in the doorway. In her most imperious voice she dispensed with orders for hot water, clean rags, and some broth to be served when Lady Meg woke up. Lady Beverly did not know the first thing about nursing humans, but knew enough about sick horseflesh to initiate some rudimentary protocol of first aid.

Her own fear dissipating, Mrs. Carrey was all practicality. "Madam, why don't ye let me and Maureen tend t'Lady Meg, you bein' shocked right out o'yer bed an'all. 'Tis yerself that needs a cup o'tea right now."

Before Lady Beverly could protest, Mrs. Carrey again held her gaze and added,

" 'Tis what his Lordship ordered, Mum, after he, uh, oh dear heaven after he .."

"Are you trying to tell me that my husband knows about this?"

Lady Beverly felt as though she were retching as the words spilled out of her mouth in one last effort to deny the truth.

"Aye Mum, that is the truth of the matter, sure an'it is. Ye see, M'Lady, Lord Wynn, if ye don't mind me sayin' so, well let's just say he was there when it happened."

At this, Lady Beverly Wynn, overcome by the truth of her suspicions, found herself lowering herself into the chair, and whispered,

"Yes, I will take that cup of tea."

Maureen thought of all this now, as she dressed Lady Meg's wounds. She really wished she could leave this place and return to her Uncle Pat's farm in Sligo. There was nothing there for her though, and her soft brown eyes misted over when she remembered the night her brother Luke had begged her to go with him across the sea to America. Her brother had been all she had after her uncle died, and he believed in the hope of a new world. But Maureen was born to the green land of Ireland and could not bear to leave.

When, at the age of twelve, she had found herself hungry and alone on the doorstep of Assumption Church, on the outskirts of the village of Clydagh Glyn, she had reached the end of her wanderings. If she did not find respectable work she would die. When the kindly pastor, Father Matt Gaskin arranged this position as maid in the grand house of Lord and Lady Wynn, she thought she had arrived in the land of Canaan.

What did she want with America anyway, great dirty old land full of red Indians who would as soon take her thick red hair and make headdresses out of it. No, she had been in Clydagh Glyn for five years. She would stay, maybe take work in the village, anything to get away from himself.

She finished rolling the clean rags and wiped the ointment on her apron. The night had silently filled the room with shadows while she had ministered to Lady Meg and as she lit a candle she was surprised to hear the little mantel clock chime nine times.

Maureen drew the deep rose velvet drapes against the night chill, and settled into a rocking chair to wait for her ladyship to wake up and take some broth. She had hardly begun her mending when she heard the latch release on the bedroom door. Pretending not to hear, she kept her head bent to her work. Ignoring the sound of the bootsteps on the hardwood floor, she sat frozen in her seat. It was not until she felt the coldness of his hand loosening her hair that Maureen looked up. With one snap of his fingers, she was on her feet, and wordlessly Lord Jeffrey pushed her toward the door.

Chapter Five

It was fully dark by the time Tom reached the back stable door leading to the two upstairs rooms where Old Ben had lived ever since Tom had known him. He emptied his cold clay pipe and slipped it into his coat pocket. As he waited for Ben to answer his knock, he thought dismally how little he knew of this man who would play such a crucial role in his plan. He grew impatient as his knock went unanswered and his thoughts turned to panic again.

What if Ben would not help him get Meg out of the house? What if he turned on Tom and went to Lord Jeffrey? That was unthinkable. Tom chastised himself for even entertaining the thought. He rapped again on the thick slats that served as protection against wind and rain and kept Lady Beverly's horses safe and dry. When he continued to be met by silent darkness, he softly called Ben's name, fearful of disturbing the animals, or worse yet the household.

He finally decided that Ben was not up there and crept around the side of the stable to peer in the window. He dared not go around the front. Someone might see him from the kitchen, where voices indicated that the last work of the evening was still not done. He heard a giggle as one of the kitchen maids warded off the attentions of a suitor, whose voice he recognized as Cory Reilly, the gardener apprentice. Scurrying across the yard, away from the young man's pleading promises, the girl spilled the contents of a slop pot close enough to Tom's feet to dampen his trousers. He ducked behind the door of a tiny windowless shed used to store old harness and hardware. Hastily closing the door behind him, he was surprised to find it lit by a lantern and occupied by Ben and his puppy. Ben looked up as startled to see Tom as he was to see Ben. Pip, the young retriever wagged her tail when she saw Tom and Ben franticly shushed her to keep her from announcing their surprise visitor. Pip settled down at Ben's feet.

Returning to his harness mending, Ben waited for Tom to speak.

"I imagine you know why I've come," Tom said, blinking in the light of the lantern.

Without responding, Ben leaned over and moved the lantern off the stoop so that Tom could sit down. He relit his clay pipe, and puffing away, raised his eyes to meet Tom's. With an impatient wave of his pipe, he motioned for Tom to sit on the stoop.

"I do," he exhaled in a cloud of sweet gray smoke.

"Have ye heard anythin' from th'house?"

"Aye, I have. Biddy Carrey was just out here and gave me all th'details, of course, accordin' t'Biddy Carrey. Ye can decide fer yerself what of her palaver is really th'truth."

Leaning forward to show Ben that he wanted to hear every word of Biddy Carrey's report, Tom reined in his mounting impatience and nodded for Ben to go on.

Ben, relishing his new role as messenger, took a few puffs of his pipe and began.

From Mrs. Carrey's report, replete with tears and great signs of the cross, Ben had surmised that Lady Meg was indeed suffering from severe pain, and was slipping in and out of awareness, and had perhaps a broken right arm. She was not taking any nourishment, but Maureen and Mrs. Carrey had been able to care for her wounds. There had been no further contact with Lord Jeffrey, who had demanded his horse be saddled immediately after tea, and had not spoken to any of the servants upon his return only moments ago.

As far as Ben knew, Tom's unborn child was still all right, and it seemed to be the opinion of the caretakers that Lady Meg would recover, though it was still too soon to tell. Ben did not know if she had been seen by a doctor, but Mrs. Carrey did think she would be able to move a bit in a few days.

Tom cursed as he ran his hands through his thick black curls. He wanted to get Meg out of there as soon as he could. It was pure torture to know exactly which window she lay beyond and be helpless to see her, to take her in his arms and shield her from her pain.

"Do ye want t'know all th'gory details, as Biddy Carrey told them t'me Boyo? She was after all, one of the eye witnesses, so to speak."

"Aye, please spare me nothin'. Tell me everythin' th'bastard did t'her. I need t'hate him as much as I can, not that I need any more reason."

Tom turned his weary eyes toward Ben's wrinkled old face, and braced himself as every word fell across his heart, like the lash across Meg's shoulders.

When Ben was finished, his voice hardly a croak, he placed his hand on Tom's knee, and at his touch Tom closed his eyes, but not before Ben saw the hatred that flared in them, like the flicker of the lantern at his feet. He shivered in the face of Tom's resolve and knew that he was inexorably involved in one man's personal crusade to destroy another. He wished he could despise Lord Jeffrey the way Tom did, it would make his role easier. As it was, he owed the Wynn family his life, a debt for which Lord Jeffrey had exacted payment for thirty years, as his father, Lord Henry Wynn had before him.

Ben set down the mended harness and leaned closer to Tom. It was very hard for him to accept the part he suspected Tom wanted him to play. He was a very old man and had accepted it as fate that he would simply care for these horses and mend old harnesses until he died peacefully and was laid to rest in a pauper's grave. He cared not for crusades or vendettas, had shielded himself from any fondness for man or woman, and was content to live out his days well fed and rested on this beautiful land. He had not been born in Ireland but would be content to die there, having no desire to return to his native France. He learned English from the Irish and so spoke with a thick brogue but the hot blood of the Celtic tribesman did not run in his veins. Nor had he the passion for the land for which these natives were so willing to fall on the sword.

Now he looked upon the face of a man he'd known as long as he'd known Lord Jeffrey, a man who had suffered the same sort of blind injustice that had killed his own mother and father, and leaning toward him, felt stirring in his tired old breast the beginnings of anger, an anger he had not felt since the sight of the Normandy coast had faded from his black eyes over eighty years ago.

Perhaps he did not burn with the passion of the Celt, but there lay smoldering in him the Frenchman's love of justice and the plain awakening of excitement that he may just do one noble thing before he died. He realized then that he cared deeply for his young friend despite his efforts to remain indifferent.

Tom met his gaze and in the silent exchange, there was born a pact. Ben knew then that his grave may not be in Ireland, nor for that matter might his death be peaceful, but he was in it now. Tom reached out. Ben set down his clay pipe and clasped Tom's hand with his own gnarled grip, thus sealing, in the ages old ritual of men, the bond of friendship and loyalty.

Tom rose to leave and they made arrangements to meet after dark the next evening by the pond between the properties, when they would reassess their situation and outline their plan.

Ben extinguished the lantern, plunging them both into darkness just as Tom reached for the door. Without turning he said "Just tell Biddy Carrey to be sure Meg knows I was here and that I will not stay away."

Before Old Ben could reply, Tom was gone into the pitch-black shadows. Ben gently prodded the dog to her feet and closed up the shed. It was time for bed, but he thought as he turned toward the light of the kitchen that a nice cup of tea would be a good idea first. Besides, he had a message to deliver.

Thomas Phalen was coming in the front door from McPhinney's at just the same time young Tom opened the kitchen door of the little cottage. He was drunker than usual due to the tensions of the day, and stood swaying in the doorway trying to focus on Tom's face.

"Well Da, ye're in a state are ye?"

Tom hung his coat on the third hook and walked over to the hearth to stir the dying embers.

"That I am and 'twould be a far bether thing if ye'd find yerself in one too."

Tom smiled in spite of himself and gazed into the flames licking around the smoldering turf he had scraped into a pile for one last burst of warmth. His father was the dearest man he had ever known and even in his misery, the sight of him in his baggy corduroy jacket squinting over his red pug nose was enough to lighten his mood.

"Da, what would I ever do without ye?"

He turned toward his father and with his old familiar gesture, put his arm around the shoulders of the smaller man. His father looked bemused by the question, as though he had never given it a thought. He also looked as though he had forgotten the troubles of the day. Seeing this, Tom sought to remind him.

"I saw Ben tonight as I said I would and I believe he'll help me get Meg out o'that prison of a house but she's pretty bad off from what he told me and not t'be moved for a few days at least. So, it looks like ye'll be recitin' Aves and novenas 'til I can do somethin' about it.

"Aye, aye, ye'd best not rush into anything Boyo, time is all ye have. She'll not be goin' anywhere without ye fer sure, and ye need time to make a solid plan ye do. God knows ye'll only have one shot at it."

"And Tom," his father said, peering at him heavily, "'Twouldn't hurt ye t'say a few novena's yerself."

Shaking off Tom's arm, Thomas stretched and eased himself onto the straw mat that served as his bed, ended any further conversation with a snorting yawn. Tom returned to the tiny fire and sat brooding until the last spark died. His plan growing and taking shape in his mind, he snuffed the candle and went to bed.

Chapter Six

Lady Beverly Wynn made one of her rare appearances in her kitchen just as Ben was finishing his second cup of tea. Mrs. Carrey, exhausted from the day's events, sat nursing a piece of barm brack. Both stood up guiltily when Lady Beverly swept into the room, her gown held high to avoid contact with the immaculate floor. It was clear to Biddy Carrey that, immaculate or not, the bare slate was not an acceptable surface to rub against the violet wool.

It was clear too, that the day had taken a terrible toll on Her Ladyship. Lady Beverly was a cold fish to be sure, but there was nothing cruel or evil about her as there was about Lord Jeffrey. Mrs. Carrey actually felt the stirrings of pity as she saw the red eyes and swollen cheeks of her mistress. This was not the first time she had seen Her Ladyship after tears, but it was the first time she had made no attempt to conceal it. There was nothing aristocratic about the beleaguered woman in the doorway, despite the haughty way she raised her skirts up off the floor. Here was a woman to be pitied; a woman brought down to the level of a peasant slave by the brutality of a cold-blooded serpent of a man. And Mrs. Biddy Carrey, self-appointed ministering angel, was just the woman to bring her comfort.

The cook was on her feet in a flash.

"M'Lady, we was just about t'hot th'pot again. Can I fix ye' somethin' fer a bed lunch?" she asked as she set the kettle on the big burner of the huge black Robinson Stove.

"Yes, tea and a piece of that barm brack would be fine. Plenty of butter." Looking at Old Ben, Lady Beverly marked the late hour and wondered if it was his habit to visit her kitchen every night, eating up her food and drinking her expensive tea, or was this too a visit born of stress over the day's calamitous events. She knew instinctively that she had interrupted some conversation, and while she cared not a fig for the opinions of her servants, she wondered what their impressions might be of the immediate future. Wishing she had taken the time to eavesdrop before entering the kitchen, she feigned indifference and took a chair near the old hearth.

"Ben, do something about this." She said with a careless nod toward the dying embers.

The old stableman ambled to the turf box and placed a small brick toward the back of the fire, and with the bellows, brought it to a crackling glow. As if she were always lounging around the kitchen, Lady Beverly slouched in her chair mulling over her thoughts as she waited for her tea.

"If there's nothin' else Yer Ladyship."

Unaccustomed to his role as house servant, Ben tried to bow his already stooped shoulders, but Lady Beverly dismissed him with a wave of her hand.

"I thought he'd never leave," she sighed as Mrs. Carrey placed the china cup and saucer before her and turned to bring over the tea.

"I actually came to see you Mrs.Carrey. We must work out some sort of schedule for Lady Meg's care. My husband is reluctant to permit anyone, myself included, to help her. He consents only to having that half-witted Maureen in there. No doctor, in fact no visitors of any kind. I do not trust Maureen, she is young and knows nothing of nursing the sick. It is my wish that you and you alone will supervise Maureen. I have made arrangements with Lady Parker to lend us her second cook, to relieve you in the kitchen for a few days."

"Of course," Lady Beverly said, giving Mrs. Carrey a penetrating look, "His Lordship must know nothing of this.

She picked at the barm brack and tentatively sipped the scalding tea.

"My husband has made it very clear to me that there will be serious repercussions if his wishes are not followed to the letter. It is no use pretending that I am exempt from his wrath, Mrs. Carrey, so you can lower your eyebrows. We've all seen a side of His Lordship today that changes the rules of the game a bit don't you agree? It is essential that you cooperate with me. No stairwell gossip or back fence talk, Mrs. Carrey, or we will all suffer."

"Lady Meg is fighting for her life right now. I just came from her room and she is very feverish. That useless Maureen was not at her post, and I realized that she was not to be trusted alone with my daughter. I want you to spend the night with Lady Meg and I will supervise Maureen in the morning while you get some rest. Remember, Lord Jeffrey must have no idea we are ministering to Lady Meg. Is that clear?"

"Of course, M'Lady. I'll go t'her at once."

"Good, then I am going to bed. Call me if there is any change for the worse."

With this Lady Beverly rose and left Mrs. Carrey to stare behind her, fear galvanizing her to duty, her fatigue replaced by the adrenalin of conspiracy.

Leaving the tea dishes on the sideboard, she gathered her rosary and her shawl and slowly climbed the back stairs to the second floor. As she trundled awkwardly up the stairs, her dress gathered up in front of her so she would not trip, she noted with a wry smile, that her Ladyship had neglected to lift her lovely wool skirt on her way out of the kitchen.

Mrs. Carrey had dozed in the chair next to Lady Meg's bed, when she was startled awake by the sound of the key turning in the bedroom door. The room was lit by the soft glow of a candle, and her heart pounding, Mrs. Carrey saw a form slide silently into the room. She stole a glance at the sleeping form of her charge, and shrinking back as far as she could into the shadows, she tried to make out the identity of the interloper.

A soft sob broke the air of suspense as Maureen approached Lady Meg's bedside. Mrs. Carrey shifted in her chair, her rosary beads slipping to the floor with a clatter, and the sob was choked off by a little scream. Maureen froze mid-step and Mrs. Carrey stood up. Relief flooded the girl's body and her shoulders sagged, but with two steps Mrs. Carrey was across the room with her hand poised to slap Maureen's face.

One look at her eyes stopped the older woman's assault as she took in the hunted, guilty look that Maureen's tears could not erase.

"Where have ye been, ye foolish, stupid wench? How could ye leave this poor girl alone in here, and her barely alive on th'bed?"

The cook's hands were tight on the maid's shoulders now, and with a jolt, she realized that they were bare.

Dragging Maureen into the light, she saw that the girl was completely without clothes, and merely held her uniform in front of her. She took in the torn bodice of the uniform and the tangled mass of red hair that hung loosely over Maureen's shoulders.

"Mother Mary preserve us, what have ye done?"

Mrs. Carrey cuffed the sobbing girl on the side of the head, shook her by the shoulders until, teeth chattering, shaking like a rag doll, she slipped to the floor still clutching the ripped uniform protectively across her front.

"Please," sobbed the terrified girl, "Please Mrs. Carrey, ye must listen t'me. I don't do it because I want to. Really I don't! He makes me I swear! I can't resist him. He's too strong. Besides where would I go? I have no other job! He told me he'd kill me if I told, and now ye know and I'll be killed if ye tell, and I hate him and ever since th'first time he keeps after me. I hate him Mrs. Carrey ye have t'believe me. I'm a good girl ye must believe me! I have no choice but t'do his biddin'. I swear on me mither's grave he forces me t'have his way with me."

"Stop this now 'afore I slap ye again girl! Stop this bellowin' 'afore he's down on us both in this very room. Ye'll be disturbin' the dead, much less Himself, and think of poor Lady Meg, if ye please!"

Mrs. Carrey heaved a great sigh, and threw herself down in the bedside chair. Her exhaustion threatened to overcome her as she took in this new bit of information. She had suspected that Lord Jeffrey was pleasing himself with the kitchen maids now and then and had thought herself wise to turn a blind eye to such goings on as she had no control over. And now Maureen! And as it would seem on a regular basis and for a long time now! She had suspected as much, but seeing the evidence was still a rude shock for sure.

Truly this was more than her staunch Catholic heart could absorb. How often had she stood beside the girl in church unaware of the business of the night before with that wicked terrible man. Her own frame of reference for such doings was very slim, for Mr. Carrey had been a man of great discretion except where politics was involved, and after a brief marriage, during which his gropings were few and fairly endurable, he was arrested and sent without her to Australia for inciting a riot in Dublin town.

She tried in vain to find the right words to address this issue with Maureen. The girl was essentially her responsibility, the Wynns having no official housekeeper, and Stiller the butler being over the menservants only. What could she do for the dreadful creature? And how did she know that the girl even spoke the truth, when she herself had caught her in the root cellar making plans for a rendezvous behind the stables last spring with her own nephew, Cory? Not that she had actually caught her in the act mind you, but there was always that element of suspicion.

Looking across the room at the naked maid shivering behind her crumpled uniform, Mrs. Carrey dismissed the thought of blaming her for her wretched situation. After Himself showing his true colors for all to see this morning and with his own daughter, never mind a parlor maid, she would believe anything of him, no matter how vile or base. But it still remained her duty to deal with Miss Maureen with the wild red hair and the beautiful creamy skin.

The sight of that milk white skin in the candle light prompted Mrs. Carrey to action. She pulled herself together and assuming the role of stern mother superior, ordered Maureen to get up at once and go to bed. They could discuss this further in the light of day. Maureen was to report to Lady Meg's room no later than six o'clock to relieve Mrs. Carrey. She would then be given her orders by none other than Lady Beverly herself.

Even in her present state of crisis, Maureen recognized this for the unusual turn of events that it was and hastened to obey Mrs. Carrey's orders. Lord Jeffrey was to be forgotten for the time being as once again Maureen crept silently to her room to wash the sickening sweet scent of his cologne from her body.

Lady Beverly leaned back into the deep plump cushions of her chaise and absently smoothed the peach silk with her fingertips, over and over outlining the paisley pattern. She looked around her beautiful bedroom with its cream wallpaper and delicate murals depicting the ethereal and mysterious mountains of the Far East. Reina, her maid had already drawn the peach silk drapes, and turned down the embroidered counterpane. She was surrounded by softness, in the colors, in the fabrics, in the lacquered sheen of her furniture, bought in Japan on her wedding trip.

Decorated entirely in creamy pastels and white, her bedchamber was surely the most beautiful room in the house. Her floors were polished to a rich caramel sheen and carpeted with rare, plush Persian rugs intricately woven in a green ivy pattern on a white background. She had had everything made for her when she and Jeffrey were in the Orient, and particularly loved the unusual ivory furniture. Most of what she had seen in

Japan was sleek and hard and black, but this set was so different she had coveted it from the start, and Jeffrey had obliged her willingly, as long as her father was paying for it.

The sconces on the wall were of burnished brass, and the lit candles threw a warm glow across the dainty scrollwork and painted scenes of beautiful geishas surrounded by flowering trees and flocks of delicate birds. The light flickered and danced bringing life to the characters whose stories decorated the doors and drawers of her dresser and desk.

Beverly loved this room and usually enjoyed her moments of solitude admiring the fine craftsmanship of her carefully chosen pieces. The beauty was lost on her tonight, however, as she stared absently, seeing nothing. She was still reeling from the shocking events of the day and her left arm ached where Jeffrey had twisted it earlier in the drawing room. There was a tiredness in her chest, and a hollowness around her heart that had settled in when she visited Meg's room and realized again just how badly hurt her daughter was. She had just returned from the kitchen and was mulling over her decision to confide in the cook. She felt odd about recruiting Mrs. Carrey as an ally in Meg's care. She and the cook had never cared much for each other and now she found herself depending on her.

Beverly sighed and burrowed deeper into the soft lacey bolsters. She gently traced first the large curve, then the small twisted end of the paisley and sighed. Exhausted, she closed her eyes. She thought of the tea Mrs. Carrey had offered her and regretted not finishing it. She ought to ring for Reina. She could use a fresh cup of tea right about now.

She reached for the sherry bottle on her bedside table, deciding that what she really needed was something more substantial than a cup of tea. She admired the russet color as the sherry splashed into the hand cut crystal glass, and savored the familiar flavor like the kiss of an old flame.

Jeffrey said that she drank too much. Well, she couldn't really look to him for comfort could she? The sweet smooth wine soothed her as she welcomed the warm rush in her chest. The hollow feeling began to fade and she poured herself another glass. No, she certainly could not turn to Jeffrey for comfort. She let out an unladylike snort as she thought of the bitter pill the day had been, and how much worse his wickedness had made it. This had been a terrible spring and this business with Meg had thrust the whole house into a state of crisis.

What to do about Meg? She was seriously hurt! What if she died? There was not a great deal of affection between her and her daughter, but she had had a surprisingly strong maternal response to this whole event. But what could she do? She had come up against an immovable object in Jeffrey, and dared not defy him openly. He really frightened her these days. He had been terribly vile and nasty in all of his dealings with her lately and his threatening attitude had filled her with true fear.

She knew he was unaware that she had disobeyed his orders about Meg's care and was certain Mrs. Carrey would keep quiet if only to protect herself. But she knew Meg needed a doctor and Jeffrey had forbidden it. Beverly shivered despite her sherry and drew a beige chenille shawl over the bodice of her dress, mindful of how light this violet wool was and how chilly the weather continued to be. She wished Sharon had started a nice cozy fire in the marble fireplace when she had come in to light the candles.

There was a clear possibility that she may be responsible for greater harm by obeying Jeffrey. He had cruelly reminded her of her shortcomings as a mother for years, but she was not uncaring and she had never been neglectful. Tonight she felt for the first time, a squeamish fear that she might be the unwilling accomplice to a crime.

She shuddered again when she recalled how Meg could barely stand earlier in the evening when Jeffrey had dragged her down to see Tom Phalen in the drawing room. The deep purple bruises around her eyes were an alarming contrast to the extreme pallor of her skin. After Jeffrey had had Meg's lover bodily removed from their home, Meg had not been able to stand at all. Jeffrey had forbidden George and Stiller to assist her and Beverly had had to call Cory in to carry Meg to her room. She had given her some laudanum and Meg had slipped into a deep sleep.

She hated Jeffrey with ice-cold loathing and often in her dreams he had no face. She lived in constant fear that he might come to her some night, but she suspected that he satisfied himself with an assortment of young girls, especially that foolish redheaded Maureen. She supposed she ought to be grateful that Maureen had relieved her of the impossible task of pleasing Jeffrey, but she was a healthy woman and had at one time fancied herself in love with him. In fact she had once found that part of marriage very satisfying.

She shook off this train of thought and rang for Reina. Despite the three glasses of sherry she had downed, she was still cold and was pining for her tea and a warm fire. While the wine dulled the ache around her heart, it was a good cup of tea that would really make her feel better. She realized that she was hungry too, for she had only picked at her supper.

Jeffrey had insisted that she take her evening meal with him, despite his obvious abhorrence of her. He used the meal as an opportunity to continue his tirade against her, at one point rising to his feet and coming around behind her chair, placing his hands on her shoulders menacingly. He had stroked her bare neck with cold hard fingers as he emphasized that Meg should be made to suffer for her sinfulness.

He blamed Meg's weakness on her and Beverly had felt a cold rage rise inside her that he could be such a hypocrite. She had often wondered if he was aware of her suspicions of his many liaisons and trysts. As he leaned over the corner of the dining room table and bullied her throughout the meal, she had wanted to spit in his face and burn him with the venom in her heart. But as she had during every argument since they were married, she kept silent. She had always been afraid of Jeffrey. After seeing what he did to their daughter, she was terrified.

She eased herself up from her cushions and crossed over to her dressing table. She knocked on the thin wall separating her chambers from Reina's narrow sleeping cubicle, and began to take the pins out of her long blond hair while she waited for Reina to come. She combed out her hair and thought how fortunate she was to have very little silver mixed in with her golden waves. A pang of loneliness swept over her as she was reminded again how her beauty was wasted in Jeffrey's house.

There was a knock on her door and she bid Reina to enter. The door opened to reveal a round bronze face, set atop a plump neck that rolled over the white lace collar of a massive black dress.

"*Madame?*"

"Reina, I want you to prepare me a tray with tea and a light meal. I'm sure Cook has gone to bed and I find myself with quite an appetite. Before you go you can start a nice fire and warm this room for me."

Beverly took in Reina's blank expression. She knew the maid felt it beneath her to do the work of another member of the staff but she also knew that Reina was both her servant and her friend, and would do as she was bidden. Reina stood for a moment gazing steadily at her mistress without speaking. When it became clear that Lady Beverly was not going to discuss the events of the day, she quickly dropped a short curtsy.

"*Oui, Madame.* But of course."

With slow measured steps the big maid crossed over to the fireplace and hastened to prepare the fire. Before long a warm blaze was crackling and she stood up. Wiping her hands on her apron, she turned toward Beverly and again looked her straight in the face. Reina's big black eyes probed Lady Beverly's cool blue ones.

"Forgive me *Madame*, but *Mlle. Marguerite*, she is improved?"

"No, Reina, she has not, but she is resting. Perhaps a good healing sleep is what she needs. Lord Jeffrey wants no one with her but Maureen. I have ordered her to wake me immediately if Lady Meg needs me."

"*Oui,* but of course, Maureen."

Reina averted her gaze and Beverly felt her face flush. She suspected Reina knew she was lying about Mrs. Carrey being asleep, and she felt annoyed at being in a position of looking the fool.

"*Pardonez moi, Madame,* I must see to your tray. Will there be anything else for *Madame* before I go?"

"No, thank you. When you return you can help me out of these miserable stays."

Chapter Seven

In the weeks while Meg was recovering her strength, Tom had been laying the groundwork for her escape. He had revealed his plan to Ben, and had been heartened by the old man's commitment. Ben had assured Tom of the cooperation of some members of the household staff, including Mrs. Carrey and her niece Sharon, and nephew Cory.

The weather, so unusually inclement in May had warmed to fill June with sweet wild roses and honeysuckle. The mists burned off early to reveal a gorgeous vista of blue skies and scudding white clouds that cast little gray shadows across the lush pastures. Tom's spirits had risen steadily as his plan unfolded, though he could hardly bear to imagine Meg so close and yet so inaccessible. Her room was located in the front of the big house and he could not see it from his rendezvous point behind the stables. Only under the cover of night could he creep up the winding drive and gaze up at her window from behind the giant flowering rhododendrons that bordered the front lawn.

Once he saw her pass across the yellow square and his heart almost stopped with the sight of her. But this only happened once, though he tried to communicate through Sharon when he would be coming back. He knew that both Stiller and George were deeply indebted and fiercely loyal to Lord Jeffrey and could not be trusted under any circumstances. Tom had his doubts about Cory, but Ben assured him that Biddy Carrey would tan his hide herself if he so much as drew breath at the wrong time. So Tom relaxed and was glad for his help.

Lord Jeffrey himself was gone a great deal but revealed nothing to anyone about his whereabouts or his schedule. Ben warned Tom to be careful, and speculated that Lord Jeffrey must know Tom would be planning some way to rescue Meg and his child. After all, he was no fool. Though he himself loved no one enough to risk rescuing them, Lord Jeffrey did know the childish passions of the Irish led them to try heroics as a matter of course. Tom had no intention of falling into any traps and had patiently and thoroughly refined his plan.

He was relieved that Old Thomas was in Swinford at Dinty Barnes's funeral, but he winced at the memory of his father's hurt expression when Tom told him he would not be going with him to pay his respects to his old friend. Old Tom knew that Dinty Barnes had been like a second father to Tom, and his daughter Fiona had set her cap for Tom years ago. Tom had used Fiona's overbearing affection as his excuse to stay home but he didn't think his father believed him. It still jarred him to remember the suspicious look his father gave him as he pulled away in the borrowed wagon with young Philip as his escort.

Tomorrow there would be no moon and under cover of darkness before the new moon, he hoped to spirit Meg out of her father's prison but really had no idea where to go from there. All along, he had thought to take Meg to one of the islands off the west coast. He had thought of hiding her with nuns or disguising her as a poor peasant and hiding her in plain sight. Nothing appealed to him. Lord Wynn would find her and he'd find himself on a prison ship headed for Australia. He and Ben had formed and dismissed ideas for weeks. Now that it was time Tom felt ill with indecision. There was so much at risk and the best plan he had so far was to take Meg to Achill Island. In his mind, this was as dangerous and hazardous as taking her across the ocean to America. True, Achill was remote but Meg's father could intercept them anywhere along the route and even on the island he could find them. His only comfort was in Mrs. Carrey's assurance that Meg was strong enough to travel. That was one worry put to rest.

At the cook's insistence, Tom had recruited the help of one of the gardeners, her nephew Cory and her niece Sharon, one of the upstairs maids. Cory had reinforced the ancient vines of English ivy that climbed up the side of the house under Meg's window. He was absolutely convinced the thick vines would both bear Meg's weight and conceal the noise of her climbing down to the lawn. Sharon would be the sentry in the hall where Meg slept. Not even Maureen, the maid charged with Meg's personal care was to know. Tom felt strongly that Maureen was too likely to panic and put them all in danger. Sharon was just a child but Mrs. Carrey had every confidence in her ability to safely carry out the plan.

The young maid had already been trusted to pass information to Lady Meg in the form of cryptic notes concealed in boxes of Meg's favorite lemon verbena soap or folded into her dinner napkin. Meg was to wait for the night when Tom felt the time was right. Sharon would wait until Maureen left her mistress's room for the night and slip one last note beneath Her Ladyship's door with instructions for her escape. Sharon had never been told what that note would say nor did she want to know. The frightened girl knew her Aunt Biddy would not let her endanger herself by blurting out information under pressure. When the time was right, she would simply need to do as she was told.

The plan depended upon distracting Lord and Lady Wynn. It seemed that the fairies had smiled on his plan. Tomorrow, Lady Beverly and her maid, Reina were planning a shopping trip to Castlebar that would keep them there overnight. Lord Jeffrey had one of his all-night poker games planned. There would be strangers in the house but once they adjourned to the drawing room and plunged themselves into their wagering, no one would hear from them until dawn. Even George would be occupied behind the heavy mahogany doors pouring drinks and emptying ashtrays all night. Tom knew his plan was very dangerous. Already, it threatened to unravel with Mrs. Carrey's hasty departure to help her sister tend to an injured husband. When Ben loaded her and Sharon into the dray, the cook had reassured him that they would be back by morning. Tom knew that tomorrow night offered an opportunity that would not be repeated. No matter what, they had to go tomorrow. Tonight with his heart in his throat, he would meet with Ben and Cory to run through the motions one last time.

What he thought of now, as he approached the back of the stable, was that Ben was late for their meeting. He was immediately concerned and began listening for any sound that would indicate why he might be delayed. He heard nothing from the kitchen, and thinking that perhaps the old man had fallen asleep in the harness shed, cautiously rounded the corner of the building.

A loud whinny and the sound of hoof beats nearly cost him his life. Tom was so startled to see Lord Jeffrey ride into the stable yard that he cried out and almost stumbled directly into the path of his master's horse, Angus. It was a direct blessing from God that, at the same time he cried out, the hounds began to howl at their master's return. Ducking back into the shadows, he waited until he heard Ben wish His Lordship a good night.

Those moments when he stood in the black hole of panic, the smell of his sweat belying the chill of his blood, he almost abandoned all plans to rescue Meg. He could feel his bowels churning as he melted into the deep shadow of the yew trees. He prayed that Ben would not speak his name, because from his vantage point in the woods, he could see Lord Jeffrey lingering in the doorway pestering one of the scullery maids. He wanted to horsewhip him for bothering an innocent sweet thing like Peggy Crahen, and was much relieved when Mrs. Carrey appeared and Lord Jeffrey let go of her arm.

He heard what Lord Jeffrey said as young Peggy rubbed her slender white forearm. He heard what Mrs. Carrey always chose not to hear by turning on her heel and pretending she saw nothing. He heard that monster promise to catch up with her another night, and pay her well for resisting him so boldly. He also heard Lord Jeffrey laugh as he bellowed out the name of

Maureen, and his laugh echoed through the kitchen as he wove his drunken path to the stairs.

To Meg's relief, over the last several weeks, her father had resumed his air of indifference to the life of his household, with the exception of daily visits to her room to see that his orders were followed as to her exile and isolation. He need not have worried about his daughter overstepping the bounds of her imprisonment. Lady Meg's recovery was gradual and combined with the nausea of pregnancy, kept her confined to her room by her own choosing.

Whether he was aware of Lady Beverly's deceit or not, he made no mention of it. On her part, his order of silence made it easier to conceal. When he did invade Lady Meg's private domain, his cruel remarks and occasional physical threat left her ill with loathing. She grew increasingly repulsed by her father and one night when the lone remaining scab on her shoulder was particularly tender, his visit reawakened in her some of her old fighting spirit.

That night, her father had come searching for Maureen, complaining that the linens on his bed were not properly turned down. It was obvious that he had been drinking and the stale odor of the pub assaulted Meg's heightened sense of smell. She was perturbed at his rude interruption of her bath, the one amenity he had allowed. She had had the impertinence to suggest that he take it up with his own man George, or with Genevieve the upstairs maid. Certainly he need not interfere with Maureen, who had no responsibility on the second floor save that of attending herself.

He had roared that Maureen would obey his every command and barreling across the room to where she was standing combing out Lady Meg's hair, had grabbed the poor girl and dragged her protesting from the room. Lady Meg, stunned out of her chair by this display had stood staring from the door of her bedroom, listening to muffled screams and curses from her father's rooms down the hall.

She felt responsible for causing this eruption of rage and completely naive to Lord Jeffrey's real intentions, followed after them to see if she could somehow placate her father or at least deflect some of his anger away from Maureen until she could arrange the bed linens to his satisfaction. The effect of her isolation and Lord Jeffrey's general indifference to her had lulled her into a false sense of normalcy, and she had so effectively buried her fear of another beating, she actually believed it had been an isolated incident.

As she slid silently along the corridor, her damp waist-length hair left small wet swipes across the wall. Centaurs and nymphs gazed down from gilded frames as she passed beneath them. They played and celebrated in bacchanalian splendor in the soft candlelight of a dozen sconces along the wall. Meg had always thought the paintings odd, but somehow stirring in their licentious sensuality. In the last few months, as her own body had relished the awakenings of passion, she had even begun to enjoy them. The pastel colors and ephemeral fairies gave a lightness to the sex act that she had never even imagined existed before she and Tom came together. Her parents had certainly never behaved toward each other with any sort of pleasure and she had always wondered why her father had bought the collection in the first place. She recalled as she slid along the ivory silk wall covering, that her mother had insisted that he keep his vulgar lascivious paintings away from her private quarters, and how he had laughed at her delicate sensibilities. As she neared the juncture of the east and north wings, she found herself beneath the intense gaze of a particularly large man-beast about to descend upon a sleeping nymph. This was the one painting that troubled Meg and she recoiled as she passed under it.

Fear now returned to draw her like a magnet toward the terrible sounds coming from her father's room but as in a dream, her feet made slow progress. It seemed to take Meg forever to make her way to the corner of the east wing corridor and turn into the north wing where Lord Jeffrey's suite was the first door on the right.

As she shivered outside her father's bedroom door, Meg realized that this was the first time she had left her own room since her father had taken his crop to her. She stood rigid, afraid to move in any direction, as she listened to her father's low growled commands and Maureen's whimpered responses. She could hear the panic in Maureen's voice as she begged her master's mercy. Meg felt herself sway as she listened to her father's laughter. The sounds of scuffling and Maureen's muffled cries brought a wave of nausea so strong Meg doubled over.

She was damp, having just stepped from her bath and the evening breeze in the corridor combined with her surging adrenalin sent little quivers through her and weakened her knees so that she reached a trembling hand toward the doorframe for support. As she tried to steady herself, she was shocked to feel the door give way beneath the pressure of her arm.

Time began to slow down. Lady Meg, when she recalled the memory of these endless moments, would always see them bathed in a blood red veil, and feel them with the cold rigidity of rigor mortis. What she witnessed in that slender space within the amber frame of highly polished wood, changed her forever.

She backed away from her father's door a stranger. She stumbled back to the haven of her childhood bed, a stick woman, whose body refused to conform to the natural contours of its skin. The grinning centaurs and flitting fairies along the corridor took on a life of their own and the soft pink curves of the wood nymphs cowered in fear as she staggered past them toward the sanctuary of her room. She finally reached her door and flung herself on the white silk counterpane. Drawing her knees up to her chest, she tried to become small, invisible to the specter that threatened to steal her cowardly soul and leave her wandering forever in search of forgiveness. Meg, having just escaped the jaws of hell, buried her face in the bedclothes and howled.

The banshee on the moors heard her and howled back in sorrowful acknowledgement that one of their own was mourning, for the call of the banshee was not of the flesh but of the spirit. When Meg joined her spirit to Tom's and took the soul of his child into her, she had indeed joined the sisterhood of Ireland; all those who had ever loved a son of the sod, both living and dead.

After what seemed like hours, Meg raised herself up on her elbows and looked around her room, half-expecting that someone had heard her. A primal fear overcame her as she realized how very isolated she really was up here in this ivory tower, how this place which had at one time seemed such a peaceful sanctuary far from the bustle of daily life had now become a prison, a cell from which she could not even be heard screaming.

Her right shoulder and arm throbbed as she got up and hastened to close her door against the looming silence of the corridor. She knew that the silence meant that her father had finished with poor Maureen or at least Maureen was no longer able to cry out. She ran her hands through her long blond hair, tearing at it and pulling it until tears came to her eyes, but she still could not erase the horror. She poured herself a glass of water from the crystal pitcher on the table and sighed as the cool beads spilled over her parched lips. She felt very old, and very oddly detached from all that had ever been her life.

A blank white plain spread before her as her mind searched for images to define her future. She could imagine no future because her mind had slammed the door on her past. The only vision her mind could conjure up was the sight of a devil in her father's body torturing an innocent young girl, surrounded by all the trappings of gentility, the fine furniture and carpet, the glittering mirrors and graceful satin drapes receding into the fringes of her mind, the soft candle light taking on hellish dimensions until she imagined she had actually seen the licking tongues and abysmal shadows of Hades surrounding the two forms as they carried out the performance of some hideous dance. Her temples pulsed as she remembered. Her head felt too heavy, and her neck threatened to snap with the weight of the memory.

She could not sit for fear of the devil himself creeping up

the legs of the chair to grab her by the ankles and drag her back into the flaming room where her father had sold his soul forever to burn in hell. Nor could she lie down again. In doing so she would suffocate, her chest crushed by the weight of legions of demons released in that terrible moment when she witnessed the gates of the abyss open up and swallow her father whole.

Nowhere in her mind could Meg find reason to believe her father was himself when he did what he did to Maureen. Even as a victim herself of his terrible violent temper, she could not reckon what she had seen with the man who had raised her, had taught her to ride, to play the piano, to appreciate the fine and gracious life to which she had been born.

She had never deluded herself that he loved her, or even cared for her or her mother, but she had accepted his cold, harsh demeanor and learned from her mother to pacify him and obey him. When the women of Lord Jeffrey's household were wise enough to submit to his authority, without questioning his rules and demands, he left them alone, and was not ungenerous with his wealth.

But now, as she paced feverishly around her bedroom, she doubted every impression she had ever had, every conclusion she had ever drawn about her father. She was tormented by questions. Had he always been like this? The young girls in their service had always been uneducated daughters of poor Irish tenant farmers. Had he abused them all? She recalled with a shudder how pretty so many of them were and how some of them had left abruptly after finding themselves expecting a baby. Were these the children of her father, left to be raised in poverty and oblivion though they were born of blood as blue as her own? Were these her brothers and sisters she saw ragged and begging in the village square?

No answers came to her, only questions shouted from deep within her mind, accusing her of compliance through ignorance, of guilt by association. Her mind beat against her skull. She pressed harder and harder with her hands until she thought she would crush her head, but still the questions came. Shrieking demons with pointing fingers cavorted around her imagination, followed by exhaustion that forced her, finally, to fall onto her bed. Despite eyes blinded by white terror, her mind viewed and reviewed the depraved act she had unwillingly beheld.

The room had been suffused in gold candlelight, the red oriental carpet and rich, crimson upholstery of the furniture accentuated by the contrast of light and shadow thrown by the candelabra on her father's massive mahogany desk. As Meg's mind had tried to take in what her eyes could not deny, the sounds of her father violently subduing Maureen had assaulted her ears. She could hear the tearing of clothing and the unmistakable thud of the serving girl's body being thrown against the desk. In a vivid recollection of her own beating at the hands of this monster, she had stifled a scream as she heard the sound of his crop lash out at Maureen, and her knees had threatened to fail her as Maureen's muffled wails followed.

What Meg then saw was in silhouette, the shadows of the maid and the master long and distorted against the wall behind the desk. Maureen appeared on the wall first, thrown face down over the desktop by Lord Jeffrey, fighting and clawing to throw off the heavy skirt and petticoat that enshrouded her head. Her futile efforts took on the dimensions of some macabre demonic sacrifice, the desk the altar, Maureen the victim, played out in black against the wavering light of the sputtering candles.

The towering shadow of her father followed as Lord Jeffrey's arms, long and thick as an octopus crisscrossed the golden wall, forcing the smaller shadow into a position of helpless submission. Meg stifled a scream as she watched the black octopus arm plunge the long slender handle of the riding crop into the rounded shadow of the defenseless girl. Maureen reared up in a convulsion of agony letting out a shriek that was stifled by the thud of her head being smashed on the desktop, as the riding crop clattered onto the chair.

Then the two shadows melded into one as the vertical lines of the master took on enormous dimensions, completely obliterating the distinction between the quaking black mound of the prey, and the long reaching claws of the predator. The vision on the wall was etched in Meg's mind like the charred remains of a funeral pyre, and the animal sounds of conquest took on the primal grunting of victory. Meg could see neither faces nor bodies, but what she heard were the screams of the damned, as the tall flickering shadow pounced and plunged in a sickening cadence over and over into the vanquished black heap that was Maureen.

Meg had stood riveted to the floor as it began to crawl beneath her, moving like a million tiny living organisms. She had felt these organisms climb into her and invade the most private parts of her soul. Instinctively she had cupped her hand across her swollen belly to shield her baby from the grisly sight of its grandfather's demonic frenzy. Terror had gripped her then, as she realized that he may turn and see her and that viewing his face filled with evil darkness would taint the spirit of her unborn child. With a mother's fierce protectiveness she had torn her eyes away from the grisly spectacle and fled from the hall just as the shadows separated, the tall one straightening to the ceiling the small one sliding silently to the floor.

Lying as still as death on her icy bed, Meg was overpowered by a single thought. She must escape. She must leave this place tonight before her father could stop her. She knew Tom was trying to set up some sort of rescue, that Ben and Mrs. Carrey were helping him and could be trusted. This hope had been all that had kept her sane for weeks, but she feared she couldn't wait for him now. Thinking of him brought hot tears to her eyes as she longed for his strong arms around her. He was her life, the only one in her world who really loved her. She was desperate to join him, to have their child and be rid of this life which had held no meaning for her since her father had expelled Tom from his home, and now after tonight, held only terror and revulsion.

She tried to imagine the last time Tom had held her, the tenderness of his soft, blue eyes as she had told him of the baby. She tried to blot out the horror of this night with the soft glow of the other so many eons ago. She could not even conjure up his face. The shadows clouded her memory and Maureen's pleading voice filled her mind.

Maureen! If she went, she had to take Maureen too. After tonight, there was no telling what her father would do to her if he found Meg gone. She could not leave that poor, hapless creature to suffer for her actions. Never could she live with herself if she abandoned Maureen now. But how? How could she even begin to plan an escape that would work for both of them?

There was no way she could reach the outside, no way to signal Ben. Cory and Mrs. Carrey and Sharon had been called to Mrs. Carrey's sister Mary's house where her husband had taken a fall from a ladder that afternoon, and been seriously hurt.

The only ally she had in the house was Maureen. Her mother, while she had defied Lord Jeffrey's orders by occasionally visiting Meg would immediately close ranks with him against her if she were threatened. Meg wondered if Maureen was still in her father's room, and if so, whether he was still with her. She glanced at her mantel clock. It was almost ten. The men of the house would probably be in their rooms on the third floor of the north wing. The maids' quarters were on the third floor right over Meg's room, but both sets of servants shared a common stairwell at the junction of the two wings.

The only servants elevated to the position of sleeping on the second floor were Reina, George and Maureen. With a jolt, Meg recalled the fierce argument her parents had had when her father had decided to move Maureen down from the third floor last spring. Was her mother aware that her father had installed Maureen right down the hall for his own personal use? Did she care? Of course her father had prevailed. She knew and cared nothing about the private side of her parents' marriage, but she had long suspected that there was no affection or even common sexual behavior between them.

While her own rooms were across the front of the east wing, with only the lawns and tree shrouded drive to look out on, Meg's mother's rooms faced the back of the vast property. Her mother's private chambers were way over in the west wing where she could lock herself away from the rest of the house.

Meg tried to concentrate on her plan. She would need to act

quickly. Opening her wardrobe she selected a very simple riding habit and sturdy boots. Her shoulder burned and her right arm, which had taken a very long time to heal from the bruises to the muscles, ached deeply as she gingerly slipped on her skirt and jacket. She had no strength to lace a corset and she almost fainted trying to fasten her boots but she finally struggled into the last of her costume just as the clock struck half past the hour. She was aware of the tightness across her middle as she smoothed her skirt with her hands. Soon she would not be able to wear any of her old clothes, though it mattered little. Meg had no idea even where she would be after tonight.

Maureen had brought her supper, which she was to have eaten after her bath, and Meg now carefully wrapped the cold meat and cheese in a towel. She took everything that was on the tray, fruit and cakes and a small bottle of sherry. For once she was grateful that Mrs. Carrey had insisted on sending heavy trays laden with all sorts of tempting nourishment and mashing a meat pie into her mouth she realized with a pang that her nausea had been replaced by a terrific hunger of a sort she had never known. She was desperately thirsty too, and finished the cold tea Maureen had poured for her to drink while she had brushed out and tied back her hair.

Meg thought of taking a warm blanket, but realizing that it would encumber her and slow her down, she chose instead a sleek seal coat that would probably be too warm but would be good to sleep under if need be. She stuffed her jewelry into a silk lingerie bag and tied it around her waist, letting it hang behind her beneath the coat.

Now for the part that Meg still had not worked out in her mind. Leaving the safety of her room, she noted that her father had not returned to lock her in again, and wondered what this meant. Was he still in his room tormenting Maureen, or had he gone off, his rage sated, to drink himself to sleep somewhere else?

The candles lighting the corridor burned low as she once again inched her way toward her father's rooms. She realized that it was growing late and the upstairs maid would be coming to snuff them at eleven o'clock. Despite her paralyzing fear Meg knew she had to hurry to avoid being seen.

Beads of sweat formed on Meg's brow as she rounded the corner to Lord Jeffrey's room. She shivered as a trickle crept down between her shoulder blades. The seal coat was very hot and she cursed herself for bringing it, but there was no time to go back and leave it. She had to get to Maureen and get out of the house before last rounds were made at eleven. She had only moments and still had no clear idea how she would do it.

As she approached her father's door, Lady Meg saw that it was still ajar. This filled her with a new fear as a wave of revulsion threatened to bring her to her knees. If only she could know what she would find inside the room. Was Maureen dead? Surely Lord Jeffrey's attack didn't appear to be lethal, but what had he done after Meg had fled the hall?

She heard nothing as she peered through the same slim space through which she had witnessed the rape. Holding her breath, she gently pressed the door opening it another foot one inch at a time. She saw Maureen lying on her back next to the desk, her skirts still up around her shoulders. Her face, now uncovered, revealed nothing but a blank stare. Dry eyed with shock, Meg shifted her gaze to Maureen's belly and with a start, realized that it was at least as rounded as her own. Maureen's torn bodice revealed the full blue veined evidence of pregnancy.

The sight of this broken battered girl filled Meg with a resolve stronger than anger, more powerful than fear. This was her sister lying here, bleeding and breathing, suffering untold shame and degradation while daily ministering to her needs. This was a sister, a girl whose body looked the same as her own, moved and stopped moving, ate drank and slept with the same hunger and need as her own. Was there a sweetheart that Maureen longed to escape with? Did she know she was pregnant? Did she crawl to her chamber pot and retch every morning before coming to Meg's room with her breakfast tray? How many of those mornings, those crisply starched curtain opening, 'How is your ladyship?' mornings had followed nights like this? How many times did Maureen listen to Meg vilify her father for his cruel imprisonment, and churn with anguish for fear her own terrible secret would be revealed.

Meg had never known. Was she simply so selfish that she had never seen past her own pain, her own loneliness to see before her a young girl whose spent her life as a virtual prisoner to a maniac, who was forced to lie with every breath, pretending to be naive, chaste and youthful, while every moment that ticked on the big mantel clock brought her closer to another night of torture, another assault upon her most private self, her body and her soul? She had never really thought of Maureen as anything but a servant before she heard her screaming. She had actually felt considerable impatience with her on days when she moved too slowly and responded in that vague manner of hers. But that was before she saw the deep bruises on her thighs, the bloody stick of torture on the chair. Meg felt herself blush with shame as she realized how wrong she had been about Maureen, about all of her servants, about the poor in general. She had always been kind, as was her duty, to those of a lesser station but nowhere in her frame of reference was there room for any kind of equality or kindred spirit with them.

Standing in the doorway of her father's room, her eyes riveted to the pale, spiritless body of an Irish orphan girl, she realized that she had more in common with Maureen than anyone else. Her life was in great peril, and she was throwing herself upon the mercy of a man who had the power to make or destroy her. She realized too, that she saw not only Maureen raped and left to carry on in service to her master, but all Ireland, torn open and left to bleed by the same vicious master, who cared nothing for her heart or soul, who would welcome her death as a chance to subdue yet another victim and continue in the brutal cycle of conquest and enslavement. As she watched the gentle rise and fall of Maureen's chest, a great prayer welled up within her, a submission to God, if He did exist and a promise to survive with Tom as she hoped or without him as she feared. If her sister, lying on the carpet of her father's bedroom could survive and carry on, so too could she.

Maureen groaned and began to move around, drawing Meg

away from her thoughts. She peered around the door and scanned the room. Her father was passed out cold on his bed and Meg realized that she would have to move very quietly if she were to get Maureen out without waking him. She prayed that he was really dead and realized with a shiver that she could burn in hell for such a prayer.

A loud snore startled her to attention as her father began to stir. She had entered the bedroom and was in full view of her father's bed and holding her breath, stood frozen as he attempted to climb out and stand up. He fell with a crash against his wardrobe and slid unconscious to the floor. With a sigh that trembled dangerously with hysteria, Meg relaxed her shoulders. Turning toward Maureen, she started at the sight of the girl sitting up staring at her.

Meg whispered, "Maureen, come with me, we have to get away from here. Can you stand?"

The terrorized maid looked furtively at the sleeping master and mimicked her mistress's hushed tone.

"M'Lady, where are we goin'?"

The tremor in her voice told Meg that the shock of what had happened tonight combined with the amazing appearance of Lady Meg on the scene, could well put her over the edge and she could begin screaming.

"Listen Maureen, dear, we haven't much time. We have to leave this place at once. We have no choice."

"M'Lady, what are ye' thinkin? He'll be after us on horseback and be chasin' us down with the constable and half the English army!"

Meg smoothed the younger girl's hair and patted her purple cheek gently in an effort to soothe her. Looking straight at her, Meg's expression convinced Maureen that this was indeed going to happen.

"Aye, Ma'm, whatever ye say, but how can I go like...oh Ma'm tis that shameful fer ye to see me like this!"

Meg shushed the maid and reached over to the desk chair where Lord Jeffrey had tossed his jacket and attempted to place it around Maureen's bare shoulders, again whispering, "Here, cover yourself with this. It will hide you well in the dark."

Maureen struggled to keep her voice from rising.

"No, M'Lady, please not his jacket, please not a thing of his, I can't even bear the smell of him!"

Realizing she was speaking to her captor's daughter, she clamped her hand over her mouth and her eyes widened in horror.

Meg was unfazed by Maureen's words. She was much more concerned with the maid's near hysteria.

"Maureen, you must stop this. I am not a bit scandalized by your words. I saw everything my father did to you tonight, and I am also aware that you carry a child."

Maureen gasped behind her hand, as Meg continued in a low whisper.

"We have to work together tonight. If we are caught, I am in as much danger as you are. Now please put this on so we can get out of here."

"Yes, M'Lady."

Maureen shook with loathing as Meg gently lifted her arms into the sleeves of the jacket. As she buttoned it up the front, she saw Maureen's breast heave with a sob that threatened to become a wail. Taking the girl's head, she placed it softly on her shoulder and tenderly stroked her back.

Meg murmured into the tangle of red curls.

"We will get out of here Maureen. Trust me and we'll both trust Tom. We will escape this place and go where my father will never find us again."

With much more confidence than she felt, she ushered Maureen into the hall, closing the door behind her. She was mindful of the approaching upstairs maid as she heard the big grandfather clock strike eleven in the foyer downstairs. She did not dare enter the stairwell until she was sure Genevieve had left it so she hurried Maureen down the hall to the guestroom nearest the stairs. The two women hovered behind the big oak door and to Meg, their breathing sounded as ragged and loud as the wind on All Hallows Eve.

Meg heard the maid enter from the stairwell and turn down

the corridor toward her room. She prayed that she had remembered to close her bedroom door when she left her room, and felt her blood turn to ice when she heard the maid call out her name. The young girl hurried around the corner of the corridor, alarm in her step and Meg knew she had forgotten the door.

She had no time to panic and breathed a loud sigh of relief when she saw the maid was Sharon. Sharon turned at the sound and before she could say a word, Meg had a hand over her mouth and was dragging her into the guestroom.

Sharon's strength surprised Meg, and almost set her off balance, but she managed to get her into the room and close the door without hurting herself.

"Listen to me Sharon," Meg hissed, her hand still firmly over the maid's mouth.

"It's Lady Meg and Maureen and we need your help."

With this, Sharon immediately stopped struggling and turned toward Meg's voice in the dark.

"Oh, M'am, 'tis that glad I am 'tis yerself. Ye gave me a terrible fright."

"Well, we are all in grave danger. I am leaving this place tonight, and Maureen is coming with me. There is no time to explain anything to you. Simply answer my questions and do what I say."

"Aye, M'am, certainly, M'am."

"Good. Now, first of all, why are you home? I thought you were at your Aunt Mary's."

Meg strained to see Sharon's face in the pitch-black room.

"I felt poorly, M'am and Aunt Biddy, I mean Cook let Cory bring me back. She stayed on though. Uncle John died. Aunt Biddy says he broke his neck and all his bones."

Meg had the briefest pang of sorrow but there was no time for grief now. She had to think of her escape plan. Maureen was so silent, Meg was concerned that she might have fainted until she stepped back and stepped on her toe. A stifled squeal of pain let Meg know she was right there with her.

"Sharon this is what I want you to do. Go back into the

hallway and extinguish the candles as you always do, but before you do, light the chamberstick on my bed table and bring it to me. Go now and hurry!"

Meg spoke with assurance but she could feel the cold prickle of fear along her spine as she tried to think of the next step in her plan. She had difficulty staying calm because she really had no idea how they would get out unobserved.

While Sharon did as she was told, Meg decided what they would do. Sharon returned with the lit candle and passed it to Maureen, who gave it to Meg as though it would burn her hand. After Sharon returned to the corridor to extinguish the rest of the candles, Meg turned to Maureen and in a few hastily whispered sentences, worked out a plan. Maureen's eyes grew wide with terror at the thought of leaving the safety of the guestroom.

Sharon finally returned and Meg gave her the candle. She told the girls that Sharon would scout for them, and they would use the servant's stairs to get to the kitchen. They hoped the kitchen would be empty at this hour and they planned to hide there in the keeping room that had been used years ago for giving birth and was now a sort of sitting room next to Mrs. Carrey's bedroom.

Maureen pulled a rosary out of her skirt pocket and put it around her neck. Meg envied her this small comfort, and wished she too had some talisman to rub for luck. Sharon took the candle and softly crept into the hall, the two others casting long flowing shadows along the wall as they followed. Sharon slowly drew open the door and disappeared as Meg held her breath and Maureen clutched the back of Meg's seal coat.

It seemed an eternity before Sharon opened the door again and beckoned them with the sliver of light to follow. Their hearts thundering against their chests, Meg and Maureen obeyed, never giving a thought to the fact that they were entrusting their lives to a twelve-year-old girl.

Chapter Eight

Lady Beverly played with the tiny green tendrils that were beginning to poke out of the branches of her wisteria bush. She was spread out on a comfortable summer couch enjoying the soft evening breeze. This was her favorite time of year, and she was in her favorite place, the balcony off her bedroom.

This lovely spot had everything she could want. Tucked away in the juncture of the west and north wings of the huge stone mansion, her private retreat provided shade all during the day and a view of the breathtaking sunset every evening. As the season grew warmer and the foliage around a great climbing wisteria became fuller, she could freely walk the wide veranda that commanded a clear view of the formal gardens and bridal paths.

Lady Beverly also had chosen her suite of rooms because they afforded a good view of the stables and yard immediately behind the house. As any good horsewoman would, Lady Beverly observed carefully the care and grooming of her precious animals. Watching the traffic around the stables also gave her a sense of control over the coming and going of her staff as they congregated by the kitchen door directly beneath her balcony. She could see most of what went on and hear a great deal by eavesdropping behind the wisteria that both shaded her and shielded her from sight.

She loved sinking back into the shadows and hiding from her whole household, listening and spying on all of her staff as they went about their business day and night. The only person who knew how many hours Lady Beverly spent observing the goings on around her kitchen door was Reina, who never revealed her mistress's secret hideaway to any of the other staff. Not even Mrs. Carrey knew that Lady Beverly eavesdropped on her kitchen door gossip every afternoon.

The night was very cool for June, and Beverly pulled her fringed silk shawl around her. Her thoughts drifted to Jeffrey, taking a gentle turn brought on perhaps by the fragrant breeze reminiscent of their time in the Orient.

He had been her only lover, as the marriage had been arranged by her father and his. She had come with a remarkable dowry, not the least of which was this beautiful land and farm. She never had understood his disappointment when they had arrived here after their wedding trip. It seemed to her that as soon as they left Japan, Jeffrey had abandoned the role of lover. Was it the new role of landowner or father that had changed him? Either way, Beverly had become a commodity, simply one more item on Jeffrey's list of possessions.

She sighed aloud when she recalled how abruptly it all ended. She felt overwhelming physical loss when she thought of the long nights of lovemaking, looking out over the odd, slender mountains of Japan, of bathing each other with jasmine scented water in the porcelain lined cedar tub set out on a balcony much like this one, overlooking the perfect symmetry of the dainty, Japanese gardens. She remembered vividly a tea ceremony during which she and Jeffrey knelt on straw mats, feeding each other sweet meats, and sipping scalding green tea from tiny cups with no handles. They had made love for hours after that and had laughingly promised each other that they would drink green tea daily to enhance their passion.

As her mind drifted back to the time and place of her greatest happiness, she felt a chill come across her heart. The face of the beautiful Japanese serving girl on the voyage from

Nagasaki to Bombay crossed her mind.

They were finally returning to England after almost a year of idyllic paradise, she feeling the full-blown nausea of early pregnancy, Jeffrey anxious to return and get on with life as a country gentleman.

He had not been at all receptive to the news of the coming baby, and despite her almost constant sickness, had insisted on normal marital relations even on that wretched boat with all those odd foreigners around them. She had finally flatly refused him one night, after heaving and retching the better part of the day. Standing over the washbasin, leaning heavily on the hired serving girl, whose name she had forgotten, she had told him to please take his interests elsewhere, as he could see she was in no condition to please him that night.

What she had intended him to do was to go to the game room and amuse himself at the tables, or head for the company of the other men aboard ship and drown his frustrations in Saki. What he did was find a physician to sedate her, and in the very same cubicle in which she slept, satisfy himself with the serving girl. She awoke to find herself pushed far back against the wall of the berth, and her husband heartily enjoying the unusual talents of this most willing flower of the Orient. She had taken her heart that night and packed it on ice, never permitting his filthy hands to touch her again, never offering an explanation and never, ever speaking of what she had seen. By the time Meg was born they had become so estranged that he never even saw his daughter until she was a week old, and never showed any real affection for her until she was able to walk and talk.

As for herself, of course she loved Meg, as was her duty as a mother, but no one could force her to lavish kisses on the child who caused her so much misery and forced her to push her handsome young husband into the arms of another woman.

Meg had been a good child, obedient and very likable. She had been a beautiful baby with thick blond curls and clear green eyes. As a girl she had been demure and submissive, winning the approval if not the love of her father. She had studied well, trained well at the knee of Beverly's own nurse, and had never done anything to embarrass or shame her family until now.

When she was little, Meg had always asked for a baby brother or sister and when she realized this was not going to happen, contented herself with the children of the servants and those daughters of the few friends with whom Lord and Lady Wynn associated. This was the only trait that had always troubled Beverly, this penchant for the lower classes that Meg seemed to have. Throughout her youth she had preferred the company of the young maids and servant children to the more appropriate young ladies and gentlemen of her own social class. Beverly had spoken to Jeffrey about it many times, only to be scolded for permitting it, without being given any ideas as to how to avoid it.

When Jeffrey hired Tom Phalen as his stablehand back when Meg was just growing into an impressionable young lady, Beverly had shuddered at the possibilities. It was then that she took to sitting out on this balcony and keeping her eyes and ears open to all that went on in the stables, especially after dark.

How could she protect Meg when she could hardly trust herself around the tall, powerful Irishman with his wide, deep set eyes that could change from soft grey to dark blue just as a cloud casts a shadow across the sun. It had taken her a long time to feel comfortable around big Tom Phalen. He was crude and rugged but well-mannered and respectful. There was never a time when she could have pointed to him and accused him of an untoward remark or gesture, but he stirred in her desires that were long dormant, and she had often observed him gazing across the countryside with the same sort of longing on his face.

When Meg had first shown an interest in Tom Phalen, Beverly had thought to tell Jeffrey and have him dismissed but she really wanted him to stay in her own life. He occasionally entered her dreams and she awoke from those dreams restless and unable to return to sleep. But she found herself wishing for the dreams to return, so she could freely have him, to do what she wished with him and fill the void that Jeffrey had created.

In her waking hours she contented herself with her horses, which satisfied her need to touch and love another living creature. Tom Phalen was always there of course, his lean, hard muscles straining under the rough, homespun fabric of his shirt; his huge arms with their ruddy skin and thick, curly hair rhythmically brushing the satin coat of a beautiful animal; his broad, gentle hands entwined in the bridle as he led her horse from the stable.

Tom had that peculiar coloring of the Irish, that rosy fair complexion so like her own porcelain skin, and the dark black hair of the Moors, a combination she found very attractive. She had once thought Jeffrey a handsome man, with his soft, brown hair and green eyes, but his complexion was sallow and there always appeared to be a shadow across his face, giving him an unhealthy, anemic appearance.

Beverly tried to ignore Tom, tried not to feel his hand under her boot as he helped her into the saddle, tried not to appreciate the fullness of his lips and the wide breadth of his smile. Most of the time she succeeded. His unrefined mannerisms often confused her and his sly little humorisms were beyond her ken, leaving her puzzled and embarrassed at times. He was physically attractive but not enough to turn her head. She was a lady after all and if she ever would entertain the thought of taking a lover, it would be someone worthy of her station and not some sweaty Irish bumpkin with big shoulders and pretty eyes.

Still, she had not wanted to be without him. He was not only nice to look at he was excellent with her horses and she trusted him as she would no other in the county. Even her brother Robert had remarked once that he had never seen someone so gifted in the art of animal husbandry, and had more than once offered to take him on as his own groomsman if she ever decided to let him go.

Years ago Lord and Lady Wynn had arranged a convenient marriage between Meg and young Daniel Parker the son of old friends of theirs. Meg had voiced no objection to the sweet-faced boy with the blushing complexion and the perpetual smile. As they grew and matured, both Daniel and Meg had anticipated the joining of their families and fortunes with excitement, and grew as companions and friends. When Meg came of age, a formal engagement was announced. Daniel had given Meg a beautiful, sweet-tempered gelding as an engagement gift. She loved her horse and named him Jewel. Two months before the wedding, while returning from a trip abroad, Daniel was shot in a dockside robbery and had lost a leg. Lord Jeffrey had withdrawn his daughter's hand in marriage as the young man poured glass after glass of rye whiskey into himself in an attempt to stop the pain of the leg that wasn't there.

Later, when Meg's girlish infatuation with Tom had begun to become evident to Beverly, she wrote to her mother who had summoned Meg to London for an extended visit. Meg had been more than anxious to go and Beverly was more than happy to send her. She had never regretted the lengthy stay that Meg had been forced to endure but she was shocked at the change in her daughter when she next saw her.

When Beverly had arrived in London for her mother's funeral, the young woman she had sent away was no more. In her place was a woman whose body had blossomed from the sweet lightness of healthy youth into the full ripeness of maturity. Meg had grown in stature and in fullness, with a high round bosom and a slender waist which tapered into hips much narrower than her own, the hips of a virgin, of a woman whose belly had never borne the burden of a child. At the time, Beverly had thought with some alarm, that at twenty three, Meg had made her debut in London society too late and had not found a suitable match, and now she beheld a woman almost thirty years old still unmarried and seemingly content to remain so.

When she left Ireland, Meg had worn her hair in the youthful style of sausage curls and earlocks. Here was a young lady with a sophisticated coiffure, parted in the middle and twisted into a smooth chignon at the base of her long slender neck. Her dress, though made of plain black silk, was the latest fashion, the waist cut in a deep point and an ample bustle in the back. The shimmering black rushing at the bosom only served to accentuate the creamy whiteness of her skin. Her jet earrings and a plain cameo only emphasized her maturity.

Beverly's hand absently went to her own throat as she

remembered. She was still beautiful too, she really believed that. Despite Jeffrey's disinterest and brutish behavior, Beverly knew when she stepped from her bath or combed out her hair that she would be found attractive by many a man. It only served to make her sad to think about her wasted beauty. She had tried to find Jeffrey attractive after Meg was born, had tried to forget the days of his blatant betrayal, but she could not forget and she could never forgive him. She had simply decided to coexist with him, allowing him to provide her with luxuries befitting a lady of her station.

She sighed as she remembered the few years right after they came to GlynMor Castle when the one thing they were able to enjoy together was their common interest in horses. They had been much closer to her brother Robert and his wife Adelaide then, and had traveled often between the two households and to races and fairs together. They had spent almost every holiday in London with her parents and summered at her mother's farm in the Scottish highlands for many years. Then his father and hers both died in the Autumn of 1820 and Robert lost both Adelaide and his only child on Christmas Eve the very same year.

It had taken years for Robert to even speak of Adelaide and the baby, the only one she had ever taken to term, and Beverly's mother went to her grave blaming the double tragedy on herself because her own private physician was so drunk on Christmas punch that he never made it to her house in time to attend to her daughter-in-law. Robert never blamed his beloved mother and kept his pain to himself over the years. If it were not for their mutual love of horses, the true legacy of their father, she would have lost complete contact with Robert. She was grateful for this common bond. He was the only person who really understood her and allowed her to bear her own pain in silence. He understood and respected her way of keeping to herself the things she could not share. She could not bear to have lost him then and could not bear to lose him now.

Beverly faithfully attended the Anglican Church of Ireland with Jeffrey as was his wish though she never knew him to be a man of faith. Her attendance at church was born more of tradition and persisted out of habit but she had no objection to going. She never understood the passion for religion that the native Irish had, both Catholic and Protestant. To her it was ridiculous to get so riled up over an old man in Rome. It seemed to her that the Irish needed something to get excited about all the time and for some reason their religion provided them with an endless source of this excitement.

The Irish were a puzzle to Beverly. She was amused by them. They made her laugh with their odd little ways and their notions about life. She enjoyed their superstitions and their stories and she sincerely wished that they would accept their rightful place as subjects of the crown and stop their endless struggling. They were like naughty children who refused to obey and then blamed their parents for punishing them.

Beverly, however, did not share Jeffrey's terrible hatred of the Irish and she really did not understand why he felt as he did. She hated no one except Jeffrey and even tried to suppress that. It was simply too much effort and life was so pleasant when the nasty parts were ignored and left dormant. Beverly believed in keeping things simple. She did what Jeffrey ordered her to do and her household did the same for her.

This had been her domain, her castle until the last few months. Then Meg had returned from London to begin an illicit affair with an Irish Catholic right under their noses. The damning proof of it was his child.

It really mattered little to Beverly if their daughter ran off and married a dervish but Meg had disrupted the peace and quiet of her home and caused terrible difficulties between her and Jeffrey. She wanted Meg out of the house. She wanted no more to do with her. Let her take her Irish sod kicker and go. Let her raise a passel of loud brawling peasants just like him. Just do it somewhere else.

Living with Jeffrey was difficult enough without his constant harping about her slut of a daughter and her failure to be a mother, her drinking and her coldness. No matter which harangue he started with, it always came around to her locked bedroom door, the one topic Beverly refused to discuss and the one thing Jeffrey refused to let die. They had lived in this house for twenty-seven years and he still ended every argument with a slur against her virtue, sometimes accompanied by a slap or a threat of force. He had never accepted her refusal of his advances but though he rarely tried to force himself on her, he would remind her of her worthlessness and ugliness and lost youth every moment of every day until one of them died.

Meg's sin and her unborn baby had made his rage unbearable. He left the house every night and returned drunk and howling. Sometimes he would come and stand outside her bedroom door and just beat on it until he exhausted himself. Other times, when he suspected she was on the balcony he would stand in the stable yard and scream insults at her, swaying and slobbering in the dust. Beverly blamed Meg for this demise. Whatever dignity Jeffrey pretended to have had been stripped away by her coupling with this Irishman.

Jeffrey hated Tom Phalen so much that he wanted to set fire to all Ireland. He wailed and threatened to throw every last man woman and child with a drop of Irish blood into the sea. He sometimes ranted and weaved around the stable yard until George came and took him off to bed, and when he wasn't tearing Ireland to the ground, he was hollering for Maureen.

As for Beverly, she was simply tired. Her stamina for chaos was spent. Her tolerance for violent outbursts was dried up. She longed to be rid of the whole lot of them and just ride her horses through the green Mayo countryside.

It was that bone weary fatigue that Beverly felt on this soft June night as she sat stretched out in her favorite place on her most comfortable couch. She opened her eyes to a sky awash with starlight and realized with a shiver that she had fallen sound asleep. The yard was quiet and she could hear the heavy sounds of Ben putting gear away in the stable for the night. Jeffrey must be home then. She had not heard him come in. She strained to listen for kitchen conversation but heard none. She pulled out the heavy German silver watch she wore in her bodice and was very surprised to see that it was after ten. Feeling really chilled now, Beverly dragged herself to her feet and went in to prepare for bed.

As she crossed to her dressing table, Beverly knocked on the wall for Reina. She had a taste for something sweet with her tea and knew Reina would find her some confections somewhere. Reina was her favorite servant for the single reason that she was completely and totally devoted to her.

They went back a long way, to the night Meg was born, years before in London. Beverly had wanted to be near her mother and she and Jeffrey had spent the last months of her confinement living with the Cushings at their beautiful Georgian townhouse in the West End. When Beverly went into labor, it was apparent that there were some difficulties ahead and Jeffrey had sent for the doctor. He was attending another birth, and Jeffrey panicked, searching for anyone who could help. Reina was the first person he thought of and he hastened to the gaudy brothel where he often took his evening comfort in her arms. She had extracted a large sum from her favorite customer to come and attend to his wife. This was surely not her usual line of work. Reina was her own woman, used to making the rules of her own game and did this for Jeffrey because there might be something in it for herself. She was not an African, nor had she ever been a slave and she did only what she considered worthy of her time and effort.

The maid was the daughter of a beautiful Jamaican courtesan and a Spanish sailor who never knew she existed. Her mother, Miina, had been heiress to the fortune of a wealthy rum dealer until he died in a duel brought on by bad debt and dishonest dealings with the wrong man. When her father's estate was taken in payment of his debt, the pregnant Miina was left to fend for herself turning to the age old profession of beautiful, desperate women. Eventually Reina's proud Mama rose to the top of the house, inheriting it from Madam Sylvia when she died.

When Reina was eighteen, she and her mother left Jamaica. A hurricane had destroyed Miina's house but the two women were undaunted, knowing that they could take their remarkable gifts anywhere and find plenty of business. They sailed to London where they opened a new house.

By the time Jeffrey met her, Reina had become the madam of the house. The night before Meg was born, she had confided in Jeffrey just that evening that her heart was not in the business anymore and she would probably be selling it and moving on. He had offered to buy it, but she just laughed and rolled on top of him to show him what she thought of his offer. Instead she told him she wanted to live in Ireland, and it was his turn to laugh. What would Ireland do with a wild, black madam when all those papists were so busy making babies with the whitest women in the world?

When he had to find someone to help Beverly, Reina was the first woman he thought of. He knew a woman like Reina would know about birthing and had no qualms about bringing her into his in-laws' home to attend to Beverly. Beverly never knew where he had found her and it was years later when she discovered what Reina had been doing before she arrived on her parents' doorstep to deliver Meg. As for Jeffrey, he lost his favorite playmate. During the long hours of labor and the perilous delivery of their daughter, Beverly and Reina forged a deep and abiding relationship that excluded him entirely.

Now as Beverly opened the door to greet her maid, she once again felt a rush of deep affection for her friend.

"*Oui, Madame?*" spoke Reina with a slight curtsy.

"Yes, Reina, I wonder if you could get me fresh tea and find me some candy? I have a desire for something sweet."

"Of course, *Madame,* would *Madame* like perhaps, some nutmeats as well?"

Beverly put out her foot for Reina to slip off her shoes and stockings.

"Certainly, whatever treats you can find. Thank you. And Reina, I've had a nap outdoors and have really taken a chill. It's too nice an evening to light a fire. If you would heat a bed warmer for me too, I'll just put it at my feet while I have my tea."

"But of course, *Madame,*" Reina said, straightening up and tucking a soft wool throw around Beverly's feet.

Lady Beverly watched the maid retreat to the hallway that

led from the west wing to the servant's stairwell at the center of the house. As she listened to Reina's footfalls, she shook her head. It never ceased to amaze her how light Reina was on her feet for a woman of such large dimensions in both height and girth.

Chapter Nine

Tom waited in rigid silence for Lord Jeffrey to disappear well into the house before emerging from the woods into the slanted light of the stable window. He hissed Ben's name into the shadow of the stable doorway. Ben appeared like a sylph, silently sliding from the deeper darkness of an empty stall. Though he was hoping and expecting to meet Ben right there in the doorway, a chill passed through him at the sight of his friend's craggy face in the thin shaft of light.

Ben looked stricken at what had just happened. Beads of sweat marked his forehead as he gestured for Tom to join him in the shadows.

Tom, still afraid he might be heard, whispered.

"I don't like this Ben. That bastard is in a rare foul mood tonight. He's liable to do anything. Let's be quick about this and I'll be going home."

"Just take a deep breath, Boyo, and clear yer head. We just need to be clear on our set up and you can go. The moon is gettin' thin and by week's end 'twill be gone altogether. Ye know as well as I do that with a well laid plan we go, but one wrong move…"

Ben's voice faltered and he let out a deep sigh.

"I am too old t'fail at this. If we fail in this attempt t'rescue Lady Meg, ye're lookin' at a dead man. So, mark me well, and remember everything, every detail."

Ben's raspy voice rumbled in the blackness like the low growling of a cornered animal. Tom's temper flared and threatened to release his hold on the tight control he had so carefully established over the long weeks of planning this escape.

"Ye're a dead man? What d'ye think he'll do t'me if we're caught? 'Tis I who will be dead, or wish I were!"

He was exhausted and feeling ill from lack of sleep. The month of Meg's captivity had strained his emotions into a taut rope about to snap and he needed to keep a vise around his feelings

Tom and Ben slipped out the door and continued discussing their plan in the deep shadows behind the stable. They had every detail ironed out but Tom was frantic that Cory was gone with Cook. He keenly needed to confirm the final details with him. Without Cory, they couldn't even get Meg out of her room.

Meanwhile, Meg and Maureen crept silently behind Sharon as the three fugitives made their way down the narrow flight of stairs. The stale odors of cooking a thousand meals hung in the dry dead space connecting the cool stone kitchen with the lofty corridors of the upstairs. Maureen stifled a gag as the unadorned walls closed in on her and the bobbing candle threw off her sense of depth. Twice she grabbed the back of Meg's coat as dizziness and nausea swept over her. Countless times she had bolted up or tripped down these stairs in a hurry to do the bidding of her master or mistress, but this trip was like a descent into hell and she ground her teeth together to hold the scream crawling up the back of her throat.

Meg herself could barely contain her terror as she tried to follow the weaving maid in front of her. With each step she felt her foot reach out into a void, never knowing just where it would set down until it hit the narrow flagstone step below. The stairwell was so narrow and the spiral was so steep that there were times when Meg felt her heel touch the step while her toe was in midair. Twice, when Maureen clutched at her back, she thought she would lose her footing and career to the bottom taking all three of them with her. Sharon led with the candle and could see her way. The other two women were forced to follow in deep shadow and guess which way the light would lead them as it darted from one gray wall to the other down, down into the world of the servant class.

Meg sorrowfully acknowledged the irony of her new circumstances. It was fitting that she be heading downward in a spiral of darkness and flickering light. She had all but descended to the nether world and this was the end of her road, the final descent, the fitting end for a woman who had fallen so quickly and so willingly from grace. She stifled the urge to sob as they picked their way toward the cavernous kitchen.

What would they find there? Each woman instinctively inhaled as they rounded the last of the spiral and Sharon stepped gingerly onto the clean slate floor. The servants' stairwell ended to the left of the huge stove, connected to the kitchen proper by an archway deep enough to conceal Meg and Maureen while Sharon entered the vast room, the candle shaking in her trembling hand. Finding the room empty, Sharon motioned for the others to follow.

First Meg, then Maureen crept into the ring of light thrown by Sharon's flickering candle. Maureen let out a deep sigh that threatened to extinguish the pale flame, and realizing this, commenced to soft weeping. Meg hastily gathered up supplies for the journey. She grabbed two market sacks and filled one with a plate of sweets, a bowl of fruit and a few vegetables. Lastly, she grabbed some cakes from a plate on the table. Almost as an afterthought, she threw in the plates and bowl as well. She then went to a large sideboard and emptied the top drawer of fresh candles and utensils adding several cups and bowls and for no real reason a silver platter.

Turning to the stove, she helped herself to a large pot and two small ones. Just as she filled the second sack with two cheeses from the larder, and slipped a bottle of wine into her coat sleeve, Meg heard footsteps on the servant's staircase. Sharon gasped and Maureen blanched in the wan candlelight, as they stood frozen for a split second that seemed like eternity. Sharon grabbed Maureen and Meg and pushed them both into the keeping room. They no sooner pulled the door closed and snuffed the candle than the footsteps arrived on the cold floor where they had stood only seconds before. To avoid being heard, Meg had purposely left the door ajar. Now she could watch the maid undetected through the slender sliver of space

"*Quesque-ce?* What have we here?" they heard Reina ask aloud when she saw cook's empty table. Where were the treats cook always left for Lady Beverly's evening tea?

Meg knew Reina had instincts like a hawk and could sense the suspicion emanating from the big maid's body. She heard the rustle of Reina's petticoat as she searched drawers and cupboards for the missing food. A chair creaked under her weight as she stood and searched the shelf over the big Robinson Stove, and a ladle clanged to the floor as she lost her balance and almost fell. The noise startled the three women behind the keeping room door and they gasped. At the same time, Reina, as startled as they were, let out a little shriek. The fugitives could only hope that the noise in the kitchen drowned out their own.

Meg had no way of knowing whether Reina noticed the missing utensils or shopping sacks. She could only hope that her mother's maid, who rarely associated with the kitchen help, would not be familiar enough with the storage system to notice a few missing items. She shuddered, though, at the thought of Reina entering the larder, because the maid took great pains to reserve a supply of cold meats and cheese for Beverly, who often preferred these for her midday meal. Whether Reina noticed the two cheeses missing, Meg could not know, though she did hear Reina open and close the larder door.

Meg could hear the kitchen clock and the swishing of Reina's skirts as the maid began making tea for Lady Beverly. Cook had left the kettle full as she always did at the end of the day, and Meg heard Reina bank fresh bog fir sticks beneath it. She called out to a scullery maid who had taken advantage of Cook's absence to delay emptying slop jars from the kitchen. Collaring the girl, Reina cursed her for being lazy and demanded that she pull down the bed warmer from its hook next to the stove and fetch some turf from the pile in the yard. The three women listened as the young maid set the brass bed warmer on the table and then dragged the full turf basket across the kitchen floor. Bridey received a slap for her efforts when it scraped against Reina's ankle.

Meg peered through the tiny space

"*Isi, Bete!* Stupid fool! Put it here."

Reina pointed to the bench next to the stove.

"But Mademoiselle Reina, I can't lift it. 'Tis too heavy fer me."

"*Avec moi, imbecile! Quelle Bete!* Together we do!"

Together they set the basket on the bench with a thud and Reina demanded another brick to stoke under the burner cover. As the kettle began to boil, Reina scraped glowing coals from the pan beneath the oven and filled the bed warmer.

"So, *petit cochon*, you are the thief taking Madame's sweets from the table, eh? Eh, little pig, you are the one?"

Maureen caught her breath when she realized that the wretched girl was going to take the punishment for their foraging.

"No, no, M'am, Cook would flay me alive if ever I stole!"

The child was whimpering now, and Maureen had resumed her weeping. From their hiding place, the three could hear Reina pull up a chair and shove the frightened scullery maid into it.

"*Assiez.*"

As if she had a choice, the girl sat as she was commanded. What do you call yourself, filthy child? The little maid answered in a tiny voice, "Bridey, M'am."

Meg watched the older maid walk again to the stove, and set down the heavy bed warmer. Like a bird of prey she swooped down on the frightened girl.

"So, you do not steal, eh? We will see. Lift your dress, *Mademoiselle* Bridey. I want to see if you have anything tied to your skinny waist."

The girl, audibly crying by now, stood up and did as she was ordered.

The three women heard the sound of ripping, as Reina,

impatient with the child's trembling attempt, tore the thin material.

"Open your legs, little thief!"

Bridey sobbed as the older woman fumbled between her legs and reached up under her tunic in search of contraband. Satisfied that she had nothing to hide, Reina ordered her again to sit at the table.

"*Donnez moi!.*" Reina commanded reaching for Bridey's hand. The young girl pulled her hand away and only sobbed louder.

"I said put it out! The hand!" Reina ordered, grabbing Bridey's hand and smacking it, palm down, on the wooden slab.

"So, what have you done with the fruit and cakes?"

Meg and her companions huddled into their tiny space as they anticipated the course of the interrogation. They could imagine, each in her own mind, the triumphant gleam in Reina's eyes as she terrorized the child before her. Reina, usually so aloof with the other servants, seemed to savor this unexpected moment of power. As they waited in silent stillness for the inevitable blow to fall, they could almost feel Reina's breath as it must have felt hot and moist on Bridey's face.

"I have no fruit, M'am, truly I niver touched it. No, Ma'm, not the paddle! 'Tis nothin' I've done t'get the wood on me!"

Holding their breath, the three winced as they heard the loud smack. Before Bridey could retract her outstretched hand, down came the paddle across her knuckles. The scullery maid let out a howl and they heard the sound of her chair topple as she got to her feet. Reina, herself, let out a little squeal. Never having struck a servant before, she was as shocked as Bridey at her own behavior.

"*Allez, allez!* Go! Get away from me!"

Reina dismissed the girl with a scornful stream of French expletives, and the women heard Bridey scurry off to the safety of her room at the top of the house. The three women slumped against each other with relief as they listened to the sounds of Reina sitting down at the table, muttering aloud in a mix of French and English at the disappearance of the fruit. Soon they heard the familiar sounds of bread being sliced, the filling of the cream pitcher, the setting of the tea tray on the stove while the kettle boiled. Finally, they heard the splashing of the boiling water into the teapot and the clink of china as Reina secured the lid. Each one, in her own small parcel of space, held her breath as she waited to hear Reina leave the kitchen.

Within minutes, Lady Beverly's tea was on its way upstairs, and Meg cautiously opened the door of the keeping room and peered into the kitchen. A candle still burned where Reina had left it.

"She will be back for that bed warmer soon," Meg whispered to Maureen and Sharon.

"Sharon, you need to go now to your room. Be quick about it and may God go with you. You have saved our lives for sure. Remember, you know nothing. You simply arrived home from helping your Aunt Biddy, put out the candles in the upstairs hall and went to bed."

Meg embraced Sharon and watched nervously as she relit her candle from the one on the table and raced up the stairs toward her own room.

Maureen and Meg divided the bundles between them and crept into the yard, staying deep in the shadows along the walls. Meg could only hope Ben hadn't already closed the big stable doors. She knew if they were closed, someone would be likely to hear them dragging the heavy wood across the ground. The house threw the yard into the shadow of the waning moon and gave them the cover they needed to remain unseen until they were safely inside the stable. Meg's relief at finding the gaping entrance to the stable was replaced by panic when she realized that the same dark that was their friend in the yard became their enemy inside the stable. There was not a single shaft of light to illuminate the dank, fetid building. The women could feel the warmth of the horses and hear the large animals snorting softly in their stalls, though they could see neither wood nor flesh.

Meg's one remaining scab burned under the weight of the food sack and Maureen hovered so closely Meg felt as though she had added herself to the sack. Meg worried that Maureen would have trouble navigating the tools and equipment in the dark and knew silence was essential for them to get through the stable and out the other side. If they could manage to leave her father's property undetected, she was confident they could get to Tom's cottage and he would find a way to spirit them away.

The two women inched across the dirt floor, the sounds from either side closing in on them. The curious beasts acknowledged their presence with soft whinnying and foot stomping. Meg gently shushed them and tenderly said her goodbyes as she picked her way through both real and imagined obstacles. She knew there were two doors in the rear of the stable, a double sliding door matching the front doors usually locked at this hour and a small door to the right of these, leading to the grain bins. It was this smaller door, always unlocked, that Meg was trying to find.

The area between the two rows of stalls was wide but the darkness was so thick and the air so heavy with the smell of horseflesh, the Meg felt as though the walls were within arm's reach. She was almost overwhelmed with relief when they finally reached the other side of the stable without tripping or falling. Meg had just reached out to feel the latch on the grain room door when the door was flung open from the outside. She lost her balance knocking both of them into a stack of empty wooden crates.

Meg landed first, her fall broken by the sack of food and pans, while Maureen landed across her legs. Neither woman was hurt, but the crates made a clatter, startling the horses in a loud flurry of stomping and neighing. Added to the shocked exclamations of the two women, was the loud cursing expletive of a male voice on the other side of the door. Two men pushed their way into the darkness, one ready to defend the property of his Lordship, the other simply ready to fight whomever he found in his way.

Chapter Ten

The finalization of the plan to rescue Meg had gone poorly, with a stalemate over whether to take horses or not. Ben was deathly afraid of being hanged for a horse thief, and Tom could not see how they would get away fast enough without horses. They still could not devise a way to get Meg out of her room undetected, and Tom's frustration had reached a point bordering on panic. Ben, while still loyal to Tom's cause, knew the plan was weak and feared the consequences of their likely failure. The one part of the plan they agreed upon, though it did them no good to do so, was the timing. Both men knew the rescue had to take place at the end of the week when there was no moon. They could not wait another month until they would have the cover of darkness again. Tom had followed Ben around as he closed up for the night, and Ben was losing patience with him. He was tired and his bones ached. Lord Wynn had been in a most foul mood tonight and Ben just wanted to check the animals, close up the front doors and go to bed.

When they opened the storeroom door they were greeted by two intruders. Ben could tell by the scent of Lord Jeffrey's cologne that one of the interlopers was his master. The other, he surmised from the screaming, was a woman. Behind Ben, Tom stood frozen in place, no possible alibi to excuse his presence.

His fear again turned his insides to a running river and he prayed desperately for control.

Ben had no illusions about his lordship, but he had never encountered him in an adulterous act before. It occurred to him that he may have some leverage here, but he dismissed this idea as nonsense, given Lord Jeffrey's current frame of mind.

Meg did not know what to do. Having made an extraordinary amount of noise, and obviously having no reason to be where she was, she could think of nothing to do but lay still. Like a rabbit caught in the garden gate, she held still in silent terror, hoping this would render her invisible. Maureen, groaning, simply rolled onto the floor.

"My Lord!" Ben exclaimed. "I had no idea ye were in here, sir. Can I help ye? Can I get yer horse fer ye?" Ben knew he was sputtering and feared his shock would give away his own subterfuge. Behind him Tom bolted toward home, leaving Ben to deal with Meg's father. He literally ran for his life, not stopping for breath until he was well along the path and out of suspicious range.

Ben did not know whether to help Lord Jeffrey to his feet, or whether his master was on the floor with this woman intentionally. In the many decades he had lived on the earth, Ben had never found himself in quite such a quandary. When he heard Maureen groaning, he became even more flustered. This was not a scene he wanted to witness but he was a part of it now, so he had better play it to the end.

"Lord Wynn, sir, I'll just be closin' the door and returnin' later. No need t' trouble yerself, I mean, sir, I'll not be any trouble, uh, not goin' t'speak of it atall, if ye know what I mean, sir." Ben hastened to close the door and stood leaning against it gasping for air.

Inside, Meg's fear had galvanized her to action. She was angry at this unexpected turn of events. Dragging Maureen to her feet, Meg felt around for their parcels. Steadying herself and scowling at Maureen to stop making so much noise, Meg pushed against the door. With Ben leaning against it, the door, at first refused to give. This sent waves of panic through Meg and she began to cry. She beat on the door, crying for Ben to let them out, forgetting entirely their grave need for silence.

Shocked to hear Lady Meg's voice and believing that the other party was Lord Jeffrey, Ben was sickened to think what his lordship was doing with his daughter on the stable floor at this hour. He wanted to open the door but feared the wrath of his master. He could hardly let Lady Meg remain in there with that monster but he had no idea what Lord Jeffrey would do to him if he interfered.

He need not have worried. Meg finally pushed hard enough on the door to open it. From the pitch darkness of the stable into the relative light of the waning moon, two figures tumbled out. Ben found himself catching Lord Jeffrey as he passed out. He realized with a start that this was not his master at all but a woman dressed as Lord Jeffrey. He gripped the familiar tweed jacket around slender shoulders collapsed against his chest. Gently placing the woman on the ground, Ben turned to Meg for an explanation. Offering none, she simply rested her head on his ancient leather vest and sighed.

The few seconds it took for Meg to pull herself together seemed like eternal damnation to Ben. If the woman was not Lord Jeffrey, as she surely was not, then who was she and why was she wearing his jacket? Where was Lord Jeffrey and would he be coming for these fugitives any time soon? How was he going to explain his involvement in this bizarre mess? And where was Tom, now that Meg had actually gotten herself out the door of her room? If he had ever doubted his suspicion that he was too old for this business, Ben was convinced now. He was so wrapped up being finished with this ridiculous rescue, that he did not hear Lady Meg when she finally spoke to him.

"Are you listening Ben? Where is Tom? We need to get out of here now!"

Before he could answer, Lady Beverly called out from her balcony wanting to know what all the noise was. Ben came to his senses then and ducked back into the stable and out the front door. He called up into the darkness in the direction of the house,

"Only meself, M'Lady. I'm so awful clumsy in me dotage that I tipped a few crates o'harness is all."

With annoyance in her voice, Lady Beverly replied, "Well, settle down, old man and go to bed like the rest of us." She then turned and went back to the peaceful haven of her room, drawing her peach silk draperies closed against the night.

The deep shadows behind the stables made it hard for Meg to see Ben but together they helped Maureen to her feet.

"Whatever are ye' doin' here, M'Lady?" asked Ben as he steadied Maureen against the stable wall.

"We have to leave. I was able to get away from my father and I intend to take Maureen out of here as well. You must help us, Ben. My father lies in a drunken stupor in his room but there is no telling when he will awaken. Where is Tom, do you know?"

Meg gently took Maureen by the right arm and led her a few feet away from the stable where the moonlight was a bit brighter. Ben followed her, supporting Maureen under her other arm. Together, they coaxed the maid to arouse herself and look at them.

"Ben, do you have any whiskey?"

Meg smoothed the damp strands of hair from Maureen's face.

"This poor wretch could really use something to stir her vitals. I must take her and I cannot take her the way she is, for sure."

Maureen opened her eyes and murmured something neither of the others could understand.

Leaning closer to her face, Ben asked, "What is it ye said, girl? Speak up so we can hear ye."

Shaking her head slowly, Maureen again opened her eyes, this time forcing herself to engage their eyes.

"'Tis a poor wretch I am, indeed."

She barely spoke above a whisper.

"Ye need not trouble yerself with me. I am just excess baggage and I will only slow ye down."

She sighed, the effort of speaking almost too much for her.

Ben produced a small flask of whiskey from his back pocket

and wiped the mouth of it with a dirty kerchief. Meg almost smiled when she saw this futile attempt to wipe away years of back pocket dust and tobacco stains from the lip of the filthy bottle.

"You are a true gentleman, Ben."

She nodded as she raised the smelly spirits to Maureen's lips. The jolt of strong drink brought Maureen around so well, Meg herself took a healthy draught from the flask. She gasped and coughed a bit but was grateful for the sudden heat coursing across her chest.

Returning the flask to Ben, Meg repeated her question.

"Where is Tom?"

Ben nodded in the direction of Phalen's cottage.

"He was here when ye' were in the stable, but while ye were still inside we thought ye were his lordship. Tom thought better of stayin' to find out, and is off home by now. If I were in yer shoes I would be on me way there m'self. Tell him I'll try t'join ye with horses later tonight, but 'tis very dangerous. Tell him t'think hard about the next step we must take t'save our skins, beggin' yer pardon M'Lady, because Himself, Lord Jeffrey, will have murder in his eye once he finds out ye're gone. And remind Mr. Tom Phalen fer me that I am a very old man who wants to become an older man still so he had better think fast."

Beverly sat at her tea table looking puzzled at her bed lunch. Reina had brought her tea, though oddly she had forgotten the sweets Beverly had requested. She had returned to the kitchen to retrieve the bed warmer and promised a nice refreshing sponge bath when she returned, so Beverly was content to eat bread and butter.

The household was very restless tonight. She had sensed an unsettling energy just now when she had spoken to Ben. Her peace had been disrupted by the loud clatter of the falling crates and the horses neighing in the stable. It always disturbed her when anything disturbed her horses. She hoped by drawing her drapes and allowing Reina to bathe her with scented soap, she would recapture the serenity of the earlier evening.

Beverly poured herself a cup of the steaming amber brew. She took a sip of scalding tea and was buttering a thick slice of brown bread, when she was jolted upright by a most unusual thundering from deep within the house, followed by a chorus of horrible screams. Almost immediately there was silence but Beverly's mind echoed with the chilling sound of an animal in agony.

She ran toward the bedroom door, but the howls had ceased as suddenly as they had started. A sense of dread came over her and she became confused about what she had heard. Was this mysterious happening the culmination of the recent events that had so deeply threatened Beverly's peaceful existence? What had she just heard? The deathly quiet that followed the screaming was every bit as terrifying as the sounds themselves. Who would help her find out what was going on? Reina; yes, Reina was in the kitchen. She would know. Reina! Reina had gone for a bed warmer! Beverly raced to the servants' stairwell, little mewling sounds escaping from her throat, some sort of prayer perhaps, that her dear friend and only ally in this horrible house was not the one who had made those hideous sounds.

Arriving at the top of the servants' stairwell she flung open the door. She had forgotten to grab a candle and she realized that there was no way she could descend into the gaping cavern before her. Taking stock of the situation, she realized that she was surrounded by pitch darkness. Beverly crept along the wall until she found a door. She recognized the scent of her husband's cologne and puzzled at how she might have arrived in his room, she fumbled around for the candle sconce alongside the doorframe. There was none. This was so odd that she felt almost as though she were dreaming all of this and would wake up in her chaise any minute. There was a small washstand to her right. Feeling around she found a candle and a match. She struck the match along the rough bottom of the pewter candleholder and in a second there was light enough to see that this was indeed not Jeffrey's room, but a maid's room. Of course,

Maureen slept here. Yes, she remembered that Jeffrey had insisted on bringing her down from the third floor. Without another thought, she knew with sickening instinct why the room smelled of his cologne.

With a thud against her chest, Beverly slammed the door on that train of thought and applied herself to the task at hand. There would be time for self-pity later. Now, she had to find Reina. She returned to the top of the stairwell just as Jeffrey's man, George, appeared in the corridor with a candle of his own. He was soon joined by the butler, Stiller and Peter, Stiller's nephew, recently arrived from Dover, hired to replace Tom.

"M'Lady, whatever is the trouble?" asked George as he struggled to fasten his robe one handed.

"I heard an awful sound, a crash or an explosion and screams. I think it may have been from the kitchen." Beverly replied, afraid of the note of hysteria in her voice.

George and Stiller heard that edge and gave each other a look.

Stiller took command, coaxing Beverly as if she were a child.

"Mum, you stay here with Peter and we'll have a looksee. No use you tryin' to take these awful stairs in the dark of night. Peter, you get her Ladyship to a chair and a blanket for her lap."

Beverly realized with a blush that she was in her bare feet and allowed Peter to spread a shawl across her lap once he had dragged over a bench from under one of the bay windows. Again she smelled Jeffrey's cologne and almost retched when she realized that Peter, oblivious, had grabbed one of Maureen's shawls to lay across her knees. She began to protest, but Peter had busied himself lighting the wall sconces.

By this time, Stiller and George had descended the stairs and come upon the scene of the disaster. Beverly strained to hear what was being said, but all she could hear was the sound of a woman softly crying and the murmuring voices of the two men. She tried to go down the stairs with her own candle to light her way but Peter, as bold as you please, put his hand on her arm and stopped her.

"Mum, I think you'd better wait until they come back. You

may not wish to see what they're seeing now." His earnest face was all that prevented her from slapping him.

Instead, she called down into the darkness and demanded to know what was going on. In reply, she heard the grunting of the men lifting a heavy burden, and Reina cry out in pain as they lifted her.

"You take care of her," Stiller, ever the senior butler, said to George.

"Get her upstairs and send Peter down to help me." With this, the hulking forms of George and Reina emerged from the dark stairwell into the bright corridor.

"Reina, what happened to you?" Lady Beverly was off the bench in a flash, noting with alarm the blood covering the right half of Reina's face. George practically carried Reina and she winced and cried out with pain in her right ankle.

"Where are you hurt, what can I do? Take her into my room and put her on the chaise." Now that she could see her friend and attend to her, she had regained the authority to which she was accustomed.

The transformation had the desired effect on Peter, as she ordered the boy to go down and do whatever his uncle needed done. But Stiller, unable to manage, had returned for both George and Peter. Despite the pallor of his face and the trembling of his hands, George ignored her authority as he always had, but anxious to be rid of his heavy charge, deposited Reina on the chaise as Beverly had demanded.

"M'Lady, Lord Jeffrey..." Stiller began.

"I don't care about Lord Jeffrey!" Beverly shrieked. "I want a poultice for Reina's ankle and some whiskey for her pain. And send me a maid, whomever you can haul out of bed. I'll need help dressing this gash on her head."

Beverly's temper astonished all three of the adults in her room.

None of them had ever heard her raise her voice. Neither Reina nor Stiller was half as shocked as Beverly herself. Reina, despite the pain in her ankle registered a deep satisfaction that her mistress had such loyalty toward her. Her long-held suspicion that she had actually displaced Lord Jeffrey in Beverly's affections had just now been confirmed. George, on the other hand only hated Beverly more after her outburst. His loyalty had always belonged to Jeffrey. He had listened to the private lamenting of his drunken master, and had stored deep inside him the words of a husband scorned by his beautiful wife. For twenty-seven years George had attended to Lord Jeffrey, cleaning up after his drinking bouts, vicariously partaking in his sexual exploits. Lord Jeffrey regaled George with the details of his particular conquests, while George listened with feigned detachment. He knew that what was for Lord Jeffrey would never be for George. That was the way it was and that was the way it should be. He also knew that what His Lordship did was a vain attempt to heap coals upon Beverly. Her rejection had turned his heart cold and his feelings toward women had become twisted and hard like petrified wood. He shuddered as he remembered some of the hateful spewing he had listened to as Jeffrey slobbered and cried into his bathwater after a night of drunken decadence. While Stiller had assumed an air of indifference to his master's marital difficulties, George blamed Beverly entirely for her husband's demise. He had gone from a capable and intelligent master of his life, to a sot, obsessed with deflowering innocent girls and holding them up like trophies for Beverly to see. The greatest pain of all was that Beverly never even noticed.

Now, as his master and friend lay grievously injured in the servant's stairwell, the cold-hearted Beverly wanted to know nothing. She had frozen Jeffrey out of her heart twenty-seven years ago and George was right to hate her for it. It was his turn to bellow.

"Lady Beverly, if I may! My Lord Jeffrey lies at the foot of the stairwell so badly injured as to be in mortal danger. I insist you allow me to send for Dr. Simmons at once. Believe me Madam, he may not live the night."

George stood trembling with shock at both her Ladyship's attitude and his own boldness. Stiller simply stared at the two of them, saying nothing.

Lady Beverly was stunned into silence. Reina sat with her head in her hands moaning. George stood perfectly straight, defying his mistress to do other than his command. The moment, only sixty seconds long, was fleeting and with it went the last threads of normalcy Lady Beverly would ever know. In those sixty seconds, as she stood there staring at George, his voice echoing his newfound authority, she suddenly felt herself sucked into a vortex. Even though she stood, an adult woman, dressed in silk, her hair done up and her waist corseted, she was a child again. She heard the voice of her father scolding her for her selfishness. She was filled with dismay at her own mean spirit and overwhelmed by her sinful behavior. She had just been cruel to a boy she had been entertaining. She did not like him and her father was admonishing her for tormenting him with a stick covered in sticky tar. She felt herself running, waving her stick and retreating into the garden, sobbing at the humiliation of her unworthiness. Remorse overpowered her and she wanted to hide. She soiled her party dress with the tar and threw herself down on the pebbled ground. The stones hurt her tender skin and she scraped herself on a bramble bush as she tried to crawl out of sight. The pain felt good, banishing her wrongdoing, cleansing her, redeeming her. As she became smaller and smaller, praying to be invisible, she felt gentle hands tugging on her.

"*Madame, Madame, s'il vous plaît!* You must hear me. *Madame,* come back, you do hear me, no?" The soft voice caressed her ears.

Slowly, Beverly's body was dragged through time, back into her bedroom. Weighing what seemed to be tons, her mind was drawn back into reality. The heaviness of her mind threatened to force her back into the garden, back into the brambles, but the gentle urgency in Reina's voice insisted that she return to the present. She wanted desperately to stay in the garden. She needed the pebbles and the tar covered stick to absolve her miserable selfishness. She felt the release of hot tears as she realized that she must not, could not stay. Her father was not going to come and take her on his lap. No one was going to forgive her and soothe her ravaged soul. She blinked and saw the angry defiant George, his mouth still moving but she heard only the tender entreaties of her friend and maid. She turned her head gently as if it would fall off her neck, and gazed at Reina's face.

"*Madame*? Beverly?" Reina reached her hand up and tugged on Beverly's sleeve. The warmth of the maid's fingers brought Beverly back into the room. She looked at her arm where Reina had touched her. There was blood smeared on the silk lace. The sight jolted Beverly completely into actuality.

Stiller was hollering at someone now. Beverly realized that she had completely lost control of the situation and that Stiller had taken charge. She stood back and let him manage things. She was exhausted and Reina needed her help. Awakened by the shouting, Sharon and Genevieve had both arrived. Stiller barked orders at them as well as George and Peter, as the three men returned to bring her husband up from the stairwell.

Reina was directing Sharon and Genevieve to get her water and rags. The girls hurried to do as she bid. To Beverly, Reina said, "*Madame*, please, go with Stiller and George. You must be brave, but you must go there. Let these two assist me. I will be fine. *Allez!* You belong with your husband."

Beverly thought of protesting, but the look of pity on Reina's face stopped her cold. Why would Reina pity her? What could possibly have happened to Jeffrey that would be that bad? Why pity her? She didn't even care about Jeffrey. Reina knew that.

Beverly turned and arrived at the top of the stairwell just as Stiller and George eased Jeffrey's limp body through the door. It was at once the oddest and the most repulsive sight she had ever seen. There was something terribly unnatural about the way Jeffrey was bent and there was her bed warmer wrapped in the shawl Beverly had just had over her knees. The two men were handling Jeffrey as though he would break, and the stable boy gingerly steadied the hot bed warmer against Jeffrey's face. She followed them into Jeffrey's room. As she closed the door behind her, she felt mechanical, like a tin toy or a marionette.

Despite the bizarre sight of three men trying to squeeze her husband through his bedroom door, her thoughts refused to stop. She knew she should be concentrating on what was before her but her mind wanted only to deal with her own needs. She thought of her tea getting cold. She thought of her cold feet and her longing for her bed. She registered disappointment that she would not have her nice sponge bath now. She made a mental note to speak to Jeffrey about George's unacceptable tone of voice. She was just about to sneer at the thought of his reaction, when she caught sight of Peter and George lowering him onto the bed. Faced with the full spectrum of her husband's injuries, she felt the vomit rise in her throat. Grabbing a chamber pot, she heaved again and again. When she finally composed herself, she looked up and saw George looking at her with unbridled disgust.

"Lady Beverly, we're sending Peter for the doctor. I see that the sight of your husband sickens you, so you really must retreat to your own rooms. Mr. Stiller and I will minister to His Lordship ourselves until Dr. Simmons arrives. We will, of course, come for you immediately upon his arrival." George actually had his hand against Beverly's back as he ushered her into the corridor.

Beverly stood staring at the closed door, wondering how her household had been put on its head in a matter of minutes. Determined to find out, she gathered her skirts and barefoot, padded back to her room.

Chapter Eleven

Meg never heard the crash that woke the house. She was running toward Tom's cottage, dragging Maureen in tow, urging and coaxing her all the way. Maureen was openly sobbing by this time and stumbling so much that Meg was terrified that she would cause them to be captured. Meg herself was weak with exhaustion and when she wasn't heaving Maureen along behind her, she was heisting the bundles onto her shoulder to keep her precious booty from being destroyed. Finally, unable to balance the sacks anymore, she laid them down and gathered them all into her skirt, securing the hem under her waistband. With this ungainly bulk added to her swelling waist, she waddled and careened along the narrow path, driven by pure terror and a fierce animal instinct to survive.

What Meg and Maureen could not know, was that Ben had heard the commotion at the house and having dispatched the two women to Tom's, had gone into the kitchen to see what was happening. He entered the dimly lit room, noting the short candle left on the kitchen table by Reina. Then, hearing groans and muffled crying from the stairwell, he grabbed the candle and peered around the archway, and up the stairs. In the flickering light he made out the form of Lord Jeffrey slumped against the wall. He was crumpled, head down on the bottom stair, his face pressed hard against something brass. He lay perfectly still, not making a sound, and yet Ben could still hear crying. Holding the candle higher, he tried to make out who might be further up the stairs, but Lord Jeffrey blocked his way from entering the stairwell. A most awful smell came from the brass vessel and smoke filled the stairwell. Almost tripping on a glowing chunk of smoldering turf, Ben realized with a jolt what he smelled and where the smoke came from. There was no way he could assist his master from where he stood.

As he tried to figure out how he would help His Lordship, Ben heard Stiller and George enter the stairwell from above. His first reaction was to call out to them, but he was afraid to call attention to himself. He realized this would lead to the discovery of the night's treachery, which would be disastrous for Lady Meg and could even be fatal for Tom. He darted back into the kitchen out into the stable yard, praying that no one had seen him. Gathering his wits about him, he realized that with the whole household up, and Lord Jeffrey critically injured, it was up to him to cover for Lady Meg and Maureen. He lit a lantern and snuffed the candle as he waited for the next move from within the house. He agonized over the real need to warn the refugees of their terrible danger and the equally real need to pretend that he actually was simply up late, puttering around the stable. Within minutes, Peter, the new stable hand, was tearing a saddle from the hook, hollering to Ben as he pulled a mare from her stall.

"What are ye' doin' ye spalpeen? Who told ye' to be tearin' around in here like that?" Ben exploded at the boy.

Peter looked at him like a doe about to be sacrificed, and stammered out his explanation.

"Lord Wynn has been terrible hurt, and Uncle Stiller sent me for the doctor!"

"Well, ye'll not go far on that old lady. Take Bay Rum, he's the fastest fer sure. And be quick about it, boyo! We can't let the master wait forever."

As they saddled up Bay Rum, the boy's teeth chattered with fear. Ben had to ask him twice what happened before he could get a straight answer from him.

"We heard a terrible sound, me and Uncle Stiller and George. We were playin' poker in George's room and I had just dealt m'self a great hand. Before we could even toss a chip onto the table, a great crashin' came from the stairwell and we were off for downstairs. But when we came around the corner of the corridor, there we saw Lady Wynn already there, and her in her bare feet too. Uncle Stiller and George, they went down the stairs to see what happened and they found the big black maid, you know, the Frenchie one, and Lord Wynn all mangled on the stairs. I mean she wasn't mangled, she was just hurt, but he was in a mess. Christ save us, I never seen anythin' like it! When they brought him up the stairs, he was wearin' a bed warmer. I mean it was like a part of his face. I was trying to hold it in place and balance His Lordship's head and I did a good enough job if I may say so, until we put him on the bed. Uncle Stiller was at the feet, and George had his shoulders and I couldn't get to the head of the bed and hold onto the thing anymore, it was bloody hot I'll tell you. When I tried to set down his head it just slid off him, like. Not his head, mind ye' the warmer. God save us, it was broke open and hot turf fallin' out almost set the bed on fire too! The thing just rolled off his face, but then he had no face."

Peter"s voice was a whisper by the time he said these last words, and Ben wasn't sure he heard him correctly.

"What did ye' say, boyo?"

Ben took him by the shoulders and shook him.

"Is it lyin' yer up to? What form of trickery is this, that ye'd stand here and tell me such a tale?"

"But it's true! I tell you he had no face!"

The boy was pale and trembling.

"You gotta' believe me, gov, I'm not lyin! I swear on Mad George's crown! The warmer was stuck to him, like, and when I set his head down on the pillow, I couldn't hold it and His Lordship's head both, and the thing rolled off him with his face still stuck to it."

At this, the boy ran from the stable. Ben could hear him gagging and retching in the woods. The old stableman felt his knees go out from under him and sat down hard on a hewn bench. Running his hands through his thin grey hair he called out to Peter.

"Why are ye' goin' fer the doctor, boyo? Are they fools enough t'think he lives?"

Peter returned, wiping his mouth on his sleeve.

`"Oh, he lives, gov. He's breathin' and the like. Uncle Stiller thinks maybe he has some broken bones, but he lives. The face is the worst of it, truly."

Peter sniffled as he tightened the cinch around the horse's belly.

"I never seen anything like it and I hope I never do again. I really have to go. I really do."

With another loud sniffle he mounted the big horse and headed out the drive toward the road.

Ben sat for a long time before he realized that this horrible turn of events had caused him to forget Tom and the girls. With Lord Jeffrey so badly injured, and Reina hurt as well, he knew the household would be occupied for several hours. Now was the time to go! What there was of the moon was high enough; he could saddle up Jewel and Angus and get them to Tom's. Then he could return to his room above the stable and pretend to sleep. No, that would never work. Peter had already seen him up and would make a connection to him and the missing horses. He would get the horses to Tom and return to the house. With cook gone, he could step in and help out. Then, if two horses were discovered stolen in the night, he would have a reason for not noticing. He could not go with Tom as planned but he could be of more use to Tom right here at home.

He dragged himself to his feet and saddled the two horses. With a weary heart, he led them out the back stable door and mounted Angus. Jewel was a sweet tempered horse and would be a gentle ride, but he felt the weight of the world on his shoulders as he sat astride Lord Wynn's horse and led the smaller pony into the night. Angus was irritable after his hard ride earlier in the evening. He seemed to sense that he was involved in some strange behavior and balked at being coaxed through the dense yews.

Ben felt like he had been swallowed up by a peat bog. The darkness was so thick you could cut it in chunks and warm your house with it. He hoped he had chosen wisely by taking Angus, but he knew the old mare, Lily, would never cooperate and he needed the strong Arabian to carry Tom and the maid if Lady Meg were to ride Jewel. Lady Meg should probably not ride at all in her condition. Thinking about his ladyship's condition embarrassed Ben and he felt his face flush in the cool night air. He wondered as he listened to the soft footfall of the horses, how his peaceful existence on this glorious farm had come to this.

He thought about Lady Meg as a child, so soft and bouncy as he put her in the saddle. He remembered how keen she was to learn to ride and her first pony, Davy-boy. How she had loved that pony, and how she and had cried when she outgrew him. Ben smiled to himself as he remembered her thirteenth birthday, how gorgeous his little Lady had looked atop her first real horse, the old mare he had decided to leave behind. When Meg had received Jewel as a gift from her young man, long before his tragedy had ruined her chances of marriage, he and Lily had had a long talk. Lily missed Meg and never had any patience with Jewel but eventually Jewel became Meg's first choice and Lily was relegated to guests and buggy pulling. Now, he could only hope that Jewel would carry her and her baby out of here where she could start a new life with Tom. The light in Tom's distant window blurred as he felt his old heart break inside his chest.

Lady Beverly allowed Sharon and Genevieve to wash and dress the wound on Reina's head while she watched, exhausted, from her green velvet wing chair. The gash turned out to be less serious than it had appeared and in moments Sharon had tied the bandage securely.

"My word, there's a lot of blood." She remarked as Sharon gathered the basin and rags.

"*Oui*, I am like butchered meat, *non*?"

Reina felt the bulky dressing on her forehead, pressing tenderly on the gauze.

Genevieve tried to wring out the hot poultice, fumbling as it burned her fingers.

"*Non, Non, Genevieve*, I will do it, *s'il vous plait.*"

The big black maid took the poultice from the little maid and slapped it on her swollen ankle. The hot pack stung and Reina gasped at the pain.

"I fear *je suis casse, Madame! Oui,* she looks broken. Perhaps just a sprain but she looks odd in her shape. And not much swollen like a sprain."

"I'm inclined to agree, Reina. It does look broken and when Dr. Simmons is through with Lord Jeffrey, we'll have him look at it. Meanwhile, keep the poultice on it and maybe it won't get too big."

Lady Beverly watched as the two maids carried out the last of the supplies, leaving them alone.

"Now, tell me what happened."

Reina stopped fussing with the poultice and looked directly at her mistress and friend. She was not a woman given to emotion but her eyes filled with tears as she eased back against the bolster.

"*Madame,* he came out of nowhere. He was flying like *un ouiseau*, a huge dark bird. I had filled the bed warmer and had her by the handle. Of course, she was *tres chaud*, steaming with coals inside. I was, maybe, half up the stairs when Lord Wynn, he come flying down from above! I could not even cry out! He collided *avec moi* and ripped the bed warmer right out of my hands. I too became flying! Down, down we fell."

Reina was crying hard now and leaned forward, holding her bandaged head in her hands. Beverly looked in astonishment at Reina. In almost thirty years she had never seen her cry.

"*Madame,* I could not believe. He was screaming and screaming, it was *tres, tres horrible*. I fell on him, *Madame,* I could not help myself. I fell on him, my Lord Jeffrey. That must have been when I cut my head. O*ui,* I hit it on the stone. And his face, *Mon Dieu*, he was pressed on her, the bed warmer, *oui*? When I fell on him I …*Oh, Madame* Beverly, Lord Jeffrey, he screamed no more! I thought *il fait mort*! I am killing him. But Stiller and George, when they brought me in here said he still lived. *Madame*, what will you do to me? Had I not…"

"Nonsense, Reina! This is in no way your fault. My Lord Jeffrey is a grown man. I smelled the whiskey all over him. If he chooses to drink to excess and then go tearing around the servants' stairwell then it would have happened sooner or later that he would be injured. You were simply doing what you had been told. Don't you think I know that? Of course, a bed warmer is an awkward thing to carry upstairs full of hot cinders but there were no coals up here to fill it. You could never have known my husband was going to choose that moment to career down the back stairs inebriated and obviously in a mad rush. Why, Jeffrey never uses that stairwell! He has often said he cannot bear the stench of cabbage that lingers there. I have no idea why he was there at the time you were coming upstairs and I am sure you don't either."

Beverly had had about enough of this whole scene. She just wanted to retire to her pillow and her counterpane. She got up and poured herself a glass of sherry. Seeing Reina dabbing her eyes made her feel sorry for her friend and she poured one for her too. Handing her the crystal glass, she patted Reina's shoulder.

"Never mind about this, Reina. I can make do with Sharon until you're on your feet and I guarantee no one will blame you for any of this. His Lordship just had a terrible accident. I'm sure Dr. Simmons will be able to make him good as new. I'm more concerned for you right now. I wonder what's keeping the doctor? How long can it take to bandage a man's face?"

Tom was still in a state of shock when Ben called softly to him through the kitchen door. He had found the two women dragging themselves across the stony yard, and by the time he had Meg in the house and propped against the hearth, Maureen had fainted again, her body slipping down alongside the pigsty wall. He had carried her into the house and set her gently next to Meg. He could hardly make sense of what Meg was saying and he had no idea what he was supposed to do with these two women. His primary concern was getting them out of his house and away from Clydagh Glyn without getting them all killed. How was it that they came to be here now? How did they get here? Who knew they were here? His head swam with questions and all Meg could do was plead for help.

Tom washed Meg's face and hands and noted the bundles of food and utensils in her skirt. When he wiped Maureen's face with the same cold rag, he roused her a bit. She looked at him but he wondered if she really saw him. What had happened to these girls? What, especially, had happened to Maureen? She looked as if she had been beaten, or worse, had had the spirit beaten out of her. Meg spoke again and Tom crouched low to hear the whispered words. She told him that they had escaped the main house, that Maureen was badly hurt and that her own shoulder had begun to bleed again from the heavy sack she had carried. He wanted, needed so much more information from her, but she too looked at him with such a dazed expression that he wanted to wail with frustration. Where was Ben? How was it that they were here alone?

Just moments ago, he was barging into the stable door and coming upon Lord Jeffrey and another intruder. Now, out of nowhere, Meg and her silly friend pour themselves onto his kitchen floor, endangering all of their lives. No one could tell him anything. He turned again to Maureen and summed her up in one quick glance. He realized that she was wearing Lord Jeffrey's own riding jacket. How odd, that this should be so! But why not, on a night when everything normal had been put to the test and failed?

The little people or even the gremlins were on the prowl for sure this night. He felt real fear at the thought of their fate being left to the mercy of the fairies. He had scorned since his youth the very idea of leprechauns and had waved away the warnings of the old folks that to deny them was to incur their wrath. He could not afford to dwell on them now nor could he shake the sense that they were somehow watching him to see if he would humble himself before them. He was so desperate to know just what was going on that he almost asked aloud for their assistance. He checked himself just as someone rode up to his door. At first, thinking the small voice was indeed one of them, he gasped but then he realized what a fool he was as he recognized Ben's gravelly whisper.

With one more look to see that the women were safely resting, he went out to meet Ben. Maybe the old man could shed a little light on this mess.

"Tom, here take th'horses, ye've got t'get out of here right now!" Ben emerged from the dark into the pale yellow patch that fell across Tom's doorway.

Tom took the reins from the old groom.

"Here, let me tie 'em. What's goin' on here Ben? I've got two half dead women in there and I can't get a word o'sense out of either o'them."

Ben shifted from one foot to the other.

"Well, first off, those two are the same two we interrupted in th'stable. They had somehow found a way out of th'house and were lookin' fer us. I sent them on t'ye but oh, Tommy me boy, 'tis not th'half of it."

Ben inhaled deeply and took his cap off. Twisting it around and around in his hands, until Tom wanted to rip it away and heave it on the ground, Ben told the whole story as rapidly as his old lungs would allow.

Tom stood slack-jawed as Ben finished the most macabre tale he had ever heard.

"Are ye sure man, that he'll not be comin' fer us then?"

Tom squinted to be sure Ben looked to be in his right mind.

"Fer certain, I'm sure, Boyo, are ye daft? Do ye' really think I'd be here if I thought Stiller was about catchin' up with me? Ye must think I have no brain atall!"

Ben sputtered with indignation.

"No disrespect meant t'ye Ben, but ye must admit, it sounds as though ye've taken a leave all right. What am I t'do with these two? No way they're walkin' anywhere and even ridin'll be hard. Meg can't ride astride, so I'll carry her, and I suppose Maureen can ride with yerself, but she's not likely t'have ever been on a horse before."

Ben looked at the ground.

"Tom, I'm not goin'. I brought ye the two horses so ye could get away fast but I can't go. I have t'go back and cover fer ye' man. If they suspect that I went with ye, ye'll never get t'the next county. But if I can be there in th'thick of it all, I can steer them away from ye. They'll not connect th'pieces right away to be sure, they have enough t'do with Himself all burned t'hell the way he is. He may not even live th'night and if he does, Lady B. will be just as glad t'be rid o'Meg and Maureen anyhow. I imagine Stiller will be far more interested in His Lordship than yerself or meself, and I'm hopin', because Lord Jeffrey won't be needin' Angus fer awhile that he won't be missed. Ye can always send him back when ye get someplace safe."

Ben stood looking very old and very frightened, his cap finally still in his gnarled hands.

Tom gazed upon him as if seeing him for the first time as he really was. He was just a very old man, small and wiry, stronger than men half his age, but nonetheless, frail inside. He stood at Tom's threshold, quaking at the thought of spending his last moments swinging from the end of a rope. Tom turned his head and tried to see past the little yard before him. He knew this place like his own body, and even in the dark he knew just where the sow was lying in her muddy bed, and how many paces it was to the chicken house. He and his father had never had to keep animals in the house like so many of their neighbors. He had his grandfather to thank for that. A generation ago, before the English burned down his home, his Granda had built this little cottage for his daughter Clare and young Tommy Phalen. He thought of his Da and his Granda setting stone upon stone to build a separate place for their prize pig and the few chickens they kept for eggs. Tommy Phalen would not have his bride waking to the grunt of a pig wandering around her kitchen on a Sunday morning! No sir, not his Clare. So, Tom and his Da, despite the very humble interior of their little home, still kept a pig in the sty. Tom had always managed to mate the sows and kept the line going. It kept them from starving and provided a bit of income, though that bastard Jeffrey took a mittful of extra rent for keeping the sty on his property.

"I suppose I should take th'pig, though Da will need it come winter. Da! What is t'become of him?"

Suddenly Tom was painfully alert.

"Ben, what will they do t'me Da once they find out I've run off with Meg? We must get word t'me brothers. Da can stay with Paul or Davey. Davey would be better he's all the way over in Swinford. Da is there now, anyway, fer a funeral. They'll not likely go after him there. I'll go t'Father Dunleavy. He'll surely help. D'ye think he'll help me Ben. I don't go much ye know, t'church, I mean."

"What am I thinkin'? I have no time t'waste talkin' to a priest! Ben, could ye go t'the father fer me? If we can just get out of here tonight, maybe as far as St. Anselm's Abbey, there's a bit of roof there in case it rains. Then we can go west by daylight. I guess I want to get them to Achill Island. Aye, t'would be safer than the mainland and the Arans are too far. If you could git to Fr. Dunleavy fer me and he can get word t'Fiona Barnes in Swinford where me da's stayin', Da could go directly t'Davey and Mary and never have t'come back here again."

Ben nodded, though he thought that an old Jew going into Fr. Dunleavy's apartment in the rectory on a weekday morning would cause quite a stir. He knew Fr. Dunleavy's cook would lose her mind trying to keep a lid on that one.

"How long is yer da plannin' t'be away?" Ben asked.

"He just left for Dinny Barnes's funeral and had talked about stayin' in Swinford till the end o'the month. He even talked about stoppin' in t'see Davey. He has young Philip with him. Now, I know Paulie and Anna will be needin' Phil back here fer th'harvest, but not sooner. I think there will be plenty o'time t'reach him."

"Then this is what we'll do."

Ben put his cap on with a definitive tug and looked Tom

square in the face.

"I'll get word t'Biddy Carrey t'come home straight away. She's at her sister's and I may not even need t'send word, she'll be summoned anyway because of all th'fuss over there. In any event she'll be home within th'day, and she can go t'the priest fer ye. It'll be perfectly natural fer her t'go. Sharon told me when she came in that her uncle died today, so Biddy'll be wantin' t'help her sister with the arrangements. She can git yer message t'Fr. Dunleavy and he'll git it t'Swinford. 'Tis that simple."

"Meanwhile ye'll be off t'yer island with th'ladies and th'horses. I'll leave it up to yerself t' figure out how ye'll get th'horses, or at least Angus, back t'Clydagh Glyn. Take yer pig. She'll be good fer bargaining, or eatin'. Take yer chickens, too. Better yer dinner than a fox's."

Ben stood straight and proud to have fleshed out a plan for his friend. He had discovered over the last month that he loved Tom like a son. He could hardly bear the thought of losing him to the wandering life, as his would surely become. Ben knew he would probably be dead before Tom ever returned to this part of Ireland again and his heart split again in his chest as he realized that he must say goodbye to Tom now. He had never wanted to go with him on this leg of the journey, but now that the moment had come, he wished he were going after all. He had envisioned dying somewhere along the road and Tom and Meg burying him. He never saw himself as the one saying goodbye, left to stay home.

As he looked up at Tom, so strong and handsome, he could not bear losing him. He had trained him as a youth to handle horses, to love the smell of their sweat and the feel of their hides. He had enjoyed countless hours watching Tom brush their glowing amber coats, and soothe the mares during foaling. Ah, there, Tom had a magic touch. But Ben had never told him how that impressed him. He had never really shared himself with Tom. He had never told him he loved him, of course. The man wasn't even his own son, though Ben had known that if he were ever to have had a son, he would have wanted one just like Tom.

He saw in the furrows between Tom's dark brows, and in

the downward curve of his lips that Tom had carried far too heavily the burden of the last month. He saw the strength in Tom's expression, but felt afraid for him. His anger was so raw, his passion so unbridled. Tom had a part of him that had never grown up, had never learned to take the world in stride. He was a powerful man, his arms like tree trunks, his chest wide and hard. Ben had seen this strength many times, and marveled at how one so mighty could be so tender with a horse in pain, or a child in trouble. This man, this complex friend of his, his protégé, his son by proxy, stood before him for the last time in the dim pool of light thrown by a turf fire.

He tried to absorb him, to draw Tom into himself, to somehow capture his essence to take back to his lonely little room above the stable. This whole venture, from the time Tom had appeared, angry and awkward in the shed that night and hatched his plan to rescue Lady Meg, had energized Ben. He had felt a resurgence of the pride and courage that had made his own youth an adventure. There were times when they had huddled over a lantern and plotted, their sponc smoke filling the little shed with a blue haze, when he felt twenty years old again. His heart would swell with the passion born of pain that had filled his early years. He would recall the loss of his mother, the chanting and rioting against his and the other Jewish families in Lyons. The memories would wash over him, painful but somehow invigorating and life giving. He had loved his mother deeply, a widow with six sons. He had been her youngest and he would never forget the day she died. With his brothers either jailed or far from home, he alone sat shiva for her, his dear sweet Maman.

He lay in bed on those nights when he and Tom would share a pipe, and the hymns he sang for her would wander like ghosts through his head. The old psalms were the only French he still remembered. He would feel his heart beating hard in his chest, where it had lain dead for decades. There were nights when, after arguing with Tom and bickering back and forth about a plan, Ben would lay awake just basking in memories so real that his aching old body felt lithe and sinewy again. This man, with the heart of a boy, had made him feel like a boy again, weightless and immortal. What would he do without him?

Every one of his years weighed on his chest, every hurt, every fear, every disappointment settled itself on his back as he gazed into the face of his young friend. For the last time he searched the face he loved. He memorized the curl of his hair, the curve of his nose, his lips. He could not love this man more if he were his own true flesh. And now he was going. Now, Tom was leaving him to live in the wreckage of his life. His master would probably be dead by morning, the household he served was collapsing around him, the little girl he had so dearly served was leaving in a shameful state and Tom, his dear, dear friend was standing before him for the last time.

He knew Tom had no idea he felt this way about him. He had never given Tom any reason to believe theirs was anything but a basic working friendship. Indeed, he had taken great pains to conceal not only his feelings, but his personal history from everyone who lived at GlynMor Castle. It was simply easier that way and no one cared anyway about the rambling life of an old Jewish man from France, who spoke English like an Irishman, and had been assimilated silently and completely into the very soil of this lonely little windswept island. Now, he would return to life as it was before Tom barged into his shed that night and try to pick up the pieces as though it were every day that tragedy struck and those you loved left forever.

Tom looked intently at Ben. The old man had the most peculiar expression on his face. He would miss his mentor. He appreciated all Ben had done for him while he anguished over Meg and his child. Now, in one final act of courage and caring, Ben was giving him the means to get her away from here. He knew that Ben could suffer greatly for this and burned with shame to have ever doubted his loyalty. Now, as he was caught in the old man's gaze, Tom felt as though a web had wound itself around him and Meg. A protective mantle covered them and he somehow knew that they would be safe for years to come because of this man. He felt oddly like he did with Da, a tender dearness that he could not express.

He reached out and gently placed his big hands on the smaller man's shoulders, and embraced him. He felt Ben give a shuddering breath, a silent sob that touched his heart more than any words. As the two men met in this timeless ritual of departure, each drew from the other a new strength and resolve. They had met along life's long road and had done well by each other. They had no regrets, no debts to pay and now, pulling away from each other, each took a part of the other with him.

Ben had brought two small storm lanterns tied to Jewel's saddle. One he gave to Tom, the other, he lit with a lucifer from his pocket. With one more silent glance at Tom's face, he turned and walked around the pigsty and out of sight.

Chapter Twelve

T om turned at the sound of Meg's voice.

"Tom, who was that? Has my father found me?"

"No, Meg, yer father is not going t'be comin' after ye."

Taking a deep breath, Tom told her all that Ben had said.

Meg stood silent while the room swirled around her. The shock of hearing about her father's accident made her breathless. For a fleeting second she thought she would have to go home and the thought caused an involuntary shiver. Slowly she realized that Tom was speaking again and it was clear that they would not be returning to Glyn Mor despite her father's desperate state

Tom looked intently at her, his face a battleground of emotions.

"Now, I have a few questions of me own fer ye. Ye can explain while ye help me pull together a few things fer this trip we must take."

He helped Meg to her feet, as Maureen began to stir.

"And, ye can begin by tellin' me what she's doin' here."

Meg looked hard at Tom. It was clear that he was angry, but she could not understand why. He had not even touched her, other than to help her to her feet, and he was certainly not as glad to see her as she had expected. She wanted to cry with fatigue and disappointment. Surely, even with all the urgency and danger that this unexpected turn of events brought with it, he could, at least, be glad to see her.

She wondered what she was doing here in this shabby cottage her life in the hands of a peasant who knew nothing of her father's real power. She was afraid for all of them but mostly for herself. Meg recognized with ice-cold logic that the die was cast for her. She could not turn back. Whatever Tom was, he was her future. The lines between her class and the servant class, so cleanly defined in her father's house were invisible to Meg when she had lain with Tom.

She had told herself Tom was different, that somehow he had escaped the influences of rudeness and drink that somehow he had risen above the superstition and piety of his papist faith. Blinded by the passion that infused their love with a brilliance she had never known possible, Meg had ignored the real evidence of Tom's origins, the brogue he spoke with, the temper he showed as quickly and as unrestrainedly as his desire for her. She paid little attention to his clothing, and never saw the red creep over his face as he humbly took the cast off garments she got for him from Uncle Robert. She had never explored his past, nor had she ever had any interest in his reasons for his beliefs. There had never been time in their clandestine meetings to really learn of each other, to grow in understanding. They had never had the luxury of a normal interchange of ideas and so, had no idea of how they agreed and disagreed.

She realized that he was no different from any other rough, brawny Irish peasant and she knew that she was the same as any other spoiled aristocrat. A new fear crept into her heart. She was about to run into the arms of a man who said he loved her but was a stranger in every way but one. Again, the cold truth nestled near her heart as she realized that if Tom ever decided not to have her for any reason, she would be a misfit, welcome in neither his world nor hers, orphaned and widowed at once, without love or honor.

Tom busied himself gathering his few belongings, packing them with Meg's in the sacks she brought. He separated out the perishable food from the supplies, and tied them together so he could hang them both on Jewel's saddle. He was not sure about the lantern nor was he certain he wanted to take livestock, as Ben had suggested. He paused to think on these decisions and Meg began to tell her story. As she began, she started to tremble and he realized that her flight from her father's house was not planned nor did she have any idea of what to do next. The burden of forcing the terrible words from her mouth one after the other, describing the horrors of the night, made her knees buckle and instinctively, Tom reached out to steady her. Feeling his grip on her arms, Meg was shocked at the lack of tenderness in his hands and looking up into his eyes, she beheld an expression she had never seen there. She saw in the steely gray-blue, a vacant, recessed expression, as if he had gone far into himself where she could not, dared not, try to venture. He was a stranger, and she depended upon him for her very life.

Meg had imagined many reunions, laying in her bed these last weeks, and none of them were like this. She could not hide her crushing disappointment. She had fought valiantly, through pain and isolation, mortal danger and gut grinding fear to arrive at this hollow, crackling moment, in a void filled with paralyzing coldness. Who was this man and why did he no longer want her? What would he do with her and Maureen? Would he be willing to take them to safety, risking his own life to do so? Did he care about their baby and still want to marry her? Fear like a black-gloved thief crept into her heart and snatched away her hopes of a joyous reunion. What a fool she had been to think that he could still care for her after all this time. When her father had banished Tom from her life, of course he had had to abandon his feelings for her. How could she expect him to love her now? Lord Jeffrey had squelched their dreams; dreams she had shared with a man she hardly knew. Now, looking at his grave, unreadable expression, she felt her knees weaken again. Where had the old Tom gone? Would she ever get him back?

Tom could not fathom Meg's disappointment and fear. At

the feel of Meg's flesh in his hands again, he was overcome with a sense of awesome responsibility. Despite the fierce, endless nights waiting for her to be in his arms again, to hold her and love her tenderly, he felt neither fierce longing nor tender romance. He grasped her shoulders tightly, saving her from tumbling to the earthen floor, while he felt as though he, himself, was wading through deep water, his legs heavy as lead. Whatever was he to do with these two sick, vulnerable women? When he and Ben had hatched their plan, he had envisioned himself in control, the captain of their fate, provider and executor of the plan. Now there was no plan. No one was in control. No one knew what the next step should be. Ben had given him a lantern, suggested he take a pig and chickens. What nonsense was that? He should bring a pig to slow them down, chickens to announce them, and a lantern to light the way for anyone to pursue them; fine ideas, all. On a night filled with wild goings on, he was about to take two women on horseback across land that had no real hiding places to speak of and arrive safely, where?

Meg's face was filled with sorrow and shame. He wanted to tell her that he would protect her and their child, evident beneath her skirt. He wished he could invite her to sit on his knee and pour out the long story of her incarceration, to soothe her and murmur promises of his love and protection into her hair. Instead, he gripped her shoulders as if he could not let go and saw her face from deep within himself. He hardly recognized this dirty, frightened female as the woman he loved above all others. Together they stood, each wrapped in private agony, neither able to reach the other, neither able to let go.

Maureen stirred and began to moan. Tom relaxed his grip on Meg's shoulders and turned see Maureen struggling to stand up. At the sight of Tom, Maureen reeled, and clutched her throat. Tom immediately let go of Meg and she felt a cold draft of finality in his turning away. As Tom helped Maureen to her feet, he noticed for the first time her own swollen belly. Astonished he searched Meg's face for explanation. Maureen began to stammer, as Tom stood frozen in place at this new development. Maureen hung on him and begged him to leave her behind, her voice becoming hysterical and shrill. Meg turned and slapped Maureen hard, silencing her protests.

Shocked, Tom had to steady the maid on her feet again

"What is this all about? What is this, Meg?" he demanded, turning and seizing Meg by the shoulders again. Her voice flat, Meg explained Maureen's situation. Tom dropped his hold on Meg and walked away tearing his fingers through his hair. This was more than he could comprehend. Lord Jeffrey deserved to be shot. Obviously Ben had not known that Maureen could not ride astride any more than Meg could for he had provided only one woman's saddle. Now what was he to do? He had to put Maureen astride; he had no choice.

Tom was furiously snapping the necks of the chickens and tying them to Angus's saddle when Meg and Maureen came out to the yard. Meg gagged at the sight of the limp birds. Tom brushed past them and returned with a rag for each of them to wrap as many eggs as they could gather. It steadied them to have something to do and they were relieved to be out of his way. He stomped around, flinging and hoisting the bundles of supplies onto the horse's backs. He piled Angus like a field horse hanging two slip-bottom creels, one filled with potatoes the other with turf bricks, across his broad back. The horse, unused to these burdens, danced and bucked. Tom whispered softly as he steadied the rattled animal. He knew he could never put Maureen atop the huge bundles and almost despaired of a way to seat her safely on Angus's back until he remembered the old slide-car he had just mended for Danny Geary, the turf-cutter. He dragged it from behind the chicken coop and secured it behind Jewel.

The slide-car was a typical double forked model with broad slats forming a bed to carry the turf. He had re-tethered the old bog-timber shafts and runners with leather thongs made from a worn harness Ben had given him. He cushioned the slatted flatbed with the ticking he had taken from his bed, securing it with a rope around the shaft. This would be cushion enough for Maureen. At the last minute he decided to take both the lantern and the pig. The pig would slow them down but they had to go slow anyway with these women in their condition. He hoped he wasn't making a mistake but Ben was right. His da had always called the pig "the gentleman who pays the rent". This pig was no gentleman nor was she a lady either but the sow may bring money or shelter down the road. Besides, she would tear this place apart once she got hungry. He motioned for the women to follow him.

Maureen mutely trailed behind as Meg followed Tom across the yard. Meg allowed herself to be lifted onto her horse and Tom helped Maureen onto the slide-car. She immediately turned onto her side and drew her knees up. There was nothing she could do to make herself comfortable even on the plump sack of straw. She was afraid she would slide off the slide–car and held onto the shaft for dear life bracing her foot against one of the wide slats for balance. Meg tossed down the seal coat and Tom wrapped it around the shivering maid. He tied the pig up behind Angus, adjusted the pack straps and heaved himself up on the horse's back. After one last look at his home his gaze fell on the pigsty, barely visible in the scant moonlight. The sight of that crumbling old stone wall brought back the night he vowed to get Meg back and his hatred for Lord Jeffrey surged through him causing his knuckles to throb with the memory of pounding them bloody. If he wasn't sure how he would get these poor women away from that monster, he knew without a doubt that he would find a way.

Wordlessly, he prodded the horse and the little group began to move. He figured it was about eleven o'clock. Hopefully they'd be at St. Anselm's in an hour. The ruins would be a good place to rest but he feared it wasn't far enough. On the other hand, staying there tonight would give him a chance to think through the next part of his plan. He was grateful for the many trips he and Ben had taken with Lady Beverly buying and selling horses. He knew the land well and where there would be places to sleep along the way.

The territory he was taking them through was rough and sparsely inhabited. He believed as did Ben that this would be safer than taking the girls through towns where they may be recognized. Ben had convinced him that Lord Jeffrey would not pursue Meg. What did he want with her anyway? But Angus, that was a different story. He was a prize-winning stud worth a great deal of money to Lord Jeffrey. Even if Himself wasn't able to go after him, his men would surely be out here looking for him. If Ben didn't get hanged for a horse thief, Tom surely would. To think that he was in greater danger of dying for a horse than for the taking of the man's own daughter disgusted Tom but he knew it was true.

And so, west it was. He would drag these women south along the Clydagh River and west through the rocks of County Mayo to Clew Bay where they would cross to Achill Island, one of the roughest and most remote places he knew. The island would be the least likely place that lazy pair of house servants would venture even for the property of their precious master. This was where he wanted to take Meg and Maureen. This was where he wanted to hide them and work out the next step of their plan. For the first time he wished he were a praying man for he needed divine guidance now. He looked at the moon on the crest of its rising and silently signed himself with a cross.

Chapter Thirteen

The thin crescent moon was high in the sky when they reached the shadowy ruins of St. Anselm's Abbey. The huge cross loomed against the night sky behind the crumbling apse. The ancient stones seemed to wave and shimmy in the light thrown across the wind-whipped trees. As Tom had known, the roof over the altar was intact and there was a good space where they could sleep under it. He could smell a storm coming but the thin moonlight was still good. As they carried their bundles into the ruin and Tom fed and brushed the horses, clouds began to course overhead and thunder rolled in the distance. He thanked himself for deciding to bring the storm lantern and gratefully lit the wick as the moonlight disappeared behind the gathering clouds. He tethered the horses to the rusted grill of the old cloistered partition where they would be out of the rain. The pig, he barricaded in a stone walled cubicle that once echoed the confessions of the sinful heart. He hoped the sow would be quiet. This was a better place than any she had ever slept in, a fact he pointed out to her as he prodded her fat hind end through the narrow doorway. They grunted in unison as the sow settled down on the stone floor and Tom shoved a massive old door into place to prevent her escaping.

For Meg he used the horse blankets to cover the floor and covered the rough blankets with the fur coat that he took from

Maureen. His heart pounded in his chest with recognition when he rolled the hem to make a pillow for her head. How many times had he thrown this same coat on the ground, filled with heady passion, feverish with desire for the woman who would lie on its silky black fur tonight? The irony of their miserable circumstances made him dizzy. He wondered how Meg could be so calm as she pried Maureen from the slide-car.

"Come on, Maureen, sleep next to me. We'll keep each other warm." she coaxed. But Maureen clung to the slide-car and refused to let go. She left Maureen and found Tom piling the last of the sacks under the eaves away from the threatening rain.

"Tom, can you help me? She's half out of her mind. She won't come off the slide-car and I'm too tired to force her and you can do it and..." Meg's face crumpled and she began to cry.

Like a shot of strong whiskey her despair filled him with hot tenderness. He reached for her to take her in his arms and without another word she silently vented her tears against his chest.

"Meg," he began. "I'm truly that..."

His words trailed off when he saw Maureen slip to the ground as she struggled to lift herself off the slide-car. As quickly as Meg had fallen into Tom's arms, she was out of them, alone and crying. Furiously she wiped her eyes and set about gathering the straw mat to add to their bed. Tom half-carried Maureen to the makeshift bed and gently laid her down. Meg turned away from Maureen and looked up at the gathering clouds scudding across the moon. She hated both Tom and Maureen at that moment. Never had she imagined her life taking this turn. Despair clawed at her and she shivered against it. She watched numbly as Tom dragged the slide-car into the old abbey, banking it into a corner formed by one crumbling wall and the partially collapsed stone of another. The second wall had fallen at an angle and formed a small shelter where it had wedged against a sarcophagus. He shoved the slide-car under this wall hoping it would escape most of the rain.

Meg adjusted the coat over the straw mat and sat down on her rude bed. Maureen still wore Lord Jeffrey's tweed jacket and the scent of his cologne was almost overpowering to Meg.

"Maureen, let's take off that jacket, you'll get too warm." Meg suggested.

"Ach! I forgot I even had it on." Maureen cried, "Get it off me!"

She sat up and began tearing at the sleeves as Meg pulled it off her shoulders. Meg involuntarily shivered at the sight of Maureen's torn bodice. Tomorrow she would find a blouse in her bag for Maureen to wear.

"There, now," Meg whispered as she flung the coat over in the corner of the sanctuary, "You don't have to smell him tonight."

But Maureen never heard her. She was already slipping into an exhausted sleep. Meg pulled up the blanket and tried to sleep herself but she kept hearing Tom slamming the slide-car into the corner in an attempt to shield as much of it as possible from the coming rain. Bad enough Maureen would need to ride on it, she didn't need it to be soaking wet.

Meg lay awake, trying to imagine what Tom had started to say. He had finally been willing to comfort her and she had finally been able to go to him when the moment had been destroyed. What had he meant to say? He was truly that what? She tried to stay awake to ask him but even as her eyes failed her, she knew the moment was gone and he would say no more tonight.

Tom checked on the horses again and settled himself on the cold floor resting against one of the saddles. Within minutes, a hard rain started to beat on the slate roof and pool on the floor around them. Tom thanked the fates for giving them the elevated sanctuary to sleep in. He thought of trying to recapture the tender fleeting moment with Meg but he was just too tired. He rolled over on his side and fell into a deep and dreamless slumber. Meg slept fitfully, her dreams full of centaurs and beasts prowling around her mother's kitchen frightening the scullery maids and nipping at a pale light from under the keeping room door.

Maureen had no comfort. As soon as she fell asleep, she was

awake again. She somehow dragged herself to the other side of the grill. From the beginning of the ride to this haunted old church she had been having hard cramps in her belly, occasionally at first, then regularly. She lay wide-eyed and terrified by the intense, rhythmic pain that began in her sides and gathered in her belly causing her to draw up her knees and shift from side to side in an effort to find comfort. Nothing she did helped and she began to panic when the cramps came closer and closer together and took her breath away. She stuffed her skirt into her mouth until she gagged trying to quiet her cries and her tears mingled with sweat to soak her face and hair. No matter how she willed them to stop the pains came again and again, tearing and pressing at the same time, longer and closer together. She thought of calling out to Meg but she was too ashamed to have Tom Phalen see her like this. More so, she felt a fierce possessiveness of her misery. She had suffered her pain alone for so many years she would not, could not share it now.

Hour after hour she writhed behind the grate with only the horses to hear her groans. Every so often one of them would nuzzle her and whinny sympathetically. Around dawn the rain stopped and the black silence was punctuated only by the dripping of the trees. Wrapping her arms around her belly she felt the rise and fall of each contraction. She knew her baby was coming too soon. She longed to scream with every wringing twist of her insides but a terror stronger than her pain kept her in its grip, forcing her to silence her anguish and suffer her loss in secret. She thought she could stand it no longer and became unable to remain quiet when she finally felt a gush between her legs. The warmth of life and the cold hand of death came to her at the same time. Like a silent chorus hitting a soundless crescendo, one agonizing convulsion after another wrenched her insides and forced out what felt to her like everything that lived in her. And then it was over.

She lay panting, soaked with perspiration but the pains were gone. Her body was calm and relaxed, her eyes heavy with the sleep that had eluded her for hours. She dozed in bliss so foreign to her she imagined she had died. As if dying, her consciousness of all around her slipped away from her as she sank deeper and deeper into soft nothingness. She knew in the pit of her soul that hers was a false bliss and even as she lost herself in sleep, a black despair as deep and silent as the bogs of all Ireland flooded her, starting at the roots of her hair and creeping through her gut, seizing her entrails as its sticky ooze leaked out of her taking the life of her child with it into the night.

Maureen lay still as stone. She thought she was dying but she awakened with her heart still mercilessly pounding in her cold chest. Frightening tremors shook her and rattled her teeth. She could smell her blood as it seeped beneath her skirt and no amount of stillness could stop it. Maureen knew she would have to look but she could not bear it. After several attempts, she found the strength to raise herself up. The next step was impossible and she sat for the longest time just staring at her lap. The eerie light of dawn fell across her and hands that she could not feel tugged gently, tentatively at her skirt. Her mouth opened in a silent sob as she drew back the layer of filthy homespun and bile crept up the back of her throat when she saw her petticoat stained deep crimson. She flung back her head and with her eyes closed tightly she ripped the bloody shroud away.

Uncontrollable trembling overtook her as she willed herself to open her eyes and lower her head. Eyes wide, Maureen gazed with tender horror upon a spectacle of death. Beneath her skirts lay the body of her baby, in a pool of clotted blood, its little cord still attached to the useless piece of womb that had failed it. At the sight, her heart fell to pieces within her and the chilling tremors turned to waves of heat that burned through her marrow to the very fingertips that drew back the cover from this tomb. As Maureen sat in the presence of this little person, this hapless being that had suffered both birth and death in the same moment of existence, her horror left her and only a deep, yearning tenderness remained.

This was her baby, the only living part of her that she had ever had for herself. No matter how brutal its conception, she had grown to love this child. Despite the sickening truth of it being half Lord Jeffrey, she had prayed to the Virgin mother that the half that was of her would make it a good person, worthy of life. Now she had her answer. Not even the blood from her veins or the love from her heart was worthy of life. When she awoke to find her baby, so tiny and purple, lying between her thighs, silently and anonymously delivered into immediate death, her grief was paralyzing.

She sat in the dawn light barely able to comprehend this new sorrow. She tried to touch it, to see if there was any hope of life in its still form but she could not make her fingers connect with the wrinkled skin. She strained to see any sign of familiar features that would show that this doomed creature was actually of her blood but she found nothing recognizable in the tiny wizened face. Only the long narrow fingers seemed to be of her and she strained in the dimness, unable to see if she had lost a son or a daughter. She sat numbly for what seemed like hours, unable to conjure tears or even rage at the terrible reality that months of torture and degradation at the hands of Lord Jeffrey had ended in this final, crushing, annihilation of life.

When the rain started again and Tom and Meg began to stir, Maureen simply covered her repulsive treasure again beneath her skirts. She was suddenly afraid that Tom and Meg would take it away from her, would bury it here in this evil place that sucked it from her in the night. As fever burned a phosphorescent glow around her eyes, she silently gathered her child into her skirt and defying anyone to try and disturb this bloody grave, fled into the night.

⊹

Tom groaned as he awoke stiff and sore sometime before dawn. The rain had stopped and the lowering moon was barely visible through the vacant skeleton of the ancient rose window above him. Meg still slept and he could just make out her profile in the thin light. Maureen he couldn't see at all in the deep shadows of the sanctuary. He felt a rush of guilty longing to take Meg in his arms. She slept deeply and he watched her for several minutes, his thoughts a jumble of sad speculation and regret that he had ever put them both in this awful position.

What was he thinking, a peasant Catholic like himself, so many years older than Meg, taking advantage of her the way he had? He had been a moderate man until that cold morning in the stable. That seemed like another life belonging to other people.

How had he let his passions get so far ahead of his common sense? His father had been right. There was no way this could ever be. She carried his child, yes, but only by his sin and her foolishness. She had given her heart to a man who had nothing to give her. He had forgotten his place entirely and allowed himself to be duped into thinking that the wide chasm between them was bridged by their love.

What did he know of love? How could he have been so blinded by pride not to see that he could only hurt her every time he touched her and that their lust would certainly end this way? He was the worst kind of fool, besotted by the feel of her skin and the fragrance of her hair. He had taken all his years of continence and flung them like so much fairy dust into the wind and now like a bad boy caught in bed with a milkmaid, he loathed himself for his actions.

No, that wasn't really it, he thought. A bad boy would only laugh at the fate of the milkmaid and run to another barn and tell his lies to the next pretty face. He had always cared for Meg. He thought he loved her but now he couldn't trust anything he thought. He wasn't a bad man; he really cared about Meg. Hadn't he planned and plotted to rescue her from her father? Yes, but in the end he had been too slow about it and she had risked everything to get away herself.

He deserved to feel horrible. He wasn't a holy man but he used to go to church. He used to confess thoughts that he had never even tried to put into action. Now, as he searched Meg's sleeping face for any hint that she dreamed of him, he wished he could find inside himself the man he was when she was in London. He ached for the days when it was just him and his Da, old Ben and the fellows in service at Lord Jeffrey's.

What did he ever want a woman for anyway? He had hardly thought of Meg while she was gone. God above, she was just a child when she left. How did he know she would be a full bloom of a woman when she returned? He could not blame her for seducing him. The thought that somehow she was to blame made him queasy. She was never to blame. He was the one. He should have been stronger, so much older and supposedly wiser. He had simply given in to the weakness of all men and now they both, no, there were three of them with the child, now they all would pay. The sight of the smooth fur of the coat, glossy in the moonlight, embarrassed him now. He should never have known that coat beneath him; wished he had never felt its smoothness. He saw it now for the luxurious bed that should never have been his.

He turned his back to her and shifted on the cold floor. He heard the horses whinny as his litany of self-recrimination continued its relentless beat in his head. He longed to turn back the clock to be her servant and saddle up her pony again. He lay in the gray light and tried to settle back to sleep. Finally, as the birds began to announce the dawn, fatigue claimed him. The rain came hard again as weird dreamy images cruised through his mind dissolving into sleepy wanderings along paths that all ended along the pigsty wall. His troubled mind could not get him and the girls safely away and sleep offered no relief from his phantom guilt.

Maureen staggered through the brambles that filled what once was the monastery entrance and careened into the night, oblivious to the thorns tearing at her ankles. Once she was away from the old church she pierced the air with a primal howling that filled the dawn with death and defied its wan, feeble, rain-drenched light. Onward she ran, her skirt still gathered up, wrapped around the voiceless one for whom she keened, her jarring steps punctuating her screams with shivering anguish. As the rain came hard and cruel, she wailed into the black torrents, her wordless cries lost on the twisted path, repelled by the dimly lurking trees. Small animals heard her with a fear that led to burrowing, searching for old wounds suddenly in need of licking.

She knew none of it; not the pain of her thorn torn skin, not the cold of the pummeling rain, not the putrid, fecund smell of wet soil and fresh blood. She ran into the night as one possessed, her demons close upon her, her fear overpowering. She saw nothing of the path before her; tasted nothing of her rain-soaked hair whipping across her tongue. Her agony complete, Maureen knew nothing but the dead child in her arms. Her heart was frozen to the specter of her dead baby lying between her legs. No whip to her thighs, no invasion of her inner parts had ever dealt her such a fierce blow as the loss of this child. She could not fathom why this was when the tiny creature was born of the despicable violence of Lord Jeffrey's seed. That her flesh and now her child's flesh were forever branded with his seal could not have made her loss greater. That her child was spared a life of scorn and misery could not begin to ease her pain. And so she wailed into the night despondent of mercy, despairing of justice; alone in the dark, utterly abandoned by even the littlest of companions, her last hope for love on this earth.

After aimlessly circling around and around a crumbling cistern, Maureen turned toward the river with sudden purpose. She needed to get to the tumbling waters of the Clydagh. Her thirst and her filth suddenly directing her steps, she heaved into the rain in a straight line to the water. The river was farther than she imagined but her steps never flagged. She knew what she would do and she never looked back. She still cried out to the heavens but her words now came in breathless whispers only she could hear. She had a purpose now as she trundled upward to the brink of the riverbank. She had thought it very steep and could barely catch her breath as she broke through the trees and rounded the high meadow.

Collapsing on the edge of the world, the heavy river rushing by below her, she searched her lap for her bundle. It was gone! O sweet Jesus, Mary and Joseph, please no! Had she lost it? Dear Virgin Mother, where had it gone? She unwrapped her skirt and felt among the folds. Not finding her baby there, she crawled around and patted the soaked ground until she felt a tiny cold limb the size of her thumb. Taking her sweet baby by its little arm and cradling its body in her palm she lay down among grass and wild shamrocks and closed her eyes.

Her cries turned to crooning as she held her baby to her heart and tried to protect it from the rain. It was so cold, dear Lord, could she maybe warm it next to her bosom?

"There, there little one, don't cry. Mam's got ye now. Sweet Jesus, did ye find an angel for this one? Does my darling's angel know we're here at the end of everything? Dear Jesus do ye know my little one?"

She murmured and hummed her litany of questions, just Maureen and Jesus, her baby and Mary's baby, together on the bank of the tumbling river waiting for the rain to stop so she could finish what she came for.

Meg awoke with a start, feeling a jolt of fear that instinctively caused her to reach protectively across her abdomen. Something was terribly wrong. She sat up and looked toward the corner where Tom snored softly and felt immediate relief. Shifting on the sack of straw she realized she was alone. Where was Maureen? Ambling to her feet she tried not to disturb Tom but in her clumsiness she groaned and he stirred. She looked around the grill but saw only the horses. Lighting the lantern she saw that Maureen had made a bed in the straw but was no longer there. The horses stomped and snorted when they recognized Meg but she was already through the archway that had once led to the sacristy of the old church. How thick the brambles were here, reaching even into the sacristy from the yard outside. They snared her skirt and she bent to shake them loose. She thought better of going further because the rain had started very heavily again and turned to go back into the sanctuary. It was then Meg caught the unmistakable odor of blood and noticed a slick dark pool in the straw where Maureen had made her bed.

"Tom!" she cried, now desperate to wake him. "Tom, come here!"

Tom lurched to his feet at the fear in Meg's voice and finding her not where she was supposed to be, thought he was dreaming. She called again from the other side of the grill and he rounded the old metal grate in one step.

"What, what?" He stammered, still half asleep.

"Maureen is gone and there is blood in here where she was sleeping." Meg pointed to the stain.

"But she was next to ye. What was she doin' in here?" Tom scratched his head and passed his hand across his eyes trying to focus on the scene.

"She must have moved after we were asleep," Meg said as she bent closer with the lantern.

"There is a large pool of blood here Tom, and here look there's more. I think she's had her baby and it's way too soon."

They followed the trail as far as the sacristy. Tom looked at Meg and both of them remembered the terrible state Maureen was in the night before. Maureen had run off and behind her she had left a trail of clots and bright red blood causing Tom to gasp in alarm and Meg to feel ill with horror at the speculation of what might have happened while they slept.

In a flash, Tom turned to go after Maureen. Meg called to him to wait. Instinctively she knew that Maureen would never let him catch her.

"If you catch her she will fight you and who knows what will happen to her?"

"But Meg, she could end up in th'river! She doesn't even know where it is!

"No, Tom, don't chase her. She'll run into the river for sure if she thinks you're after her. There's no baby here so she must have it with her!"

Meg stood up and came toward Tom, touching him gently on the arm.

He looked at her hard.

"Meg, I have t'go after her."

"Wait for me then, I'll follow you."

"No, ye will not! I'll not have both of ye t'carry back like drowned rats. Ye'll stay here and keep dry fer yer own sake."

But Meg was already pulling on her boots. As she looked on in disbelief, Tom stripped to his undergarments and bolted out into the rain. She watched as he disappeared in the direction of the river and tried to absorb the shock of seeing him almost naked. Of course, it made perfect sense that he would not want to soak his only clothes. Realizing how sensible this was, Meg too stripped to her chemise and headed out in search of the desperate maid.

"Pray God, please let us find her before it's too late," Meg intoned from her heart her first real prayer in a very long time.

The rain came down in sheets now and the dark of night returned. Tom cursed this damnable weather as he slipped across the mud in his haste. Plowing through underbrush and shrubs that whipped his bare legs, he raced toward the river. He suspected she wouldn't get far and he tried to see without stopping if she had fallen along the way. He was surprised that he hadn't found her yet as he heard the sound of the river getting louder.

He spotted her lying along the bank of the Clydagh where he had drawn the water for the horses last night. She was on her side, rocking back and forth crooning and keening. Her back was to the river and as he approached her she shot up on her knees and bent protectively over the bundle wrapped in her skirt. He tried to look into her eyes but they were wild and unfocussed like those of a cornered animal. As though to a wild filly, he spoke her name in his gentlest most soothing voice. Still she cowered next to the edge of the bank.

Tom was aware of the danger of this stream. He had watched a dog drown in it when he was a young boy and he knew there were currents that could pull at a woman's skirts drawing her down in seconds to the rocky bottom. Again, Tom found himself making the sign of the cross over his heart. What this meant he had no time to ponder but he knew he needed help to keep this girl from losing her life to the water tumbling and swirling behind her.

Suddenly Meg rushed past him and crouched down beside Maureen. She took the frightened girl in her arms and Tom thought for one terrifying second that he was going to lose them both to the rain-swollen river. But where he had failed to penetrate the terror that had gripped Maureen's senses, Meg had instinctively known that she would want a woman to help her. Maureen sagged against Meg's bosom and looking up at her with piercing pain, she lifted her skirt to reveal a baby no bigger than a newborn kitten. As the rain washed the blood from its little face, Maureen turned her own face to the sky, her sobs tearing through the sheets of water like thunder, her voice raised in the cry of Rachel whose child was no more.

Together they finally persuaded Maureen to return with them to the shelter of the old church and she submitted willingly though she refused to let go of her bundle. Tom settled her and her prize in a dry corner and Meg stripped off her wet clothes and wrapped her in the black fur coat. Maureen permitted Meg to cut the umbilical cord and Tom disposed of the afterbirth while Meg wrapped the little creature in a linen hanky she found in one of the coat pockets. Maureen fell into a deep sleep with her dead baby tucked safely in her arms.

Tom had been startled by Meg's sudden appearance by the river but more so by the fact, that like him, she too had stripped down to her undergarments. The obvious practicality of this was obliterated by the sight of her full, round breasts beneath the sheer fabric of the soaked chemise. He was also astonished at the little round belly that showed so clearly beneath those beautiful breasts.

As he watched her bend over Maureen, her long blond curls lay across her chest and tiny droplets of rainwater ran down to drip from her nipples. Her belly formed a curved mound that rested against her thighs and the thin wet material of her chemise stretched across her back and buttocks stirring in him an overwhelming desire to touch her.

His feelings roared around inside him. He realized he desired her more than ever. He was almost overcome with relief that this desire was still there. Gone were the voices of guilt and recrimination. It had been so long since he had had her and so many images of her had crowded out his memories of her beauty that he had feared himself unable to want her again. He especially hesitated to entertain wanting her because she carried a child.

He was totally unprepared for the longing he felt for her now, greater than any he had had for her in the past. He purposefully put behind him the feelings he had had while watching her sleep. She was his lovely Meg and he would have her. He would find a way to marry her and their child would have two parents and a life filled with their love. Thank God he had found his passion again. Thank God he had found the heart that beat with love for her.

He felt a strength he had not had since Lord Jeffrey had taken her from him and he realized that Meg was not only his lover but his friend from whom he drew his strength. He would find a way to get them all safely to Clew Bay and Achill Island. That was the haven where he planned to take her. He knew they were on the right road to that place but he also knew they had a long way to go. He would see them there or he would die trying.

Meg turned from Maureen to see Tom staring at her. She started at the raw emotion of his expression. She had seen desire on his face before but there was a nakedness about his eyes that almost frightened her. He took a step toward her but realizing her own near nakedness, she hastened to cover herself. This was enough to break the spell and Tom turned away to dry himself. Meg instantly regretted her shyness. Her pregnancy made her feel vulnerable and self-conscious and she was acutely embarrassed to be unclothed in front of Tom. His unfeeling abruptness in his father's kitchen the night before had hurt her and she felt ashamed that he would desire her now when he could not even show her tenderness then. She was embarrassed that she had later shown him the weakness of her tears.

Now, he was gone from her again and she saw her opportunity to feel his loving hands on her, the desire of her heart for all the lonely nights spent locked in her room, dissipate like breath in the wind. Silently, their backs to each other, each wrapped in their own brand of humiliation, they dried and dressed themselves.

Meg broke off a piece of cheese for each of them and unwrapped one of the cakes for them to share. Tom dug into the saddlebags until he found two small bowls they could drink from. With water from the river drawn last night for the horses, they ate their meager breakfast in silence, every so often casting a worried glance at Maureen to see that she was still breathing.

The rain had stopped and as though it had never shed a drop of water, the blue sky radiated the warmth of the summer morning. The wet grass and rocks glistened in the sun and Tom breathed deeply as he walked Jewel to a patch of oats that Angus had already found. How odd that there should be this little square of oats for the horses. He was grateful for their sakes that they could enjoy a treat instead of grazing on grass and bracken.

Returning to the sanctuary he found Meg just sitting staring at Maureen and her bundle. Without looking up at him, she asked, "What will we do with the baby?"

"We have t'bury it, if she'll let us, Meg. I was afraid she was after drownin' herself but I suppose she was just tryin' t'baptize the poor little thing. Let her sleep while we pack th'horses again. I don't know how she'll travel but we have t'get out of here. We're not nearly far enough from GlynMor t'be safe. I had hoped t'be t'Murphy's Coffin by sundown."

"Murphy's Coffin?" Where is that?" She looked at him in disbelief that there was such a place.

"'Tis at th'crossroads the English named Charlesgate and Heather Crossing. We always called it Murphy's Coffin fer old Murphy. He was hanged there by a mob back in 1803 fer disgracing th'daughter of th'constable. Th'neighbors took th'punishment when the authorities couldn't find Murphy. This stewed 'em so much they took to th'fields and farms t'find him themselves. When they did, they hanged th'fool."

"What was the punishment?" Meg almost hesitated to ask.

"Doled out by none other than yer very own granda, their homes were all burned. They rebuilt but not until they had their revenge on old Murphy. As for th'girl, th'same mob took her t'the streets and cut off her hair in th'sign of th'harlot. They say she ran off soon after and was never heard from again. They say th'little people got her and that Mrs. Murphy's spirit still wanders th'fields on th'third of July every year looking for her dead husband. Most of'em think she's wantin' t'kill him all over again herself!"

Meg searched Tom's face for any sign that he might be having her on but he looked as serious as she had ever seen him.

Chapter Fourteen

Meg hated to disturb the sleeping Maureen but by full light they were back on the road, heading west. She had given Maureen her black riding skirt and a soft white muslin blouse to wear until her own clothes, washed clean by the rain, had a chance to dry out. Meg pulled out a yellow silk Morning Robe covered with sprigs of embroidered bluebells. This was loose enough to fit her swelling middle but Meg found it cumbersome to ride sidesaddle in it. She wished Maureen had worn the Morning Robe and left her to wear the riding habit but the maid had absolutely refused to put on the fine garment. Meg had finally given up and let her have her way. She supposed the black serge skirt was better for riding on the slide car, after all.

Tom, riding high on Angus, led the little procession. The big stallion was sulky and difficult, as unhappy to be dragging the disgruntled sow as she was to be tethered to one of the slip-creels. Maureen seemed resigned to the uncomfortable ride behind Jewel. She had fashioned a sling around her waist from one of Meg's stockings and threaded it through the planks of the slide-car, tying it to support her weight. Between that and the brace usually used to hold the wicker turf creel in place, she was able to remain quite secure on the bumpy ride.

Tom called over his shoulder.

"If we can get to Turlough by day's end, I think there's an

144

abandoned shack just outside the woods near Henry House."

He squinted at the clear blue sky and nodded. The day promised to be clear after the stormy night and the morning sun felt wonderful on his back.

Meg hadn't been to Henry House since she was a child. She wondered out loud how Tom knew about it.

"Two reasons. First, me cousin Sean married the daughter of Timmy O'Reilly, the gamekeeper and yer mother bought two good fillies from Col. Thomas Fitzgerald when he was visitin' there from Turlow Park. 'Tis O'Reilly's old house I mean t'take ye to."

The road widened and he slowed down to let her pull Jewel and the slide-car alongside the huge black stallion.

"When was this?" Meg asked, her curiosity peaked.

"While ye were in London. Yer mother arranged t'meet Col. Fitzgerald through yer Uncle Robert. They were lads together at Trinity. He was a year ahead of yer uncle but they stayed close even after the Colonel graduated and went into military service."

Meg raised an eyebrow at Tom's apparent familiarity with her family's personal history.

"How do you know all this?" She asked Tom, warming to the subject.

Tom looked at her taking in her odd outfit and unkempt hair. She looked more like a tinker's daughter than the daughter of an earl and he loved her more than ever. Her long blond curls, soft and shiny from the rainwater rinse, bounced gently on her back as she sat straight and proud on the tooled leather sidesaddle. Angus towed the sow and Tom had to smile at the sight of Meg in her sweetly sprigged dressing gown perched atop Jewel, her beautiful rowan, her closest companion the smelly, grunting cargo waddling between them.

"Ah, Meg, Darlin', I know many a thing that would probably shock ye. T'is no wee mystery that the servant class knows more about the gentry than they know about us."

He chuckled when he saw he'd hit a nerve.

Taking proper umbrage, Meg straightened her shoulders and sat taller in her saddle suddenly intent upon studying the landscape. Pretending not to notice, Tom went on.

"Anyway, I remember Henry House had a grand, big kitchen and the cook took quite a fancy t'me. Sure, and I ate well the fortnight we stayed there."

He had to turn his head to keep from laughing out loud at Meg's stiff back and scowling mouth. It felt good to see her jealous.

They rode in silence until noon, following the Clydagh River as it wove its way southwest. The sun had thoroughly warmed them and dried them out. Maureen had slept for most of the trip but now was awake and hungry. Tom realized how hungry he was too and Meg seemed to have forgotten that she was miffed with him. When they stopped, he offered to start a fire but both women were content to eat a cold meal and drink fresh water from the river. Tom watered the horses while Meg took cheese and fruit out of the sack she had taken from the larder. That and some stale barm brack would be lunch.

Maureen had gained some of her strength and though stiff and sore from the slide-car, she was able to drape her wet chemise and petticoat across a stand of cattails to dry. Once she stretched the heavy homespun skirt across a big flat rock, she began walking along the riverbank until she found privacy behind a thicket of briars.

Meg, still fearful for Maureen's state of mind followed her. Maureen had allowed Meg to take her wrapped baby, a girl, and gently secure her among the bundles of supplies. She knew she had to bury her soon but couldn't bear to part with her yet. She had wept inconsolably when Tom had poured plain river water over her sweet little forehead baptizing her Mary Ellen Dougherty after Maureen's own mother. Her childhood pastor, Father McGinnis had said from the pulpit that baptism was a sacrament of the living and she shuddered to think that her little daughter probably wouldn't go to heaven with a baptism like that but she still wasn't ready to believe God would let this innocent child languish in Limbo because she hadn't lived long enough to have a proper invitation.

Tom told her that there was such a thing as baptism of

desire. He said that God would admit a baby if a mother desired her child to go to heaven even if it were not baptized in the customary way. He told her the nuns told him that. She wondered what Fr. McGinnis would say about that but she believed Tom for now because she had to. Maybe someday she would have enough courage to ask a priest if Tom was right.

When Meg and Maureen reached the thicket Meg handed Maureen some of the rags Tom had packed. Maureen tore them in narrow strips and layered them. Meg went behind a clump of twisted branches and took off her boots. As she rubbed her feet, sore from hours in the tight, fashionable boots, she wished for the ability to go barefoot like Maureen or even trudge around in brogues like the ones Tom wore. She had just rolled down her stockings when she heard a splash. Looking up, she saw Maureen in the water. Stripping off her stockings, she ran to the bank, fearing for Maureen's safety.

"Come in M'Lady, it feels so good to get clean!" Maureen called out.

The river was much quieter at this point bearing no resemblance to the wild tumult of swirls and vortexes back at St. Anselm's. Meg shook her head. She had had enough of being wet this morning. She sat down on the bank and waited until Maureen clambered out and sat down next to her to dry herself in the sun. Maureen's thick auburn hair lay like a wet fox pelt across her back. As she sat trying to sort out the snarls, Meg watched her in amazement. Maureen's belly was no longer swollen but still sagged with the excess flesh of her pregnancy. She seemed unfazed by her nakedness in front of her mistress and Meg thought to herself that this too was part of the strange turn their lives had taken.

"Maureen, how are you? I mean to ask, do you still flow?"

Meg found herself embarrassed at the maid's lack of inhibition and was shocked that she herself could even ask such a question. She quickly realized how silly this was. Hadn't she after all, found this same girl being savagely attacked by her own father less than two days ago?

She picked up a thorny branch and began running it through

Maureen's hair in an attempt to smooth the mass of curls glinting in the sun. Now it was Maureen's turn to be shocked. No one had ever touched her this way. She sat frozen in place while Meg gently loosened the tangles and smoothed the long copper curls.

"I'm much better, M'am. I'm just tired, is all. Once we, ye know, find a place fer Mary Ellen, I'll be fine."

Meg's concern resurfaced with a jolt at the frightening flatness in Maureen's voice as she spoke of burying her daughter. The two women sat for a long time as the lady gently combed the maid's hair. They said no more, lulled into a sisterhood of sorts. Their roles were reversed now by the steady rasping of the thorns through Maureen's hair.

"I had better get back to Tom," Meg said eventually.

"And you, Missy, need to put some clothes on."

She left Maureen braiding her hair into a thick red rope down her back. Maureen stood up and slowly dressed herself in her mistress's clothes. Meg joined Tom and sat down unaware of Maureen's silent tears, the only response she had to the only act of kindness she had ever known.

A low black cloud loomed menacingly in the western sky as they approached the outskirts of Turlough. The houses on the edge of town were dotted with traditional wattle and daub built in the typical fashion. Women bustled about, pulling in laundry from lines strung between the houses and backyard boolies or snatching their dried linens from low stone fences or hedgrows in an effort to beat the dark, billowing cloud that seemed to sit like a brooding hen over one small area.

There were children running about, their mams calling from half-doors painted bright green or blue. Meg looked out over the gently sloping fields, taking in the tidy stone fenced plots dotted with men and women hoeing and weeding. She marveled at the even split between the bright green fields lit by brilliant sunlight and the dusky pall cast by the threatening cloud. The stark beauty of this rugged landscape was marked by such definitive contrasts. Beyond the patchwork of tidy fenced off fields, flocks of sheep grazed in the sun on the steeper, rockier hillsides, their woolly tails painted red or blue to identify the farmer who owned them. Oblivious to the approaching storm, the little lambs frolicked around ewes munching on clover and bracken or resting in the cool grass. Rams, their massive curled horns glinting in the sun, stood like sentries, staring in the direction of the storm cloud.

Starting at the sound of a shrill whistle, Meg watched as two border collies were dispatched up the hillside to corral a herd of sheep into a pen behind a large well-kept house. Without a word, the master of the house instructed the dogs, whistling first to one then the other as they obediently moved the sheep from left to right and top to bottom forcing them to file down the hill into the pen. As the sheep rounded the corner of the property, he slammed the gate shut and turned to go into the house, tipping his cap politely at the passing strangers.

Just as he ducked into the low kitchen door, a faint rainbow arched over the thatch of his roof, dissipating as quickly as it had formed while a flock of silverbellied pidgeons in sleek formation landed on the sculpted eaves. Perhaps the black cloud would pass by after all, without leaving the land any wetter for its brief visit.

By evening they had arrived at Turlough after following the Clydagh southwest along its meandering bank. It was a beautiful journey filled with sun glinting off the water, chickadees bobbing ahead of them leading the way and the soft shushing of the breeze in the rushes and cattails along the riverbank. Meg felt the sun and breeze caress her spirit as she savored being outside after her months of confinement. They spoke little, each lost in their own reverie. Even the sow seemed content to trot along behind Angus only occasionally grunting her opinion.

They stopped for the night just past Turlough, where they found the gamekeeper's abandoned old house, the thatched roof half collapsed. The sun was just beginning to set as they unloaded the bedding and set up for the night. Maureen had gutted a chicken and began to pluck the feathers while Meg busied herself picking wild blackberries and Tom started a fire in the hearth.

Maureen wasn't as strong as she thought she was and the plucking was going far too slowly for Tom. Hungry and impatient, he pulled the chicken from her lap. Without a word he took the bird down to the riverbank. Making a paste out of mud he rolled the chicken in the paste until the feathers were completely coated. He then took the mud coated chicken and placed it in the center of the fire. He tossed in some potatoes and went to tend the horses. Meg and Maureen stared at the chicken ball in the fire. Maureen leaned over and tried to rescue the sloppy gray blob from the flames when Tom called from the doorway, "Get away from me supper!"

Maureen turned on him and cried, "What are ye' thinkin' ye poor omethon that we'll be eatin' a ball o'dirt for our meal? I may be daft but sure'n you'll never feed me that thing and me so hungry me gut is achin."

"Just get away, ye'll get yer supper when I get mine, girl," Tom scowled.

He turned and started toward the river. He was as weary as he had ever been. The long ride had given him time to reflect on all the changes that had taken place in the last few days. They were finally on their way; he was grateful enough for that but as the day wore on his mood had darkened and he had become morose and cranky. Meg had seemed fine one moment and stiff and irritable the next. Granted they were all exhausted and had put a frightful night behind them. What did he expect from two women in their state? He was the one who had to be strong. It was this reality and his mixed feelings that made him so moody.

He wondered if he would ever figure out just what Meg needed from him but Maureen was the one who really got to him. He couldn't figure out why Maureen, who admittedly had never been a favorite of his, so easily got his goat. Why did he dislike her so? Back at GlynMor Castle he had had little to do with the house servants other than common politeness at the occasional holiday gathering. Never a man to delve too deeply into others' lives, Tom took most people at face value and Maureen looked to him like a wild wood nymph, all bushy red hair and sharp glances.

Somewhere in his mind there circulated gentle words of reproach in his Da's voice. He knew she'd paid more than her dues with Lord Jeffrey and God in heaven hadn't she just lived a nightmare losing the babe and all? How could she be blamed for what that monster had done to her? Standing at the river, feeling the soft sucking bank beneath his feet, he heard the soft admonishment. Tom had always thought his Da was much too trusting, too forgiving. He would have coddled a girl like Maureen, tallying all the sadness of her years and feeling compelled to fix all her ills. Now, Tom was wishing he could feel the same. Lord knew the girl needed all the kindness she could get.

Tom wondered how he had grown so different from the man who sired in him at least some of the same compassion. There was a time when he probably would have felt tenderly toward Maureen and been compelled to make up to her for all she had suffered. Now, he couldn't see past the burden of her company. He shook his head at the silent nudging, unable to think beyond his own dilemma. His hungry belly growled and the looming responsibility of the next few days crowded his mind. These two women were his charges now, depending completely on him for their survival. He shivered as his shoulders instinctively tried to shake off the weight. Despising this unmanly cowardice, he stood by the water in a cloud of gloom.

Out of the corner of his eye, he saw Maureen walking slowly along the shallows upriver, kicking up foam as she steamed and muttered to herself. He heard Meg approach him from behind. She stood silently at his back just as she had on a winter day in another life. Then they had stood frozen in place along the bank of the chilly stream connecting the two parts of Derryhick Lough where GlynMor Castle and his own home stood.

Now, along the bank of the river Clydagh, he could feel the heat from her body as she waited just as she had then for him to speak. He could not bear it. This was a torment. Here they were alone except for that stupid maid and the gulf between them was as wide as the water before them. He longed to turn around and carry her off to that broken down cottage and throw her skirts up over her head taking her down on the moldy old bed and having her the way he did that first time. She should be sleeping with him under that rotten old thatch, not Maureen! His sulkiness turned to anger as he stood ramrod straight refusing to acknowledge Meg behind him, dying to turn and take her down right there, forget the old thatch. He'd have her right here before God and all creation on the riverbank!

As if she could hear his angry thoughts, Meg turned and walked away from him. He cursed his own temper, knowing Meg had left him standing there. He felt a draft where he had stood in her warmth. Fury with himself and his situation rooted him where he stood staring across the river, squinting in the setting sun. Realizing what a fool he was, he burned with frustration. Pretending not to notice the soft slapping of her soles on the sandy bank, he willed himself to stand alone, finally allowing his eyes to focus on the magnificent sight before him.

The setting sun sent long golden fingers across the river, caressing the gentle swirls and undulations of the current. Tom could see clearly to the bottom of the shallow water along the bank. Below the golden streaks were smooth rocks reflecting crimson and russet like coals defiantly ablaze beneath the very element that should be dousing their glow. Tom was as sensitive to symbolism as any Irishman and gazing into this strange and mesmerizing eddy, swirling with cool heat and drowning fire he felt drawn into the magical world of the fairies. Half expecting to find himself at the end of a rainbow standing with this pot of gold at his feet, he looked up.

The huge sun had shifted, casting its net across the entire surface of the water scooping up the river in a golden blanket that beckoned and dazzled him to step out and glide effortlessly to the other side. Blinded by the brilliant glare, he raised his eyes to see rings of color, a rainbow indeed, bursting and fading around the body of a hawk out for an evening forage, confident and relaxed. The hawk dipped and swooped, came to rest on a bare branch, etched black against the sheer amber haze. Suddenly, with the shrill call of noble death, the hawk dove. In one swift perfect curve he scooped up a trout and arcing high on the crest of the glowing sky claimed it as his own.

Tom stood transfixed with admiration. His shame threatened to overwhelm him. How could the creator of this magnificent creature have made him, as well? How could a bird, so small and brainless know exactly what he wanted and how to get it and he, supposed to be the most intelligent of species, be so mystified by his own feelings? Why could he not just take what he wanted like the hawk? What was it that made him so weak and indecisive about Meg? He would never be this way around an animal. He would never let even the strongest horse bully him or trump his will. Why did she get into his gut this way and twist him inside out?

Was this love? Was love really so painful it took a man's pride and devoured him like a common trout? He realized he had never really thought this way about him and Meg. His emotions had led him into a bog that threatened to swallow him whole. And now there was a child on the way. His child! His son or daughter would be born by year's end. Suddenly awash with a poignancy that threatened tears, he imagined holding his baby. He realized that this child connected him to all those who had gone before him and all those who would come after him.

He shivered again not in his shoulders but deep in his loins as he recognized for the first time the awesome power he had to give life. He wanted this child. He felt a yearning to touch it and have it for his own. Standing there awash in the setting sun he imagined Meg placing this gift in his arms; her gift to him, real in its flesh, flesh of his flesh and hers.

Slowly he felt his rage leave him. His limbs felt heavy and his feet deeply embedded in the earth as his anger seeped into the mud. He wondered how many riverbanks in Ireland had absorbed the fury of centuries of men like himself raging against fate until their bodies went limp with the futility of it all?

"You are a fool, Tom Phalen," he muttered as he turned and followed Meg up the bank to the place where they would find their separate beds tonight.

He found the two women setting bowls around the fire.

Meg had scrubbed out the kettle and set it to boil. Maureen snapped him a look that told him they had united against him in the solidarity of women wronged.

He sighed and went back outside. What he needed was a pipe. The chicken would be ready soon but he had time for a nice pipe before dinner. Let them stew in their own black mood wondering how they were to eat the clay bird. He'd take his comfort in puffing, quietly knowing how good their supper would be.

Chapter Fifteen

They had perfect weather for the next three days and followed the river like gypsies enjoying fresh fish and berries every stop along the way. They met no one but one tinker who traded a crate of eggs and two sacks of oats for two huge trout. Tom had argued for a sack of corn for the sow but it took one of Meg's baubles to satisfy the old man's price. The tinker was heading upriver but was able to tell them that they were half a day out of Newport. Tom had taken them due west to avoid Castlebar where he was afraid someone might recognize them. Lady Beverly had traded heavily around there and many people would know both him and Meg.

Under other circumstances they could have been a family group on a holiday. Meg had adopted an ordinary air that belied her privileged upbringing. Tom, who never let down his guard against being pursued by Lord Jeffrey, was actually relieved to see this. He and Meg had had no further encounters like the one by the riverbank and the trip had been without disruption. He had taught the women how to cook another chicken in clay the way he had learned from his grandfather and they were astonished at how delicious it was. That first night when he cracked open the clay shell and the steaming bird fell off the bone, they gasped in surprise at how the feathers and clay fell away from the meat leaving it juicy and wonderfully tender. Tom explained that this was an ancient method of cooking used by hunters as far back as the Druids. He expressed surprise that Maureen had never heard of it which earned him a smart retort about his barbaric upbringing.

He was growing more tolerant of Maureen but she troubled him and he could see that Meg too was watching her. Meg was right to be concerned over Maureen's casual words about finding a place to bury Mary Ellen. Maureen had still refused to open the market sack that Meg had put the little baby in and no amount of coaxing could get her to bury the baby and be done with it. Tom had grumbled more than once about the odor coming from the bag and Meg had tried several times to suggest stopping for a roadside funeral. They had even passed a ruined church with a pretty little cemetery where Maureen had wandered around for awhile. Meg thought it would finally be the right time until Maureen came back to the horses cursing the dead for being church of Ireland instead of Catholic. Now Maureen wouldn't even hear of burying her baby.

Tom took Meg aside as they approached the outlying townlands around Newport. Maureen had asked to stop so she could stretch her legs and had wandered off to the privacy of a small grove of stunted monkey trees.

"We have to bury the wee baby tonight. 'Tis no way we can enter Newport pretendin' there's nothin' wrong. Ye can see, even th'crows are startin' to flock around us. As soon as we slow down or stop they're waitin' to find th'source of th'death smell. I'll do it after she's asleep."

"Tom, you can't be serious. If she finds out that you took her baby from her she'll lose her mind!" Meg clamped her hand on his arm as if to stop him.

They turned to see Maureen standing behind them as still as a pillar and just as white.

"Ye'll not touch me daughter as long as I live" she said in a voice so flat and spiritless Meg shivered.

"Maureen, we have to bury th'child!" Tom erupted. "We have no choice. Would ye' rather it be taken from us some night by a fox or a hawk? Ye' know we've been that lucky so far!"

Meg now placed her hand on Maureen's arm only to have it shoved off.

Stung, Meg tried to reason with her.

"Maureen, we're heading into a town where we simply cannot let anyone suspect us of anything. We need to get through this place unnoticed. Can you imagine what people will think if they suspect we carry the unburied dead? Try to imagine what will happen if my father finds out we're here. We can have a service. We'll do anything you like but we have to do it soon." Meg was begging now.

"A service!" Maureen spat out the words. "That's what ye would do, is it? A high Church of Ireland funeral is it? I suppose 'twould be fittin' now wouldn't it? The babe is, after all, th'daughter of a lord!"

Her cheeks had gone dusky with rage and her pain blazed behind her brown eyes leaving them pale as isinglass. Again Meg shivered. Was Maureen going mad? Had some demon taken over her soul? Instinctively she turned away from Maureen, her hands across her belly. She prayed for deliverance and the protection of the angels. Prickly cold sweat stung the back of her neck as she shivered again at the thought of those mad, hate-filled eyes resting their gaze upon her unborn child.

Tom stepped in now and took Maureen in hand. His powerful grip gave her nowhere to turn and he spoke slowly and with absolute authority.

"We will bury th'babe. By evening we'll be in Newport. Th'child will not be with us when we arrive at th'town line. We will stop at th'first Catholic Church we find and bury her there with or without a priest. Then ye'll decide whether yer comin' with us th'rest of the way or stayin' with yer baby. 'Tis yer right and yer choice. Ye're strong enough now t'decide this. Now get back on th'horse and get movin'."

Tom took Maureen by the shoulders and pushed her toward Angus who now pulled the heavy slide-car. Slumping against his sleek black flank Maureen allowed herself to be lifted onto the horse's back. Jewel stood, patiently pawing the dusty road, the snorting sow tethered to his sadle. With a boost from Tom, Meg resumed her mount. Her horse turned to nuzzle her as he tried to understand all this business.

Tom had been either riding up behind Maureen or walking since Maureen had recovered and they had transferred the supplies to the slide-car. He would have walked rather than be anywhere near Maureen at this moment but he took his mount behind her so he could scan the horizon for a church. Within seconds he felt her sag against his chest and his anger was replaced by pity.

Meg rode behind Tom and Maureen, taking in all the different sights along the way. She had been on many trips with her parents but had never really paid attention to the people and the houses before. Now, she was heading toward her own uncertain future. What sort of house would they end up in? As they plodded on toward Newport, Meg saw every kind of house. After passing the far fields of the large landowner with the two dogs, they passed mile after mile of low stone fences interrupted by thick overgrowth of honeysuckle and wild pink roses. Ancient orchards crested the hills with stumpy, gnarled trees bearing early summer plums and peaches. Row upon row of shiny barked cherry trees had long since lost their blossoms and hung heavy with tiny, reddening orbs.

As they neared the outer townlands around Newport, isolated white houses dotted the way, some with sculpted thatch roofs and tidy gardens filled with hollyhocks of every hue and vines of early squash and ripening beans. Fields of cabbage and turnips stretched up the rocky soil of the low hills while the fresh green leaves of new potatoes filled every spare corner of every field.

Women bent to the task of tilling the cottage gardens while men harvested early wheat and rye, swinging the long scythes and piling the haycocks for later when they would load up the hay-bogy and drag the hay home. One farmer wielded a nasty looking whip that he cracked in the air over several boys who lumbered uphill under the heavy burden of hay cradles loaded on their backs. It was clear that the young men were his sons as they all had his flaming red hair and broad stocky build. Meg shuddered at the thought of him actually applying the long braided whip to any person or animal and cringed when she caught sight of his wife and daughters dutifully lugging creels of food and jugs of drink down the mountain for their lunch. Her sore shoulder burned at the sight of the girls bent under the heavy yoke of sloshing milk pails.

Most of the houses were single rooms of whitewashed wattle and daub with thatch roofs secured with twisted straw bobbins at the gable ends. If a house had any added rooms, they were always at one gabled end or the other. Meg understood from listening to Mrs. Carrey that no Irish house would ever be more than one room deep. This apparently angered the little people and brought a lifetime of bad luck. And the dung pile! She'd never forget the day Tom told her why his father had a pile of manure next to the front door of his house. He had claimed it was a sign of prosperity! The bigger a man's heap the better off he was in life. A wry thought crossed her mind that the two perpendicular wings and the lack of a dung heap at GlynMor Castle may be the reason for her own family's miserable life within its walls. Or perhaps the ancient superstitions didn't apply to gentry. They seemed quite capable of creating their own misery without any help from fairies. As they passed house after house with their low stone fences and their dung piles by the front doors, Meg knew one thing. She would like a pretty stone fence and a hedgerow of roses but she would never allow a dung heap anywhere near her front door to stink and steam in the July heat.

They rounded a bend in the road and Meg was shocked to see the landscape dramatically change. Gone were the fences and tidy fields replaced by the dank fetid depths of a turf bog. Like a huge black wound across the earth, the dense decay yielded tidy piles of peat bricks cut uniformly by long-handled slanes. Meg looked with shock upon the stark existence of the poorest of Ireland's people. Several whole families lounged in front of pathetic hovels cut into the slope of the hill; nothing more than a sod caves with livestock grazing on their grassy roofs. People in tattered rags stared from hand cut doorways in tiny windowless boolies no bigger than a chicken house. Naked children ran around paths that passed for streets in a little cluster of windowless huts. These were the turfcutters. Meg had never seen anyone so poor and ragged as these filthy people.

Families of ten and twelve children worked the flat face of the bog, stopping to stare with black smeared faces at the strangers on horseback. Haggard, stooped women piled bricks of peat into bogbarrows and loaded creels slung across the backs of donkeys or children as the men leaned into their slanes, "breasting" thick horizontal slices from the tall, black banks of the boghole. Thin grey smoke filtered through holes in the grassy roofs of the turfcutters' huts lending the whole scene a mysterious, tremulous quality.

Meg felt herself gag at the sight of the gaping black hole in the earth where people worked like animals slicing and stacking, carting and loading. As far as the eye could see, the bogs stretched across the land. Crystal clear streams running through the scarred landscape failed to wash away the filthy blackness and the whole world took on the bleak, smokey barrenness of death. This place was a place of demons and Meg realized why the spirits were so real and so frightening to the bogdwellers. She breathed a sigh of relief as they passed the bog and headed south away from the misty stench of that creepy, mysterious world.

Meg had no idea what kind of dwelling they would have. The hovels of the turf cutters were beyond her comprehension and yet she knew there would be no luxury like that which she had left behind. Tom could and would work hard to provide their family with as comfortable a life as possible and she was willing to learn anything she needed to know to make a home for him and their children. She let thoughts of a future kitchen and little garden plot fill her mind and drive out the images of the black turf bog.

A light rain had begun to drift in from the west as the little caravan approached the outskirts of Newport. Tom saw the priest before he saw the church. Jogging along a hedgerow, the young cleric hastened to get home before the rain caught him. Tom noted how dusty the hem of the priest's cassock was and thought that this place could use a bit of rain. He wasn't comfortable around priests for the simple reason that he had been lurking with the lads in the doorway of St. Columban's for years instead of entering into the nave with the women and old men. There were many Sundays when he and the boyos had celebrated the sacraments in the pub, avoiding the church altogether. Why he had left matters of faith and worship to his Da, he couldn't say but he had never been a praying man, plain and simple. He hesitated to call out; indeed didn't really know how to properly address this strange priest that looked more like an overgrown altar boy.

Meg saved him the trouble. Jerking the reins she caused a whinny from Jewel that turned the priest around and the whole unlikely procession stopped at the foot of a long, shadowy drive. The priest tipped his tattered felt hat to Meg and squinted through thick eyeglasses that made his eyes small and beady.

They regarded each other wordlessly for a moment as the rain found them and began to lob wet bits of the dusty road at their feet. The priest gestured them into the narrow drive bordered by high hedgerows that crossed each other overhead and provided natural shelter from the rain.

Tom dismounted while Maureen sat rigid on Angus's back. She looked as though she awaited a noose around her neck. Meg watched as Tom walked a few yards away with the priest, confiding in him their dilemma. Twice the priest looked back at Maureen with a blend of shock and pity. Meg hoped Tom was showing at least some discretion in his remarks. After a few moments, they returned to the women.

The priest went to Angus and stroking the long black nose, spoke softly to Maureen. Meg could not tell how much Tom had told him.

"I'm Fr. John Finnegan. I understand ye've suffered a sadness, child. I'd be much pleased if ye would permit me t'help. Why don't ye follow me now and we'll set things t'rights before

God and His Blessed Mother."

Tom was already leading Angus through the narrow space between the hedgerows toward a small stone church at the end of the curved path. As Jewel followed behind the bumping slide-car Meg thought how odd they must look to Fr. Finnegan. This unlikely troop, one huge thoroughbred dragging a farm cart and another beautiful racer towing a sow; how ridiculous they would have been if they were not so desperate. She wondered if the priest saw a parade rivaling a minstrel show or the flight of the Holy Family into Egypt?

Whatever he thought, Fr. Finnegan never swayed from his gentle solicitation. He helped Meg from her mount, bringing a blush to her cheeks when she realized that of course he would know she was pregnant. She caught his quick, almost imperceptible glance at her left hand but his face was unreadable when he saw she wore no wedding ring. Tom went to help Maureen dismount but she spurned his efforts, sliding down the wrong side of the horse and causing him to snort and dance. Tom grabbed Angus's reins and together he and Fr. Finnegan led the bedraggled procession into the churchyard.

By now the rain had started pelting the dry ground hard and the smell of dampened dirt brought Meg back into her own yard. She half expected to smell her mother's wisteria. She pulled two sacks off the slide-car making sure to avoid the small bag containing the baby. Fr. Finnegan hustled the girls into a small stone cottage while Tom took the animals into an old lean-to made of huge single pieces of slate stacked against one another like a house of cards in the corner of the yard.

He had only seen slate outbuildings like this once before on a trip south with Lady Beverly and Lord Robert. They had gone to a little town called Bunratty on the River Shannon and sold two chestnut racers to an earl whose name was lost to him. He had only been with Lady Beverly a few months and was so overwhelmed by his first trip away from Derryhick Lough that he had remembered very little about it until now.

He marveled at this slate construction so similar to that around the grounds of Bunratty House. He remembered walking up the drive toward the big stone house, leading the young horses along a gentle slope away from the town proper. On his left there had been a huge stretch of green lawn with deer and domestic animals grazing together, hawks and hooded crows swooping from the tops of majestic yew trees and tall swaying pines. The other side of the road was bordered by a fence made completely of slate planks, some as tall and wide as two men abreast. He had stood amazed at this unusual border, enclosing a large yard and several stone outbuildings. The cottage and sheds were roofed with slate as well and looked ancient but strong enough to last for generations. Now he remembered there had been ruins on the grounds too, though he never found out whether they were of a church or a castle. He just remembered the sight of a turret towering behind a yew tree across the deer park. He shook his head at the flood of memories that came back at the sight of these slate slabs. He filled the feed-bags, tossed an armful of corn to the pig and dashed across the yard to the house.

Inside he found a most inviting scene. Fr. Finnegan lived alone in the little rectory but his mother stayed in a tiny stone cottage behind the church and kept house for him. What a nice arrangement, Tom thought. Grow up, be a priest, but never part company with yer mam's home cooking. And cleaning and ironing. Not a bad life for a man to take on.

Mrs. Finnegan had made tea and was slicing thick slabs of warm soda bread. A pot of fresh sweet butter sat on the embroidered tablecloth and she had set out real china cups and plates. Fr. Finnegan sliced a ham he had been given by a grateful parishioner who credited the priest's prayers with healing his fractured leg. Slices of white potatoes snapped and sputtered in a cast iron pannie. Meg was pouring as the priest's mother beamed at her bountiful spread. Fr. Finnegan said a blessing and they all tucked into their meal with gusto. After several cups of the steaming bronze tea laced with thick yellow cream, Meg felt more normal than she had since leaving home. Even Maureen's cheeks had flushed with the warming brew.

Mrs. Finnegan was as kind and intuitive as her son and after hearing a brief version of their story and seeing the rain falling harder as evening drew near, she began making up a bed on the floor for Tom. No one protested when she said goodnight to her son and throwing her shawl over her head, indicated to the two women to do the same. Grabbing their bundles, they ducked out into the gray mist and crossed the churchyard, geese and chickens scurrying in their path.

Once inside, Mrs. Finnegan lit a candle in the front window.

"This tells Fr. John that I'm safely in," she said. "He can see th'glow from his room."

"Now, girls, let's get settled. 'Tis'nt a big place but I do have a bed in th'loft where ye' can sleep.'Tis early yet. Maybe ye'd like t'bathe a bit? Do ye have clean things in yer bundles?"

The old woman moved to the corner of the kitchen and dragged out a wooden tub big enough for a body to sit in.

"Tomorrow is Sunday and ye'll be needin' fresh things fer Holy Mass."

Tom sat staring out the tiny window of the rectory kitchen. He had not expected to stay here for the night but he could hardly insult the priest and his mother. He wished he could sleep with the animals. Of all people, a priest!

Fr. Finnegan had gone into his own room to put on a warm sweater and emerged lighting a clay pipe. He gestured to Tom to go ahead and light his own.

"Ye'll be wantin' t'stay a few days I suppose, t'set things right by th'girl and bury th'baby. Nothing t'be done about it tomorrow, bein' Sunday and all."

Tom stopped midway to striking a lucifer and sat up straight. He had not even known what day it was!

The younger man went on, "Holy Mass is at seven and me mam fixes a noon meal. Then I usually make calls on folks in the afternoon and after tea me aunts come fer cards and singin'. Not a bad way t'spend the Sabbath atall, atall."

Tom scowled at the thought of delaying the burial and being

stuck here for an extra day. The last thing he needed was a bunch of old aunties peering at Meg and clucking about her condition and him not her husband and all. He lit the lucifer and with the great drama of pipe-smokers everywhere, hid his frown behind clouds of smoke.

"Father", he began, "I'm not much of a churchgoer, if ye' want th'truth. I wonder if it's wise fer us t'stay around where we'll only upset yer people. T'be sure, we're hardly yer ordinary visitors. We could be away before they even arrive fer Mass. T'would be better fer all of us."

"I may be a young man, Tom, but I'm not a fool," Fr. John said quietly. "I've been a priest ten years and I've heard many a confession that might have set tongues t'talkin'. I've baptized babies on their birthdays only t'bury them hours later. I've even delivered a baby. Before I took vows, of course," he added with a smile, seeing Tom's eyebrows arch.

"Me own sister died in me arms after her son was born. She wasn't married either."

Fr. John looked directly at Tom as he said this and Tom, unflinching, met his gaze.

"Would ye like t'tell me about it Tom? I guarantee ye I have a very short memory and ye look like a man who needs confessin'."

At first Tom was furious at the gall of this young fool prodding him like a cranky mule. Where did he get the right to expect Tom to explain anything to him? First, he takes Tom in. Then he works his charm on him to trick him into confessing. Nice work for a lad who still lives with his mother.

The two men sat in silence for a long time. Tom sulked and kept his face turned away from the young priest as he grappled with his pride. It would feel good to get some things off his chest, he thought; but now, to this boyo in this woman's house with little curtains in the window and doilies under everything? What kind of a man would let his place be filled with this fluff? Why should he confide in him?

The evening was still, the sound of dripping boughs drawing his thoughts outward. He wondered if Meg was angry with him. He had handled this whole thing so badly. He would be surprised if she weren't angry. If they could just get where they were going and set up some sort of normal life! She must be uncomfortable riding long stretches, her baby growing heavy in her belly but she never complained. If anyone was behaving like a fool he was. He never ceased to amaze himself with his ability to act like an ass.

He wasn't sure, later, when he was lying awake in the dark, just when or how he began to tell Fr. Finnegan his story. He hadn't meant to and he was very surprised that he had but at some point his thoughts turned away from the sounds outside and tuned in to the familiar clicking of wooden rosary beads. It made him think of home and Da. Da said his beads the same way in the evening by the fire with a pipe. Maybe this smooth-cheeked boyo would have something wise to say to him after all. He didn't know how it started. He just remembered taking a deep breath and talking. He talked and talked while the silent priest listened and prayed his beads. Fifteen decades and one hundred-fifty Aves later, the young priest brought Tom a fresh handkerchief and placing his stole across his shoulders, intoned the prayers of the ancient sacrament giving Tom absolution.

Chapter Sixteen

They ended up staying with the Finnegans three weeks. Fr. John's parish covered many miles around Newport. He and Tom traveled to the homes of the main tenants of the townlands to the south. Together they came up with a reasonable plan to have the fugitives head directly to Westport and from there to Achill Island. Connor McGee, whose brewery provided the ale for the pubs of Newport was the best connected of the men. He had a huge family spread out across the whole area between Newport and Westport. He arranged for Tom to bring the women to each of his brothers along the way. Terry McGee's wife had a cousin with the Mercy Sisters on Achill who could help them once they arrived. Duffy McGee, Connor's twin brother, lived in Westport and made arrangements with his friend Gerry Shea to hide them in the boathouse at Westport House where Gerry was the head gardener. They could stay there until they could safely cross Clew Bay to the island.

The best cover they had was the huge throng of pilgrims heading south to Croagh Patrick for the annual ceremonies in honor of Ireland's patron saint. Reek Sunday was celebrated the last Sunday in July, only a few days hence. Already the road at the end of the long lane was filling with early pilgrims. Tom planned to leave within a day or two joining the heaviest flow of pilgrims on their way to climb the holy mountain. No one would suspect anything as they blended into the crowd, just another family on their way to pray to their beloved Patrick to intercede in heaven for them here on earth. Maureen was particularly excited about making the trip south. The trip was twofold for her. Of course she was escaping but for her the pilgrimage had taken on much greater importance. She had given much thought to her future over the last three weeks and hoped to find inner direction on Croagh Patrick.

Tom himself was very curious about this whole thing. His da had made the pilgrimage when he was a lad and had spoken of it in mystical terms ever since. It was on Patrick's holy mountain that he had met Tom's mother, a girl from his own townland and it was on the journey home that he had fallen in love with her raven hair and cobalt eyes. His da had always credited St. Patrick with his happy marriage to the sweet Clare Meahra and had cried aloud for the saint to take her as he held her dying body in his arms. Tom had never shared his parents' devotion to St. Patrick or any other saint. His childhood memories went back no further than the age of twelve when his family was torn to shreds by the evil tyranny that killed his granda, his uncles and in the end, his mam. His da had healed of the stripes the constable had given him that day in the town square and he had even found a way to move on after his wife died but Tom had been too young to grow past the anger and the pain. Every time he had looked at his crippled brother Francis, the hatred had bubbled up in him. When Francis died, mercifully young and unaware, Tom's heart closed around the vision of him being born on the bog in a haze of smoke and stink from their burning home. In many ways he was still twelve years old, confused by feelings and mistrustful of love. He, of course had never confided these things to Meg but the whole jumbled mess had spilled out before the backdrop of clicking rosary beads the first night at Fr. Finnegan's. Now Tom hoped that by making the climb up Patrick's sacred mountain he might be able to fan the tiny flame of faith that seemed to warm him as the priest had laid his hands upon his head that rainy night.

He had slept that night in a state of such complete rest that he awoke as fresh as a newborn. Now the mystery of his transformation haunted his thoughts and caused foreign stirrings in his breast. He had attended Mass the next day and found it to be rich and fulfilling. The disdain for religion he had held for most of his life was gone and he was overwhelmed by a sense of surrender when he approached the altar rail and fell to his knees to receive Holy Communion.

A month ago he would have spat in scorn if someone had told him he would ever behave this way. This was women's stuff, forgivable in his da but certainly not for him. Meg had seen the change in him and he saw how she had looked questioningly at him. His confession to Fr. Finnegan had freed him from the vice of anger and bitterness that had gripped him in her presence. His stiff, unyielding selfishness had been replaced by the same shyness he had felt with her when he had first loved her. Tom did not regret returning to that place. Rather, he felt peaceful and easy around Meg, ready to start over and try again to love her without possessing her. He still struggled to master his rekindled physical urges and no amount of praying made this any easier. As Meg's body blossomed with their child, she became more beautiful to him than ever before. The good food and deep sleep they enjoyed at St. Mary's had filled out her cheeks and brought the sheen back to her beautiful blond curls. She was growing round, but from behind, her slim frame was unchanged. He often caught himself watching her move and marveling at how she changed completely simply by turning around. If this was what he could expect from marriage he would take it.

He wanted to marry her. He knew he could never take her into his bed again without taking her as his wife. And of course, he wanted to marry the mother of his child. He had talked to Fr. Finnegan about it and the priest had offered to perform the ceremony. Tom was shocked that Meg did not have to convert to Catholicism first and planned to ask her today if she would have him. They would be heading south the day after tomorrow and he wanted more than anything to leave here with his wife by his side.

The opportunity to ask Meg came late that afternoon. She was pulling sheets off the clothesline as Mrs. Finnegan spilled out the wash water from the big wooden tub. As she piled the fresh, neatly folded linens into a basket, Tom came up behind her and put his hands on her waist.

"Let me lift that fer ye," he said to the back of her neck.

Startled she let out a squeal that made him laugh. Beads of perspiration dotted Meg's forehead as she turned around. She raised her apron to wipe her face and looked at Tom over the embroidered hem. He could see she was not amused at being startled.

"That's quite all right," she replied. "I can manage quite well, thank you."

She found herself talking to his back as he carried the basket to Mrs. Finnegan's kitchen door and ducked inside. Meg wondered how she would ever deliver a child with shoulders like his. Winding the clothesline and stashing the pins in a tattered old sock, Meg puzzled over the change in Tom. What had happened to him that first night they were here? He had woken up, literally a changed man. Certainly a good night's sleep could not account for such a transformation. To be truthful, Meg didn't quite trust this change. How does a man go from being angry all the time to wake up one morning as charming and playful as a boy? They really hadn't talked about it with Tom gone most of the day with Fr. John and she and Maureen spending their evenings helping Mrs. Finnegan with the extra work of houseguests.

Meg had more or less resigned herself to keeping a distance from Tom, giving him all the space he needed to work out his miserable mood. She was not prepared for the new Tom, so much like the Tom she had always loved. She wanted to let herself go, to return his overtures but he had frightened her away with his thunderous brow and snapping eyes. He had rejected her when she was most vulnerable. He'd have to earn her trust again. She hoped her own bleak mood would pass. Now that she was feeling better Meg found the old attraction almost overpowering.

Despite her growing size and the strange surroundings, Meg hoped for opportunities to touch Tom and felt a thrill whenever he brushed up against her or touched her hand. This only added to her confusion. She remembered only a few short weeks ago standing in his father's cottage desperate for some sign of affection from Tom, receiving none. She had not forgotten the bitter tears she had cried riding behind him and Maureen, watching the muscles of his back tighten and relax under his thin shirt. She had longed to run her hands over those broad shoulders, to feel the strength and safety of his arms. But he would have none of her then. Now he was all friendly and full of romance. Musha! He could just wait until she was good and ready.

It was a straight back and stiff neck Tom saw from the kitchen door as he decided to approach Meg again.

"Mrs. Finnegan says supper will be awhile. Care t'walk a bit?"

Tom slipped his hand under Meg's elbow and steered her toward an opening in the slate fence that led to a peach orchard behind the church.

Meg slipped her arm away from his grasp and nodded.

"Sure, I could use a stretch of the legs."

They walked side by side but not together, each one wrapped in silence waiting for the other to speak first.

Tom felt like a school-boy courting a pigtailed girl. At first he was irritated by Meg's rebuff but then he found a perverse humor in it. Here was a woman who had made love like a wanton nymph with him and now she wouldn't even speak to him. He envisioned her thrashing around naked on her silky black coat while he coaxed and aroused her to a frenzy. Now she glided beside him as stiff as a nun, her chin high and her sanctimony intact. He knew he had perplexed her and the thought caught him in a funny place. He found himself humming a little tune he and his da had sung many a time at McPhinny's.

"Lada da dee, th'humor is off her now, th'humor is off her

now."

He chuckled at the lyrics about the woman who wanted nothing more than to marry until the mood left her and she just as surely wanted no more to do with it.

"Ah, Meg Darlin', is it that th'humor is off ye now?"

He chuckled again at the silly ditty and Meg's pinched profile. When she didn't return his good humor he straightened up to his full height and composed himself. Oh dear, had he made a bog out of this? He tried another approach.

"I'm sorry Meg, I'm just feelin' high spirited. Ye have that effect on me, that ye do."

He reached for her hand.

"Hmmph" was all he got but she did let him take her hand. Her hand felt slim and cool in his big rough mitt and the feel of it made him decide to speak seriously.

"Meg, do ye remember what I said that day when ye followed me from th'stable and found me by th'lough?"

"Actually I remember you standing there like a tree trunk saying nothing just like you did by the river the night before we came here. I've never met another man who could be so silent and so loud at the same time. So, no, I cannot remember you saying anything at all."

She spoke steadily without looking his way.

He walked on a bit in silence, entwining his fingers in hers. Finally, deep in the orchard, out of view of the rectory, he stopped and turned to her. He took her other hand and looked at her squarely.

"Not by th'lough side, Meg, Darlin', later in th'meadow."

His voice had become husky, laced with sincerity and thick with desire.

She looked up at his handsome face finding it as pensive and serious as that first day. Just like that first time, he locked her gaze with his eyes, drawing her into himself. She could not help but sink into their azure depths and see his soul. He allowed her this after being so distant, so difficult? She could see that this was the Tom she knew, the man she had fallen in love with. Who that other Tom was she refused to explore. This one had her now. Like a pond at the winter's end, she found herself thawing, her strength pooling at her feet.

Taking her silence to mean she had forgotten, Tom felt his resolve turn to hurt and almost dropped her hands and walked away. But something inside him knew that if he did, he might never find the courage to try this again.

"Meg, d'you not recall?" he almost pleaded.

He tried to penetrate her expression, to divine her thoughts. He saw in her eyes a searching of his own, both hope and hesitation ringing the clear green irises. Golden curls lay against her temples framing her heart shaped face in damp fringe. The day was warm and her face glowed with it, moist and rosy as though fresh from her bath. He could hardly bear it. Her poignant beauty tore at his heart and aroused in him such a surge of desire he thought he'd not recover unless he could have her. Still, he never dropped her gaze. Still, he held fast to her hands.

"Meg," he barely whispered, "D'ye' not recall?"

His voice catching, he saw that she did recall but she would force him to say the words. He knew now that he had hurt her, and she would exact his repentance. Taking her gently into his arms, he spoke into her hair.

"Meg, I told ye' that if ye' came with me that day I would be having ye' fer me' own. That's the all of it and there would be no goin' back. Darlin', d'ye' not recall?"

For his answer he received her kiss. She raised her face to his and took his mouth in hers and parting her lips she opened her heart to him once again. Her mouth was sweet, her tongue soft and tender. For several long minutes they stood, hands barely touching, only their mouths locking them together. They saw nothing, felt nothing but the deep velvet of surrender as they drew from each other the very breath of life.

Finally, unable to bear any more, Tom took hold of Meg and raised her off her feet. Scooping her up, he carried her beyond the peach trees across the meadow. Laying her behind a hedgerow of sweet pink roses, he knelt next to her and began to fumble with her clothes. She was dressed in an old red skirt of Mrs. Finnegan's who was stout enough to fit her clothes to

Meg's growing figure. Her bodice was a loose peasant style blouse and she had tossed an old black apron on when she started her chores. Meg had no corset that would still fit her and wore no shoes or stockings because of the heat. Tom had promised himself he would not do this until they had married but he pulled at the apron strings like a man possessed. When he finally unloosed it he had torn one string right off. He never stopped kissing her, devouring her mouth with his and covering her face with his lips. The salty taste of her sweat urged him on with a sense of purpose that bordered on frenzy.

Meg responded with equal purpose. It was clear she had made no such promise to herself. He felt himself sinking, unable to muster any of the resolve he had felt after he had unburdened himself to God and Fr. Finnegan. He rolled onto his back and sat Meg astride him, her skirt around her hips. Meg's breasts were so full beneath the ruffled blouse he could not wait to feel them in his hands, against his mouth. Down he tugged on the blouse, trapping her arms by her sides, urging her hands below her skirt to touch his body so urgent and so hard. As he drew her breasts toward his mouth he felt her unhook his trousers and move her hands beneath the cloth. He could stand no more. His mind and body exploded at the same time flooding him with shame as he let out a harsh groan filled with so much sorrow it startled her.

Unable to free her arms from the constricting blouse Meg was helpless to move. She was too awkward, her belly and skirts too hard to maneuver. She felt his body go limp beneath her, his hands slipping off her breasts to the ground. Her tears of disappointment fell on his chest as she tried to free her arms from the blouse. All of the terrible tensions of the last month coursed down her cheeks as she wept her humiliation. She had failed him. She had tried to give herself to him but she had only made him sad. She was so clumsy and bulky she could not please him. How unfair this was! She had wanted this for so long and now that they had finally come together, her belly sat like a melon on his chest and her breasts only seconds ago a gift she offered him, bulged from her blouse, ugly to her now. She blushed with embarrassment at their nakedness.

Tom looked up at her and much to her surprise he was smiling tenderly. Gently he pulled her blouse up over her breasts and her arms swung free.

"Why are ye cryin', me darlin' girl? Please tell me ye're not sorry we came t'this end? Have I hurt ye?"

Alarm crossed his face turning his tenderness to panic, his smile fading.

"Meg, have I done wrong? Ye seemed t'want..."

She covered his mouth with her hand and looked hard at his face.

"Tom," she said evenly, trying to gain control over her tears, "We've done no wrong that I can see. I am just so sorry I couldn't please you. I'm so big and clumsy."

He slid her off of him and sat up. Taking her in his arms he sat her on his lap like a child.

"Meg, Darlin' what are ye sayin', not please me? Tis that pleased I am, indeed! I know now that ye want me th'way I want you. Now I can ask ye outright, will ye marry me, Meg? Fr. Finnegan is willin' t'do it before we leave. I could never be without ye now Meg, not after this. Why ye just restored me t'meself and I know ye love me. 'Twas me angel himself that came between us just now. I promised God Almighty I'd not' take you again until we were married and He held me t'me promise. We came awfully close but don't ye see? Tis so much better this way. Tis that ashamed I am t'have behaved like such a demon almost draggin' ye down with me. Marry me Meg and we'll have no more need fer the angels in our bed."

Searching her face for some sign of assent, he lifted her chin. Kissing her tenderly he tried to read her eyes again. What he saw in her expression was not the eagerness he hoped for but a veil of confusion. Meg turned her face away from him and refused to meet his searching gaze. When he tried again to tip her chin up so he could see her face she pushed against his chest and heaved herself to her feet.

He sat in utter disbelief as he watched her walk slowly along the hedgerow. To the casual observer, she was a woman out for a stroll, taking in the scent of the hundreds of tiny pink blossoms along the fence. To Tom she was his life! He watched his future fading like a mist before his very eyes. Black dread rooted him to the ground where he sat. He watched her wrap her arms tightly around herself and raise her face to the sky. What was she doing? He had expected her to fall into his arms, overjoyed that they were finally to be wed. Now he could only sit while she gradually ripped his heart from his chest. Tom knew he had to know now what she wanted from him. He stood and refastened his trousers. When he looked up she was gone.

Now he was angry. This was the woman he wanted and she wouldn't even give him an answer. He went after her, catching her half way through the orchard. Spinning her around, Tom again took her in his arms. This time there was no tenderness in his kiss. He pressed himself hard against her, bending her backward and seizing her lips with his own. He forced her mouth open with his tongue and when she tried to turn her head he took her face in his big rough hands and held her fast. Finally, feeling her go limp against him he released her, knowing she had not returned his kiss. She simply stood looking at him, her expression a mixture of sorrow and resignation.

"Is that how you mean to have it Tom? By love or by force, however it's given?

At this he bellowed.

"Meg, be fair!"

He spun around now pacing in a circle, his skin boiling with frustration.

"I just made love t'ye and asked ye t'marry me! What d'ye want from me? What has this been about? Did I risk me life and Ben's t'get ye out o'yer father's house only t'have ye spurn me now? Have I trucked you and yer maid across Ireland so ye can give me the air? Do ye have any idea how many times I could have had ye since we left Clydagh Glyn? Why, God in heaven Meg, th'first night by th'river ye were practically naked and soakin' wet! Did ye' think I didn't just about lose me mind right there on th'riverbank? What d'ye want from me? Sure'n I'm only a man!"

He stood between Meg and the rectory now, huge, immovable, facing her down. She had nowhere to go and met his glare with one of her own.

"That first night by the river? How could you even think about yourself and your urges while I was desperate to keep Maureen from jumping in? I never took you for a selfish man Tom but you're just like the rest! We came all these miles with you hardly speaking and you get with that priest and all of a sudden you're all over me with fun and affection. What did you two talk about? Did you have a good chuckle about the loose morals of Protestant women? Is that what this is, now that there's another man around, a challenge to show me you're in charge, to keep me in my place? Well, you have me in my place! Where else am I to go? Look at me!"

By now she was sobbing, waving her arms in a rampaging tirade.

Tom was dumbstruck, her words like hot spears flung at his chest. Where did she get these thoughts? How could she accuse him of such cruelty and then drag an innocent priest into the mix? Here he was, fresh from his confession, filled with hope for the marriage they had both almost died for and Meg like some strange peasant banshee stood before him tearing his dreams into shreds. He had never seen anyone behave this way. He had absolutely no idea what to do.

Meg continued rambling on but Tom just heard a humming in his ears. His mind had emptied and he felt faint. He steadied himself against one of the gnarled little trees and wondered what manner of woman could make a strong man faint? He mopped his face with his sleeve and turned to face her again.

She was still crying and hiccupped as she continued, "And you will just possess me like my father did and I'll have to obey everything you say and you will beat me and keep me a prisoner and the law will allow it. I can't, I can't! I simply cannot go back to that! With this Meg sunk to her knees and wailed.

Tom stood, shocked at what he had just heard.

"Meg, d'ye really mean t'tell me ye think I'm like yer father? Can ye really believe that?"

He reached down and pulled her to her feet. Meg, completely spent, allowed him to press her cheek to his chest. She could feel his chest heaving with every breath and his heart pounded beneath her ear. She was strangely aware of everything around her as they stood there, reeling from all that had just happened. The aroma of peaches wafted over them and Meg felt somewhere on the bottom of her foot a prick where a twig had stuck itself to her damp skin.

Tom stroked her hair and spoke slowly as to a child.

"Meg, I'm not yer da. If that's what this is about then I see now. Is that what ye thought? That I would arouse in ye needs and feelings that I would only use against ye? That I would make ye need me so much that I could own ye and force ye to bend t' me will? That I would lock ye away in a room if ye didn't please me? Is that what this is about? Back there under th'tree? Meg, I understand what happened back there but you don't. How could ye?"

She mumbled against his vest.

"I couldn't please you. I spoiled everything. I couldn't do it right."

She sniffed and fresh tears began to soak his shirt.

"Meg, if anyone did wrong, 'twas me! I promised before God and Fr. Finnegan that I'd not take ye that way again until we were properly wed. I confessed to Fr. Finnegan Meg, all th'ways I've sinned against God and against you! That's what we talked about Meg. He spoke nothin' about ye except t'defend ye. You were the innocent in his eyes and I had tarnished ye and left ye with child! Don't ye see? The confession and absolution was what made me feel so free to be meself with ye again. And then, off I go tearin' yer clothes off and ruinin' everything!

"But I wanted you to!" Meg cried looking at him now with her heart in her face. "I couldn't understand why you were so cold to me, why you weren't glad to see me in your kitchen the night I ran away. Seeing you again was all that I lived for all those days locked up in my room. The beating, the pain, the isolation! It was only bearable because you were waiting for me."

He leaned down and put his lips against her cheek,

interrupting the crooked path of a tear. Straightening up he took her chin in his hand and looked hard at the dear face he loved so much.

Trying and failing to compose herself, Meg simply let the tears fall.

"Tom, I don't understand about your confession! I'm glad for you that you feel better now. But I just want you to love me. I'm so big and awkward and not nearly as pretty as before and…"

Tom gently placed his hand over her mouth.

"Meg, ye're more beautiful t'me now than ever. Can ye just take me word for that? I see that we have some long work t'do because of th'way yer father spoiled ye toward men. As for th'way I was when ye first came to me that night with Maureen, I was just scared, Meg. I'm responsible for ye and now Maureen. And of course, our child. And it was that humiliated I was too, by me own failure to get ye out of yer house. There was never a moment when I was sorry to see ye, God strike me dead! T'be sure, I was not too glad t'see Maureen, but sure'n ye can't blame me for that!"

He was relieved to see a faint smile.

"We can do this married just as easily as not, Meg. Will ye marry me, then? Will ye let Fr. John do it tomorrow before we go? I promise ye on me life that I will love ye till I die."

In response, Meg kissed him, her warm moist breath against his cheek.

"Yes."

Her hot tears soaked his collar as she clung to him like a drowning child.

"Yes, yes, yes!"

Hot tears pricking his own eyes, Tom lifted her up again and carried her to the low stone fence along the hedgerow.

Placing her gently on a bare, worn spot, he took out a clean handkerchief from his pocket, one of the luxuries Fr. Finnegan's mother had provided. They took turns cleaning up their faces and then, pulling her to himself, Tom gathered her again in his arms and kissed her deeply. Now they were oblivious to the soft scent of peaches and the warmth of the sun on their hair. They lost themselves in the sweet, long kisses of reunited lovers. There was no need for the crashing passion of their hidden trysts. The false intensity of forbidden love had dissipated, washed away by their tears. The sun had slipped away from their hair, down their necks and begun to warm Meg's back before they pulled away from each other.

Looking deep into Tom's eyes, Meg repeated again, "Yes."

Tom eased her off the fence and together they turned and headed back for their evening meal.

Chapter Seventeen

Maureen walked alongside Angus now, preferring to join the pilgrims on foot. Tom walked too, having stockpiled Angus with supplies donated by Fr. Finnegan and his family. Meg rode Jewel whose even disposition kept him calm even in the growing throng of people headed south to Westport. Tom had given the slide-car to Fr. Finnegan and had tried to leave the sow behind as payment for their keep. Fr. Finnegan flatly refused to take her so Tom sold the sow to Connor McGee. Connor had given him a very fair price for her and Tom had negotiated for Fr. Finnegan to receive fresh meat from the slaughter of every pig born to her for as long as she bred. In the end all parties were happy and Tom was grateful for the bulge of money in his pocket.

The pilgrim troupe was a very mixed crowd. There were sisters from several convents traveling in clusters. Meg thought it odd that they didn't mingle with each other until Maureen explained that just because they were all brides of Christ they didn't necessarily have anything to talk to each other about. Meg wondered aloud if they would even like each other which struck Maureen funny enough to make her laugh.

It was good to hear her laugh. The last few weeks had been so difficult for Maureen. She grieved her baby deeply and was unwilling or unable to talk about it to anyone other than old

Mrs. Finnegan. She had spent an afternoon with Fr. Finnegan confessing the way Tom had, Meg presumed. After that, she spent every free moment with the little mother as Fr. Finnegan fondly called his mam. At first Meg had felt a little left out but she was so relieved that Maureen had found a soul-mate that she kept her distance.

They had buried little Mary Ellen Dougherty early on the Monday afternoon after they arrived at St. Mary's rectory. Maureen had been inconsolable despite the beautiful little gown Mrs. Finnegan had made for the tiny body and the cap of lace Meg had crocheted for her head. Connor McGee had hastily prepared a casket from a birdhouse he had been making and his wife, Brigid had lined it with eiderdown she had been saving for a pillow.

Maureen had been speechless at the kindness of these strangers. So long removed from family and friends, in the service of the tyrant Lord Jeffrey since she was twelve, Maureen could not remember ever being treated with the tender pity these good people extended to her now. She was grateful beyond words to Meg for taking her away from Clydagh Glyn but had not been able to tell her. Maureen still associated Meg with servitude and their undeniable class difference made her sure they could never be equals and would never be true friends.

Maureen didn't know how to feel about Tom Phalen. He had never had much time for her when they both worked for the Wynn's and now she couldn't help feeling his judgment and scorn. Granted, he too had provided her with all she had needed to escape and didn't he treat her decently along the difficult journey? He had taken care to make her comfortable and safe but she felt deep humiliation at his presence during her miscarriage and emotional breakdown.

There were among the classes in Ireland, whether the servant class or the gentry, clear and definite rules of behavior. When classes mixed, as when a gentleman took up with a servant girl, the rules all favored him. His peers would never question his right to despoil her but among those of her own class she was shamed and shunned for her sin.

Maureen had felt this from Mrs. Carrey and some of the other servant girls, especially when she began to show her pregnancy. When Lord Jeffrey moved her downstairs so he could have her at will, her shame was overwhelming. She certainly wasn't the first girl Lord Jeffrey had taken as his own personal property but she was the only one still living at GlynMor. The others had been dismissed when he tired of them or they too had become pregnant and left. So, despite the rumors among the servants and the people of Clydagh Glyn regarding Lord Jeffrey's former victims, Maureen's name was the one on their tongues now and she had thanked God and the Holy Virgin when Meg's imprisonment had kept her busy and away from the rest of the house.

She had stopped going to church when she began to show. The women of the parish had begun to turn their backs on her as soon as the news was out about her being His Lordship's whore and when her bulging belly gave proof to the rumor the spitting began. Not a man dared to take up her cause. They risked scandalizing the very women they hoped to marry by even speaking to Maureen.

Young men she had been in service with and had been friends with for five years now disregarded her so thoroughly she ached to be treated like a stranger, even a stray animal. Instead they caved beneath the weight of the glares shot them by their mothers, sisters and sweethearts. One boy, slow to catch on to the scandal received a hard cuff on the head for smiling at her.

Not even the priest would intervene. This was the man who had given her Communion for five years, the man who had prepared her for confirmation and had praised her beautiful singing voice. Rules were rules and for a woman like Maureen, no matter how much an individual might want to show compassion, the mob ruled and every girl she had ever giggled with now spat in the dirt before she passed by. Had they not, they would have paid the price of a tongue- lashing or even a switching when they got home.

It wasn't that the mores on sexual behavior were even that

strict because Maureen knew they weren't. And surely childbearing was not in itself the problem. The inability to have a child was a worse scandal than having one outside of marriage. Maureen even knew couples who tried each other out before marriage to be certain that barrenness would not be a problem.

The scandal went deeper than that. Maureen's sin was their collective sin. They saw in her themselves, oppressed, without choices, trapped in the net of servitude by the class that owned them. They saw in her shame their own shame, the price of which was way too dear to pay.

When the rumors started, they had served a very valuable purpose. The woman who started them became an authority among her peers. She knew a secret that gave her a perverse power over the other women. When they spread the rumor they took on some of that power for themselves. Each one who leaned into the face of the next one ensured her place in their little circle by passing the test of telling. Each woman, by smearing Maureen's name and character wiped a little smudge off her own reputation. The more they talked the cleaner they became until finally, months after Lord Jeffrey stole Maureen's innocence and no one listened to her screams, they forced her to accept the silent stoning of the woman caught in adultery.

They had to shun her; her pregnancy was proof of her sin. They had to show her they were without sin, agreeing that they had no proof she had ever resisted. Moreover they had to show each other and their husbands and sons that they were good women, upstanding and virtuous. It had been ever thus since the first woman was tempted by the serpent. The fall of mankind was placed on the shoulders of Eve, as Adam, before God, blamed her for his own sin.

They knew no other way to survive the raw truth that if not Maureen then any one of their daughters or sisters might have fallen prey. Even more terrifying, in the dark of night upon their beds, in their own worst nightmares Maureen's screams became their own. If Jesus could forgive her, well then, He was God. But they were the women whose lives were governed by the unspoken fear that a man with a buggy whip could force their skirts up. They were the ones whose fathers and brothers had taken the whipping in the town square, the clubbing outside the pub, the bullet in the head behind the graves of their mothers.

They could not bear to face the sound of the boots coming for them, the paralyzing terror of the torch to their roof.

Did they not place the charms in the cradle and dress their sons in girls clothing to protect their babies from the fairies taking them? Even more reason, then, to insulate themselves from the bitter gall of truth. Any one of them might find herself in Maureen's place but no way could they admit that. They, just like generations of women before them, had found safety in blaming the victim, security in dragging her still further into hell while keeping their own faces lifted heavenward.

None of them knew this, of course. The rules of survival among men and women, between one class and another were clear and best obeyed. There was no time or energy for analyzing the rules. The ruling class knew the best guarantee of obeisance was punishment by one's peers.

The ruling class had learned this early on. It was a universal tool of oppression to keep the many under the control of the few. If the rulers doled out the punishment, they provoked fear, which was only good for a while. Eventually rebellion would foment among those who feared them. A wise tyrant made sure the rules seeped down into the very warp and woof of daily life among the common folk.

By allowing the lower classes their own leaders and their own petty rules the oppressors accomplished two things. First there was no need to enforce tyranny if the people would do it for them thus freeing the tyrants to severely punish randomly for select infractions. Secondly, they kept the servant class busy enforcing their own class structure leaving them little time for organized rebellion. This was the strong underpinning of class society. The strong became the strongest exploiting the dignity and pride of the weak.

Maureen was weak, this she knew. But walking along beside people like herself, free and unfettered by the prison walls of beautiful GlynMor Castle, she felt for the first time the prospect of a future. Each step she took away from her former life strengthened her and fed her resolve. Along this dusty road she breathed easily and with each breath felt a little more hope enter her heart.

The pounding rain the night of her miscarriage had washed her past away. Her grief remained, to be sure, and her shame was ever with her but she was with strangers on this journey, people who would never have to know what had happened to her. Would she run across anyone from her past along the road or among the pilgrims climbing the holy mountain? This was surely possible but she refused to worry about it. Instead she kept to herself, contemplating the possibilities of a real life. It seemed to Maureen that a dark curtain had fallen across the land to the east and reborn, she had only one direction to go from here and that was away.

There were whole families traveling like gypsies atop carts laden with belongings, old men and women atop bedding and sacks filled with potatoes and turnips probably hoarded from last year's harvest just for this trip. Dozens of barefoot children ran between families. Babies cried and mother's chased unruly toddlers away from the dangers of horses and donkeys, carts and tramping people.

From her perch above the crowd as far as Meg could see, a sea of white blouses and black shawls dotted the road. These were worn with skirts in a lively mix of reds and blues, and tweeds of all hues. Many women wore several layers of skirts. Some of the better- dressed women had pretty white petticoats peeking from under their skirts. There were very few women in dresses, certainly not like any Meg had back in her wardrobe at home. Meg was grateful for the castoffs of Mrs. Finnegan. Her waist was swelling steadily now but the little mother had taken good care of her, making over several skirts and blouses for Meg to grow into. She had also sewn several lovely shifts and nightgowns from some of the useless finery Meg had thrown into her bag the night she ran away. The older woman had embroidered these sweet underthings with soft pink roses and decorated them with tiny ribbons saved years ago for the little girl she had never had. Meanwhile, Meg had taken the scraps of silk and fashioned little baby frocks and bonnets. In the evenings she had crocheted with the tiniest hook soft stockings and blankets for her little stranger. Meg had some skill at lace making learned from a Belgian neighbor of her grandmother during the months she had lived in London. This she used to trim a Christening gown fashioned from an old bodice of Brigid McGee's.

She thought of these simple, generous people as she looked out over the mass of pilgrims from her perch on Jewel's back. How odd she felt up there. Her life had taken such a dramatic turn that this place, high above the ground, her body fitting snugly in the fine leather saddle, no longer felt right to her. This horse was her prize, her friend; the one animal she trusted. Now, from her place above the heads of these peasants and priests, nuns and tinkers, she felt caught between two worlds, no longer welcome in one, unsure of her role in the other. She knew she would have to raise her child Catholic. Fr. Finnegan had told her that when he married her and Tom. She was somewhat surprised at how little this bothered her. She had been raised to despise Catholics, to treat them as fools who obeyed a foolish old man in Rome. Nothing in her scant, formal religious formation had prepared her for what she had witnessed of their freedom, their sacraments and certainly not their strength.

The confession was the thing that had really impressed her. This ritual of telling your sins to a man behind a screen and coming away somehow cleansed and refreshed was very disquieting to Meg. No one had ever cared to relieve her of her guilt. Rather, any transgression was met with stern reinforcement of her sinfulness and her shame before God. How was it that these people were able to simply go to a priest and let it all out and come away pure and ready to start fresh? Who were these men and who gave them this power?

Meg thought about the druids of Irish history. She had read that they had had this sort of power. They had been the priests of the ancients who were somehow able to go before the gods on behalf of the mortal world. How were these priests different?

Had St. Patrick, whose mountain they were hoping to scale, somehow tapped into the great store of influence these early priests had over their gods? Was he the one responsible for their ability to take a man's guilt and cast it away into the sea? She believed that Jesus saved mankind but no one had prepared her for the ease with which these simple papists accepted this salvation upon the word of a man just like themselves.

She had gleaned some of the ancient stories from her reading and the tales told by her governess when she was young. While Reina had filled her head with the grand pirate tales of the Caribbean, Miss Carney, who had grown up in the great story-telling county of Kerry, enthralled the young Lady Meg with stories of fairies and druids, of the high kings of Tara and the chiefs of the ancient clans of O'Neill and O'Brien, Maher and O'Connor. Now, having had only a taste of this papist faith, Meg found herself very keen to know more.

Thinking about Catholics and her own child's faith turned her thoughts to Tom. She was astounded at the change in him. She had never known him among his own people, indeed had never cared about him beyond her yard and stables. Now, feeling like a fickle schoolgirl, she sought him out in the crowd, anxious to have him in her sights, to feel a part of this foreign world by his reassuring presence. Men in homespun britches and leather or homespun vests prodded their families and animals along, anxious to reach Croagh Patrick in time for the solemn Mass at the top of the mountain. She searched the crowd for the familiar form, so dear to her but so anonymous among hundreds of men all dressed in a sort of peasant uniform, their faces shielded by wool caps. The sun was warm and the pilgrims suffered dearly from the heat. Almost everyone was barefoot and the children wore outfits similar to their parents. Only the very small children looked comfortable in light summer shifts that left them free to run around the crowded road without becoming overheated.

She scanned the sea of caps and shawls but could not see him. Then she heard him right behind her, his voice raised high in exclamation followed by a laugh so hearty and full she craned her neck to see what was so funny. What a sound he made when he laughed! This too was a new element of her husband that she had not known. He had been so serious when they had been secret lovers. Now that they were free, secure in their vows and able to enjoy each other guiltlessly, laughter had exploded into their relationship. She shook her head at this new Tom, so at ease with and so energized by the company of strangers who behaved like they had been lads together. Content to know he was nearby, Meg settled herself on Jewel's back and took a deep satisfying breath of air, fragrant with summer flowers and the familiar pungency of warm horseflesh. Her thoughts never even entertained the image of home or anyone within those cold walls.

They had left St. Mary's Friday morning just as the sun rose. The road was already crowded but many travelers lined the hedgerows, some still cooking their breakfast and packing their carts. Meg had marveled at the distance some of these people had come. She chatted with a woman all the way from the Liffey valley near Dublin. Another family was bringing ten children and both sets of grandparents from Ulster and had been on the road two weeks. One of the grandfathers was feverish so Meg kept her distance from their group.

Tom wasn't surprised at the distance. He knew St. Patrick was so beloved by the Irish that they would travel twice as far to honor him in the place he was said to have fasted and prayed for them. As they bid farewell to Fr. Finnegan and his mother, Tom had been aware of a deep sadness in their leaving. Fr. Finnegan and his boyish face had started Tom on a pilgrimage of his own. He had married Tom and Meg before the altar of God just the day before and Tom was so deeply grateful he could find no words to say.

Everyone had been so good to them at St. Mary's. Connor McGee and Maureen had witnessed their vows and Brigid's nephew Sean sang a beautiful melody. They had no proper wedding feast, no games or racing for the bottle. Tom did treat the few men present to a pint at Mulroy's. It was the least he could do and now that he had sold the pig he had the means to do it.

After the wedding, Meg and the women had retired to the kitchen for a cup of tea and fresh buttered scones. Mrs. Finnegan was quite upset that Meg and Tom would have no proper wedding festivities and had made an oatcake anyway to break over Meg's head. The women cheered as Mrs. Finnegan broke the cake on Meg's head and in the age-old custom they each took a piece for themselves to put under their pillows. Meg didn't understand this at all until Maureen explained how it pleased the fairies and must be done to protect Tom and Meg's marriage and the children born of it. Besides, the women who attended deserved the good luck the little pieces of oatcake would bring them. Mrs. Finnegan made Meg promise to have a full-blown wedding once they were settled on Achill Island.

Tom and Meg spent their wedding night alone in the little cottage while Maureen and Mrs. Finnegan went to McGee's for the night. They made love by the fire, slowly and without words, finishing what they had started in the meadow. Content and deeply satisfied, they slept on the old fur coat, Tom's arm drawn protectively around Meg's swollen belly, his child asleep beneath his hand.

Now, they approached Westport House in the rain, hours later than they had planned. The crowds from the south and west had converged along the Louisburg road and had barely found a place to camp when the sky opened and drenched everyone in a typical Irish downpour. By now the crowds were so huge that no one expected to find a camping place closer than the outskirts of the town and no one thought anything of squatting on the open road for the next few days. But the rain had made people irritable and Tom had continued on. He hoped to get safely into the boathouse at Westport House before the next rain came. He had smelled it on the wind off Clew Bay and from the bluff over Westport could see the roiling black clouds out over the ocean. It was late Saturday afternoon when they finally arrived at the entrance to Lord Sligo's property.

They had come down into the town along a narrow winding road banked on one side by a steep hill and on the other by an apron of land leading to a small bay. Westport Bay was overflowing with pilgrims on foot and horseback, dray and common market cart. Waves of well-dressed gentry arrived by every kind of seagoing vessel. They saw traditional curraghs by the dozens ferrying pilgrims from larger sailing ships anchored farther out in Clew Bay. These majestic beauties had brought wealthy Catholics and clergy from areas along the Atlantic coast and even some from as far away as Dublin.

This was the biggest religious event in the lives of the Irish and if an Irishmen could not come every year, to have made it once was enough for a lifetime. They could see crowds in the street dancing and drinking. Tom knew the women were hungry and tired and despite the threatening sky out over the bay they entered the throng and bought meat pies and sweet pastries washing them down with rich bronze stout. Admiring Meg over the thick creamy head of a fresh pint, Tom thought himself the richest man in the world and let out a yelp of laughter at the sight of her screwed up face as she tasted her first Guinness.

Maureen looked radiant as she turned the heads of many a young man until one of them lazily put his arm across her shoulder and she fled back to the protection of Tom and Meg. There she stayed as they wandered among the colorful sojourners. Hucksters hawked their wares and tinkers clanged their pots and hollered out their bargains while others stood on the tops of colorful wagons that doubled as homes, promising everything from cures for gout to tonic that would replace a man's hair in ten days.

Over near the break wall there was a fight going on. Tom craned his neck to see who it was and one of the pilgrims said it was Brian McPhilbin, a local boy who had made a name for himself in America and returned to claim his proper place among the great Irish pugilists. A man weaving through the crowd was taking bets, claiming that the opposing contender was the son of the great Dan Donnelly, the greatest of all, whose arm had been severed at his death and preserved for all times. Tom waved him away as he approached proclaiming Pat Donnelly the greatest pugilist on two feet.

Fishmongers and bakers, children trading everything from

seashells to sweets mingled along the twin quays leading to the bay. They barely escaped being trampled by the horse of a man so drunk he thought everyone was in his bedroom and accidentally hit his horse in an attempt to evict the crowd with his buggy whip.

This was enough for Meg. She begged Tom to take them out of there and he reluctantly pulled himself away from the makeshift ring where the two fighters pummeled each other. It was clear that McPhilbin was the winner and that the fellow claiming to be Donnelly's son had none of the great one's blood in his veins. They turned away from the bay and wended their way through a ring of gypsies on hand for the festivities, always willing to read a fortune or sell one of their colorful shawls. Maureen tried to coax Tom into letting her have her palm read for a halfpenny but he looked at the threatening sky and said no, promising her the chance before they left Westport.

They found a narrow alley that led to the park-like estate of Lord Sligo. The Marquis of Sligo was known as a good landlord, attentive to his tenancy and compassionate with the poor. Tom was confident that even had they made themselves known on his property he would have treated them well but he intended to keep their arrival secret lest Lord Sligo recognize Meg and alert her father to her whereabouts. Connor McGee had told them the lay of the land and where to expect his brother Duffy to meet them.

They passed a short row of shops and a small inn just outside Lord Sligo's park. A boy was tossing pebbles at the name 'Browne's' scrolled in bright blue paint on a black sign trimmed with red. Above the name was a coat of arms and the words 'Cead mile Failte'. While Tom went into the inn to enquire after Duffy McGee, Meg and Maureen strolled across the road, down to a little fresh water inlet where the Carrowbeg River emptied into the sea. They let the horses drink the cool fresh water while they waded along the marshy bank soothing their tired feet.

This small inlet was extraordinarily beautiful even in the gray light of the approaching storm. Along the bank were two curraghs, left overturned until needed by their owner. Meg leaned against the curved hull of one of the boats. She could smell the tar coating that made it leak proof. Looking across the water she admired the long narrowness of the inlet and the trees that lined the shore. There were so few trees in Ireland the sight of these lovely willows bending down to kiss their reflection in the water made her homesick for the sycamores and yews of GlynMor. Not until she had been on the open road had she realized how fortunate she had been to be born to the luxury of trees. She had missed the fragrant yews while she lived in London and she missed them now. She imagined how the graceful willows would look in a proper sunset.

Maureen rested on a small stack of mussel traps and threw her head back letting her hair fall freely down her back. Meg's hair had dried quickly after the rain but Maureen's thick mane took forever to dry. Now as she watched her former maid shake loose the red waves Meg wondered what Maureen would do with her newfound freedom.

The rain started again just as Tom emerged from the inn followed by a tall, burly man. Meg guessed him to be in his early twenties. He wore baggy tweed pants and a collarless white work shirt opened to reveal a powerful chest covered in a thick mat of blond curls. He had carelessly slung a worn leather vest over his shoulder. Meg felt a surge of energy from Maureen as he approached. Duffy McGee looked nothing like his twin brother Connor. While Connor was built the same, he had a good, plain face and had already lost some of his hair. His brother Duffy was perhaps the handsomest man Meg had ever laid eyes on, and her chest constricted as she reminded herself that Tom too, was a handsome man, indeed. Duffy's curls were thinning but that only enhanced his fine broad forehead and deep-set blue eyes. Like his brother, Duffy's hair was golden red like new straw only slightly darker than the hair on his chest. Meg redeemed her thoughts by marking her husband's thick black curls against the younger man's thinner blond ones.

Meg had never seen any man's chest other than Tom's. By the way Maureen was blushing; she guessed that Maureen had never seen any man's chest at all. She felt a quick flash of pity for the maid, so experienced in the worst of all physical encounters without ever having any other knowledge of what a man could be. Duffy McGee helped Tom take the horses and Meg and Maureen followed as they scurried into the entrance of the dense park.

The trees shielded them from the worst of the rain but the woods were dark and suddenly very threatening. The horses were skittish as Tom and Duffy tried to lead them to the small cottage that served as the gardener's home. Duffy's friends, Gerry and Katie Shea lived in a tidy stone cottage nestled in the midst of a typical Irish country garden. A shaft of soft yellow light cast by a storm lantern led the travelers to a door, recently painted green and festooned with fresh flowers. The Shea's were in town enjoying the festivities and had left instructions for Duffy to get everyone settled.

There was no way to house the horses down near the boathouse so Gerry Shea had cleared a small area behind his cottage and erected a shelter of saplings and cast off thatch for them. Once Duffy and Tom had tethered them and brushed them down, the tired animals settled into their new home. Meg and Maureen unloaded sacks of clothing and bedding they expected to need for the night. Duffy explained to them that the inn where Tom found him had been in the Browne family for generations. The Marquis of Sligo, one of several descendants of this well respected family, owned the inn now but preferred to keep the family name on the sign. Duffy McGee ran it for him and Lord Sligo let him keep a percentage of the income in exchange for the upkeep of the inlet across from it.

The little finger of water was a far better source of income for the marquis, filled as it was with the flat oysters whose flavor was unmatched in all Ireland. These oysters were native to Ireland and were found where salt and fresh water met and mixed. Here in this inlet, where the waters of the Carrowbeg River met and mixed with the Atlantic, the oysters were a plentiful and profitable harvest. The mix of fresh and salt water was credited with the extraordinary fineness of their flavor. Lord Sligo had great reason to protect the delicate balance in his little bay and Duffy McGee had proven the man to do it.

This had been the way of it since Duffy had arrived in Westport at the age of sixteen. Duffy McGee was a naturalist who had an almost mystical way with plants and herbs and the diseases of trees. The Marquis' son George, only a few years younger than Duffy was the heir to all of this beauty and had learned from Duffy the ways of horticulture. The young marquis respected the older youth mightily even as he approached young manhood and began to question his own father's wisdom. Duffy coached young George in the ways of nature, taking him often to Achill Island to study the habits and ways of the islanders and the natural rhythms of the mighty Atlantic.

Duffy was a bachelor boy, an announcement that brought color again to Maureen's cheek. Perhaps sensing her interest, he hastily added that he would never marry. He loved the work of innkeeper, particularly the freedom it afforded him to care for the inlet and the woods. Meg thought it criminal that a man so beautiful as Duffy McGee would never marry but guessing his age at around twenty-five, knew he had plenty of time to have his mind changed. If she was disappointed, Maureen hid it well, thought Meg, even though it was clear that the auburn haired maid admired him.

The rain had again been brief and Meg could see stars twinkling through the treetops as they wended their way through the dense forest. The women felt quite safe as Duffy led them along a narrow path lighting their way with the lantern. Tom brought up the rear with his own lantern given to him by Ben. Finally they came to a clearing and in the thin light of the new moon they could see the outline of a huge square house. Maureen gasped when she saw it looming in the night. It was much larger than GlynMor Castle and much more imposing.

Meg just thought it was heavy and glum, the same way she remembered her Uncle Robert describe it. Before he met Adelaide DuBois, he had briefly courted Louisa Beaufort, the daughter of Daniel Beaufort the clergyman and entrepreneur, famous for his innovative farming methods and beautiful maps. It was said that he designed the gardens for a great many of the finest houses in Ireland and was a great friend of the Marquis. Louisa herself had already been an accomplished artist when she had visited Westport House in 1808 with her parents on a cross-country jaunt to view some of the Charter Schools established by the Church of Ireland. When Uncle Robert had found out that the object of his affections was coming to Westport House, he made certain to be there, selling the Marquis a fine horse. Young Robert Cushing had fallen hard for Louisa Beaufort but in the end, she spurned his affections in pursuit of her art. As Meg looked at the great house, looming like a fort against the night sky, she understood why Uncle Robert had thought it so plain.

By the time they walked around the large lawn and through the formal gardens Meg was ready for a good night's sleep. They had slept out the last two nights and she was looking forward to a roof over her head. The boathouse was beyond the garden at the bottom of a terraced piazza leading to a shimmering lake. The night had become so clear after the rain that the stars reflected in the lake, darting and skipping across the clear black surface as the breeze gently churned the water into little ripples. Meg thought the whole effect very mysterious and half-expected to see little leaves and plant pods transporting fairies and leprechauns across the starlit water.

Duffy led them down a broad stone staircase to a clump of trees at the right of a low stone railing. The railing separated the last tier from the water and was split in the center allowing for the staircase to extend to the water's edge. The small grove concealed the boathouse from both the main house and the water. Duffy knew they would be very safe there, as the Marquis and his wife had gone abroad for the duration of the holy festival.

Lady Sligo had at one time been very hospitable, welcoming both Great Folk and lesser gentry alike to be her guests and view her property. She had especially liked to show off her vast dairy and much to the bemused pleasure of the townsfolk, actually had two sets of dishes that she used for the different classes. The servants had reported that she used china for the high born and simple Wedgewood for the gentry. It was often laughed about in the pubs that the lower classes, if they were ever to be invited would be treated to the use of cow patties personally flattened for their use. They never got their invitation though, as Lady Sligo had developed bad nerves and the Marquis very often removed her from the bustle of his beloved great house to stay in a small Swiss cottage near Cashel, in the county of Cork.

The boathouse was more than suitable. Gerry had taken several curraghs out to make room for them and had brought in two old iron beds. His wife had hung drapes from the overhead beams to afford their guests some privacy. A washtub and a commode were set apart from the sleeping area. Their own damp bedding would not even be needed as Katie Shea had borrowed fresh bedding from the servants' quarters and made up the beds with clean white sheets and colorful quilts. Meg's eyes filled when she saw fresh flowers on the pillow of the double bed made up for her and Tom. She sighed aloud at the simple decency of the many people who had cared for them since they left home.

Duffy said his goodnights advising them to go to sleep early. They would have to rise at dawn to begin the climb up the mountain in time to get to the chapel for Mass. As she fell into a deep and satisfying sleep, Meg thought they'd never get anywhere near the mountain with all the people she saw in the town.

✣

Reek Sunday dawned clear and warm. By three o'clock the sun beat from a cloudless sky. Only the breeze off the bay saved the pilgrims from sweltering in the late afternoon heat. Meg fell exhausted onto a small patch of lawn she found in the shadow of a parked carriage at the foot of Croagh Patrick. Pilgrims were milling everywhere forming long lines at the wagons of venders and hucksters. Old women in black shawls ladled out soup and scooped mussels and oysters, steamed or on the half-shell for the hungry pilgrims. Men, women and children quenched their thirst with mugs of cold cider and pints of ale.

Meg looked around at the crowd. People who had approached the holy mountain in the cool damp dawn, singing and reciting litanies and Aves were now stumbling down the stony path in the heat of late afternoon, hungry, thirsty and desperate for shade. Many pilgrims nursed bleeding feet or knees that had taken them up and down the mountain. She wondered at such physical punishment and marveled that people would voluntarily cause themselves such pain. She herself, had worn her boots and still had not been able to make it half way up the path. Faint with the effort she had turned around and spent the remainder of the day following the shade as the sun beat down on the heads of the faithful.

At times she felt queasy at the heaviness of their piety. It seemed to her incredible that the demonstrations of personal mortification could be sincere. Yet, these people for the most part seemed very simple and unpretentious, uncaring of what she or anyone else thought. She had seen women bent under the weight of children carried up the mountain in straw turf baskets, strapped around them with a woven band across the midriff. Men older than Tom's father or Ben on their knees, literally crawled to the top of the mountain, perhaps believing that they would never have another opportunity to make this journey. Families, many with mothers far greater with child than she, pressed sons and daughters onward and upward in pursuit of the graces of the holy blessing at the top. Her heart was full as she watched them all while her mind cried out,

"Why?"

At first she felt shame that she did not have the stamina to make the climb. She actually had to look away from a woman who looked much older than she, greatly pregnant, carrying a small child in a turf basket strapped across her chest and leading two little girls by the hands. The woman's husband, presumably the reason for the pilgrimage, was being carried on a blanket slung between two boys about fifteen who struggled to keep him from hitting the ground while they climbed. The heavily bandaged man had obviously been terribly injured and was in a great deal of pain. His family plodded toward heaven to place him before the altar of Holy Patrick and beg healing for him from God. What caused Meg to turn her head away was not the rags they wore or even the sight of the poor woman's huge belly straining with every step but the tender way she led her children and her lovely voice coaxing her older sons to be gentle with their da.

Meg wondered if that little band of saints had made it to the top and if their da had been restored to them. As she scanned the crowd for Tom and Maureen, she saw the woman unwrap a meat pie and break it up among her children. Their father was not with them and Meg felt dread that perhaps he had not survived the trek. But, as a pair of horses split the crowd, she saw the twin boys propping him gently against a wagon wheel. He looked near death but they continued to minister to him one son wiping the sweat from his face while the other held fresh water to his lips. Meg had never witnessed such filial love. She had never known such tenderness and sacrifice was possible.

These boys must have been exhausted from their climb. They must have been hungry as all growing boys are hungry. Yet they showed nothing but the utmost love and deference to this man whom they had dragged over four thousand feet uphill and back. What kind of love could make two youths do this without complaint, without reward and from the unchanged appearance of their father, without success?

Meg marveled at the whole scene. Families just like this one were everywhere. Love and sacrifice was the order of the day. This man was just one of hundreds carried by devoted families to the top of Croagh Patrick. Now as the weary travelers pooled at the base of the mountain in the heat of the July sun, Meg could almost hear the angels singing, the feeling of peace and graciousness was so strong.

Maureen and Tom came around the wagon with parcels of food and tankards of fresh water. They smiled to see Meg scrunched in her little patch of shade. She felt a wave of relief that they had found her so easily, and laughed when Tom said they had watched her move from one shady spot to another as they came down the path and knew exactly where she was. She asked Tom if he could buy something for the two hungry boys and their father but when he turned to look in their direction, they were gone. Meg was astonished that they had disappeared so quickly and stood up to see where they were. They had vanished into the throng and she never saw them again.

Back in the boathouse, Katie Shea brought ointment for Tom and Maureen to soothe their feet. Meg's feet had begun to swell when the weather turned warm and she gratefully soaked them in a bucket of cool water. Around nine, Duffy McGee and Gerry Shea arrived to talk to Tom about the plan to cross over to Achill. The marquis and his wife would be returning in a few days now that the pilgrims were drifting back to their homes. Meg had in her reticule a letter that Brigid McGee had written to her cousin and the men did not think there would be any problems from this point on. The sticking point would be returning Angus to GlynMor and deciding what to do with Jewel. They agreed that Jewel was no plow horse. The men weighed the value of trying to get him over to the island and decided that it would be too risky. Jewel was a thoroughbred, a lady's horse, bred and trained for Lady Meg. Tom knew they could not afford to keep him. He hated to break the news to Meg but she would need to say goodbye to her sweet tempered friend. There was no place for him on the island and selling him here would give them a good sum to get settled there. Tom would immediately return Angus to GlynMor. He could see Ben and find out what had actually followed their escape. Perhaps he might find out how Da was doing, too.

Meg stood frozen as she heard him say the words that would separate them again. They had finally made it to safety! She was simply aghast, stunned. How could he think of leaving her here among all these strangers? Her baby wasn't due until October but what if something happened to delay him? What if her father caught him and had him hanged? Furious that he would take such a chance, Meg watched in stony silence as the men took their planning outside, lighting their pipes and heading for a pint at Duffy's inn, leaving her to stew as they decided her future.

Maureen and Katie caught Meg as she stumbled, speechless, from the door where the men had left and she had begun to follow. With a stern look Tom had stopped her in her tracks forcing her to seek solace in the arms of these two women. Katie sat her down and took her hands in her own. Meg shook off the gesture and stared across the makeshift bedroom, her eyes resting on the wildflowers now wilting on the double bed where she and Tom had slept the night before. Fat, salty tears began to slide down her cheeks.

Looking confused, she turned to Maureen.

"Do you plan to leave me too?" she asked plaintively.

"Of course not M'Lady I owe you me life. I'm not goin' anywhere!"

"How could he go? For the sake of a horse!" Meg cried in disbelief.

"Well, Ma'm, d'ye think he'd really do that, now?" Katie asked as Meg shrugged her hand off her shoulder. Meg suddenly felt smothered by the tender solicitousness she had so recently appreciated. She was tired, and Katie kept trying to touch her.

Rebuffed, Katie stood up.

"Ma'm, if there is nothing else, I'll be going."

Katie, too, immediately reverted to her servant role when Meg's high birth surfaced.

Meg's predicament and her new role as the wife of an Irish Catholic peasant had forced her to publicly assume the same status as Maureen and Katie. What had so recently been a huge gap between the classes, where each woman knew the rules and fell into position, had now narrowed to a very fine line, with sheer need the equalizer. Most of the visible trappings of Meg's aristocracy had been replaced by her peasant skirts and blouses but when Katie had helped Meg remove her boots, she had been well aware of the fineness of the kid and the soft whiteness of Meg's delicate feet.

Maureen and Katie tiptoed very carefully around this new

friendship with Meg. It was clear to them that she needed friends more than servants and they were happy to give her their friendship but when Meg became irritable or demanding, they instinctively retreated into the safer role of maid. Meg's own struggle was clearly evident to them, though not so evident to her. Meg, who had played with Irish children, who had sincerely tried to understand their ways, displayed none of the prejudices of her parents. Hadn't she gone so far as to fall in love with one of their own? Hadn't she married him and agreed to rear her children in his church? Meg's own upbringing, surrounded by privilege and wealth would be the greatest obstacle to her new role as peasant wife. She could not change herself any more than Maureen or Katie could rise above their servitude. Katie looked with pity at this woman, so used to having all her whims met, all of her comforts provided for her, sitting in this drafty boathouse, pretending to be satisfied with a few flowers and a patchwork quilt. Katie had grown up a servant in this household and knew full well that despite tender words of gratitude and lovely Christmas treats every year, even the nicest, most sincere mistress controlled every moment of her life.

The trust between servant and mistress was clearly one-sided. There was no doubt in the mind of a high-born woman that her maid or cook would simply do as she commanded. The servant would simply obey or be turned out without references to starve in the street. The mistress trusted the servant with the most intimate of her needs, assuming her place in society guaranteed her the loyalty of her underlings. This loyalty was born of her servants' need to survive. The blind spot in the eye of the aristocracy was mistaking the work of survival for true affection and gratitude. No doubt many servants did develop affection for their masters and mistresses but Katie knew, as every maid, cook, gardener or liveryman, that this was a fleeting emotion. She had stood in the kitchen doorway through too many gossip sessions to believe for a moment that any servant truly loved the one who literally held their lives in his hands. It was and had always been the greatest defense of the servant class to foster in their masters the greatest dependency on them. The aristocracy with all their social mores, all their petty proprieties, feared offending each other as the greatest threat to their security. But it was their blind arrogance that was their true Achilles heel. The servants who drew their water and washed their undergarments often held them in contempt, feigning fealty and falling asleep dreaming of gruesome comeuppances for their silk-clad keepers.

Katie, who had always been treated well by her master and mistress, knew her good fortune. She was satisfied with her lot. Maybe she was a fool to enjoy the life of a virtual captive. But she had married her childhood love. She had a lovely little home in a glorious parkland. She was not only allowed but encouraged to keep her own beautiful garden. She had been given a pup from her master's pedigreed collie as a wedding gift. When she needed to dress up she had her pick from a closet full of her mistresses cast-off dresses. Indeed, from Maureen's description of Tom and Meg's hasty wedding, her own perfect day, drenched in golden sunlight, dressed in a beautiful white lawn dress and flower studded bonnet seemed to reverse their roles entirely.

Katie Shea was no fool. Every Sunday in the tiny stone church she could look around at her peers and see that many of them were barely living. She knew she had great fortune to be the servant of the Marquis of Sligo. Now, as she withdrew her hand from Meg's shoulder and began to retreat toward the door of the old boathouse, Katie felt a keen desire for these guests to leave this place. Meg's inner turmoil had upset Katie's equilibrium. She wasn't used to feeling sorry for her betters and was confused as to the proper response.

"Ma'm, is there anything else I can do for you?" she asked as she turned toward the door. Meg did not answer but Maureen shook her head. Katie slipped out into the grove and ran up the stairs and around the main house into the woods, never slowing down until she saw the light in her window.

Meg continued to be cranky with Maureen, demanding a bath and acting as if she were back in her bedroom at GlynMor. Maureen complied, filling the tub with soothing cool water and washing Meg's back with lavender scented soap. Maureen slipped into the water herself after tucking Meg into her bed. Meg's mood had improved some when Tom returned to their makeshift room and finding Maureen and Meg refreshed by their bath, decided to take one himself. He was amazed at how often Meg bathed. Most people among his class believed that bathing was actually harmful to a person's health. But since he had married Meg, she had demanded he regularly clean and refresh himself. Now, he actually enjoyed the feeling of being clean. As he soaked in his refreshing bath, Tom mulled over various ways he could broach the topic of leaving to return Angus to Glyn Mor. He also needed to see his da once more before he settled with Meg on Achill. He could only imagine the old man's shock at the sudden developments in his life. He tried to think of words that would soften the reality of his departure and finally decided to be simple and straightforward. Some things were best said bluntly.

Returning from dumping the water, Tom slipped into the big iron bed next to Meg and took her in his arms. Maureen was snoring softly behind her curtain so Tom felt free to speak.

"Meg, ye know I have t'go back. We talked about it."

She stiffened but did not pull away from him.

"I can't believe you care more about a horse than you do about me and our baby," she whispered into his fragrant chest.

He stroked her damp hair, winding a golden curl around his thumb.

"Oh, Meg, sure'n ye know t'isn't about th'horse!"

She looked up to see him actually laughing and she stiffened again.

"Meg?" He enfolded her deeper in a tight embrace that forced her to relax against him again.

Her face against his thick chest, she mumbled, "What?"

Now he put her away from him and looking directly at her said,

"What d'ye mean what? We've known from the beginin' that I would have t'be goin' back t'return Angus. Duffy and I decided tonight that I would sell Jewel before I leave. T'is a man from

Ballinisloe at the inn tonight who offered t'take a look at him in th'mornin'. Between th'price we get fer Jewel and that fine saddle o'yers and th'money we got fer the pig we can get a good start."

"My saddle too?" Meg squeaked.

"Of course, Meg! What good is a lady's sidesaddle to ye when ye'll be lucky to sit on th'back of an arse?"

He knew by her downcast eyes that he had really done this last part badly.

Meg pulled herself away from his arms and sat with her back to him shrugging off his hand when he reached for her. For several minutes neither of them spoke.

Finally, she turned to him and with her chin firm and her eyes focused directly on his, said,

"I've had to trust you for everything since that horrid day in my father's study and you have never let me down. Tom, I know you have to go back. Just get us safely settled on the island and go."

Her resolve crumpled with a single tear as she continued, "But if you don't come back, if something happens to you I will never recover."

Tom gathered her again in his arms.

"Meg, me darlin', me dearest girl, I will come back! I'll be here for th'birth of our child. Please believe me. Please don't be afraid."

At this he kissed her with a tenderness that quickly turned to urgency. Drawing her fully into his embrace he reached for the lace hem of her nightgown raising it above her hips with one hand while unfastening the buttons of her collar with the other. Together they slipped beneath the crisp white sheets and slid against each other. Meg urged him on, placing his hands where she needed to feel them and Tom like a man starved, devoured her with his lips. She covered her mouth to keep from disturbing Maureen, as Tom aroused in her sensations she had never known, his warm mouth finding its way everywhere and beyond. When he finally could wait no longer he came into her with such a force she feared he'd hurt the baby but couldn't, wouldn't dream of trying to stop him. With a muffled cry, Meg felt herself and Tom surrender together. When they were finished, he looked intently into her eyes and barely audibly, breathed, "I'll love ye forever, darlin' Meg Phalen."

He gently kissed her belly, then her mouth and settled onto his own side of the bed.

Chapter Eighteen

Maureen straightened herself up from the beach and scanned the horizon for Seamus Foy's curragh. Her back ached and her bare feet throbbed from the weight of the straw basket slung over her left shoulder. She had been gathering periwinkle and dulse for Friday supper but the tide was starting to come in and she needed to head back to the kitchen. Seamus Foy had promised limpets today, said he had found a spot where there were more than a whole town could eat. Bending down to scoop up the small pile of sloke she had scrambled to find, she thought of how good this meal would be. It was a favorite island dish, this cruasach and she and Meg had grown quite accustomed to it. She had actually spent this long September day gathering the three seaweed types for Meg, who was nearing her time and needing the strength promised by the locals to those who ate the meal. The basket was heavier than usual. Maureen came often to gather these gifts of the sea but usually she dried the leaves before bringing them in. Today she had gotten a late start and the seaweed was still wet. Dark briny juice dripped from the bottom of the basket as she hoisted it on her back for the short walk home.

She turned again in the small yard and scanned the bay for Seamus. If he didn't bring limpets they could always do with oatcakes and taters but Meg wouldn't be the only one disappointed. Seamus had boasted all over the place last night about his find and more than one kitchen was filled with women chopping and simmering the purple and crimson leaves.

"Here I am Meg!" she called, bending next to the well to rinse the salty leaves. The sand and grit spilled at her feet as she tore the tougher more fibrous leaves into small pieces.

She poked her head into the kitchen expecting to see the pot on the boil. It sometimes took hours to soften the seaweed, especially the dulse and Meg had said she would get things started. Maureen could smell the oatcakes and saw scrubbed potatoes on the kitchen table.

"Meg?" Hello, where are ye? I'm here with the dulse!" Maureen rinsed the last of the flat leaves and gathering them up, carried them into the cottage.

"Meg?

Irritated when she found the pot cold and the fire left to smolder, Maureen dumped her gatherings on the table next to the potatoes and threw more turf on the fire. She grabbed the metal crane with her left hand and swung it forward. She adjusted the pot-hook to hold the largest bastible Meg had. She filled the bastible with fresh water and swung the crane back over the fire. Maureen had seldom been asked to help with the cooking at GlynMor but from her meager experience she thought the crane and hake set-up in this cottage's wide, open hearth was every bit as efficient as the old Robinson stove Mrs. Carrey used.

The crane was made to swing up to three pots in almost any position over the fire while the pot-hook was used to adjust how high or low the pot was suspended. Maureen hoped Clive Hampton, the old village smithy would soon deliver their new pot-hook. The one they were using now was old and corroded and there were only two positions that were safe to use. With a new pot-hook, or hake as the smithy insisted on calling it, referring smugly to his personal knowledge of the Norse roots of the word, she and Meg would be able to safely adjust the pots in any of several positions over the flame.

She did wish they had a boiler for hot water and even a poker oven would be better than the tin oven Duffy had brought from Westport. Maureen had gotten used to fluffy white bread at GlynMor and had never grown to like the smoky flavor of the hearth-baked bread. She and Meg were much happier making soda bread in the covered bastible which, when hung way back in the hearth, kept out the smoke altogether.

Once she had swung the big pot in place Maureen went out to look for Meg. Coming around the side of the house where the two women had planted turnips, carrots and potatoes, she found Meg on her knees pulling thorny weeds from the tidy rows of feathery carrot tops.

"Meg! What are ye doin'? Ye know I'll do that. Ye can't be doin' that so close t'yer time."

Maureen bent to help her friend to her feet.

"Oh, bother, Maureen, I'm fine. I'm trying to have this baby not keep it inside. I'm ready for this to be over, no?" Meg turned unsteadily and allowed Maureen to hold her arm while she trundled into the kitchen.

"Yes, m'Lady, but ye do want yer husband t'be here do ye not? And isn't he after sendin' word that he's at least a week away?"

Even after several weeks of living as rustics, Maureen still slipped into her servant role when Meg acted cross. But now Meg only laughed.

"Maureen, I am so far from m'Lady I can't tell you what it does to me to hear you call me that. Tom has been gone for so long and I do miss him awfully, but I want this baby out! Besides, the message came yesterday and who knows how long ago it was written. He could be here by dinner time tonight!"

Meg's eyes were bright at the possibility that she might see Tom in a matter of hours. Maureen, seeing her friend so hopeful put her arm around her shoulders and squeezed.

"M'Lady, we decided not t'get excited until we saw his face at th'door now, didn't we?"

Meg nodded, "Didn't we just, didn't we just that."

Once inside the house, Meg collapsed onto a three-legged creepie, threatening to topple it and her into the fire. Maureen grabbed her and steadied her into a straw chair. They were both laughing so hard they nearly toppled each other. Breathlessly, Maureen tried to compliment Meg on being able to tip the untippable stool but she couldn't get the words out. Instead, she threw her head back in a hoot of laughter that made Meg howl.

The thought of Tom coming anytime and the reality of the imminent birth of Meg's child had made them giddy. Nearly doubled over and bursting into new gales every time they looked at each other, neither of them heard the sound of the man calling from the yard. Seamus was in the doorway dripping salt water on the floor when they looked up, tears of laughter on their cheeks.

He was a very old man, grizzled and bent with a long gray beard and a thatch of shoulder length hair sticking out the back of a seamen's cap. A stoic old bachelor, Seamus was unperturbed at the sight of the two women dissolved in giggles and observing the usual proprieties, took his cap off to reveal a shiny bald dome. Townsfolk had always said that old Seamus grew his hair so long in the back because there was none at all in the front. Now he stood squinting soberly at them, his hat in one hand and a small sack filled with limpets in the other.

"If ye ladies would just be makin' yer selection, if ye please? I have other customers waitin,' don't ye know," he said with a slight bow.

He stood, dripping salt water all over their floor, holding out a bag of slithering limpets like a nosegay of sweet violets. The sight of him, hat in hand like a suitor, made them convulse in laughter again. Neither of them could help it. They had started with the tipped stool and now everything was so very funny.

Meg could hardly breathe and finally, gulping noisily, managed to bring herself under control.

"Thank you Seamus, thank you. Will you take eggs or bread?" she asked, still trying to compose her mouth.

"Bread, if ye please, Ma'm."

Meg took the limpets and handed him a fresh loaf of soda bread.

"Thank you again, Seamus, they look lovely."

Maureen had to face the hearth as laughter threatened to return at the sound of Meg's Lady Wynn voice.

"If ye have a few eggs, Ma'm, I'd be obliged t'trade 'em fer some oysters," Seamus Foy said, fondling the warm loaf.

Meg nodded toward the bowl on the table.

"Take six, and leave me a potful."

Maureen handed him a pot and he left to fetch the oysters from his cart.

In a few moments, Seamus returned from his cart, the oysters mounded in the pot. He tipped his cap ceremoniously, took his eggs and departed without another word.

"Oh, sweet Mother, I'm spent," Meg sighed.

"No more laughing!"

"Why don't we sit outside where it's fresher? Much as I love it, dulse and sloke make a terrible stink cookin'."

Maureen had cleaned the limpets and was heading out the door with the pot of oysters and a sharp knife.

"I'll shuck these and you just rest."

Meg nodded and heaved herself out of her chair.

It was breezy outside and Meg never tired of sitting and watching the tide roll in. Living on this island was hard but the views of the ocean and the indescribable sunsets, the gannets swooping against a backdrop of silver and white clouds made up for the endless toil. She had developed the ability to see in the clouds and feel in the breeze the sudden, wild and blustery storms off the ocean. She could feel one coming on now. The sky was gray and heavy and the clouds scudded across the horizon. She had an image of a children's book she once owned that showed the chubby face of a playful god blowing the clouds across the sky.

"There's a big one brewing, Maureen. Just look at that sky."

Meg leaned forward to catch the breeze. August had been warmer than usual and now, midway through September, she welcomed any sign of cooler weather.

Maureen just kept shucking. Meg marveled at the speed with which Maureen could work. She could have the wash boiling before breakfast, clean the cottage from top to bottom before noon and weave a basket while supper boiled. Since they had arrived, she had woven three hearth chairs and several baskets including the big kelp basket she had filled with dulse this afternoon. She had offered to weave a Moses cradle for the baby but Tom said he would pick one up in Westport when he laid in the supplies for the winter. He had seen Meg admire a pretty little swing-cradle in a shop when they were there for the street fair.

Maureen pampered Meg and Meg knew it. No other woman on the island, pregnant or not, got away with so little work. No one was wise to their previous status as maid and mistress but in the privacy of their home neither of them minded playing their former roles. Meg promised herself that after the baby was born she would allow no more of this coddling, but truth be known, there was so much she didn't know about running a house it seemed logical to let Maureen do it. And Maureen seemed happy to do it. She was indefatigable. Up at dawn and squinting late into the night mending by the weak light of an oil lamp she never stopped working.

The house had been in fairly good condition when they arrived. It had been recently vacated by a young widower who went to America. Made in the traditional coastal farmhouse style, it had elements of both the Donnegal longhouse and the typical midland architecture. It was bigger than the average cottage and Tom knew he could make a comfortable home for a good-sized family in it. The house sat overlooking the bay about a hundred feet from the water and backed up to a nice yard surrounded by a stone wall, long since overgrown with berry vines and hedgerows of honeysuckle.

Beyond the wall were acres of potato fields that led to an orchard bordered by nut trees. Finally, in the distance, the land sloped upward to grazing pastures dotted with sheep. The foundation and lower half of the house was stone like a Donnegal house but had wattle and daub all the way to the thatch roof. The front door jutted out from the house a bit providing an attractive interruption to the roofline and formed a little shelter for any guest waiting at the door. The thatch was in fairly good condition and the sod that lined the rafters was tight and secure.

Tom did want to have the thatcher repair a few weak spots

in the roof before the winter rains started but the whitewash both inside and out was fresh and the three windows on the sea side of the house were in good condition. Two of these windows were the only source of light for the kitchen and bedroom. The third window, Meg was delighted to discover, was in a parlor that even had its own small hearth and chimney.

As in every house of its kind, this house was built one room deep and any additions went on the gable ends. It was clear that the parlor had been added on across the kitchen from the bedroom and a good- sized loft opened into the space above it. The front door, which faced the sea rather than the road, opened into a generous kitchen flanked by a wide, canopied hearth on the right and a wall with a ladder leading up to the loft on the left.

The little bedroom shared the hearth wall. Meg knew it would keep them cozy on a cold night. Two stone seats on each side of the fireplace were built into the frame of the canopy in the Galway style and whitewashed to a glistening sheen. This formed a very pretty area for sitting and visiting and Meg could picture her little children sitting on the stone seats warming their feet on a winter day. Above the canopy was a deep shelf that promised to hold everything from winter vegetables to warm woolens. Another little cubby to the right was perfect for keeping their precious supply of sugar and salt dry.

Meg had left home knowing nothing about the running of a kitchen but Mrs. Finnegan had taught her much in the three short weeks at St. Mary's. She could plainly see, however, that Maureen was thrilled with the supply of utensils and pots being sold with the house.

In addition to a shiny copper pitcher, there was a mortar and pestle, a sieve, two griddle pans, a heavy cast iron pannie for frying bacon, and a smaller one for eggs. In the cubby they found a bastible and single farl toaster for quarter loaves as well as a hardening stand for toasting single slices. There was a straw potato basket with a well in the center for salt, a hob-kettle and trivet, and two cauldrons were set in the back of the hearth. Meg followed Maureen's cue and explored every corner of their new kitchen. Deep in the shelf above the canopy, she found a basket full of small implements that would do everything from grind meat to whisk eggs. As excited as a child, she pulled out her treasures to show Maureen. Maureen stood in the center of the kitchen with her hands on her hips and proclaimed that there was little they would need to set up a very efficient kitchen.

Turning around, Meg saw a dresser painted yellow with three shelves above for dishes and a deep cupboard below for storage. The top of the piece extended over the other shelves forming a deeper ledge for larger bowls and basins. The whole dresser was trimmed in pretty scallops painted white. There were three hundred-eye lamps, three chambersticks with candles already in them, a butter-cooler and a small meat safe. Next to the dresser stood a dash churn for making butter and a food ark with bins for both white and brown flour.

Meg could not believe their good fortune. She could not imagine anyone having a wonderful little home like this and simply selling it completely furnished. There was only a small truckle bed in the bedroom but there was a fine looking settle bed along the far wall next to the hearth. Maureen scrambled up the ladder to see what was in the loft and exclaimed at the discovery of a tester bed and several quilts along with a lampstand and a washstand.

The young man had lived there all his life and had worked hard to make it clean and fresh for his wife who had obviously come with a substantial dowry. When, only one short week after moving here, young Mrs. Hanley wandered too far offshore to escape the rising tide, Billy Hanley was consumed with guilt. He knew he should never have brought a girl from Killarney back here to live. She knew nothing about the sea and despite his warning had insisted on gathering just a few more mussels for their supper. He had been tightening up one of the ropes at the far corner of the roof when he realized that she had been out too long. By the time he had raced to the beach she was gone.

Her body had washed up the next day and after the funeral he packed up and moved out. It was Tom's good fortune that the poor man had buried his wife the day the three strangers set foot on the island. They paid him what he asked and watched in disbelief as he simply climbed into Duffy's McGee's boat and left everything behind. The young bride was buried in the cemetery of St. Dymphna's church. Meg always walked around the far side of the church on Sunday to avoid the risk of her spirit laying eyes on the baby.

Meg's thoughts drifted back to Maureen's messy job. Her hands flew as she shucked the pot of oysters. And she wasted nothing. The shells that dropped to the ground would become a project for a strong lad. Maureen would bake him a tart if he would crush the shells beneath a wagon wheel for her. Tedious work but Maureen's fruit tarts were delicious and all the island boys were anxious for the work. Then Meg, whose special gifts were found in the garden, would mix the crushed shells into the sandy soil and hope for enough time to harvest at least a few vegetables for the winter.

Duffy McGee had taught her this when he had planted bulbs for her to enjoy in the spring. Meg was also grateful to Duffy for repairing the soot-house which, according to the locals, was somehow kept smoldering all winter producing soot later used to fertilize the soil. This was only one local practice that had both Meg and Maureen shaking their heads. There was much to see and learn from the land and the people of this remote windswept place. This island was breathtaking in its beauty. Meg had never seen such vistas as the beaches along the south coast where they had settled a few miles east of the little fishing village of Dooega.

They could see from their front door all the way to Clew Bay with Clare Island marking the beginning of the great Atlantic Ocean. Up and down the strand as far as they could see there were no other houses. In the far distance Croaghaun Mountain rose to mark Achill's western tip where it met the ocean at Achill Head.

Tom had set his sights on the north shore and had expected to shelter Meg and Maureen at the convent of the Mercy Sisters but that was before he had money to provide for them himself. When the little house by the sea was offered for sale his decision was made. Meg wasn't sure about being so close to Westport Bay but Duffy had assured them that the people of southern Achill would close ranks against someone of Lord Jeffrey's ilk.

The north part of the island was another story. There was a Protestant missionary group up in Dugort that was upsetting the Catholics across the whole north shore. The Church Missionary Society of the Church of Ireland had leased land at the foot of Mt. Slievemore. A Rev. Edward Nangle had founded a place called The Settlement about a year ago and made all sorts of promises. He tried to lure good Catholics into his mission by offering them cheap rent and free schools. He said he planned to build an orphanage and had even dragged a huge printing press over the mountains to start a newspaper. It was better that Tom and Meg settled on the south shore just to stay away from Rev. Nangle and his cronies. If anyone would reveal their whereabouts to Lord Jeffrey he was the type to do it. Better to stay away from Church of Ireland folks and make the weekly trek to St. Dymphna's even if Meg wasn't Catholic.

At first the women were disoriented by the ocean at their doorstep, the endless sound of the lapping surf and the austere beauty of the landscape. But soon they began to relax and their bodies responded well to the ebb and flow of seaside life. Maureen had taken to the work of housekeeping immediately despite having recently been Meg's personal maid. Prior to that she had spent plenty of time in the scullery and beneath the yoke of the sheer hard labor of the lower servants. She had learned to cook and bake under the expert eye of Mrs. Carrey. She had honed the skills of ironing, polishing and scrubbing by enduring the sharp pain of cook's heavy ladle across her knuckles for every scorched collar or tarnished piece of silver she produced. Now, the days unfolded gently bringing cool mornings and high blue skies over the bay. Maureen awoke feeling free of everything that had ever frightened or oppressed her. She was like one of the strong graceful gannets whose cries woke her at dawn and called her to her hearth at dusk. Her days were filled with new chores, hard tasks but things that energized her and filled her with a sense of self-worth.

She loved this place and had charmed even the staunchest of spinsters, the storekeeper and post-mistress Cora Foy, Seamus's younger sister. The day Cora sprained her finger trying to lift an unwieldy package, Maureen was in her shop trying vainly to find just the right knife to fillet a fine fat salmon she had purchased from Seamus that morning. She had splinted the finger for Miss Foy and finished sorting and unloading the post for her. Maureen even rescued a stew Miss Foy had begun for supper by peeling her onions and spuds for her. The older woman was so pleased that she had given Maureen one of her own fish knives from her kitchen drawer. This same knife, Maureen now used to skewer a plump oyster, popping it in her mouth and letting it slide across her tongue, swallowing it whole the way Duffy McGee had taught her. Meg cringed at the sight of Maureen eating the raw shellfish. She loved oysters but only thoroughly cooked ones.

Duffy McGee came by every so often to bring them provisions or news and eat Maureen's gooseberry fool. Maureen enjoyed his visits immensely. He had not displayed any particular interest in walking out with her or spending time engaging her in private conversation but Maureen was content to feed him and listen to his beautiful tenor as they sang around the fire in the evening. He never stayed in the house, preferring to sleep in his curragh and scoffed at the warnings from both Meg and Maureen about the dangers of the night air. Just looking at his perfect face in the firelight as he plied his squeezebox was enough to make Meg's heart ache for Tom but Maureen was content to just feast her eyes and ears and leave the rest of her body in peace.

"Done!" Maureen said as she stood up, shaking bits of oyster shell from her apron.

"Let me take them to the booley," Meg said taking the pot from Maureen. "It's the least I can do. Unless you're planning to make the stew tonight?"

"No, go ahead. Just let me have one more," Maureen scooped out another slimy oyster and slipped it into her mouth.

Meg could hardly watch her. She gagged every time she

thought about her first attempt to eat one of the awful, gray oysters off the half-shell. The whole idea was repulsive. With a little shudder she turned to walk down to the ancient stone outbuilding that served to keep perishable foods cool. The booley was at the back of the little yard and was easily one of the oldest structures around. Many of the local people had these stone huts in their yards and they used them to stock joints of meat, bricks of butter and milk for the winter months. In the warmer days of summer, they kept these things cool and away from animals. They dated from the days of the druids and the early Christian monks had used them for living quarters. Meg had never seen one until she came here and delighted in having a larder as big as the one at GlynMor and with a much more interesting history.

The two women had made a lovely home of this little cottage. The architecture of the house was nothing special, a typical seaside cottage with the roped thatch roof required by beach dwellings. When the winds off the ocean became fierce, the network of bog-fir ropes held the thatch securely. Tom had paid Finn Kelly, the local thatcher to finish repairing the ropes with the promise that he would return in time to repair the weak spots with him in the fall. He paid Finn to repair the ancient stone chicken house too.

The cottage had been built sensibly with one gable side angled toward the ocean. This provided both a sturdy face to the weather and bit of shade along the front to sit in during the evening and watch the sun go down. There had been no flowers planted when they arrived at the end of July but luck and hard work had begun to revive the fledgling vegetable garden. Maureen felt sure that added to the acres of potatoes, they would have enough for the winter and Tom planned to bring more supplies from Westport when he returned.

Inside the cottage there was a fairly large room that doubled as kitchen and sitting room. Tom had sold the sow and was not in the habit of keeping animals indoors as did many of his countrymen and he had planned to replenish their chickens. Meg was much relieved to have only people in her house. She still could not get used to visiting a neighbor and being obliged to visit her cows as well.

The two women worked every moment of daylight to make soft lace curtains for the windows and a crocheted cloth for the table. Maureen repaired the old falling-leaf table herself replacing the rusted hinges with a pair she found in a box of tools left behind by Billy Hanley. Folding the leaf down against the wall gave them more room around the fire, but both women were used to having furniture and preferred to leave the leaf up covering the tabletop with the pretty cloth and placing an arrangement of shells and wildflowers in the center.

People on the island did not warm easily to strangers but they were equally respectful of a newcomer's privacy as they were of their own. Meg's lace-making skills did not go unnoticed and her accent gave away her high birth but no one had come out and said anything. Tom gave the letter of introduction from Fr. Finnegan along with the letter from Sr. Clothilde's cousin Brigid O'Shea to Fr. O'Boyle, the priest at St. Dymphna's. This had gone far in winning the acceptance of the townspeople, if not their affection. Meg attended St. Dymphna's with Maureen but did not take communion, a fact that was not lost on the other ladies. There was work to be done, Meg knew but she believed time would take care of much of it. Meanwhile, she had brought a bit of finery to the town and was more than happy to share her skills with anyone who wanted them. She had acquired a lovely hearthrug and an eiderdown comforter for two crocheted christening gowns and a wedding veil. She was almost finished with a pair of new surplices for the monsignor from Newport who had visited his mother last month and admired her work. For this work, she and Tom would receive a good iron bed and ticking, and Maureen would take the other bed into the loft. For now, Maureen slept on a straw filled ticking on the little tester bed and Meg slept in the truckle bed made soft by the comforter she had earned for her first real work.

She and Maureen had scoured and whitewashed the loft overlooking the kitchen and Maureen had made it her private space. Duffy McGee had been over to the island several times, during which he painted the ladder for the loft, repaired the front door and secured fresh turf in the eaves and under the thatch to keep out the cool evening drafts. While he was at it, to Meg's eternal debt, he banished a family of mice from the eaves. His visits were always a cause for a special meal and as she watched Maureen shuck the oysters Meg had wondered out loud if she was expecting company.

Maureen had sidestepped the question, saying simply that if Meg was going to have her baby anytime soon they had better have a few meals prepared. Meg knew this was nonsense and said so, to which Maureen replied that Tom would be home soon and who would be bringing him but Duffy McGee? And didn't Mr. McGee just about lay down in the dust for a bowl of Maureen's oyster stew? And hadn't she been skimming the cream off the top of the milk for just this pot of the creamy white concoction?

Meg smiled to herself as she tried awkwardly to duck into the small booley house door. She still had about two weeks to go by her estimation but she was so large even the smallest stoop felt like a contortion. Setting the pot on an upturned basket, she backed out into the yard. Straightening up she scanned the changing sky. The clouds to the west looked wicked now and the wind had picked up. The first fat raindrops had begun to fall as she rounded the stone fence and began the incline toward the house. The wind whipped her hair across her eyes and she clutched her shawl around her, bending now into the fury of the squall.

Just as she rounded the northeast corner of the house Meg was seized by a searing pain in the fold above her right thigh. She doubled over and grabbed her belly. She had sneezed early in her pregnancy while lying on her back and this muscle had bothered her ever since. Thinking this was another spasm she continued along the wall of the house. There was some respite from the wind back here and breathless, Meg leaned against the wall. She was suddenly weak and lightheaded. She called out to Maureen but there were no windows on this side of the house and the storm was howling by now. A second sharper pain drove her to her knees and she felt a gush of wetness between her legs.

"My God, the Baby!" she cried into the wind. 'Maureen, Maureen!"

It seemed as soon as the pain came it was gone again. Meg clambered to her feet as the sky opened, drenching her from head to toe. She staggered into the wall of wind, finally coming to the front door just as Maureen threw it open.

"Oh, sweet mother Mary, look at ye!" she cried when she saw Meg.

Maureen brought Meg in and threw all her weight against the door to close it against the wind. She put her arm around Meg and sat her by the fire. As she stripped off Meg's wet clothes Meg told her about the pains. Maureen had no time to say anything when another pain brought a loud groan from Meg. Maureen held her hand until it passed and together they got Meg into a fresh nightgown.

The pains came steadily through the night as Maureen walked Meg around and around the little house. She made tea and tried to coax Meg to drink some but Meg's appetite had simply ceased. The furious storm beat against the little house and the wind whistled and howled as rain lashed against the little window in Maureen's loft.

Around dawn both the storm and Meg's contractions suddenly stopped. She and Maureen both napped until Maureen was awakened around eight o'clock by another round of wind and rain worse than the first. Maureen tried to see out toward the beach but the rain bathed the windowpane. She sat alone at the hearthside and sipped a cup of cold tea. Tea was a luxury over here and she could hardly be wasting it. She got up and rolled out a couple of oatcakes and put them on the fire. Let Meg sleep, she thought. She'd need all her strength when the pains came back. She wondered where Tom was, hoping he hadn't been caught out in this storm. He should be arriving soon, given his message.

This was the worst weather Maureen and Meg had experienced yet on Achill and Maureen wasn't sure what to expect. Did seasoned villagers go on about their business or did this kind of storm keep them indoors too? She wished she had someone else to help her with Meg. The closest farm was way down the road and she didn't know the woman there very well. Her husband was a brutish type who lived for his whiskey. Mary Feeney, the midwife, lived clear on the other side of the village. Meg had planned for Tom to fetch her when the time came but now Maureen couldn't even imagine finding a child to run for help.

The storm was unrelenting and around nine o'clock with the deafening wind roaring around outside, Meg's pains started again in earnest. Maureen had to force her to get out of bed and walk around. She had told Mary Feeney she had never assisted a baby into the world before and had listened carefully to Mary's advice. Walking helped speed things along, the midwife had insisted. It did seem to Maureen that Meg had progressed more while she slept but she faithfully dragged Meg around and around the little room. She recognized the wild swings between irritability and sweetness and when Meg began to shake and begged Maureen to let her go back to bed, Maureen knew that things had changed.

By noon, the storm had let up again and Maureen prayed that someone would come by as she mopped Meg's face with a rag dipped in cool water. Meg writhed and groaned during the contractions and Maureen's heart ached for her, remembering all too clearly her own torturous delivery in the ruins of the old abbey. At least Meg didn't have to stifle the screams that had taken the place of groans with the last two pains. The pains were coming very close together now and Maureen saw a lot of fresh blood on the sheet. Meg strained against the contractions arching her back and begging for her baby to be born.

"Get it out of me!" She shrieked grabbing Maureen by the bodice and pulling her to her. "I can't do this! Where is Tom? Where is the doctor?"

Meg's head fell back in a mass of sweat-drenched curls and went limp as soon as the contraction released her. In the quiet, Maureen heard a commotion outside and with a flood of relief got up to answer the door. Near tears herself, she flung open the door hoping to see Tom or at least a neighbor who could help her. Oblivious to her own sweat and blood stained apron, she saw Charlie O'Malley, the local constable staring at her in shock.

"What?" he managed to stammer before Meg's pain returned and her screams filled the house and yard both.

Maureen just glared at him like a madwoman.

"Thank God ye're here. Please get Mary Feeney fer me. M'Lady's time is almost here!"

Seeing what was going on, Charlie collared a small boy and sent him off to get the midwife. With Meg moaning in the background and Charlie talking very fast, Maureen had the odd revelation that the beach was full of people. People were running from the village to gawk at the sea and women held their aprons up to their mouths as they stared. Her head spinning, she caught the words curragh and storm and pieces. Horrified, she realized that Charlie was there to announce some terrible accident that had him standing in her doorway with a shredded piece of tar coated wood, when Meg began screaming again that the baby was coming.

Maureen raced back into the bedroom to find Meg propped up on her elbows, thrashing like a banshee trying to shake off the pain. Taking her by the shoulders, Maureen said as calmly as she could,

"M'Lady, if th'baby is comin' ye have to calm down and help it come."

She wiped a layer of spit off of Meg's upper lip and soothed her the way she had when Meg lay motionless after her father beat her with his riding crop. Maureen remembered how well she had cared for her mistress throughout that terrible time. Spine stiffened, Maureen took control over this new crisis. Bending near Meg's face she said in the gentlest voice she could muster, the words Mary Feeney had given her to say.

"M'Lady, ye can do this. Ye just need to blow th'pains away until Mary gets here and can tell ye if it's time t'push."

Meg clutched Maureen's shoulders.

"No, no, I can't do that Maureen! No it hurts too much. It burns like fire! No! Here it comes!"

With the next pain Meg threw her head back and grunted,

arching her back and holding Maureen's arm in a death grip. Maureen could see that whatever Meg was doing it would not bring this child into the world. With the next contraction Maureen held Meg steady and spoke gently into her ear,

"Blow, M"Lady! Blow like th'storm. Blow th'roof off. That's it, no pushin' yet."

But Meg was overwhelmed by the pressure tearing at her loins and with a great grunt pushed again. It went on this way for almost an hour and still no baby came. The front door finally opened and in came Mary Feeney with, of all people, Cora Foy. Maureen would not have thought Miss Foy had ever witnessed a birth before. Mary smiled at the expression on Maureen's face and said,

"I'd like ye t'meet the woman who taught me all I know about deliverin' babies."

Before Maureen could reply, Meg started again to strain and grunt, pushing against the pain that consumed her. Mary tried to intervene but Cora stopped her saying,

"Let this one pass. I can see that she's fightin' th'pains instead of workin' with them. Sure'n we'll have her turned around by th'next one."

Approaching the head of the bed, Cora introduced herself and wiped Meg's forehead with the rag as the contraction subsided.

"And this is Mary Feeney who needs t'check ye and see if its time fer all this pushin'."

Maureen was astounded that this dry tempered spinster was so easily transformed into a calm and compassionate nurse. Sensing that things were finally under control, she stepped back and let the experts do their job.

Mary washed and dried her hands and raised the hem of Meg's soaked nightgown. With swift competence she inserted her fingers deep into the birth canal and felt for the baby's head. Meg tried to push her hand away but Mary, speaking steadily and softly, told her that she needed to feel things during a contraction to get the best idea of how far along Meg was.

She didn't have to wait long.

Almost as soon as the pain stopped another one took its place. Meg started to arch her back but Cora, speaking into her ear, convinced her to take one leg in each hand and draw them back toward her head. Maureen couldn't believe that Meg actually obeyed the old midwife but she did as she was told. Mary could now see and feel much better and Maureen saw concern cross her face as she felt around for the familiar landmarks. When the contraction ended Mary withdrew her hand and turned to wash herself in the basin.

'T'won't be long now fer sure, Mrs. Phalen. Yer doin' fine but 'tis too soon to push. Try t'pant like a dog or blow through th'next few pains."

She motioned for Maureen to come into the kitchen with her as another contraction started and Meg began to scream.

"Let her scream," Mary said to Maureen as they left the bedroom. "At least if she's screamin' she ain't pushin'. Cora is with her."

Maureen was deeply disturbed by the sound of Meg howling and screaming in what seemed a constant barrage of pains. Mary explained to Maureen that two things were wrong. First, the baby was face up, making the delivery much harder on Meg. To make matters worse, Meg had started to push before the womb was fully ready and now the opening was almost swollen closed. If she continued to push she would bear down for hours against the swollen opening and probably tear it. She could also harm the baby by doing that because the baby could not get out and it was ready to come.

Hearing this, Maureen began to cry.

"I tried all I could, I tried t'remember what ye told me but she couldn't wait atall. What if I did somethin' wrong and now th'baby is ruined?"

Memories of her own dead daughter flooded back and threatened to overwhelm her. Mary, however, was calmly putting a kettle on for tea. She turned from the hearth and gave Maureen's shoulders a squeeze.

"Ye need a break, Maureen. Ye've done a fine job! We're here now and things are goin' t'go very slowly, I'm afraid. Let me fix ye somethin' to eat and we'll let Cora work her magic on Mrs. Phalen."

Reluctantly, Maureen let Mary feed her and as she washed down sweet soda bread with a cup of good, strong tea, she realized that there were neither screams nor grunts coming from the bedroom. All they could hear in the kitchen were the low tones of Cora Foy's voice reciting like a mantra, instructions for Meg to pant and blow followed by the sound of Meg trying to blow the thatch right into the sea.

The afternoon droned on as the sun filled the humid little room with steamy heat. Meg wavered between faithfully obeying Cora and Mary and dissolving into screams and sobs of frustration. But however much she wanted to, she didn't try to push again. Cora had explained to her in simple terms what was going on and Meg understood how important it was for her to avoid the overwhelming urge to bear down. Maureen was in and out of the sweltering bedroom bringing cool water and whatever fresh linens she could find. Meg had soaked through all of the nightgowns, both hers and Maureen's and now lay naked on the bed. The expert coaching of the midwives and Meg's herculean efforts to control her urge to push had paid off. The swelling had gone down and the womb was about half way open. Maureen had rinsed and hung linens by the fire and was about to bring a fresh dry gown and sheet to her friend when she sprang up and went to the door.

It was the noise outside that suddenly got Maureen's attention. She had forgotten about Charlie O'Malley. The crowd on the beach had drifted out of hearing. Now they were back with twice as many people milling around outside her house. They were all scanning the sea and several of the fishermen were combing the bay in curraghs and hookers.

She approached Mrs. Trent, the vicar's wife.

"Whatever is it?" she asked the older woman.

"They found the wreckage of a curragh washed up on the beach this morning after the storm. They've accounted for every fisherman in Dooega, thanks be to God, but they're searching for the poor soul whose boat it is."

She looked hard at Maureen's filthy apron and matted hair and started to say something else but Maureen could only hear humming and everything around her had slowed down. The people on the beach had taken on a silvery sheen and the sea seemed miles away. Wordlessly, she left Mrs. Trent on the beach.

Somehow she found her way into the house without fainting. The sound of Meg wailing again snapped her back to her senses. The poor soul who owns that curragh? Christ save us, could it be Duffy McGee? Could Tom be lying at the bottom of the bay along with her new friend and companion? The thought was unbearable! Here was Meg, laboring in agony to deliver his child and Tom Phalen may be dead at the bottom of the sea trying to get home in time to be there! God wouldn't do this to them! Not after she just buried her own sweet Mary Ellen. Not when Meg and Tom had finally gotten married! And they all had just made their pilgrimage to the holy mountain. This could not be!

After she helped Mary and Cora change the bed and dress Meg in the fresh nightgown, Maureen returned to the door and scanned the sea herself. The fishermen were coming in now, followed closely by another evil looking storm. The wives on the shore called and pleaded with them to hurry as the storm boiled across the bay, threatening to catch them all at sea. Maureen stood riveted and watched as, one by one the women ran into the shallows and helped their men drag their vessels onto the sand. Raising the curraghs over their heads they scurried back to the safety of their homes. Just as the last hooker was dragged up on the beach, the wind began to tear into the little village and the drenching rains started again. Maureen simply could not believe how quickly the weather could change around here. Whoever the poor sod was who lost his boat last night, he'd have to wait until this passed through for the search to resume.

As the clock chimed three, Mary called Maureen to bring some fresh water and she slowly turned away from the door. Needed for more urgent business, she left behind the thundering sky and the naked beach, which only seconds ago had been bustling with the urgency of life.

Chapter Nineteen

At the time Meg's labor started, Tom Phalen stood under the poor shelter of the doorway of Browne's Inn and scowled at the rain. He had wanted to get back to Achill tonight but the weather was just awful. Duffy was inside drawing pints for the locals. The season for tourists had waned and the little port was settling in for the quiet of the off-season. From now on, storms like this would be the norm and only the most adventurous men and folks visiting family would venture this way until late spring. He had tried to strong-arm Duffy into taking him across but he shook his head.

"No way would I be fool enough t'take a boat out in this," he said, waving his clay pipe in the direction of the door. The men around the bar nodded, grunting their agreement over pint glasses raised to salt-chapped lips. This was a favorite pub for fishermen and as long as they minded their manners and did not disturb the guests, Duffy was delighted to have them, especially on Friday when they had money in their pockets.

There were two other pubs along the strand, Gilly's and Marie's but Gilly's was a filthy hole of a place with a fighting reputation and Marie's was known to offer much more than a pint of stout. Most of these men were married and wanted no more than good male company with which to share their pipe and pint. Both Fr. Timon at St. Peter's and the Reverend Mr.

Gibbs at St. Ambrose were petitioning to close Marie's down but neither of those men needed to worry about these fishermen crossing the line. Even if they were of a mind to sneak in and out, these stalwart husbands and sons were more afraid of getting caught by their wives or someone else's to even glance in the direction of the place. Besides, some of the younger, single fellows, no one local mind you, had reported that the girls at Marie's weren't worth a second look.

Tom wasn't interested in any of this talk tonight. He had arrived this morning hoping to make short work of his trip across to Achill. If he had gotten away when he had hoped, he'd be there now instead of stranded by the miserable weather. As luck would have it, the curragh that brought Tom into Westport Bay from Newport had also delivered a huge cargo of winter supplies for Browne's Inn. Tom himself had secured his passage by loading the sacks of potatoes and flour and kegs of ale and stout. He was astonished at how much cargo a curragh could carry and when the captain pointed out another curragh filled with sheep he shook his head in disbelief. He had earned a considerable sum working his way back to Newport these last six weeks and had actually arranged the purchase of a dozen sheep and two heifers from the man with the sheep load. The man's son was about an hour behind, bringing a cargo of three cows and more sheep. He had no buyers lined up for the cows and Tom wouldn't mind buying them all if he could buy a bull somewhere. He wished he could replace his sow but that would have to wait till spring.

By afternoon, the day's earlier luck had turned sour. Duffy was alone at the inn when Tom arrived. His apprentice had gone off to join the seminary and his cook had burned his hand on a hot pannie. Duffy was running the house and was on deck for the unloading.

"Sorry, me lad, but ye can see th'pile I've got t'move. I might be free by early evenin' but I'll have t'get someone t'mind th'pub."

Duffy grimaced as he bent to slice a sack of cabbages and tumble them down the shoot into the root cellar.

"Give me a hand and maybe our luck will change."

Tom was already knee-deep in potatoes. He sliced the sacks and poured the contents into a similar chute that serviced another room-sized cavern in the cellar of the inn. He had never imagined the number of potatoes a place like Browne's could go through. Duffy was pleased to replenish his supply with the first of the fall harvest.

The flour and kegs were stored in an upstairs loft at the back of the taproom and it was mid-afternoon when they had lugged the last of them up the dark, narrow stairway. Tom had done most of the carting and had worked up a good sweat and an even better appetite.

"So," he had asked Duffy, as he plowed through a thick slice of fresh poached salmon wrapped in coarse brown bread and butter, "Any luck?"

Duffy shook his head.

"The only one available is me cook's nephew and he's just too young. Besides, th'lad who just left came in from Clew Bay just a while ago and said there's a wicked storm brewing t'th'west. At this time o'year, ye can't be too careful, Tom. Let's see if this blows through quickly. They often do. If it's clear later, maybe one of the other lads can take ye over."

Now, the afternoon long spent, the clock behind Browne's bar struck six. The storm had hit Westport a few moments ago with a demonic fury and Tom's mood had turned black. He was dying to see Meg again. Not only so he could be there when she had her baby, Tom knew he would be ushered right out of the house by the womenfolk, but he had so much to tell her. He had seen and learned more in the past weeks than he had in his entire thirty-eight years. He had traveled to Clydagh Glyn and well beyond. He had had to work at jobs he knew nothing about, had even taken a shallow flesh wound to the thigh from the gun of a jealous husband who had mistaken him for his wife's lover. He still carried the wound in his left thigh though it was healing slowly now that the infection had cleared up. He'd spare Meg the part about the maggots the pub keeper's wife had used to devour the fetid decaying tissue that had threatened to lose him his leg. Thank the fairies he had a strong enough stomach for the disgusting creatures crawling around his wounded flesh. He was just grateful they did the job. The man who shot him did indeed find the rogue who bedded his wife and did indeed kill him with one shot. Tom knew he had been very lucky that that husband had been so drunk when he pulled the trigger on him.

He couldn't wait to tell her about how he found the folks at GlynMor Castle. He had news for both Meg and Maureen. Old Ben had been ill when he had arrived but had improved immediately upon seeing Tom. All Ben could tell him about his da was that Mrs. Carrey had passed on the message to Fr. Dunleavey. Beyond that Ben couldn't say.

Tom's own house was unharmed and he had been able to bring a few more items back with him. He was especially delighted to have his violin back again. He had learned to play at his granda's knee and had regretted terribly leaving it behind. He had brought the old family bible with him and the sketches done of his mother and him. These tiny pen sketches had been tucked into the bible after his mam died. They had been drawn years ago by a wandering tinker who had traded his skills for a hot meal. Tom had been only a wee lad when they had posed by his mother's flower box and had their images preserved on paper.

He remembered the care his father had taken to place them right above the hearth where anyone sitting around the fire could admire them. These prints, one of her alone and one of them together, had filled him with longing when he found them. He was very disappointed that Ben had no word of his da and he wanted badly to squeeze in a visit to his brother. He ached for Meg, for Da, and even after all these years for his beautiful mam. He and Meg had chosen the name Anselm for their baby if it was a boy, hoping that the saint who had protected them the night of their flight would forgive them for using his honorable ruins as the very place where this child had been conceived. They had not decided on a girl's name yet but now he knew he liked Clare after his mother.

Tom smacked the bright blue lintel with his fist as he turned to go back into the inn. The change in the weather had made his leg throb and he needed a pint badly. He drained his glass and looked up as a noisy braggart of a whelp began swaggering around, challenging everyone to a game of cards. He claimed he had a sack of coins that was burning his hand and dared any man to win it off him. Duffy did not look pleased and warned him that he'd better not start trouble but he just laughed and swung his little bag around temptingly.

Tom asked Duffy who he was but Duffy didn't know him. One of the old salts waiting out the storm said he was a mean kid out of Newport who would take on dangerous loads and contraband for a price. He was a skilled sailor, the old man granted but not to be trusted. Rumor had it that he would take on huge loads of livestock and then dump some of the poor creatures overboard to keep his speed. Duffy had only seen him in here a few times and admitted that he was more bluster than truth but he still didn't like his looks.

Tom had seen tougher lads on his trek across Ireland and suggested that if he was so brave maybe he'd take him to Achill after the storm cleared. Duffy shook his head at the idea.

"Tom, are ye daft, man? He'd just as soon kill ye as deliver ye."

"Now, Duffy, I think I can hold me own. I'm twice his age and half again his size!"

The several pints Tom had downed made him indignant.

Now the old sailor stepped in on Duffy's side of the argument.

"No lad, Duff here is right. I wouldn't want him at th'helm. He's been drinkin' all afternoon."

"Ach, but I want t'get home man! I need t'get home!" Tom said, his jaw set.

Hoping time would make Tom see reason, Duffy said,

"Let's see what th'weather does. Nobody's goin' out on th' street in this storm, never mind th'sea. Treat us to a bito'fiddlin'while ye're waitin'."

Tom nodded and picked up his fiddle. As he tuned the old instrument, he kept his eye on the skinny boyo with the swinging sack of coins.

When it was clear the storm would last into the night, Tom gave up his hope of going across and accepted a room at Browne's. In spite of Duffy's warning, he did talk to the lad about taking him over and the boy agreed, for a price, to leave as soon as the weather cleared. But he wasn't about to take Tom's cows and sheep. They would have to come over with somebody else. Disappointed, Tom played slow, mournful dirges on his violin until Duffy begged him to play something cheery or stop.

Duffy agreed to bring over Tom's supplies as soon as his cook was able to take over the pub. It was already late September and Duffy warned his friend that the weather was going to be changeable from here on in but he did want to see Maureen and Meg again before the winter set in and of course, he needed to celebrate the arrival of Tom's first baby.

"Tom, if ye're fool enough t'let this divil take ye across th'bay then I can't stop ye. But I'll take yer livestock. I wouldn't want yer widow t'starve."

Tom cuffed him one for saying that and Duffy laughed at him.

"Ah, inlanders are so superstitious. Live by th'sea fer a while and ye'll see some real spirits at work. Not little fairies but great sea monsters and th'ghosts of pirates. Why, ye may even be treated to a visit by th'ghost of Grace O'Malley, the Pirate Queen of Kildownet Castle!"

He chuckled at Tom's stricken face, just drunk enough to believe him.

Around six the next morning, Tom awoke with a wicked headache to find the storm had passed. The slick young sailor was asleep in the bed across from him. He remembered with a scowl that he had bargained with him to pay for his stay at the inn in exchange for the trip across the bay. Duffy gladly accepted the money for two rooms and they had gone their separate ways. How this edgit came to be in his room was a mystery to Tom. Anxiously he checked his vest pocket for his money. Finding it there he realized how stupid he was to think this fool would rob him and then decide to stay with him for the night. He took the leather pouch and fastened it securely around his waist, under his shirt.

He kicked the sleeping lump, causing him to grunt and snort.

"Come on, get up. Th'birds are up and we need t'set out."

Tom realized he didn't even know the lad's name.

"Get up ye spalpeen, and keep yer end of th'bargain."

A shower of salty curses was his reward for prodding the boy in the ribs.

"Come on, you, I'm not impressed with yer fine education. I have a few things I can say too, if I were of a mind."

With this he pulled the sputtering lad to his feet.

"Lord, do ye stink, lad!"

Tom plunged the sailor's head into the chilly wash water sitting on the dresser.

"Ach! What are ye doin' man, trying t'drown me?"

He hollered and sprayed water all over like a dog.

"Just get goin'. I bought ye yer room and now yer goin' t'give me that ride. Take me across and ye'll never have t'lay eyes on me pretty face again."

The boy squinted at Tom, whose own head wobbled like a melon on his neck.

"What kind of a bastard are ye?" he exclaimed.

"Give a man a chance t'wake up, fer crissake."

"Mind yer tongue, boyo," Tom replied with a shove toward the door.

The sailor smoothed his wet hair, plopped a cap on his head and stumbled toward the stairs.

"Ye're daft is what ye are. It's th'bloody middle of th'night! Me head is th'size o'Galway and ye're sendin' me out t'sea!"

Tom ignored this as he poured two short shots to clear their heads and left some coins on the bar. Handing him his hair of the dog, Tom paused to look at this loud, foul-mouthed fool.

"Have ye a name, boyo?" he asked, as he tossed back the whiskey and tried to focus his own eyes in the wan early light.

"Johnny. Johnny O'Neill, of th'great clan of O'Neill's, I'll have ye know."

At this, Tom laughed.

"Well, Johnny O'Neill, ye'll have t'learn how t'drink more and suffer less fer it if ye want t'make me or anyone else believe that!"

"So, where is this craft ye so highly prize, Johnny O'Neill?" Tom asked as they went out into the thin gray light.

"Right across by the inlet."

He pointed at an upturned curragh lined up along with half a dozen others.

"Let's go, then. I want me woman, that I do."

Tom headed for the line of boats.

They were out on the open sea when they spoke again. Tom had snagged a few biscuits from the bar and offered Johnny one of them. Gnawing on the stale brown bread, Johnny asked Tom why he was in such a hurry, anyway. Tom explained that his wife was due to deliver a baby, which did not seem to impress his companion. He was annoyed with himself to find that it mattered to him that this selfish, ignorant boy cared little about his reason. He anxiously scanned the horizon as the sun came up and revealed huge dark clouds out over the Atlantic.

The trip across should not have taken long but they were rowing into a stiff wind coming in from the ocean. Tom and the boy, strong as they were, made slow progress against the steady wind. At times it seemed they were rowing with all their strength and standing still.

Finally with the sun starting to warm their backs they came around Clare Island and sighted land. Tom guessed it to be about eight or nine o'clock. He could almost taste the big plate of brown bread and fresh eggs he knew Meg would put in front of him when he walked in. He imagined the welcome he would receive and the image of her beautiful face made him row harder.

The clouds to the west had turned ominous but Johnny O'Neill swore he'd seen worse and they just kept rowing. Tom didn't know when it was that he realized they were no closer to land than they were several long minutes ago and he asked again what Johnny thought. Johnny wasn't as cocky when he answered this time. Both men were very tired from two hours of hard rowing and Johnny looked at the sky with concern.

"We're not makin' enough time t'hit land 'afore that storm catches us," he hollered over the wind.

"What can we do?" Tom yelled back, his heart in his throat.

He couldn't believe they were close enough to see the shore but were being propelled away from instead of toward it. For the first time Tom felt afraid and the taste of bile burned his throat. He knew nothing about sailing and now his young captain looked like he was about to pee himself.

The clouds were rolling in like billows of black smoke across the sky and the wind was pushing the boat like a toy back across Clew Bay. Caught between Achill and Clare Islands, both shores were disappearing before their eyes and soon they could no longer hear each other yelling.

Johnny was in a full panic now, trying to keep the boat steady. They abandoned rowing when Tom's oar was ripped from his hands and the rain began in torrents. Tom had never seen such weather. The rain was coming from every direction, stinging and blinding the two men. The waves swelled and crashed around them and the wind screamed with an ungodly shriek.

Johnny tried to hang on but within minutes was flung overboard. Tom screamed as he saw him disappear beneath the waves. Try as he might, he could not even move to the side of the boat to see where the boy had gone. There was no saving him. He had simply vanished.

For what seemed like hours, Tom hunkered down in the prow of the curragh clinging to the sides of the thrashing vessel. The curragh, true to its reputation, rode the waves now coming in sickening swells and deep devouring dips. Tom prayed like a child, begging for his life, pleading for the mercy of the God he had just rediscovered. He called out to his mother and Meg, to Christ's mother Mary and to his da. The tearing and wrenching wind flipped the boat around and around in dizzying circles and Tom's stomach emptied itself in a whirl of bile that was immediately torn away on the wind.

He slipped down into the hull of the boat trying desperately to keep from being tossed overboard. Hanging on to the seat he had been sitting on he felt the rough wood tear open his hands. He could smell the iron in his blood as the saltwater washed over his face. The healing wound on his leg burned like the devil and throbbed with cold. Realizing that the curragh was filling up with water, he knew it would not be long until it rose over his face. There was nothing he could do to stop the rising water. He had nothing to bail the boat out with and when he raised his body up to get out of the pool, the remaining oar slid clear across a fresh wave and came crashing back into the boat smacking him square on the head.

The pain blinded him and he lost his hold on the plank of wood. A massive swell upended the boat and the oar came flying back again, clipping him on the shoulder. This time it rent the curragh's canvas skin and the water poured into the hull freely. Tom knew he was going to die. The last thing he was aware of was deep, searing pain as his arm broke through the torn canvas and caught itself between two of the hull's ribs. The world went black as the boat came apart with an ear-splitting shriek and flipped Tom into the sea like a fish.

Chapter Twenty

The last gasp of the storm had lasted only about an hour and the sun finally moved away from the little bedroom. The three women tried in vain to keep the laboring mother comfortable in the lingering heat. Around six o'clock Mary checked Meg again and pronounced her ready to push.

"Mrs. Phalen, with the next pain, take th'deepest breath ye can and bear down hard."

Mary's voice was just a hoarse whisper and her own dress was soaked with sweat.

As a contraction rose to a crescendo, Meg began to howl and thrash.

"No, Mrs. Phalen. Now ye must push th'baby down, 'tis time now. Push!"

"I can't," Meg groaned. "I just can't. Oh God, just let me die!"

The midwives looked at each other, exhaustion on their faces. Maureen could not believe how long Meg had been laboring. It had been twenty-four hours since the first pain had brought Meg in from the yard and she was beyond her strength. Maureen herself was completely spent. She could not imagine how Meg was going to deliver this baby when she lay like a wet rag in the bed.

Earlier in the day, the women had pulled the bed away from

the wall to make it easier to change the sheet and minister to Meg. Now, Cora went around the foot of the bed and crossed over to the other side. As a new pain wracked Meg's body, Cora took Meg's left leg and bent it back toward her head. Maureen raised Meg's other leg the same way and watched in awe as her friend's belly rose almost to a point at the peak of the contraction. Mary had placed one hand on Meg's rising belly and the other into the birth canal. At the peak of the contraction Mary did something that made Meg shriek with pain.

"I'm tryin' t'turn th'baby, Mrs. Phalen. I'm so sorry t'hurt ye."

The contraction ended and Meg fell limp. Maureen and Cora let her legs down and she fell immediately into a deep sleep. Maureen worried that Meg might have fainted but with the next pain she immediately awoke and they lifted her legs again. This time though, Meg bore down with a strength that defied her exhaustion.

"Good, Mrs. Phalen! Good push!" Mary cried, her hand beneath the sheet. "I felt the head move with that one. Yer baby is on its way, Mrs. Phalen. Just keep pushin' like that and 'twill be here in no time!"

On and on it went like that. Every time Meg had a contraction she pushed with all her might. And every push brought the little head down. But the baby just wouldn't come out. At the end of every pain the little head slipped back up. The baby was coming down but progress was very slow.

Finally as the room began to darken, Meg was getting angry. With the last two contractions, Mary had again tried to turn the head and the pain was excruciating for Meg. She demanded that Mary stop trying and when her belly began to rise again, Cora nodded and Mary tried something different. She took Maureen's left hand and placed it on Meg's belly right below the ribs. On the other side Cora placed her right hand the same way.

Mary reached up into the birth canal and said, "Now!"

Maureen and Cora pushed as hard as they could on Meg's belly and Mary felt the baby's skull push down. In one last attempt to turn the head around, she hooked her finger around the little forehead and pushed toward the right at the same time the others were pushing from above. Meg let out an earsplitting wail and tried to push them all away but it worked. The baby spun around and by the end of the contraction was in good position for delivery. There was a great deal of blood after this and Maureen felt herself get queasy but there was no time for that.

Another pain overtook Meg and she pushed with all her might. Maureen gasped as she saw the little head begin to slide out of the birth canal. With each contraction the head came further and further down until Maureen could see a mass of black curls all matted with blood and water. Her shrieks of delight spurred Meg on to finish the job and when Maureen took Meg's hand and helped her reach down and feel the damp little head, Meg pushed with a ferocity that shocked Maureen but only made the midwives smile. They knew this was it. Meg would have her baby within the next few contractions.

At the stroke of eight, with a gush of red water, Tom and Meg's daughter came into the world howling and punching. In seconds she was pink as a rose and lying across her mother's breast. Maureen was sobbing, Mary was busy tying and cutting the cord and Cora was quickly and deftly drying the slippery baby off. Meg lay limp on the bed, simply beaming. Where seconds ago there was only searing pain, here was her sweet baby, the most beautiful little girl in the world.

Mary delivered the afterbirth and told Maureen to bury it in the garden. There was nothing quite like it to fertilize Meg's flowers. As she massaged Meg's womb bringing it to a nice firmness, Mary chatted easily with the new mother. Meg asked what she was doing and Mary explained that her womb needed to tighten so she wouldn't bleed. She showed Maureen and Meg both how to feel for the suddenly tiny womb and rub it until it was as firm as a potato. Cora coached Meg as she tried to put her little girl to her breast and they all cheered as the feisty babe latched on and immediately began to suckle.

As the baby nursed, Meg felt the contractions start again. This time they weren't as sharp but she was shocked to have them back. A look of panic crossed her pale face and she exclaimed, "Is there another one coming?"

For the first time Cora laughed out loud.

"No dear, 'tis the effect of th'sucklin'. That will tighten yer womb more than any rubbing."

Meg frowned, "Oh, but it's so uncomfortable!"

"That will only last a while, Mrs. Phalen. Once yer milk comes in all this will settle down," Mary said, omitting the fact that Meg's milk would not come in for a few days.

Once mother and baby were bathed and freshly dressed, Maureen brought Meg a pot of steaming tea and a big bowl of cruasach. Meg tucked into it like a dying man and together they raised their cups in a solemn toast to the new lady of the house. As Maureen set aside the dirty bowl, Meg sipped her tea and gazed at the sleeping baby at her side. Fatigue had overcome her and she longed for Tom in a way she that reminded her of the months locked in her room.

"How I wish he had made it back in time," she sighed. She could hardly be angry but she was wistfully sad. Her time was really about two weeks away and there had been the storm to delay him but now that their baby was finally here her heart broke not to show him. Maureen said nothing, afraid anything she said would betray her deep fear for Tom's safety. Meg knew nothing of the alarming discovery of the curragh. Maureen silently helped Meg settle into the bed and watched her friend drift into a deep, sweet sleep.

Maureen herself was bone tired. Mary and Cora had left after a snack of soda bread and buttermilk. Meg had set aside coins to pay their fee weeks ago and Maureen counted it out before they left. Because there were two of them, Maureen tried to add a few pennies. They protested saying that Cora was there only to supervise Mary. Maureen knew this was malarkey. She had seen herself the yeoman's share Cora had carried during this long, difficult birth. She finally persuaded them to accept the remaining eggs and a large portion of the cruasach. After all, they had been at Meg's side all day and no one was fixing supper at their houses.

After the two women left, Maureen sponged herself off and changed her clothes. She was starving and took the last of the cruasach and a heel of soda bread out to the bench by the front door. The evening was beautiful. The sky was clear and the air smelled sharp and salty after the storm. As she wiped the bottom of her bowl with the crust she wondered if there was any news about the accident.

Before she could think about how she would find out, the vicar's wife appeared, rounding the corner of the house, startling Maureen.

"I thought you should know they found a man washed up on the beach between here and Achill Sound," Mrs. Trent said softly.

Maureen felt her heart miss a beat.

"Do they, could they?" she couldn't get the words out.

"No, he was a stranger to everyone here and no one so far has been able to say who he is."

The expression on Mrs. Trent's face told Maureen that she thought this news would be comforting. Perhaps it was to the women whose men were known up and down the coast but to her and Meg this meant only one thing. The man was a stranger. So was Tom Phalen and to most, Duffy McGee.

"Thank you for telling me. Was there any description of the poor man?"

The older woman shook her head.

"They say he died of drowning though he was badly hurt as well. The pieces of his boat are still washing up."

"Where is he?" Maureen asked.

"My husband took him to the vicarage at St. Mary's until Mr. O'Rourke picked him up. No one was sure what to do. No one knows where he's from or if there is a family."

At this, all of the day's emotions overcame Maureen and she began to weep.

Mrs. Trent was puzzled and reached for the girl's arm.

"Why do you cry for him? Do you think you know him?" she questioned.

Maureen dried her eyes.

"Mrs. Phalen's husband has been away on business and sent word a few days ago that he would be crossing from Westport any day now."

She began to cry again, sobbing, "He wanted to be here in time for the baby!"

"What baby?"

Now it was Mrs. Trent's turn to be shocked.

"Mr. Phalen brought Mrs. Phalen and me here in th'beginning of August. She wasn't due until th'middle of next month but I think th'storm brought th'babe early. Mr. Phalen had t'sell a horse and see t'his family near Castlebar and he planned t'be back in time fer her confinement. But th'baby came a few hours ago and now ye tell me he could be drowned!"

Maureen sat down on the bench and put her head in her hands.

"Well, dear, why don't you go and see for yourself? He is at Mr. O' Rourke's funeral parlor. I'll stay with Mrs. Phalen while you're gone. You can take my trap, it's around back."

Maureen was touched by the kindness in the woman's face. Why was she fussing so over a distraught Catholic maid? She was a Protestant vicar's wife for heaven's sake.

"Ye're very kind but I'll walk into town. Th'fresh air will do me good."

Maureen stood to go, looking anxiously at the sky, half expecting a new storm to be approaching. Instead, she found a clear, cloudless sky aglow with the setting sun.

"Promise me ye won't mention any o'this t'Mrs. Phalen if she wakes up. She's been in labor since yesterday and probably doesn't even remember th'storm. Just tell her I went fer a walk and I'll be back soon."

With this Maureen slipped off into the dusk.

She decided to walk along the beach to catch the last of the waning sunlight. She would barely make it back before dark. The thought of laying eyes upon a drowned man repulsed her. The possibility of it being either Tom or Duffy terrified her. She hastened across the cool wet sand, each step of her bare feet slapping down with a plop. About half way to the village she stopped in her tracks. A figure was dragging itself toward her along the shore. She couldn't make out whether it was a man or a woman and in the dusky light it wavered and floated in and out of focus. There was no question that the form was definitely coming directly at her and she stood rooted in the sand.

She could feel the cold sand oozing between her toes as she stood in terror watching this specter weaving sylph-like along the shore. It raised one arm and she saw it had a huge claw, which it waved at her in the lowering sun. It seemed to recognize her and began to trip and stumble as it hurried toward her. She tried to turn back and run to the safety of the house but she was frozen in place. Her mind raced as she tried to remember the few legends she had heard since coming to the island. This didn't look like the pirate queen, and what form of sea monster walked on two legs? The closer the creature came, the more she could feel her feet sinking into the sand. She was chilled to the ankles now and she could hear her teeth chattering with cold and fear.

As the creature dragged itself closer and closer she could see with the setting sun lighting it from behind that it was very large and waved madly with its black claw against the deep orange backdrop of the falling night. Soon it was close enough for her to hear it calling, its raspy, hoarse voice grating like metal on metal across the strand. She could not make out what it was saying but it continued to call out desperately waving and weaving as it plunged in her direction. She felt her knees buckle when she saw its face and at the same time heard it call her by name. This ghostly figure knew her! Her last thought before she fainted was the certainty that this creature from the dead was here to take her to Hades and she'd never know who the drowned man was after all.

Chapter Twenty-One

Tom roused gradually, dazed by the oozing wound on his head and blinded by the sun on the water. He tried to reckon his situation but nothing made sense. Was this what being dead felt like? He finally focused on the tar-coated canvas in front of him. He realized that his right arm was stuck in the foremost part of the boat's prow and his good arm rested across the inverted bottom of the boat. The rounded shape of the hull and the air pocket beneath it had kept it and him afloat. Once he had his bearings he could see that it was very late in the day. The sun was low in the western sky and he was facing due north. He was too low in the water to tell how far he was from land and he had no idea how far east or west of Dooegh he had drifted. He kicked a bit and felt both legs working. Aside from a colossal headache and his arm jammed tight into the split canvas he could see nothing critically wrong with him. He did worry that he could not extract his arm from the broken remnant of the curragh. He wondered what kept it so tightly in place.

He was very thirsty and not a little hungry. He estimated that he had been in the water about ten hours; not counting the time spent crashing around in the storm. His face felt raw with salt and sunburn and the rest of him was numb with cold. When he realized how long he'd been floating alone in the sea his heart shrank with fear. Night was falling and he could smell his own blood. He had heard of great man-eating fish that saw poorly but could smell blood for miles. Whether there were any in this part of the Atlantic he didn't know. He hoped he would be rescued long before he found out.

His thoughts drifted to Meg and their little home on the beach. Would she be standing there now scanning the horizon for some sign of him? Maybe she didn't get the note he sent with the package boat from Newport. It would be better if she hadn't. Otherwise she'd be expecting him by now. He wondered how she looked now that her time was getting close. She was just nice and round when he left. Now she must be very big and filled with baby. He smiled at the thought of their baby. He hoped he would look like her, all soft blond curls and deep dimples. But a girl with his dark hair and fair eyes would be a beauty too. He couldn't wait to see both Meg and his child.

He knew Maureen would take good care of Meg. They had finally gotten used to each other and he saw before he left how devoted she was to Meg. He had had no qualms whatever leaving her in the younger woman's care. He, himself, had had some extraordinary adventures crisscrossing the countryside. He had even gotten to see his father. He had been shocked to see how old Da looked after being away so long but he still sprang to his feet at the sound of Tom's voice and despite his near blindness, grabbed his hand pumping it in a strong grip repeating, " Tommy, me boyo' how are ye?"

The best news he had for Meg was that her father would never bother them again. He was just thinking of a way to tell her when he felt a light bump against the back of his legs. He tried to look behind him but his arm was stuck fast. He felt another bump and then a gray snout broke the surface next to his left hip.

The silly face that looked at him had intelligent eyes but he was so shocked he could only yelp when he saw the sea monster at his side. Within seconds there was another one on his right and he could feel smaller ones skirting his feet beneath the piece of upturned boat. The little ones caused the broken curragh to spin around and he saw dozens more surrounding him in a huge school of snub nosed gray faces. Some of them leaped and splashed with a strength and grace that took his breath away.

What were these huge fish? They certainly didn't look like they were planning to eat him. They just seemed to want to play. They communicated in high- pitched squeals that all of them seemed to understand. They were very animated and seemed to be discussing what to do with him. Apparently they agreed because at once they all began heading in one direction and unbelievably, they were taking him with them!

The large one that first popped up next to him seemed to be the leader and dove under Tom. Before he realized what was happening the sleek silver-gray beast was carrying him along while he and the broken boat skimmed the water. He knew now he had to be dead. Nothing like this happened on earth! He didn't even feel any pain. He saw just beneath the surface of the water the two little gray ones bearing the weight of the curragh bow and realized that he felt no pain because they protected him from the friction of this very rapid swim.

He hoped they knew what they were doing. What if they were taking him further out to sea? What if he was going to be drowned after all by these playful creatures trying to take him home with them? He didn't have time to worry long. Almost as soon his wild ride began, it was over. The dolphins had carried Tom to the point where they could go no further. He could feel the seaweed tangle around his feet and knew he was very close to shore. The two little dolphins poked and prodded him until he could touch the sea floor with his toes.

Once he could stand with his head above water his new friends swam out to sea again. He watched them play and cavort in the foam, screeching and calling to him and each other. Tears of awe and gratitude flowed from his eyes as he watched their gorgeous silver bodies arcing against the setting sun. Not only had they saved his life, they were putting on the most breathtaking spectacle he had ever seen. If Tom had not already been convinced by Fr. Finnegan that God loved him; he surely would have believed these holy fish. As they disappeared from sight, Tom dragged himself out of the water and started the long walk home.

It was Charlie O'Malley himself who alerted the men of Doeega. He had been leaning on the wall behind his mother's house having a pipe and mulling over the events of the day. His ever-present glass of rye whiskey sat next to him on the wall. He felt pretty important having taken charge of so many critical details throughout the day. He had organized the search party the minute the Creahan lad had brought him the torn piece of curragh just as he had sat down for his midday meal. The rest of the afternoon had been a blur of activity between more findings along the beach and that new woman having her baby up near the strand. He still grimaced at the sight of that comely lass who stayed with her, all covered in blood and mess when he came to her door. This day had been filled with entirely too much blood and mess for Charlie. When the body of the skinny lad washed up on the beach he had just sat down to his supper. God bless his sainted mother! Never in his time as constable had he missed two meals in a row! Doeega just wasn't that exciting a place. He finally had his supper at eight o'clock and now with his pipe and the sound of Mam humming a church hymn in the kitchen, he began to relax.

His mam came out to dump the wash water just as his eye caught a most bizarre spectacle. They watched together as a creature from the sea emerged west of the village and began heading east across the beach. What manner of creature was this? His mam gasped at the sight of the half-man, half-clawed sea dweller. They watched for almost thirty minutes as the creature stumbled and fell, got up and tried again. It was clearly wounded but Charlie was not about to get close enough to help. Both he and his mother stood and stared, each wrapped in silent terror at the strange sight.

Charlie and his mother lived on the beach some distance from the village and the view from their back wall afforded them a clear vista across the entire strand. It was for this reason the townsfolk asked Charlie to be constable ten years ago when the island fishermen were having trouble with a group of blackguards from Westport pirating their curraghs and poaching their fishing spots. Charlie liked to think his chums selected him for his brawn and bravery but his mother reminded him regularly that he had neither in much abundance.

He had served them well though, enabling them to catch the thieves by simply enjoying a pipe and observing the activities on the strand from his yard. Most recently he had assigned himself the task of observing the goings on at the old Hanley house since Billy Hanley had sold it to the lad from out Castlebar way. He had seen the fellow's wife about ready to have her baby but it was the other one, the pretty redhead that he watched most of the time. Never can be too careful about folks, he always said, especially strange redheads. Many a night since they arrived Charlie had mulled over his approach to making her acquaintance. He had learned her name and that was about all he knew about her.

Dooega had its matchmaker and decent couples stepping out had to do their courting according to the proper custom over the designated time. The widower, Tommy Toohill, had inherited the role of matchmaker when old Timmy Mahany died thirty years ago. Now the town looked to old Tommy to keep the ways of courting as they always had been. Tommy had been after Charlie to let him inquire about Miss Maureen Dougherty, discreetly and without her knowledge, of course. Charlie had just last week hinted to Tommy that he might be ready to meet the young lady at that. There would be an opportunity in a few weeks at the harvest hooley and he was a patient man. But oh, how her hair glinted in the sunlight!

Now he blushed to himself at the thought of her hair all wild and damp with sweat the way it was when she opened the door to her house this afternoon. Charlie had hoped to appear cool and capable when he approached the house to warn the ladies of the accident but had been completely flummoxed by what appeared to be a crazed axe murderer flinging open the door. Charlie had never been familiar with and never hoped to contemplate the doings of women and birth. He had hardly contemplated women at all until the lovely Maureen Dougherty came on the scene. He knew that for a proper courtship Tommy would have to speak to the man of the house and he had been gone all summer.

The tongues wagged around Cora Foy's about the two women who lived alone on the strand and spoke so little of themselves. The women wondered if they were sisters or friends. That was until Lizzie Ballard, an old bat who made it her business to know everything about all the island folk and made up anything she felt she ought to know but didn't, said the fine Mrs. Phalen was not so fine atall and the young Miss Dougherty had been seen having much too good a time with a big blond lad from Westport one afternoon on the beach. Why, they were even splashing each other with water! And the other one, a married woman mind you, encouraging them when she should have been keeping herself indoors where decent women in her condition should be. That's what happens when the man of the house is not around to keep the women in line.

Most of the women suspected that Maureen was Meg's sister but Lizzie wasn't so sure. She could swear she heard the young miss call the elder one "M'Lady" one day at church. This sent a ripple of alarm through the women of Dooega. Why would a Lady be on their island in their village and wouldn't she be Church of Ireland? But then, she never receives at Mass, don't ye know! And if she was fine born, then what of her husband? Was he going to be a landlord? He did after all buy the Hanley House outright. Didn't Billy Hanley show them all the cash money himself? She did speak as one with education and didn't she turn out a fine piece of lace, now? She must have learned that somewhere!

The women were all in a dither whenever the topic of the newcomers came up in the daily review of happenings about town. The only thing that quieted them was today's terrible events and the threat that one of their own might be missing. In every little stone house in the village, suppers tonight were prefaced by tearful prayers of gratitude that the poor man washed up on the beach was none of theirs. No one, not even

Lizzie Ballard, suspected that Miss Maureen would be making her way toward town herself pleading to the Virgin to spare her own.

Now, Charlie O'Malley watched in disbelief as a sea monster, sure as he stood in his yard, plunged headlong toward the very same Miss Dougherty of his dreams.

"Charlie, get down there! Ye can't let it get t'the young lady!" his mam cried.

"Sure'n, yer th'constable," she said pushing him away from the wall.

Charlie was filled with sudden strength and purpose as he saw the evil creature waving and lunging at his sweet Miss Dougherty while she, Jesus save us, fainted dead away in the sand. He knew he had only seconds to act before the sea creature lifted her and dragged her into the briny deep. No longer was he shy about his love for the red haired maiden. He, Charlie O'Malley, of the same great bloodline of the pirate queen Grace, would save her and thereby win her hand, Tommy Toohill or no Tommy Toohill.

He tossed back his whiskey and with the courage of better men he vaulted over the stone wall and frantically blew the whistle he always wore around his neck. He flew like the wind to her side. The damp sand caused his fine brogans to slip and slide giving him more the look of a drunken gull with a broken wing than a powerful hero but little did he care. His lady fair was in grave danger and he was getting closer to her with every step. He noted with fury that other, far less worthy men, were nearing Miss Dougherty before him as the furious shriek of his official whistle filled the air. Breathless, he came to a skidding halt next to Miss Dougherty just as Rev. Trent reached down and helped her to her feet. She was as white as a sheet and trembling from head to toe as the vicar steadied her.

Seeing the Protestant vicar rescue his red haired princess almost sent Charlie into a fit but when several other men and three women arrived he had to hide his crushed ambitions and direct them to take her to his mam's house. At least he would be able to introduce her to his mam. Under the safe cover of the rescue mission, he could actually have her closer to him than he could otherwise ever hope for. He hardly noticed the fishman on the beach croaking and pleading for help. It was almost dark and the monster had fallen, exhausted, onto the sand several feet from Miss Dougherty. Three of the men were tending to him but Charlie had eyes for Miss Dougherty alone. As he watched the women steady her on her feet and half-carry her to his house, one of the men called out to him.

"Charlie, look what we have here!"

Reluctant to pull his eyes off the procession of women, he slowly turned to focus on the others. He squinted at the men as they stood around the body of the fishman and shook their heads. Coming closer he realized that this was no sea creature but a seriously injured man who looked near death. Two men had gone for a blanket to drag him up the beach but Dooley Creahan, the biggest lad in the village simply squatted down and the other men carefully laid the unconscious victim across his shoulders. Dooley lugged the man, his right arm dangling the broken bow of the curragh, up the beach to his own house nestled next door to Charlie O'Malley's.

At Creahan's they carefully laid him on two benches pushed together in front of the hearth. He was unconscious and shivering fiercely. Someone had called Cora Foy and she came immediately. Cora looked ready to drop from her long day at Meg's delivery. When she saw the injured man, Cora blessed herself and began immediately to take charge.

She ordered all but Charlie and Dooley to leave and put them to work filling the washtub and gathering rags. She herself banked the fire to warm his dusky blue limbs. She gently washed the caked blood and salt off the man's face revealing a serious gash in his forehead, the source of the vast amount of blood that glued his hair into long spikes and coated his shirt into a stiff shell across his chest. She dressed his head wound and wound a rag around his head tearing the end with her teeth and tying it fast. Satisfied that she had stanched the bleeding for now, Cora concentrated on his mangled arm.

Dooley had cut away the canvas and realized that the man's

arm was wedged between two half lengths of ribbing. This was why he could not pull it out. This half-dead stranger owed his life to the design of the boat that carried him.The Achill curragh was made with no full ribs in the hull. Instead, the whole skeleton of the boat was made from half-lengths of ribbing that overlapped. The force of the wave had rammed Tom's arm between two of these overlapping pieces and the two pieces had snapped tight around him refusing to let him go. Now, the arm was so swollen that Dooley had to cut the piece of curragh off with Finn Kelly's thatching knife. Dooley separated the two ribs and Cora gently slid the piece of the boat from the man's forearm. Dooley and Cora then washed the battered flesh. It did not appear to be broken which was a testimony to the man's strength. Together they swathed the arm in soft rags and bound it to his chest.

Cora bathed him and Charlie took the filthy red water outside and dumped it. This was not what Charlie usually did of an evening and his stomach wanted to revolt with the gory task. What he needed was a stiff belt. He decided Cora and Dooley could manage without him and went next door to see how things went with the girl. He knew he would find his bottle right where he left it. He entered his mother's house to find Miss Dougherty sitting in a straw chair by the fire sipping some of his very own whiskey from a teacup. At first he was scandalized by the sight of a woman knowing spirits. Especially his spirits! Then he saw how very pale and frightened she was and he realized that his mother had given the whiskey to her for medicinal purposes. The women were clucking around her like so many hens but they couldn't get a word out of her. Lizzie Ballard, kept prattling about the scary creature from the sea and every time she started to carry on, Miss Dougherty's eyes glazed over and she began to shake.

Charlie finally threw the babbling women out, using his most officious constable voice. He needed to talk to the young lady himself, he said. The women went out muttering and twittering about the whole event and he pulled up a creepie and sat down facing Maureen. Mrs. O'Malley started to follow her friends outdoors, calling excuses for Charlie's behavior, bein' the constable and all, but decided she was of more use to Charlie inside. After all ye could never tell how a woman might get all funny with a hero like her son the constable. She parked herself on the wooden settle along the wall and picked up a clean pannie just in case.

Charlie leaned forward. In his role as constable he was remarkably competent and self-assured. The shy suitor was well camouflaged by the abrupt and efficient officer of the law as he cleared his voice and began to speak.

"Miss Dougherty, 'twas no sea creature chasin' ye down on th'strand. 'Twas a man. Most likely washed up in the accident that took th'life of th'lad we found this afternoon. God rest his soul."

Charlie paused as he and his mother both blessed themselves.

"He's very bad off, sad to say but he is just a man and ye have nothin' more t'fear."

He straightened up and filled his pipe.

Maureen's eyes took on a searching expression as though she didn't quite believe him but wanted desperately to do so. She watched him tamp down the tobacco and followed the billows of smoke that shrouded his head as he lit it. Still she didn't speak. The terrifying incident on the beach had shocked her so that she couldn't even remember why she had gone down there in the first place. She didn't even remember about Meg and the baby! She just sipped her whiskey and watched the smoke curl around this stranger's head wondering what he wanted her to say.

It wasn't until the front door opened and Cora Foy poked her head in that Maureen showed some sign of recognition. Cora wanted to see how the girl was and was shocked to find Maureen sitting there. Seeing the older woman brought Maureen back to the present and she lurched to her feet, stumbling and almost falling. Charlie reached out to steady her but Cora already had her by the arms.

"Maureen!" she cried, "Whatever are ye doin' out here? Ye

need t'get home and rest! Mrs. Phalen will be needin' ye."

At the mention of Meg's name, everything flooded back and Maureen gasped.

"Miss Foy, I was goin' t'see if I knew th'man ye found this afternoon. Mr. Phalen was due any day, remember? I needed t'know if he was th'drowned man. I still need t'know."

She pulled away and headed for the door but Charlie blocked her path.

"Miss Dougherty, there are now two men. As I was tellin' ye the man we thought was a sea creature is bein' taken care of next door at Creahan's. Let me take ye there and see if ye can identify him."

"Of course."

Maureen wiped her clammy, damp hands on her skirt. Even as she heard herself say the words, Maureen felt a surge of lightheaded nausea and had to fight the urge to run home. Cora moved to assist her but Charlie stepped between them.

"I'm afraid this as a matter fer th'law, Miss Foy. Please allow me to escort Miss Dougherty myself."

Cora Foy stood dumbstruck, not closing her mouth until Philomena O'Malley handed her a cup of tea.

Maureen let Constable O'Malley walk her out into the cool evening but she deliberately moved very slowly. He assumed it was due to her weakened state but Maureen simply dreaded the task ahead of her. Charlie hoped she would lean against him but she made no attempt to do so. The hero of Dooegh had to satisfy himself with holding her by the lovely elbow so very evident beneath the light fabric of her blouse.

Maureen's mind raced as they approached the house next door. The man on the beach had called her by name. The only men who would do that were Duffy and Tom. One of them was lying in the house they approached. The other was dead. She could hardly bear to find out which was which. There was no way she could tell Meg if it was Tom who had died. But she could not bear it to be Duffy either. She was surprised that it mattered so much that it not be Duffy. She hadn't realized how much she cared for him. Her knees shook and she was forced to lean heavily on Mr. O'Malley's arm as they clambered over the short, rocky span between the two houses.

As they approached the door, Dooley came out to meet them and Maureen covered her mouth and let out a little scream. She was certain he meant to tell them this man had died too. Instead, he asked Charlie where Cora was. The man was burning up and he didn't know what to do.

Charlie sent Dooley over to his house and held the door for Maureen. She shook like she was the one with the fever and could hardly put one foot in front of the other as she crossed the stoop. There was no way to tell who it was in the dim house and the form on the bench was lit from behind by the hearth. Creeping closer, she saw a face badly battered and blistered from hours in the sun. The man's hair was still matted with blood and his forehead was bandaged from his crown to his eyes. But she knew who it was. The man who survived the boating accident was not Duffy McGee. She was swept by terrible grief and overwhelming relief at the same time. Once she saw that it was Tom she fell to her knees next to him and began to sob as though her heart would break.

Charlie could not fathom what to do. He could hardly leave her like this but he could hardly stay either. He leaned to reach out to her but stopped short, his hands inches from her shoulders. What was he thinking? Here was a woman who had haunted his dreams and filled his waking thoughts, sobbing over this stranger. He felt his blood run like sand to his feet as he watched his possibilities evaporate in the face of her obvious affection for the man. Here he had hoped to save her from this very creature and now she knelt weeping for his life.

A new feeling came over Charlie. He wheeled away from Maureen filled with fury. Disgust flooded him as his affection for Maureen twisted into a loathing of her and women in general. His mother was right. Even in her badgering to find a wife, she had always told him there wasn't a woman worthy of him. He was that fine a fellow. He turned to storm out the door just as Cora rushed in and took the situation in hand again. She went directly to Maureen never seeing Charlie at all.

"Maureen, who is he? Pull yerself together girl, we need ye and so does Mrs. Phalen. Is this Mr. Phalen?"

The old nurse held Maureen's shoulders and spoke directly into her face just the way Maureen had seen her speak to Meg only hours ago.

Maureen nodded and Cora gave Charlie a grave look over her shoulder.

He was still in the shadows and glad of it as his pale face filled with color at his misreading of the scene before him. Hope washed back like the tide, pushing away all the rage he had felt only seconds before. Gradually he gathered himself again and approached the two women in the circle of light. He wished he knew where Dooley Creahan kept his whiskey.

Cora straightened up and wearily assessed the situation.

"Sure'n he's one who's been kissed by a fairy t'have survived that accident but he's not out of danger yet. There's many a slip 'twixt the cup and the lip."

Philomena O'Malley nodded in agreement.

"Sure'n no truer words were ever spoken. Nothin' is certain about this man's future."

Cora shook her head gravely.

"He took in a lot of seawater and a terrible blow t'th' head. His arm is terrible bruised and his face is awful burned from th'salt and th'sun. If his injuries don't kill him he may die from th'lung fever. Ye need t'know these things and ye need t'decide how much o'this Mrs. Phalen needs t'know."

Maureen stood up and sank into a straw chair. Her voice barely audible, she spoke.

"If 'tis I must decide then I decide t'tell her nothin' till morning. If he dies then that'll be soon enough fer her t'know. She doesn't even know about the accident. If he lives and wakes up of course I'll tell her right away. If he lives th'night and does not wake up, I'll tell her after she rises and feeds her baby and has a meal herself. Then I'll bring her t'see him."

She stood up and headed for the door. She stopped and took Cora's shoulder. "Suren' yerself can't be the one t'sit up with him all night any more than I can."

Shaking her head again, Cora sighed.

"'Tis not yer worry, child. 'Tis already settled. I'll take th'first shift and see if I can't get th'fever down and then Dooley will take th'next shift so I can sleep. Philomena's a very early riser so she'll relieve Dooley around four o'clock and then I'll be back around eight. Ye can go home and sleep, Maureen. Ye'll be needed in th'mornin' t'care fer yer own."

Chapter Twenty-Two

Two days after Tom and Meg's baby was born a curragh arrived with the new bed from the grateful monsignor in Newport. Meg was barely strong enough to sit up and watched from the hearthside while Dooley Creahan and his young nephews moved the old bedstead up to Maureen's loft and set up the new bed in the downstairs bedroom. It almost filled the far end of the little room and Meg was delighted to have it. But as she crawled in and took her daughter from Maureen, sorrow overcame her and she began to weep. She was overwhelmed by the demands of her baby and fear for Tom's life. Maureen was wonderful, keeping her and the baby comfortable but the long, difficult birth had left Meg weak and sore. She tried to sleep when her daughter slept but her milk had still not fully come in and the baby fed often, in short spurts and Meg was exhausted.

Cora came in twice a day to see them and pronounced them both well but Meg was deeply discouraged. She still had not been to see Tom despite her determination to do so. She was simply too weak and when she tried to walk the short distance to the Trent's trap, she began to bleed heavily and had to be carried back to bed. It was still too soon to move Tom. He had not woken up yet and Meg was devastated at the description of his injuries. She longed to care for him herself and hold him in her arms. Yet all she could do was heal herself and feed the endless hunger of their baby.

Meg named the baby Rose because she was so beautiful and her little mouth was like a perfect rosebud. Tom and Meg had not decided on a girl's name before he left but Meg thought he would like Rose. Thinking of him lying in another bed without being able to see his beautiful daughter made her weep even harder. Maureen came in just as she finished feeding Rose and finding Meg in tears, took the baby from her, placing her in a borrowed Moses cradle. She gently covered the baby and sat down on the side of the bed next to Meg.

Meg sniffed and wiped her eyes with the back of her hand.

"I don't know what's wrong with me. I have this beautiful baby girl and yet I can't help crying."

She looked up at Maureen and sighed,

"I am so tired Maureen, I could sleep for a month."

Maureen just listened, smoothing the covers next to Meg.

"'Twill pass, M'Lady. Cora says 'tis natural and only lasts a few days until ye get your strength back. Sure'n ye had a very hard time of it and don't I know it! Ye didn't even have yer husband here! Now, there is all this with him too. Ye can't expect yerself to feel anywhere near normal atall, atall. Once Tom is better and ye're feelin' stronger things will sort themselves out. Just wait and see."

By the end of Rose's first week of life Meg was strong enough to go over to Creahan's to see Tom. Her milk had come in and she was very relieved to see Rose more satisfied. Maureen had noticed Mrs. Trent there and was relieved to see Meg responding to her gentle kindness. Mrs. Trent was happy to help and waited politely outside for Meg to come out after her visit. Catherine Creahan was not interested in inviting the Trents into her home and posted her daughter-in-law in front of the door to see to it they stayed outside. She had been away to see to her own sister's baby when all the commotion happened. Now she felt skittish about all the fuss caused by Tom being in her home when she was not. She was that proud of Dooley, mind ye, but strangers in her house without her there! She was very disappointed when Seamus Foy had fetched the doctor from Westport who had decreed Tom too severely injured to be moved to his own home. The young man had returned twice since but only shook his head with concern, still refusing to let Tom be moved.

Three weeks had passed with Meg coming every day to see Tom and what with the baby crying and people in and out of her house all day, Catherine was very weary of the arrangement. Dooley had been sleeping at his brother Con's and Tom had been placed in her bed. She, the lady of the house, had been relegated to Dooley's loft. This, of course, had set tongues to wagging something fierce. Even her belief that she would probably go straight to heaven for her sacrifices was poor compensation. Mrs. Creahan wanted them all to go so she could sprinkle the holy water over the whole place and get on with her life.

One day in late October, Dr. Callahan returned. This time he brought with him a tonic far greater than any potion for both Meg and Catherine Creahan. The two women had just emerged from Creahan's house and Meg was damp and tired from bathing Tom and freshening the bed. Caring for him was exhausting and while his appearance had improved, his condition had changed little. Meg was discouraged and frightened. She was tired of dragging Rose down the beach every day to care for Tom and wanted to bring him home but Dr. Callahan had forbidden it and hadn't been to see Tom in over a week. Meg wasn't sure how long he would lie in the house of strangers and felt terribly obliged to Catherine for forcing her to share her home with them.

Admittedly, Tom was looking much better. When Meg had first seen him a week after he was washed ashore, his face was still swollen and his bruises had turned ugly shades of brown and yellow. The gash on his head had been concealed by the bandage but the peeling burns on his face were angry and red. Now, he just looked like he was sleeping but had a lingering fever and his raspy breathing filled her with dread.

Dr. Callahan approached, talking animatedly to a

distinguished gentleman in a fine gray suit carrying a small black bag. Maureen came from the yard where she had been hanging freshly washed bedding. She plopped down a wicker basket which held both a stack of fresh towels and a wiggling Baby Rose.

Looking out over the beach she recognized who this man was from a conversation she had overheard the day before.

"That would be the other doctor, M'Lady. His name is Browne, like the inn. Cora says he's a cousin of th'marquis and Dr. Callahan told her he's th'best around here."

Meg had heard Dr. Callahan speaking to Cora at his last visit but she had never thought this highly regarded physician would actually come to see her Tom.

Dr. Browne was about twenty years older than Tom and handsome in a trim, refined way, meticulously dressed and clean-shaven. As he carefully picked his way across the stony beach, he stopped to talk with the Trents, smiling with even white teeth and reaching for Rev. Trent's outstretched hand, displayed the slender, gloved hand of a surgeon. He appeared to waste nothing in his presentation. There was not an ounce of him that wasn't absolutely necessary, not an inch of height nor a moment of extra preparation in his grooming. His boots were polished to a perfect shine, his coat tailored to his exact dimensions. He wore his tall beaver hat at the perfect angle and bowed to precisely the right degree as he tipped it in greeting to Mrs. Trent.

At the sight of Dr. Browne, Meg sighed with relief. Dr. Callahan was very young and had been quite overwhelmed by the extent of Tom's injuries. To his credit, he was a humble man and more than willing to call his mentor and friend to help him. While the two doctors exchanged pleasantries with the Trents, whom they obviously knew, Meg looked beyond them to the activities on the shore. When she saw two men unloading the curragh that brought the doctors, her eyes grew wide. The curragh was the biggest she had ever seen. There had to be twenty sheep being herded along the beach toward her house and crates of chickens and geese being placed into Dooley's cart.

Several villagers helped hoist jugs of molasses and honey up with the chickens. Sacks of potatoes, flour and other winter staples were already piled high in the cart. Just when she thought there could be nothing more, a man prodded two heifers and a bull over the side of the curragh and as a black and white border collie nipped at their hind legs, they followed obediently behind the sheep.

The man turned away from the cows and waved to Meg and Maureen. Maureen gasped but Meg didn't recognize Duffy McGee at first. Charlie O'Malley wandered onto the scene just as Maureen grinned and waved back. Charlie mistook her welcome as being for him and smiling, quickened his step toward her. Duffy saw the constable and smiled himself, shaking his head as he and the other men upturned the curragh on the sand.

Maureen was delighted to see Duffy. They had known since the day after Tom returned that the man who drowned was not Duffy and hoped that the unusually good weather they'd had since the storm would bring him over from Westport. He approached them with his strong legs striding effortless up the rock-strewn beach. Out of the corner of his eye, Duffy saw Charlie O'Malley's crestfallen face and wondered who the little fellow was.

When Duffy put his arms out to take baby Rose, Meg just couldn't help smiling. She had been doing an awful lot of crying these last few weeks and it felt wonderful to feel so happy. Her heart ached for Tom and the yearning to be a family again was overwhelming but just seeing Duffy gave her hope. The doctors had gone in to see Tom. Meg pulled herself away from the happy reunion to follow them. She wanted to hear what the older, more experienced man had to say. She found him listening to Tom's chest and nodding.

Meg greeted Dr. Callahan as they waited for Dr. Browne to finish his examination of the patient.

"Well, Mrs. Phalen, I'm encouraged," the younger doctor whispered. "His breathing is much easier than last time I was here. Your husband is one very strong man, I'll tell ye that."

Meg was surprised to hear that. She thought his breathing sounded awful. When she said as much, Dr. Callahan shook his head.

"He was gasping and tugging for air when I was here last. You could hear him breathing as you came in the door. What I hear today is much better."

Feeling Tom's forehead, he acknowledged the lingering fever but proclaimed that much improved also.

Dr. Browne was now almost finished with his assessment. He sat on the bed and took Tom's free hand. Squeezing the limp fingers he waited for a response. Nothing happened. Meg stared at the deadness of Tom's hand as it slipped back onto the bed. She could hardly form the question she needed desperately to ask.

"Doctor, when do you think he'll wake up?"

Dr. Browne said nothing, his back to Meg as he intently probed Tom's responses to his needles and a tuning fork.

Dr. Callahan turned to her and taking her by the elbow led her into the kitchen.

"Mrs. Phalen, he may wake up tomorrow or next week or he may not wake up at all."

His voice was flat and factual but Meg sensed compassion beneath the harsh words. Still, she gasped when she heard them.

"Doctor, what will I do if he doesn't wake up? What happens to him then?"

"Well, Mrs. Phalen, what say, we cross that bridge when we come to it? Your husband has shown himself to be a strong lad so I expect he just needs a good long rest. Let's just take one day at a time."

She stood up and looked levelly at the older doctor who had finished his examination and was putting his instruments back in his bag. She listened carefully as he repeated the same news she had heard from Dr. Callahan. Even if she had not already known who he was, Meg could tell by his accent that he was high born and well educated and knew that without the intercession of Dr. Callahan and Duffy McGee he would never be ministering to a peasant like Tom. But she was this peasant's wife and the daughter of an earl so she pulled herself up to her full height when she spoke.

"I want to bring him home and care for him myself. I'm quite recovered from the birth of my daughter and I have help. When can he be moved?"

Dr. Browne looked hard at Meg, carefully sizing her up. His good breeding kept him from asking but Meg's own obvious breeding begged the question of why she was Mrs. Tom Phalen. He could see, despite her tired eyes and peasant clothing that she was fair and beautiful with fine bones and aristocratic bearing. He thought she would have made a fine companion for his own son had she not been married to the dark haired stranger in the bed. Indeed, she looked so familiar he almost forgot his manners and asked where she was from. Before he could give it more thought, Maureen came in with the baby who was now howling to be fed.

"M'Lady, I know 'tis you she wants," Maureen said with a smile. "I'll be headin' home t'see t'th'livestock and supplies. Dooley will bring th'cart around t'fetch ye as soon as its unloaded. Duffy McGee is comin' with me and I'll have tea ready when ye get home."

With that, she flew out the door in pursuit of her friend.

Dr. Browne observed this exchange carefully and looked at Meg with deepening curiosity. When Meg saw his raised eyebrow, she became suddenly very frightened. What if he figured out who she was? What if he already knew and had informed her father? How could Maureen have made such a gaff? She was sure Maureen had simply slipped into her servant role because she was so excited to see Duffy she forgot. But, what consequences there could be for that one slip!

"M'Lady?" he asked, looking directly into Meg's face. Young Dr. Callahan looked on, his face a study in disbelief.

Meg flushed deeply and looked away, unable to think fast enough to lie.

"Yes. Maureen used to be my maid. But as you can see that has all changed now."

Turning to fix her gaze on the doctors' faces, she used all her breeding to convey that this conversation was over.

Dr. Browne gave a stiff bow, acknowledging that he

understood. Dr. Callahan quietly moved toward the window and looked out.

"Now Doctors, can I take my husband home? Our home is just down the strand."

Dr. Browne stroked his chin and looked again at Tom. "I suppose he could travel that far, what do you think Richard?" Dr. Callahan, relieved to be of use, nodded his agreement.

"How would you transport him Mrs. Phalen?" Dr. Browne asked.

Meg thought for a moment.

"The Trent's trap would probably be the most comfortable way. Now, if you'll excuse me, gentlemen, I must ready my husband for the move."

By mid-afternoon Tom was home in his own bed and Dr. Browne was on his way to the Trent's for supper. He would be staying there for the night while Duffy helped Meg and Maureen get the livestock settled. Dr. Callahan had a sister up in St. Dymphna's and wanted to have dinner with her and her family. He would join Dr. Browne at Trent's in the morning. They would return to Westport together. Dr. Browne had not broached the subject of Meg's background again but it was not a topic he would forget to pursue. He was too much the detective to leave this one alone. Good detective work was, after all, not unlike medicine was it? One just needed to ask the right questions to find out what was wrong with the patient.

The first night Tom was home, Meg could hardly peel her eyes from the sight of him. She sat up late into the night, the oil lamp sputtering in its sconce above the bed. She talked to him, massaging his good hand all the while. She told him all the news; about the different foods they had learned to enjoy, about the garden and the people they had met in the town. On and on she prattled about this one and that, about Maureen and Duffy and poor lovelorn Charlie. But mostly she whispered against his face about their beautiful baby girl and her tears dampened his growing beard as she promised her love for him and begged him to wake up. She took the sleeping Rose out of the cradle and placed her next to him, taking his fingers and caressing the baby's cheek with them. The size of his great big hand next to the pouting pink lips took her breath away. Finally, exhausted, she put baby Rose back in the cradle and lay down next to Tom. Sleep finally found her and she succumbed, broken hearted, until she was awakened by the wails of her hungry baby.

Tom had hovered between life and death for the first month of his daughter's life. The fever had come and gone, keeping Meg in a state of emotional bondage. One day his breathing would be raspy, the next day it would be clear, only to sound even worse the day after that. She and Maureen shared the huge task of caring for him, sitting him up and forcing water and broth into him with a dropper, cleaning up after him, washing the sheets and bedclothes almost hourly at first. Cora recruited the women of Doeega to help them with the piles of dirty linens but the ticking was another story.

When Tom had taken over her room, Mrs. Creahan had moved into the loft, taking her mattress and turning over Dooley's for Tom to use. By the end of the first week it was obvious that fresh linens were not enough and the soiled mattress itself needed to be regularly freshened with new straw.

With the help of a couple of village boys, the two women had lugged Maureen's mattress down to Creahan's house. Once Tom was home, Maureen would take her mattress back but for the time being, she would sleep with Meg in the new bed from the monsignor. Two weeks ago, Maureen had begun piecing together a second ticking in anticipation of Tom's homecoming. She gathered the sacks from the new supplies and rummaged around until she found the ones they had brought with them that summer. Piecing them together she would be able to make a ticking. Once that was stuffed with straw they could alternate the mattresses filling them with clean straw.

Maureen was almost finished sewing the last sack on the day Tom came home. She realized then that she had misjudged the number of pieces she needed and would come up short. She looked around over the hearth, under the lid of the settee and in the crevices of the loft ceiling. She found two patched canvas bags but they were two small. She was puzzled. Somehow she remembered a large tapestry bag, more like a carpetbag, that Meg had brought from the house the night they fled. Yes, it was Meg's own bag. She'd had it when they had arrived in the kitchen at GlynMor Castle. It was just the right size to finish the mattress cover but where was it? Maureen hadn't seen it since they first got on the road.

Now Maureen was on a mission. She needed to finish the mattress and she wanted that bag. Again she turned the little house upside down looking in places she knew were empty. She went outside and prowled around the outbuildings and kicked around the garden as though somehow Meg had buried it there. Finally she came to the chicken coop. This was the last possible place it could be. She scattered some feed on the rocky ground outside the coop to draw out the hens and crawled into the little stone hut. The stench of chickens and the flurry of feathers made her sneeze. Groping around she felt around the shelves for the bag. As her eyes adjusted themselves to the dark, Maureen saw something glitter in a shaft of soft sunlight coming through a crack in the back wall. Moving a stack of egg baskets, she saw a buckle glinting in the sun. She pulled out the sack raising a cloud of dust and chicken dander. Sneezing and gagging, she backed out of the little house.

Maureen hurried away from the choking cloud, scattering squawking chickens as she went. In front of the house she dropped the filthy bag and sneezed again. Taking a hankie from her apron pocket she blew her nose and wiped her eyes. Holy Mother, chickens bothered her nose!

Just as Maureen was pushing open the door, Meg called to her from the bedroom.

"Maureen, can you help me move Tom?"

Dusting her sleeves and shaking her apron, Maureen dropped the filthy bag on the ground and went in to help Meg. She'd deal with the dusty old thing later.

It was well after sunset that Maureen and Meg finished their chores and drifted out to the front yard for moment before going to bed. Maureen had gotten so involved helping Meg with Tom, she had forgotten all about finishing the new ticking. The weather was changing and the nights were actually cold. Meg still enjoyed a few moments of stargazing, a habit she had gotten into when Tom was far away from her. Wrapping her shawl around her against the chill, she looked heavenward.

"Do you think he'll ever wake up Maureen?" she asked.

Maureen wasn't quite sure how to answer and hugged herself tightly in her own shawl.

"Ah, Meg, only God in heaven knows that. But I believe He is a merciful God and knows how much ye need yer husband. I would have t'say that yes, in his own time He'll give Tom back to 't'ye."

"But in what condition? I know we have sinned grievously against my parents and against God but Tom confessed and we were married so I thought we were over that. I can't help but feel that God is still angry for what we did; that he will exact his just punishment. Then I come out here and see the thousands of twinkling stars and feel the sea breeze and I can't reconcile a God who cares for the sky and sea with a God who avenges people for loving each other, however lustful we were. The God I was raised to believe in would definitely be that way. Sin is sin and the sinner must pay. But this isn't just about me and my sin. This is about Tom and his sin and he believes in a God of forgiveness. Which God is it that keeps him from knowing his daughter and keeps me from seeing his eyes looking at me with love? It sounds more like my God than his and yet we believe there is only one! I can't understand this and I'm very angry. Is it a great sin to be angry with God? Were you, when you suffered your terrible loss ever angry with God, Maureen?"

Maureen shivered in the damp cool breeze. These were not the thoughts she entertained about God. To Maureen, God was a powerful father, the father she had never known in her own family. He cared for her but didn't really get involved. If he had, how could he ever let her suffer rape and torture for so many years with Lord Jeffrey? She loved God and needed to believe He loved her. Didn't he send Jesus to die for her? Didn't Fr. Finnegan say that Jesus died for Lord Jeffrey too?

That was so hard for Maureen to accept and so painful for

her to think about that she had shut her mind and heart to God having anything to do with her past. As far as she believed, God had only made her acquaintance after she had confessed to Fr. Finnegan herself. Whatever he had had to do with her before, he could never have known about Lord Jeffrey or he would have stopped it. Now, as Meg idly probed her thoughts, the past came back in such a flood of pain she swore she could smell the sweet stale odor of his cologne on the breeze.

Maureen gulped and started to answer Meg but no sound came out. She wanted to say that she didn't dare get angry with God and that it wouldn't do any good anyway. Instead, she made a little squeak and turned to sit on the bench kicking something in her way.

Thinking she was about to fall, Meg reached out to steady her friend.

"Maureen! You're trembling. Are you all right? You don't have to answer me. I was only thinking out loud. Forgive me. It was simply awful for me to bring up the past. How rude of me!"

"No, not atall, atall," Maureen replied, finding her voice.

"I do feel angry at times but not at God. I was always taught that God is good even if we're not. I'll admit I'm a wee bit afraid of Him. I mean, just talkin' about bein' angry with God made him put Lord Jeffrey's scent on th'breeze."

Meg put her hand to her throat.

"I smell it too! Maureen you can't believe God did that? Do you not think that maybe he's here, in the dark, waiting to pounce upon us? What else could it be? We know of no one on the island who wears that scent. It's far too dear for these people to afford. Oh, Maureen, what will we do?"

Meg's voice rose to a high squeak.

Maureen sprang from the bench and turned toward the door.

"Enough o'this palaver, before th'little people show up! Suren' tis the divil himself on th'breeze bringin' his stink t'this house! We'll talk no more of it tonight. We can't be givin' the divil more than his due."

As she reached to usher Meg inside with her she again

kicked the sack on the ground. She picked it up and shoved Meg into the dimly lit kitchen. Dropping the bag by the dresser she bolted the door.

Meg jumped when the bag hit the floor.

"What was that?"

"Oh, just a bag I need t'tear up t'finish th'mattress ticking."

Maureen lit an oil lamp.

"Listen, Meg, I'm not fer thinkin' yer father is anywhere near here. How could he get here without th'great Constable O'Malley seein' him on his night watch?"

Maureen knew full well there were any number of bays along the island where Lord Jeffrey could have come to shore unnoticed but she could not bear the thought nor could she allow Meg to become frightened and risk souring her milk. Making light of the possibility made it easier for her to dismiss the lingering scent of Lord Jeffrey's cologne.

Rose began to whimper and Meg picked her up.

"I'm sure you're right about my father."

She changed Rose and handed her to Maureen. Then she went into the bedroom to put on her nightgown muttering to herself about how strange it was, smelling her father's cologne.

By the time she returned, Rose was rooting and sniffling at Maureen's bodice looking for her next meal. Meg sat down in the wicker chair opposite Maureen and began nursing the hungry baby.

Kissing the little fingers and stroking the soft curls, Meg returned to her thoughts about God.

"I still don't understand about God, Maureen. How can he love me and let me drift along wondering if Tom will ever be well again? How can a loving God be so cruel? It makes much more sense to have a God like the one I was raised to believe in. At least you don't expect anything better of him!"

Maureen shifted uncomfortably on the three-legged creepie. She wished Meg would drop this train of thought.

"Meg, I think the answer t'yer questions can only be found in prayer. When I've had me doubts, and believe me I've had them, prayin' is the only thing that helps. That and th'Holy Mass and Communion. And when I can't think o'words t'say, I pray me Aves and let me mind wander t'the things I want t'bring t'God's attention. And when 'tis really bad, sure I don't even do that, I just hold me beads and let me guardian angel do th'talkin'."

They sat in silence then; the only sound that of the suckling baby and the distant lapping of the sea.

Both Baby Rose and Meg began to doze. Maureen shook Meg and told her to go to bed. They headed for their sleep, Meg in the big bed with her silent husband and Maureen up in her loft under the stars.

Meg put Rose in her cradle and knelt down next to the bed. The darkness helped her pretend that Tom was only sleeping. She reached for his hand and rested her face against his knuckles. Her heart was empty and she felt her soul all shriveled up inside her. No words came as she tried to pray to the God who had forsaken her. All that came to the surface of her mind was a fierce longing. She knelt at the bedside and poured forth a yearning so poignant and so bitter that she could taste it. She couldn't cry, she couldn't think, she couldn't speak to God. She could only kneel there, silent and dry-eyed like the Virgin in all the paintings looking up from the foot of the cross, watching, waiting and trying to understand.

This was how she found herself at dawn when Rose awoke, howling. She was glad to put the sweet smelling baby to her heavy breast. Climbing into bed she nestled down and Rose began to suck greedily. Meg smiled at her daughter's lusty appetite and felt a genuine peace come over her. How she wanted Tom to know this dear, lovely little child. She looked over at him sleeping soundly. Tom was damp with perspiration but his breathing was easy. She lay in the gray light and watched his profile against the little square backdrop of the window.

She and Maureen had removed the bandage from his head and the wound was healing well. All the time he was at Creahan's, Cora came by and enquired about him and the salve she had brought had done wonders for the blistered skin on his face. His arm was still swollen but the bruises had completely faded. If only he would wake up, she thought. As she shifted Rose to the other breast, she felt her eyelids get heavy and sleep overtook her. The last thing she remembered was the feel of Tom's hand brushing against her thigh. If only that were real, she thought and fell asleep.

While Meg's dreams were gentle and sad, Maureen's sleep was filled with terror. She too had fallen to her knees before she climbed into bed but her prayers were more like pleas for deliverance. She begged the Virgin and her Son for protection against Lord Jeffrey. She whispered tearfully to St. Michael and St. Patrick to protect her from the evil man that had terrorized her and robbed her of her innocence.

Once she was asleep, the scent of Lord Jeffrey's cologne plagued her dreams and filled her with deep fear. He walked in rooms lit from behind by candelabras, tall walls shrouded in shadow with stars and a huge angry moon for a ceiling. Nowhere could she see a door and in the background she could hear the sound of water rushing. He laughed and pulled her from her bed dragging her by the hair to a steep slippery riverbank. She could feel him unbuttoning her bodice and feeling around for her breast, squeezing and pinching her until she could not bear the pain.

She tried to pull away from him but he only grew bigger and darker, blocking her path. Now she could hear his hard breathing behind her as he pulled at her clothing and reached beneath her skirts tearing and grasping at her. Down, down he pulled her until she could feel the tug of the rushing water pulling at her hair. He took her face and pressed his hand against her chin forcing her head back. The water was cold on her forehead as he pressed her backward. When she felt it flow across her eyes she began to scream but no sound came out. He was trying to drown her with one hand even as he groped and clawed beneath her skirt with the other. The river was frigid and she felt her nose stinging as the cold water began to fill it.

God, save me! Mary! Jesus save me! She cried out in her dream as she fought in vain to free herself. Suddenly Lord Jeffrey released her head with a snap. He was so close to her face she could almost taste his cologne. The scent was overpowering and she began to feel faint. His loud, cruel laughter mocked her. His right hand was still up under her skirt and he was drawing something from beneath the folds. He brought it up to her face and forced her to look. It was her baby, cold and dead. She felt herself falling deeper and deeper into the water as he followed her, swirling black and formless in the dark. Down, down she fell. She could not breathe and yet she still screamed for someone to save her. She could make no sound but she could hear her baby crying, abandoned to her wicked father.

Now she was completely beneath the water and knew she was dying. He scolded her in hissing whispers that he would never let her die. She would be forever his prisoner beneath the rushing water. He grabbed her breast again and pulled it from beneath her gown. As he tried to force her to look she realized with a chill that he was pressing the baby to her breast. She felt a silent wail rip through her chest as he laughed in her face and flung the baby into the depths of the murky water.

Maureen awoke with a start and lay exhausted and drenched, her breast clenched in her hand. At first she mistook her sweat-soaked covers for the dregs of the riverbed and she flailed against them. Her chest felt like a great weight had sat upon it and she could hear her breath coming in loud gulps. She lay still for several minutes, feeling her bed, her arms, running her fingers through her damp hair and touching her face in the dark. Tenderly, she pulled her worn nightgown around her.

Finally, reassured that this had all been a terrible nightmare, Maureen sat up on the edge of her bed. Silently she stood and walked to her window. Peering through the tiny panes she saw that dawn was just breaking. How could she have dreamt this? Everything was so real! How could her mind be so cruel in its images?

She stood still in her little loft trying to sort it out. She wanted to forget the terrible dream but not until she had dispelled it from her mind. As she walked herself through it's ugly, disgusting images, Maureen calmed down. Eventually she realized that she would never be able to fall back to sleep and throwing her shawl over her shoulders she climbed down from the loft.

Perched on one of the whitewashed stone benches jutting out from the hearth, she stirred the ashes until the fire flared up and swung the crane out to hang the hob kettle for tea. The crane squeaked loudly and Maureen winced with the noise. The baby would be waking soon enough without her noisy help and she and Meg would start another round of caring for Rose and Tom.

When the kettle boiled, Maureen fixed a bracing cup of Meg's fine tea and settled in with her thoughts again. She leaned her back against the warm hearth and drew her knees up under her nightgown. How good the warm stone of the bench felt against her bare feet. She loved this house and no spot more than right here on the hearth. The Galway style of hearth, with its side benches and deep canopy over the fire was so efficient and attractive Maureen was surprised more homes didn't have a hearth like this. Why you could even sleep a small adult or child on the shelf above the canopy in a toasty little cubby of a bed. A small child. Yes, Maureen thought, involuntarily shivering despite the warmth of her perch, a small child was what she felt like since awakening from her dream. She wrapped her arms around her knees and rocked back and forth in the dark and long after her tea was gone she still dabbed at her salty, fat tears with her shawl. Just as Maureen reached for the poker to rouse the embers again, she heard Meg cry out from the bedroom.

"Maureen, Tom! Maureen you must come! No, Tom, no! Maureen hurry!"

Duffy McGee had had trouble sleeping that night too. He was torn between staying on Achill until Tom recovered and going back to the inn. He had an obligation to Dr. Browne to return him the next morning but he knew Meg and Maureen were hard pressed to finish preparing for the winter. Tom required a great deal of help; way more than two women could give him. Now, they had livestock to care for as well, not to mention a brand new baby. He could leave the inn with his cook. Rory, the brother of the would-be priest apprentice had proven to be a capable barkeep. If he could just have a week or two he could get them settled in and still be back in Westport before the worst of the weather.

He wandered along the beach in the dawn light, reluctant to disturb Charlie O'Malley whose mother had insisted he stay under their roof for the night. Mrs. O'Malley could not permit a nice Catholic boy like Duffy McGee to spend the night under the roof of a Protestant vicar, and to be sure he hadn't been invited. Charlie was not happy to share his bed with another man but he needn't have worried. Duffy simply lay down on the loft floor using his hands for a pillow beneath his head. Flat on his back, he said goodnight to Charlie and within minutes was snoring heartily.

Charlie tossed and turned, thinking of the attention Miss Dougherty had showered on this common innkeeper when he had first come ashore with the doctor. He felt morose and defiant as he lay in his bed listening to the big man from Westport snore. Charlie never snored. If he had, surely his mother would have pointed it out to him. This big omathon was never good enough for his Miss Dougherty. Why, she would never even get to sleep with him around! Intrigued by the thought of Miss Dougherty sleeping, Charlie lay awake for a long time following his thoughts. They moved from her sleeping in general to her sleeping specifically, to her red hair spread out on her pillow.

His belly felt strangely painful as he imagined himself touching that gorgeous hair as it spilled over onto his own pillow. Then he imagined his fingers traveling down her hair to her shoulder, pure and white in the moonlight. This was too much to contemplate and Charlie shut down his thoughts by pulling an imaginary black curtain over his mind. Miss

Dougherty was going to be his wife someday and no big lug from Westport was going to whisk her away from him. He was after all, the constable and a direct descendant of the great pirate queen Grace O'Malley. He would no more tarnish his image of her than he would insult her to her face. He would permit no more thoughts of Miss Dougherty sleeping. Enough thinking. It was time to sleep. When Duffy rose and went out, Charlie never stirred.

In the dawn light the strand looked like shimmering gold silk as it spread out before Duffy McGee. He turned and began to walk slowly toward Tom's house. He had thought of a way to fence in the sheep for the winter and there was a stone hut that he could convert into a manger for the two cows. Tom had wisely waited to buy himself a pig and the new chickens were already crowded into the little stone coop with the old ones. They would have plenty of fresh eggs and stewing chickens for the winter. Tom had bought two fine roosters too.

The sale of his old sow and Meg's horse had brought Tom a very good nest egg. If he recovered and the weather on the island served him well, he could be very comfortable, if not wealthy, in a few years. Owning his house outright was a tremendous plus. True, he had only had a few acres but he had his waterfront and if he couldn't stomach the sea again, he had his fishing rights to rent out.

What a fool he had been to go with that braggart boyo. Duffy cursed himself every day for not stopping them. What were they thinking? Tom was not a stupid man and even an inlander can read a stormy sky. He liked Tom and thought they could be good friends in the years to come. God, he hoped Tom would recover. He had never seen a gash like the one in Tom's head that hadn't killed the man who bore it. Duffy shook his head as he passed the place where Charlie had pointed out Tom's collapse. He knew why Tom would want to be home for his baby's birth but Duffy was a practical man. He would have been more cautious and made sure he got home alive even if he were late. But then, what did he know? He had no wife and no one was presenting him with his own child. He scowled at the thought as he approached the little house. No use starting that old argument with himself. He had made that decision long ago and that was the all of it.

Duffy turned his thoughts to the little house coming into view. Meg and Maureen had made a lovely home out of their house by the sea. Why, they even had curtains in the windows and flowers on the kitchen table where they took their meals. Most Irish people, especially the islanders, simply used a low bench for eating and no one had money for extras. The hearth was the real center of a home and the family was content to sit on the little three legged creepies and share their meal. Children were usually relegated to the floor where they not only ate their meal but found their sleep.

Most folks had their livestock in their house but Meg wouldn't hear of it. Meg was a lady after all and it was reflected in how she made her home. Duffy thought Meg was the most beautiful woman he had ever seen and Tom the luckiest man alive to have her. He had spent hours with her and Maureen while Tom was away. His feelings for Meg bordered on worship and he felt self-conscious and awkward around her. Even now alone on the beach in the dark Duffy felt his face burning at the thought of her.

She never even noticed him, not in that way. For this he was both grateful and sad. Fortunately, Maureen occupied most of his time and attention with her lively chatter and laughing face. He liked Maureen but she was way too much woman for him. He was by nature a shy man and preferred women to keep their distance and give him plenty of space. He smiled as Charlie O'Malley's face came into his mind. Yes, let Charlie have Maureen. She would do him a world of good and his mother would certainly keep her in line.

He knew why he could not stop thinking of Meg. Once when he was just a boy of seventeen, he had had a girl with eyes like hers, soft and green with feathery blond lashes. Her name was Mary, she had been his first love and he had fallen hard for her. He remembered her thick blond curls and felt a pang of sorrow every time he saw Meg's lovely hair catch the sun. He shuddered as he walked on the cold sand. The sight of Mary's tear-stained face looking back from her father's rented curragh came back to him as he listened to the lapping of the waves against the shore. The sea had sounded the same that day, slapping gently at low tide as his Mary had faded from his sight. She was off to one of the tall ships in Westport Harbor. Off to Liverpool and on to America. He vowed that day never to marry.

But, God save him, if Tom could not be the husband Meg needed he would break that vow without taking a breath. He liked Tom and felt terrible lusting after his wife. Duffy, unlike many of his friends, was a devout, churchgoing Catholic, and after losing Mary had once thought he would be a priest. To feel the way he did about Meg Phalen was a sin and he knew it. But it wasn't really lust he felt. After all, until today, he only knew her carrying Tom's baby. He could hardly lust after a woman like that. Dear, God, it would be like lusting after the Virgin Mother! He crossed himself in an effort to banish any thought of Meg in that way. No, if he felt lust, and he really didn't, he could satisfy that with any woman. Maureen was always glad to see him and he knew he could have a good time with her if he could corral her coltishness. But even her raucous welcome and her flaming hair couldn't touch him where his Mary had scorched a hole in his heart. Only Meg and only from afar dulled the pain of that loss. Ah, well, what good was it after all? Tom would recover and he would make more babies on his beautiful wife. Maureen would pine for him, Charlie would pine for Maureen and he would simply go back to the inn and draw drafts for the regulars.

The sun had glazed the beach in glistening bronze as Duffy picked his way across the stones and boulders strewn like nuggets across Tom's front yard. Long shadows reached with creeping fingers as the sun crawled up the horizon and the cool morning breeze promised a beautiful day. Duffy didn't mind being up and out so early. He was used to early hours at the inn. The least he could do for his friend were a few chores before he took Dr. Browne back to Westport.

"Meg?" Dropping the poker with a clang, Maureen darted into Tom and Meg's room just as the baby began to howl.

"Maureen, help me!" Meg cried when she saw the maid.

Maureen soon saw what was happening. Tom was sitting up in the dark struggling to free himself from some imaginary confines. Meg held baby Rose up in the air away from his groping hands.

"Here! Take Rose!"

Maureen was already at the bedside pulling the screaming baby out of danger. She set Rose safely in her cradle and went to help Meg calm Tom down. Rose just screamed and screamed as Meg and Maureen grappled with Tom who fought with a strength that was overpowering them both. Meg couldn't get near him from her side of the bed without getting struck by his flailing fists. Maureen struggled to lay him back down and both women coaxed and pleaded with him to lay back and relax, calling out his name and reassuring him that everything would be all right.

The more he fought the two women, the more Tom seemed to gain strength. The bedclothes were strewn and tangled around his feet, seeming to terrify him. Maureen tried to untangle him but she had to let go of his hands to reach them. Just as she exposed his feet she felt two strong hands take her from behind and shove her away from the bed. At this, she threw out her fist and struck the intruder as hard as she could in the face, knocking him across Tom's legs. At the same instant Tom grabbed Meg's gown tearing it down the front from her left shoulder to her waist.

Thus it was that Tom Phalen regained consciousness that day to the sound of three females screaming, and the sight of his wife nearly naked with milk pouring from her breast while his friend gaped up from his wife's lap blood dripping from his nose. When she realized he was awake, Meg stopped screaming his name and began screaming it again in almost the same breath. Tom stared with profound confusion at the spectacle before him. What Duffy McGee was doing in his wife's lap would require some serious bit of explaining but his head hurt fiercely and Duffy looked as if he were leaving anyway so Tom just lay back down and promptly fell asleep again.

By this time, Meg was hysterical, shaking Tom to wake him again. Duffy carefully extricated himself from beneath Rose's dripping breakfast and lifted Maureen from her place on the floor next to the cradle where she landed when he pushed her. Maureen gathered Rose up and handed her to Meg who put her to her breast thereby restoring calm to the room. Rose suckled contentedly, Tom snored quietly and Duffy submitted to having his bleeding stanched by the she-devil that walloped him. Meg watched over Tom as she nursed Rose. Her heart was torn between relief that Tom had regained consciousness and terror that he would not wake up again. She ran her hand across his arm and he reached out and took her fingers in his. She knew then that he merely slept and her terrible wait was over.

It wasn't until Meg had finished feeding Rose and placed her back in her cradle that the three of them realized how terribly funny the whole scene was. All Meg wanted to do was stare at Tom until he woke up again but all she could do was remember his expression when he saw the horrified Duffy McGee lying in her lap, his face covered in blood and milk. She began to laugh in the doorway to the kitchen and doubled over. Before they could speak, both Duffy and Maureen were laughing too, the blood spurting afresh from Duffy's swelling nose. The three of them stumbled breathless around the kitchen where every time they looked at each other they started roaring anew. Finally, as the sun began to fill the little house, Duffy went outside to get some eggs and the two women calmed themselves, sniffling and giggling as they prepared breakfast.

Tom awoke again around sunset. He didn't thrash and fight this time. In his mind, he simply woke up from a daylong nap. Much to everyone's relief, he did not remember any of the events of the morning. Over the next several weeks he pieced together his situation. He had all his faculties, could move all his limbs and see things clearly but he was very weak and couldn't remember anything after the crashing of the curragh. Talking fatigued him in minutes and he slurred some of his words.

Meg was concerned that he often used the wrong word in a sentence but Dr. Browne had told her to expect that. The morning Tom woke up Dr. Browne had stopped in looking for Duffy to take him back to Westport but when he heard of Tom's awakening, he stayed until the next day. Dr. Browne was very pleased with Tom's condition. Tom had lost several pounds and was still too weak to stand but Dr. Browne felt that with good food and care he should be in top shape by spring.

He knew Tom would be very frustrated if he couldn't get on his feet soon so he arranged for a young man from the village to come daily and exercise Tom's limbs and help him get out of bed once he was stronger. If the weather held, Tom would soon be able to walk along the beach.

Duffy would be back as often as weather and his work would allow, a pledge that put a smile on Maureen's face. Dr. Browne left a tonic for Meg to give Tom daily and with one arm wrapped around a hearty cold lunch prepared by Mrs. Trent he headed out to sea, Duffy at the oars, Himself the Doctor waving like the King of England until they were gone from sight.

All the advice, the exercise, the good meals prepared by Meg and Maureen and the fine salty air off the bay brought the color to Tom's cheeks in no time. Meg was thrilled to have him back and caught him gazing on her with a deepened love and admiration that stirred her soul. They had long hours of tender, wonderful conversation. He wanted to hear over and over how she had been while he was away, about her garden and her last weeks of confinement but he never asked her about her suffering, her childbirth and the agonizing days waiting for him to wake up.

It wasn't that he didn't care, he just couldn't bear to hear anything from her that wasn't good and uplifting. They had both waited so long for these days, this time, this place. Tom could hardly believe they were together here on this wild, beautiful island. He felt as though he had been given a great gift he didn't deserve. He remembered so little from the accident that he had trouble piecing together what happened. He wanted to know but he just couldn't get past the crashing of the sea and the splintering of the curragh beneath him. He woke often in the night caught in the vague remnants of a dream that he was somehow being bumped around gently. The dream left him feeling safe and serene but he could never remember what or who was bumping him.

He had other dreams too, more vivid and much less pleasant. Dark swirling images of water and rain, always ending with a blinding light and a sudden start. These dreams left him sweat-soaked and exhausted, grasping for Meg's hand next to him. Gradually the weeks turned into months and he gained strength in both his body and his mind.

Meg and Maureen fussed over him, which drove him mad but healed him quickly. The boy who had exercised his legs for him in the beginning later showed an aptitude for odd jobs, so Tom put him to work as a helping hand. But the greatest balm for his spirit was his daughter. Having her around him, watching her grow simply thrilled Tom. She was the light of his life and her antics filled their home with laughter. He never knew much about babies and was delighted at how funny she was. Often when he felt discouraged or weary of the cold rainy winter weather, he thought of the moment he first met little Rose, and the memory warmed his heart.

The evening he began his recovery, he had awakened thinking he was alone in the room. He could hear Meg and Maureen talking to Duffy McGee in the kitchen. Shadows had fallen across the bed and he could see that the sun was beginning to set. He had looked around at the walls, recognizing the picture of the Virgin Mother given to them by Connor and Brigid McGee on their wedding day. He then had detected movement near the foot of the bed. Straining to see what it was, he fell back onto the pillow, too weak to sit up.

Then he heard her. First she just rustled the blanket. Then she began to kick the side of the cradle and he could hear it creak as she set it to rocking. Then he heard her whimpering and fussing and realized with a start that he was listening to his own baby and didn't even know if it was a boy or a girl. Within seconds the whimpers turned to wails and Meg came in and lifted the baby out of the cradle. Tom watched as she cooed and whispered into this strange baby's ear, thinking that this was without a doubt the most beautiful sight he had ever beheld.

"Meg," he whispered.

She swayed back and forth humming to their child and he knew she hadn't heard him.

"Meg, Darlin'," he tried again, his voice hoarse and raspy.

Startled she swung around to see him looking up at her.

"What is it yer holdin' there, me son or me daughter?"

"Oh, Tom, this is your daughter Rose."

Meg felt shy all of a sudden as she leaned over the bed and pulled back the blanket to show Tom Rose's perfect little face.

"Rose meet your Papa. Tom, this is our sweet baby."

Meg gently set Rose in the crook of Tom's good arm. Her heart broke with tenderness as she watched his expression go from bemusement to gratitude to adoration. She felt her breath catch and her eyes fill when he spoke to her.

"Hello, Rose Phalen. 'Tis yer da yer lookin' at. And there ye are me own little baby girl. Aye, 'tis yer da. I'm yer da and ye're me own Lovie. Me own little Lovie, ye are."

Meg reached down and took Tom's other hand in hers. This time, Meg felt his grip tighten around her fingers. Meg knew then that Tom would recover. Looking at the two people she loved most in the world her heart broke again, this time with joy. Meg knew in her heart, Tom's Lovie was simply and purely the reason Tom would get well.

Chapter Twenty-Three

Lady Beverly woke early, the cool October breeze wafting across her counterpane, bearing the aroma of fresh baked bread. Mrs. Carrey always baked bread on Tuesdays and Thursdays reserving the other days for pastries and sweets and Saturdays for buns and biscuits. The smell was intoxicating and she knew she would not go back to sleep. She also knew that Reina would anticipate her arousal and be at the door in moments with a tray filled with thick warm slices of her favorite soda bread and sweet butter.

Since Meg ran away and Jeffrey never ventured from his room, life at GlynMor had become so peaceful that it bordered on boring. Lady Beverly had filled the last months with social calls, something she had not done in years. Jeffrey had driven away most of their friends and neighbors and systematically isolated her behind the high, stone walls of GlynMor Castle. When he was injured, people sent servants around with gifts of food and comforts. Lady Beverly knew human nature well enough to surmise a far greater curiosity than charity in their actions. Regardless of their reasons, she didn't mind and responded to each gesture as if it were a singular act of kindness. The servants were instructed to leak enough information to allow the neighbors to know that Lady Beverly was well and taking callers. She then issued invitations to tea and dinner to their old friends. Life took a sudden turn for the better the day she received her first guests in over five years.

Jeffrey took all his meals in his room and had left orders forbidding her to approach him. She ignored this command and stopped in his room every few days to see how he was. Her bitterness toward him had hardened to a keen hatred as the truth of his sadistic liaisons with Maureen and the other young maids surfaced but he was still her husband and she still needed to know what was happening to him. Her concern was hardly for Jeffrey himself. He hated her as much as she did him and despised their forced visits.

Beverly's hatred for Jeffrey had simmered quietly for years, soothed by her sherry and her horses. As long as Jeffrey didn't approach her for his pleasure she could abide living with him. She cared little for his friends. His gambling, whiskey and cigars were just filthy habits she chose to ignore. His violence was another story. The day he took his whip to their daughter Beverly Wynn had set her heart like stone. That act of savagery was so appalling she still had nightmares about it. Then, a few days after he was injured and Meg left she had interrogated Mrs. Carrey, under threat of dismissal, about what had been happening in her house that she did not know.

Biddy Carrey had spilled it all: the cruelty, the fear, the battered and bruised girls. Over the years she had lost count of the wounds she had salved and the tears she had dried. These were the maids Beverly had so summarily dismissed when they were found to be expecting a baby, or too sickly to meet her strict standards. These were the girls who had left her home in a steady stream of failed service. Why had no one told her? Why had Reina and Mrs. Carrey, her oldest and most trusted servants never said anything? Mrs. Carrey was astonished when Beverly said she had had no idea this was going on. She had never spoken of it because she assumed Lady Beverly was well aware of it. It wasn't her place, saints preserve her, to question her mistress.

As for the ruined girls, well, that was the way it was in service. It was a rare and very fortunate girl who found employment with a master who never made advances. And how would Mrs. Carrey know what Lord Jeffrey did in the privacy of his chambers? The memory of Maureen in Lady Meg's room naked and reeking of Lord Jeffrey's cologne made bile rise in her throat but she thought better of sharing it with Lady Beverly. And why should her ladyship expect her to be the watchdog for this household? She had always lived in the village. How was she to know what went on here at night? Who was she to judge the actions of folks such as the Wynns? Beverly had found the whole interview exhausting.

Reina was more circumspect. Her knowledge of the secret goings-on was complete but her reasons for keeping it secret had more to do with loyalty than fear. She was friend to both Jeffrey and Beverly and felt that silence on her part protected both of them. Reina casually dismissed the horror of this behavior as a necessary function of men and women since the beginning of time. Some men were satisfied with one woman. Beverly was startled at the snort of contempt with which Reina said this. Other men, despite genuine love for their wives, still sought out pleasures found only with much younger girls. This was usually to spare their wives of "bending to the task, n'est pas?" Reina was quite amused at her selection of words and simply shrugged when Lady Beverly stood up and demanded an immediate end to the interview. She wanted to hear no more of Lord Jeffrey's sinful liaisons and certainly none of Reina's philosophical posturing on his reasons.

Later that night, alone with her sherry, Beverly's thoughts had drifted back to the early years of their marriage. She hadn't done this in months and she didn't want to now but she couldn't help wondering whether Reina was right. Had Jeffrey simply pleasured himself with that Japanese servant girl to spare her when she was so sick with pregnancy? Had her refusal to give in to his rude appetites sent him into the arms of all these women?

Her own mother had been a paragon of propriety, even a bit stiff-necked. She had sometimes been stingy with her affection for her and Robert but Beverly knew her mother adored their father. She doubted her father ever turned on her mother the way Jeffrey had done. No, her father loved her mother and had always provided well for her. He had always been a gentleman and a wonderful companion to her and his children. He was strict and even harsh, if necessary, with his tenants but never did she remember him denying her mother his affection even when she was irritable with him.

Now it was Beverly's turn to shrug as she stood to bring the decanter into bed with her. What a ruination her household was! As she felt the sherry work its magic and sleep caused her to drop her empty glass on the carpet, Beverly had known that the dissolution of her household was nothing more than a new beginning for her. It was her turn to take control. For the first time since she married Jeffrey she felt truly free.

The first time Beverly saw her injured husband was in July, shortly after his fall. George and Stiller had tried to keep her out of his room and at first she didn't care. The day after she interrogated Mrs. Carrey and Reina, Lady Beverly shoved past a startled George and entered her husband's room, locking the door behind her. Jeffrey still had not regained consciousness at this time and she spent a long time examining him from head to foot. She pulled back his bedclothes and stared for several long minutes at his naked body stretched out on the crisp white sheet.

Her thoughts careened around her head as she took in the swollen purple face swathed in the thick gauze dressing. She scanned down to his narrow, white shoulders. He had always been such a slight man. It was no wonder she had found Tom Phalen's shoulders so attractive. Compared to Tom, Jeffrey looked like a schoolboy. His hairless chest showed bad bruises turning yellow and brown and his arms lay limp at his sides. But she hadn't come in to see his arms. She shivered with disgust as she forced her gaze to fall lower, past his navel to his manhood, now and forever useless for any purpose. She stood by the bed and stared, trying to figure out how this man lying before her, completely vulnerable to her wretched intentions and her spiteful thoughts, could have wielded such terror in the lives of so many innocent young girls. How many had there been over the years? She knew of dozens of young maids who had come and gone. Some stayed for less than two or three months. And what about them now? How many of them had children by this slender, pale creature before her? Was she feeding his bastards when she went into the village with the pastor's wife on Boxing Day?

The thought made her want to retch. How could he live with her? How could he live with himself? Every day he rose and went down the grand stairway into the dining room, ordered his breakfast, laughed and talked with Stiller, inspected his roses, read his mail, saddled his horse. How did his body feel doing all these normal things after spending the night tearing the soul out of some girl? How did he meet with his friends, discuss politics with the pastor or joke with the tailor after sowing his seed in a poor helpless girl and turning her out when he no longer had use for her? And he always hurt them! From Mrs. Carrey's report he burned them and bruised them and purposely hurt them so they would never want to be with a man again.

Beverly knew now what she had always suspected deep in her psyche. This was what he had done to her and now Beverly wanted to hurt him. She wanted to dismember him and carve scars into his skinny white chest. She wanted to cut off his offending member, so evil and hurtful yet now so useless and pathetic. Her tears fell freely onto her pink silk bodice and she covered her ears with her hands, pressing hard to stop the vile imaginings and wicked thoughts that pounded the inside of her head.

How had she come to this? She had always done what her mother had taught her, what men expected of her. First her father, in his benevolent control, arranged for her to marry young green-eyed Jeffrey, son of his good friend Lord Henry Wynn. Then Jeffrey, as he wooed her and played with her affection, drew her into the web of his depraved sexual appetites, a new bride, a naïve and innocent girl of seventeen. Even Tom, a man in her own service had had his way with her, wending his way through her dreams and fantasies, teasing her own appetites and then in the end stealing away like a coward in the night with her only child!

289

Where was her backbone? Her mother would never have allowed her life to become such a charade. Her mother, so formidable and so strong would have brought down this macabre arrangement before it had ever taken hold. Never in Lady Eleanor Cushing's household would there have been such evil, such decadence. Well, no more would it be so in her house either. She was in charge now and things were going to be different.

Jeffrey had terrorized her for the last time. Standing at his bedside, shaking with rage Beverly saw him for what he was. This broken cripple with half a face was never going to hurt her or anyone else again. Whatever made him go tearing down those stairs the night Meg ran away had freed her completely. Maybe he would die and she would nevermore have to lay eyes on him. On the other hand, she hoped he would wake up before that so he could suffer at his own hands. She deserved the opportunity to watch him helpless. She relished the thought of him pleading at her back as she walked away.

Beverly stood at the bedside and wept. Hot tears soaked her cheeks as she mourned the years she wasted being his obedient wife. Her shoulders shook as she sobbed out years of pent up fury and loss. How deeply she felt the loss of her youth, her innocence, her intelligence, her creativity! He had robbed her of her spirit that night on the ship from Japan. When he had stolen her self-worth from her, he had also stripped from her the ability to love and to care for others. This pale, naked animal lying in the bed before her had raped her soul. She cried for every opportunity lost to her, for her daughter now gone forever, for her friends so long rebuffed.

Finally, Beverly stood dry-eyed having emptied herself upon him. Her tears had soaked his chest and thighs; her rage spewed into his bandaged face. Finished, exhausted of all she had come to dump upon his bed, leaving the heavy boulders of her bitterness to crush the life out of him, she left him. It never even entered her mind to cover him. Let Stiller find him and know that the only one who had ever really had the right to his body had left it exposed to the contempt of his shame.

Now, several weeks after she had purged herself at Jeffrey's bedside, Beverly felt a spring in her step as she greeted the day. The high blue sky and cool breeze promised a beautiful day. Her husband had awakened a fortnight ago but she hadn't been to see him. Let him forbid her to come into his room! Beverly knew that were she to desire it, nothing would keep her from entering his bedchamber every day. She also knew that this would never happen. She chose to see him only when necessary and delighted in his inability to control any aspect of her visits.

Beverly walked out onto her balcony and inhaled the lingering scent of her waning wisteria. The horses were awake and Peter was whistling as he went about feeding them. Old Ben was ambling around slowly since he had suffered a summer cold. She worried about the old man as she listened to him coughing. Ever since Tom Phalen ran off with Meg, Ben seemed to have grown shorter and even more stooped. Beverly had never especially cared about Ben but he was an old and faithful servant and she wondered how long he would be with them.

The smell of the bread baking was making her stomach rumble. She returned to her room just as Reina entered with her breakfast tray. Thanking her, Beverly set upon her toast and jam with gusto and instructed Reina to return in twenty minutes to gown her and dress her hair. Lady Beverly was going out on this beautiful day and didn't know when she would be back.

Lord Jeffrey too, woke to the delicious aroma of baking bread on this fine October morning. He knew Stiller would be bringing him his usual hearty breakfast of bangers and eggs, piles of toasted soda bread oozing with melted butter, his three required jams and a pot of strong Turkish coffee. Jeffrey had lost a great deal of weight after his accident and his trim frame looked skinny and weak. Since he had awakened, his appetite had been ravenous. George and Stiller were both heartened to see him eat and Mrs. Carrey was more than willing to pack him full of extra eggs and puddings. Besides his three meals he demanded and received a mid- morning sweet bun and bacon and a second pot of coffee and an afternoon platter of cheese and fruit to wash down with port or stout.

He had been kept in a state of twilight sleep by large doses of laudanum for several weeks while his burns healed. He had awakened the first of October, the day after his fiftieth birthday. He was still shocked to realize his condition every time he awoke. His whole life was turned inside out. All of his power had been stripped from him. All the years spent trying to banish Beverly to her proper place beneath him had been wasted. She now ruled the house. She defied his orders and he was certain she laughed at his infirmity behind the cold indifference of her face. Were he able to escape her attention, he would have but he could only endure her barging into his rooms, ordering him about, making her own decisions and ignoring his authority over her.

That would all change once Lord Jeffrey got back on his feet. He had been examined by several physicians since his accident. None of the local men could offer much encouragement but one doctor visiting from Dublin had recommended a Dr. Browne over in Westport who specialized in serious injuries. Jeffrey had sustained critical burns and a paralyzing back injury when he fell down the servant stairs in June. Now that he was alert, his pain was often intolerable and he had continued taking laudanum around the clock. His loyal servants assumed all of his personal care and Dr. Simmons brought a nurse on his biweekly visits to change the bandages on his face. He thanked his stars for the laudanum. When George had refused to allow him a mirror he knew he must look hideous.

Reina had been able to tell him what he could not remember about that night. She had been carrying a bed warmer filled with hot coals up the back stairs and he stumbled and fell down taking her and the scalding brass pan with him. The weight of his falling body had ripped the bed warmer from her grip and sent it flying down the stairs. Jeffrey had fallen head first to the foot of the curved stairs where he became wedged across the archway leading into the kitchen. He had struck his back on the hard stone pediment and landed with the left side of his face pinned against the hot pan.

Stiller and George gathered him up and brought him to his room but they were reluctant to tell him much more. He despised Beverly and could hardly bear her presence but at least she was honest with him about Dr. Simmons' report. Dr. Simmons said that Jeffrey had broken his back and would never walk again. Nor did he have control over any of his lower bodily functions. The injuries were likely to be permanent and he would always require complete care. The pain he suffered from the burns on his face would ease. The scars would remain and he would never see out of his left eye again. His mouth would always drool from the left side and his speech would always be slurred.

He had recovered consciousness about a fortnight ago and on Monday, when Dr. Simmons had brought his esteemed colleagues to poke and prod him all over, they concurred with the dismal prognosis. He threw them all out of his room. As George prepared his laudanum, he wept like a baby from the one eye that still worked. Damn Beverly! Would she not even try to defy him and see to his health? He could count on one hand the number of times she had visited him.

He planned a trip to Westport to see this Dr. Browne. Dr. Simmons strongly discouraged travel for many reasons but Jeffrey was determined to go. No one wanted to tell him what he looked like or show him his face in a mirror. He had shouted and cursed as George gathered up all the mirrors from his room and Stiller had turned the one hanging over his dresser toward the wall. They had even removed his cheroot case and silver snuff box when George found him trying to see his reflection in them. He still had use of his hands and kept his pistols close to his side even when he was sleeping. Everyone, including George skirted the issue of his burns whenever it came up. If he intended to use the weapons on himself he had never said so and no one seemed interested in dissuading him from the thought. Damn them all! If they wanted him to end his life and relieve them all of looking at his ugly face he had no intention of doing so. He would outlive them all and see that they suffered along with him.

One thing he did brood about was his reason for tearing down the back stairs in the first place. He never used the servants' stairs. Even when he was engaging in his little games with the maids he never snuck around. He was the lord of his manor and offered no apology to anyone for his actions. What was he doing on those stairs at that hour? Why was he in such a hurry and where was he going? He pondered this question for hours and to his fury, could not remember. In fact the last thing he remembered clearly was sitting down at the table with a chap from America and a few of the local lads for a high stakes poker game down at The King and Crown. Angus had brought him home and he had vague memories of Maureen in his room. But he had Maureen in his room every night and they all blurred together. Where had she gone? He had no idea nor did he care. He wished he could take his crop to her thighs again though. Despite the deadness of his body, his mind was perfectly clear and one thing he did remember was the sight of Maureen's long, creamy-white thighs, welted and bruised by his own hand.

He spent most of his time savoring the memories of one maid or another. There had been countless nights when he sought to banish the pain of Beverly's rejection. He never saw their faces at the end. When he finally felt the dizzying rush of power that climaxed a night of torture and submission; when he had finally sated himself with the sound of begging and pleading he saw only Beverly, heard only her whimpering sobs. He always clenched his eyes tightly closed at the end.

He cared not who his victim was; to him it had to be Beverly. She was to blame for the man he had become. She was the one who deserved to beg. Was it Beverly he sought that night on the stairs? Not likely. Even if he had reason to want her, he would not have found her. Reina was the one she sent to fetch from the kitchen. Beverly was way too good for that stairwell. Send Reina to carry the scalding pan of coals. Let Reina risk life and limb on that treacherous stairway. Never mind the fact that Jeffrey had sent many a maid crawling to her room up that very same stairway, fully expecting her to show herself the next morning at the kitchen door ready for work. In the long hours of crushing boredom, he never remembered that. It was Beverly who ruled the servants and cared not for the dangers of their duties.

Now, because of her careless self-indulgence, he sat here a broken man. All because of Beverly's chill, her poor cold feet and hands, Reina had been on those stairs with that hot bed warmer. If not for Beverly, he would never have suffered this fate. If not for Beverly, he could be planning what new game he would play with Maureen tonight. Without that evil woman, his life would have been so different. How he hated her! What he wouldn't give to ruin her face the way she had ruined his.

When George returned to take the empty tray, Jeffrey was ready to plan his trip to Westport. George and Stiller were both concerned that a trip that long at this time of year could be dangerous for his Lordship and had decided to take no action until Dr. Simmons had made his call on Friday. When he saw George's hesitation, Jeffrey flew into a rage that in turn infuriated George. He went about his tasks in stony silence while his master railed curses at him and threatened all manner of disciplinary action. George was certainly not afraid of Lord Jeffrey. He knew there was no power behind the raving tirade but he was not used to taking any verbal abuse from anyone. George and Stiller had enjoyed a very privileged existence as trusted companions and confidantes of his Lordship. Like any smart house servant, they had always understood their position to be at the pleasure of their master but in a house so dominated by women, they alone had Lord Jeffrey's trust and affection.

Since the accident, though, they both had been subjected to the irrational and cruel outbursts that Jeffrey used to reserve for Beverly and the maids. In George's quiet fury, there was an element of real pain as the man he had so loyally served for most of his adult life, tore his head off like a common errand boy. As soon as he could, George hastened to the dining room where Stiller was supervising the rolling of carpets to be hung outdoors and beaten.

"His honor is at it again," he said to the butler out of the corner of his mouth.

Neither of them wanted the other servants to think they had lost any of their status in the household since his Lordship no longer stormed around barking orders at everyone else.

"Like a raving lunatic, I say. He's bloody crazy if you ask me!"

George hissed in an effort to whisper.

"Hell bent on going to Westport, he is! Do you think you can talk sense into him?"

Stiller listened with his back straight and his attention ever on the task at hand, nodding imperceptibly. Waving two houseboys out toward the kitchen with the heavy oriental carpet in tow, he finally turned to George.

"Yes, yes, I will speak with him but you know as well as I do he won't listen. Dr. Simmons is due to return in two days' time. Let him be the one to tell him he cannot go. Meanwhile, begin to prepare for a journey. At least that will keep him occupied. And by the way, her Ladyship is planning a trip also. She hasn't deigned to let us know where or for how long but Reina thinks she plans to go to Lord Cushing's on holiday."

He smiled frostily.

"Who knows? We may be lucky. She may decide to stay for Christmas. Now, there is a thought I could live with."

The two houseboys returned and Stiller waved George away this time. George started to go back upstairs. Hearing the grandfather clock in the foyer chime ten, he realized that he had not eaten today. Before Lord Jeffrey's fall, he would have denied his gut and heeded the duty at hand. Today, he found himself following the aroma of baking bread and turned away from the stairway toward the kitchen.

Chapter Twenty-Four

After the second week of working with Michael O'Boyle, the village lad assigned to his care, Tom was able to walk outside unassisted. He stood in front of his house and breathed deeply of the sea breeze. The day was balmy for so late in the season and the clouds formed great fluffy monsters across the bay. It had rained during the night and the strand was washed clean and smooth. He heard Meg come out the door and felt her arms circle his waist from behind and knew he was the luckiest man alive, to be loved and to love her as he did.

By Christmas Tom was able to make love to Meg again and by April she was carrying another child. Things were good on the island. He had planted Meg's garden and spring had arrived whisper soft and dearly welcome after the storms of winter. The island folk looked forward to the first currach from the mainland and contact with family and friends again. Everywhere there was restlessness as both land and sea woke up from winter's gray mist.

Tom had not yet been back out to sea and did not desire to go. His plan to thatch the roof had been delayed and he had much to do to repair the old out buildings and stone fences on his land. He wanted to clear the area around the house so Meg could have flowers wherever she looked and he needed to secure a place for Lovie to play.

Rose was growing so fast! He enjoyed her more every day. Now that Meg was pregnant again and feeling poorly, little Rose was lapping up fresh milk from their heifers. He had arranged to sell milk at Cora's and when he discussed it with her and Seamus they had expressed delight that Doeega would have its own dairy. They had had to depend on Billy Maher's farm up north to provide them with milk and he charged a very dear price for bringing the milk over the mountains. No one had ever been able to afford a cow in the village before and word quickly spread that Doeega was about to take a step up the social ladder now that Tom Phalen was planning a dairy farm. No one was more surprised to hear this announcement than Tom himself.

"All I did was offer to sell milk to Cora Foy!" he bellowed at Meg as she wiped gruel from Rose's chin. "Now she has me takin' on Billy Maher's business. Now there's a way to make friends. I don't even know Billy Maher and I'm slidin' his business right out from under him. And what do I know about it, Meg? I've spent my life with horses, not cows!"

"Now, Tom, it can't be that different. You bought a fine looking bull and the heifers are already carrying, so what would you expect people to think? Maybe this could be a great thing for you. You don't want to be a fisherman and that's what these folks do."

She handed him his daughter and began setting the table for breakfast.

"Meg, the whole village is dancin' in the streets for me milk and I feel I can hardly say no. Maybe I'd be Ireland's best milkman but I'd like to have some choice in the matter. To see them prancing about ye'd think the beasts were puttin' out stout not milk. I don't even like milk! Besides ye know the village likes t'clear out for the hills in the spring. It'll be like tryin' te' sell milk to a bunch of Arabs or gypsies. Ye remember, I'm sure, that cows make milk every day. What am I t'do when they're all in the hills sowin' corn and I got tinnies stacked up in me yard full of milk just waitin' t'sour? Suren' it'll be 'Tom do somethin' about' the stench then'. I'll be needin' t'buy a donkey, maybe two. Maybe half a dozen! Then I can rent my arses on the off season. There ye have it: 'Tom Phalen's Dairy and Arse Rental'. I'll have a sign made. I'll put an advertisement in the Westport paper. 'Yer Arse Is Cheaper at Tom Phalen's' or maybe, 'Tom Phalen's Arse is Cheaper t'Rent'. Or maybe 'Sign up at Browne's Inn for a ride on Tom Phalen's Arse'. I know, 'Want t'Ride a Really Big Arse? See Tom Phalen Today.' Ye know Duffy'll be glad te help out, that he would."

Meg was dissolved in laughter but continued to drive her point home.

"To the women and children, milk is more like gold than Guinness, Tom. The availability of milk locally will make this a much healthier community and you could be a rich man for it, too. And yes you could buy some donkeys and you can employ local boys to run the milk from here to the villagers. Just Sunday, Fr. O'Boyle was saying that the younger village boys would be in less trouble if they had more work to do. It would actually work well. In the spring when everyone goes to the hills to plant corn you could hire the boys to run the milk. When they all come back in the high summer to do their fishing and the boys are needed for that, get some girls or women to deliver the milk. The harvest will be the toughest time when they're all back up in the hills again. But you can deal with that then."

Maureen, coming down from her loft, joined the debate, laughing and tossing her head.

"Tom Phalen, ye'd not be complainin' about local milk if ye remembered Biddy Carrey's sweet bread puddin'. Don't tell me ye' never enjoyed it on a cold winter evening? Just to make ye' feel better I'll cook up a batch fer ye' while the weather is still cool. Just think of the sweet sultanas floating in some of that thick cream ye' skim off the top of the bucket. And think of the butter ye' can slather on yer toast! Yer own cows makin' the cream fer yer own butter! And don't ye ferget, I used to make cheese back on me uncle's farm, good enough to sell if I might be sayin' so."

"See, Tom, you could easily be a rich man if you just listen to the women around you." Meg stifled a chuckle as she saw this remark hit home.

Tom only grunted, "I'll be in the yard squeezin' the moneybags. If there's ever a sound that pains me ears it's that miserable groaning of the cows when they want to be milked. Thank God I finally learned how to properly squeeze a teat, and it taken' a woman t' show me!"

He turned to see Maureen shaking silently with laughter.

"And you! Ye'll be sayin' not a word to Duffy McGee about that when next ye see him!"

Plopping his cap on his head he left them laughing and shaking their heads.

Tom really didn't mind the thought of being a rich man. He had always disdained the idle rich who came into their money by birth. But to earn your own way, and set your own standards appealed to him very much. He wanted to give back to Meg all she had sacrificed for his love. How fitting would it be to someday go back to GlynMor and surprise them all. As if that mattered a fig now that he knew the whole truth about the night they left.

Tom walked to the byre summoned by the loud mooing of Maude, his large red poll cow. According to the lad who sold her to Tom she was of the highest sort of cow, regarded throughout Ireland (and across the sea, mind ye) for the sweetest, richest milk. He had been skeptical of the tiny, wizened dairyman but Duffy stood by him and proclaimed the cow as beautiful a redhead as he had ever seen. Tom smirked as he remembered that remark. Duffy needs spectacles fer sure if'n he can't find a redhead better lookin' than this mean tempered beast. And with wild Maureen throwing her copper locks around every time he pulled his curragh ashore! The man must be blind or daft or maybe not so daft. Maureen was a handful that old Duff may not want at the end of his arm at that.

Maude was the reason Tom wasn't sure about being a dairyman. She was a cranky beast that regularly smacked him with her tail when he wasn't paying enough attention to her comfort. He regularly had to tie her forelegs with a cowhair spancel to keep her quiet during milking. Thank God she had no horns! He'd be a dead man if she had horns.

He took the rinsed wooden pails from their hooks and rolled a couple of tinnies closer to her side. He couldn't argue with the men about Maude's milk. The cream was rich and yellow and the butter was the best he had ever had. And she produced huge quantities of the stuff. Duffy had told him that it would only get better once she calved in the spring. She was huge now so he thought she must be close to birthing. The thought terrified him though it couldn't be much different from foaling. Well, he would just have to learn now wouldn't he?

Maybe the girls were right. Maybe his fate was to be a cowman, God save him. Tom loved horses, plain and simple. He loved their smell, the feel of their withers beneath his hand as he brushed their coats. He took such pride in the sight of a beautiful roan or chestnut mare glinting in the sun. Talk about redheads! And then there was the tremendous feeling of triumph when a man lay down at night, bones aching, soaked with sweat after a day spent breaking a wild stallion. All his gifts for horse whispering and the tender way he could calm a foaling mare or a frightened colt was wasted on cattle. They were totally indifferent to his greetings and they had never been comforted by his touch, so far as he could tell. Horses were powerful, sleek and graceful. A horizon filled with charging horses was a sight to bring tears to the eyes of a grown man. Cows were heavy and temperamental and the sight of them dotting the hillside munching their cud only made a man want to go home to supper.

The least thing could sour their milk and the fairies were always after the cream for the butter. He was ignorant of the many superstitions about dairying until it was too late. He grunted to himself as he remembered the little man counting out his cash after selling him Maude. He was sure to have Tom's money stuffed safely in his pocket before spouting a list of warnings big enough to choke on. Give the fairies the thick yellow new milk after the calf was born. Beestings he called it. Beestings it was too from a foul tempered beast. This, right after Duffy tells him to save out the beestings for the best egg pancake ever to pass his lips. Then there was the May morning thing about the hag stealing the cream. Well, no hag was getting near his cow. She would see to that herself!

And then there were all the silly rituals done every May to keep the witches and fairies happy so they wouldn't be souring the milk or ruining the butter! Pouring milk on the threshold and all over the roots of a fairy thorn! Tying garlands of May flowers and primroses all over the byre, the house, even on the cow's tail! He'd be sure to do that so she could comb his hair with the stalks while she beat him with her tail on May Morning.

He dragged his creepie over to Maude's side and settled in to grab a teat. She was quieter than normal this morning and as the stream splashed into the waiting bucket, his mind wandered. He thought about the weeks following his awakening. Despite his loss of memory surrounding the accident at sea, he remembered everything he had done prior to leaving Duffy's the morning of the storm. He had saved the tidbits and details of his news like gold nuggets laying them before Meg and Maureen with childlike pleasure.

For Meg he had the terrible but reassuring news that Lord Jeffrey was now paralyzed and confined to his room with horrible scars and blindness. Ben had spoken of his injuries with both awe and dread. Ben himself had not seen the terrible face but Mrs. Carrey had gotten a glimpse of it and said it was monstrous. Of course, Stiller and George would say nothing to anyone if it killed them to keep silent but the staff had other ways of gaining knowledge. What they couldn't get first hand they had no trouble fabricating.

Tom had stayed hidden in Ben's room the first night and they had talked into the early morning. Ben said that the household had pretty much come to a stop when Lord Jeffrey got hurt and Lady Beverly hadn't even been riding at first. Then later, right before Tom came back, people started calling on her and she started going out. Ben was tremendously relieved that Tom had returned Angus. Her Ladyship had never asked for her husband's horse but now that she was out and about he had been afraid she would find out he was gone. Stiller and George too had been so busy with Lord Jeffrey's care that they hadn't even been to the stables but now, if they did come out they would see His Lordship's big stallion right in his stall where he belonged.

Tom had kept a very low profile while he was at GlynMor but he felt safe staying at his father's house. No one thought there was anyone there so no one ever came that way. He inquired about his da' at the rectory and Fr. Dunleavy gave him what little news he had. His da was still living with his brother Davey in Swinford and young Philip was back at Paulie and Anna's.

Tom had stayed about a week at his old home and bundling his few mementos into a rag sack, he said goodbye to Ben and set out to see his brother Paulie.

Tom walked the two-day trek to Paulie and Anna's, leaving before dawn one Saturday morning to avoid any curious neighbors. He walked halfway to Lough Cullin following a winding stream banked by the deep shade of willow trees. He slept on a huge stone slab that jutted out over the stream like a bed made just for him. By Sunday evening he had reached the south bank of the Lough and could see the smoke rising from Paulie's chimney. Their little mud and wattle home along the shore of the lough was as tidy as ever and he saw that Anna had planted a huge vegetable garden to supplement Paulie's fishing business. Paulie had always made a living from the lough. He farmed the water of Lough Cullin the way other men reaped the fruits of the land. Paulie loved the simple life of a fisherman and he and Anna had filled their tiny house on the lake shore with ten rowdy, free-spirited children. He could see half a dozen of them chasing and splashing after a dog who had snatched a sheet off the clothesline and dragged it into the water. Smiling, he approached the house with a spring in his step.

His brother and sister-in-law were shocked and overjoyed to see him.

"Tommy, Boyo! We thought suren' ye were dead or at the least gone from us fer good!" his brother exclaimed as he thumped him on the back. "Holy Mary, sure tis' good to see ye!"

"Why, what did ye hear?" Tom wanted to know how his

story had been spread about.

Anna piped in, her plain, round face animated with the telling, "Well, not a week after ye left, we got word from a tinker that there had been a grand fire at GlynMor. He said that Lady Meg and you had run off but Lord Jeffrey had shot yerself and set a lantern ablaze in the stable."

Her voice dropping to nearly a whisper, Anna leaned into her story.

"Then he was trapped and burnin' alive and him screamin' fer someone to have mercy and shoot him, if ye please. We heard that herself, Lady Beverly, did indeed shoot him but didn't kill him, Lord have mercy. And he's alive to this day screaming in pain to send the banshees fleeing the turrible sound of it all. The tinker said that the only part of GlynMor still standing is the wing where Lord Jeffrey lives and that herself has taken up quarters in the village and starvin' with it, for he won't allow her even a penny to live on."

Tom had listened to this amazing version of that evening and marveled at the ability of ordinary people to create such a great tale out of a simple accident.

"I hate to prove yer tinker a liar but the truth is much less a story, I fear. Ye can see meself here before ye, sound as ever I was."

He had smiled at Anna's dismay as he relayed the facts as he had lived them and as he knew them from Ben. As he finished he saw the crestfallen look on Anna's face and decided to tell her about Maureen and her baby. Even an abbreviated version of that story, without naming the poor victim, brought the look of pleasure back to Anna's face and when he swore her to secrecy, Anna purely glowed.

"Sure'n I'll be in me grave afore I ever breathe a word. Why St. Peter himself will be the first to know it from me!" she said signing herself with the cross of her rosary.

He had stayed with Paulie and Anna for a few days until Paulie could secure a wagon to take him to Swinford to see Old Thomas. Philip, who had just returned from there grudgingly agreed to take Tom. Tom was glad for the lift but really didn't want to spend the days on the road with Philip. He had never liked the boy, plain and simple.

He tried to convince Paulie that he would prefer to go alone but the neighbor who loaned them his wagon needed it back by the end of the week and Paulie pressed Tom to enjoy a long visit with Davey and Old Thomas.

"Mercy, Tom ye haven't seen Davey in years and Da' isn't gettin' any younger. Ye two are so close, give him a chance t'get a long look at ye."

Paulie looked up from the fish he was scaling.

"Tell Davey he can bring ye back here and bring Molly for a visit. He can leave the shop with Molly's brother. It would do that tattie hoker good to work for a change. Besides, Davey promised me a new set of hinges for the front door. That last bad storm we had nearly tore the old thing off."

"So, Davey's doin' well, I hope? He still likes bein' a smithy?" Tom asked later, lighting his pipe on the way to McGill's Pub for a pint.

Paulie nodded.

"Sure'n I never hear him complainin'. But then I never hear him atall, now do I with him all the way over in Swinford!" Paulie still had a way of teasing Tom that put him in his place.

Tom kept quiet. He had always had a fairly good relationship with Paulie but when he married Anna and left Tom and Old Thomas alone, Tom had felt that Paulie was somehow trying to escape. There had only been the three brothers when Clare Phalen had died giving birth to the fourth. At fourteen, Davey was the oldest and already gone as an apprentice to the blacksmith in Swinford. He was the image of his da and without a doubt their mam's favorite. After he lost his mam, he never returned to live in Clydagh Glyn. He had married Molly Quinn when he was only seventeen and never looked back. They had never had children and visited Da often in the early years but it had been a long time since he'd even spoken to Davey. It would be good to see him again.

Paulie was next in line followed eleven months later by Tom, so close in age that he was dubbed Paulie's "twin". They did look like twins when they were youths but the years had been kinder to Tom. Paulie was still fit but the black curls inherited from his mother were long gone. Lastly, there was Francis whose face Tom could hardly remember.

Why he and Paulie had always fought for first place in their da's affections Tom never did understand. Da had always been the kindest and most generous of men. But as he remembered it, Paulie had always felt that Tom was Old Thomas's favorite and when he had the chance to leave and join Anna Dunleavy's father in the fishing business, off he went. He and Anna visited often, frequently bringing food and fresh fish. The trip between the houses was only a day by mule and even shorter by curragh.

Tom shrugged at the thought that somehow Paulie thought fish caught from his lake was somehow better than the wonderful trout he and Da caught themselves right behind the house. Probably because Lord Lucan, Paulie's landlord thought so and Paulie was never late with the rent thanks to the endless supply from the deep cold lake. Da never refused a gift though and Anna was a far better cook than either Da or himself so they always ate well on those visiting days.

Finally, as they approached the pub door, Tom spoke.

"Now how is it dear brother, that ye haven't asked me about me wife?"

He relished the shock he saw on Paulie's face as he held open the door for him.

"Wife?" Paulie exclaimed. "Why ye dirty dog, and ye never tellin' me! When did ye do it, lad?"

"Along the way to Achill," Tom said as Paulie gestured to the barkeeper for two pints.

"I found a priest out near Newport and he married us good and proper. And we'll be parents afore long."

"I knew that was the case. Oh, Tommy, what a life ye've led behind that humble guise! The quiet stableman, bedding the wild-eyed heiress. And now ye can have her till death do ye part. I've heard she's a beauty too! Such a man ye've proven t'be, Boyo!"

Tom immediately bit the bait and red-faced with fury swiped

at Paulie. Paulie ducked the cuff he knew was coming, Tom sloshed his stout all over the barkeep's apron, cursing and hissing at his clumsiness. Paulie simply laughed, bowing and tipping his cap in admiration.

A deep chuckle rose from Tom's throat and pulled him back into the present. Shaking his head at the memory, he backed away from the cow, remembering Paulie's mischievous face. He stood up and poured the milk from the bucket into the big tinny and positioned himself to begin milking Aggie, the smaller cow. Aggie was a much easier animal than Maude and he rested his face against her warm side with pleasure rather than trepidation. She too bulged with her growing calf and her tan hide was smooth and soft against his cheek. He picked up his train of thought as he began rhythmically expressing the milk.

The next morning Tom and Philip had left before dawn for Swinford. Anna had packed them a hearty lunch and a fresh loaf of barm brack. She also packed the wagon full of fresh vegetables and some late pears and wild raspberries for Davey and Molly to enjoy. For Da she wrapped a sack of his favorite blackberry jam and a nice sharp cheese she had bought in Puntoon the week before. Tom loved Anna. She never forgot anyone's favorite things and was always willing to go far and wide to find them. The whole family was indebted to Paulie for marrying her and mothering ten children just like her. She had never been pretty and had grown plump over the years but her face could light up a room and no one he knew had a softer voice and sweeter manner. Tom, in the few days he had stayed with them had seen in her five daughters the same gentle kindness. Her sons were respectful and obviously devoted to her. This impressed Tom tremendously. He hoped someday he could be as proud of his own sons and daughters as Paulie and Anna deserved to be of theirs.

Tom had been especially attentive to the interchanges between Philip Carney and Julia, Paulie and Anna's third girl. Tom had never approved of Philip's devotion to Julia though he really had no reason to feel that way. Philip was only four when Paulie and Anna adopted him. He had lost both of his parents and his little sister to the fever and Paulie and Anna had twin boys the same age and was expecting again but her big heart opened to the little orphan boy and she swept him right into the circle of her love. Anna had twin girls and two more boys before Julia was born the day after Philip's tenth birthday. Julia had come so quickly Philip was the only one there to help Anna. Ever since, he had been fiercely possessive of the girl. Anna had supposed that he just missed his own little sister but Tom had seen Philip far more interested in Julia as they had grown older together.

Philip was a good lad. Anna had taught him the same as she had her own and he had plans to apprentice himself to the owner of the apothecary in Castlebar. The man was his mother's cousin and had kept in touch with Paulie and Anna over the years sending money once in awhile to see to his education. Philip had never met his cousin but now he was nineteen and it was time to go. Philip had always been gifted. He was very intelligent and ambitious. Even as a child, he had been a great help to Paulie in the fishing business. Tom shrugged. He knew he had no reason but he just didn't like him.

He decided to stop being bullheaded about it and struck up a conversation with the lad.

"Anna tells me yer plannin' to leave for Castlebar before the winter."

Philip nodded. "Me cousin Frank Connelly wants me to apprentice in his apothecary."

"Have ye a gift for the herbs, then?"

"Aye, Anna says I do. I've read some and spent time learning from Brother Michael from the abbey of St. Brendan up near Lough Conn."

Tom's brows went up.

"Lough Conn? Isn't that a stretch of the legs fer ye?"

"Well, it happens that I've been stayin' up there most winters since I was fifteen. There's plenty o'help at home and I'm not there to be feedin' then. I come back home t'help with the fishin' in June. The other boyos go off too, now that they're grown. Terry and Brian cut the turf down around Galway and

Aidan comes with me. He's the priest in the family I wager."

"Priest? Funny, Anna never said."

Tom scratched his chin.

"Though, if I had to guess which one, he's most like that. How old is he now?"

"I say about seventeen. Terry and Brian just turned nineteen in May. Liam is eighteen. No, Liam is seventeen. That makes Aidan fifteen. But he's been a priest since he learned to walk."

"How old is Julie, now?" Tom asked directly.

Philip smiled and replied, "Not old enough."

Seeing Tom's scowl, Philip straightened up and his face became serious.

"She will be ten next week."

Tom decided to continue to be direct with Philip. Sure'n wasn't he her godfather after all?

"Do you have intentions for Julie, Philip?" he asked, lighting his pipe.

"Intentions? D'ye mean do I want to marry her? Aye, I always have. It's never been a secret. But I can wait. She'll be old enough soon and by then I'll be able to provide fer her. We both know there's none other fer us. Even Auntie Anna and Uncle Paulie talk about the day. So unless she goes off and joins the sisters, as soon as I get me apothecary license she's mine!"

Tom sat puffing, the smoke from his pipe hanging heavily in the morning mist. Well, now he had his answer. His suspicions were correct. Philip had had designs on little Julie since the beginning and Paulie and Anna thought it was just fine. So then, it would have to be fine with him.

As he and Philip rode along in silence, Tom's thoughts had drifted back to Achill and his heart ached for Meg and the baby so close to arriving. The only experience he had ever had with babies was the nightmare of Maureen's dead child. He had been present for foaling countless times over the years but nothing, not even the terrible Easter morning loss of Lady Beverly's mare, Dame Mamie, and her colt ten years ago, could have prepared him for the horror of his experience with Maureen. He shuddered involuntarily against Aggie's side, remembering. The cow turned around and began to low mournfully as though she knew what he was thinking.

Maureen. What a complication she was. But at least she would be some help to Meg until he figured out what to do with her. Just before he left Clydagh Glyn, Ben had given him the latest tidbit for Maureen. Lord Jeffrey had apparently won the deed to some property in America and had put it in the pocket of his jacket the night of the accident. Ben remembered Maureen wearing a jacket of Lord Jeffrey's that night because he remembered thinking she was Lord Jeffrey himself. Ben begged Tom to find the jacket and leave Ireland and start a new life in a safe place far from all this trouble.

Tom could see his old friend's wrinkled face in his mind as he milked the last drop and lifted his face from the warm soft brown of the cow's side. Lugging the milk cans into the house, he shook his head at the amazing development of the American deed.

Months ago, the morning after he woke up, Tom had heard Maureen shriek in the kitchen.

"The bag, God save us 'tis the bag that carries the smell. Ah, Sweet Mother, 'tis the divil's own jacket inside!"

Meg came running from where she had been churning butter on the back stoop and Tom could hear the two of them carrying on about Lord Jeffrey and his smell and the jacket.

Maureen was wailing about the jacket and how it must be burned right away and Meg was trying to convince her that the piece had no power over her and to get a hold of herself. Tom could hear the two of them scuffling as Meg tried to wrest the jacket from Maureen. Maureen proved the stronger and tore out of the house with it, bent on setting it ablaze on the beach where the terrible smell of it wouldn't fill the house. Tom remembered what Ben had said to him about the deed and tried to call after them as he heard Meg go after Maureen. He could not bear to think that such a prize could go up in flames and them not even knowing it was in the pocket all the time!

He called and called but his voice was too weak. Finally he sank back on his pillow exhausted and grieved that their chance at a new life was about to be extinguished. As the smoke drifted past the window, he could smell the acrid scent of burning wool laced with the faint sweetness of cologne. Finally, the two women returned to the house and he told them about the deed. Maureen ran out to the strand and threw sand on the burning jacket until the jacket was no more than a smoky pile of charred plaid.

He heard her cry out and start to wail and thought surely the deed was destroyed. But she came running into the house still shrieking, the deed in her hand. It was singed around the margin but otherwise unharmed. As Tom and Maureen waited anxiously, Meg tried to make out the terms of the deed. It certainly looked authentic and outlined property in the state of Pennsylvania, United States of America. There was a plot of four acres. Tom thought it must be town property because a farm in the states would be much larger. They passed it back and forth until Rose began to cry and Meg tucked the deed into her apron pocket. Maureen wanted nothing to do with it. It still smelled of Lord Jeffrey's cologne and that was enough for her to let Meg have it. Meg busied herself with Rose and tried not to think of the impact this property could have on their lives. At the end of the day she took it out of her pocket and without another glance, slipped it into the top drawer of the dresser.

Now, as Tom came around the corner of the house, the smell of bacon and eggs called him to his breakfast. This life on the island was a good one. He had no desire to go to America and Meg hadn't mentioned the deed since the day they found it. Maybe Maureen would like it someday. Lord knows she's entitled to it, he thought as he opened the door.

My Tears, My Only Bread

The next chapters in Tom and Meg Phalen's life follow *A Tent for the Sun* in book two of the trilogy: *My Tears, My Only Bread*.

Tom struggles to support his growing family and sustain the life he has begun with Meg on Achill Island without compromising his integrity and identity as a son of Ireland. He bears his own conflicts as a man walking with one foot in each of two cultures.

Meg settles in as a wife and mother. Maureen finds herself caught between two men, one she loves and one whose determination to have her drives her away. The tension between Maureen and Duffy comes to a head, forcing one of them to make a life-changing decision, leaving the other to sort out the consequences.

Looming over all is the specter of The Great Potato Famine. *My Tears, My Only Bread* takes us deep into the anguish of starvation and casts a wide net, gathering characters from all political leanings and social classes. Tom and Meg watch their friends and neighbors succumb to the great hunger as their love for each other and their faith in God are sorely tried after death touches their own hearth and home. A turn of events and the love of one man save the surviving members of the Phalen family as the Great Hunger threatens to wipe out their future entirely.

The Phalen's story continues in book two with the addition of compelling characters and severe challenges to test Tom and Meg as their life together takes a sharp turn into the darkness of self-doubt and the discovery of inner depths neither had been aware they possessed. Walk this leg of the journey with them as they give birth and bury, triumph and weep, in the end finding that their faith and their love is all they truly have and all they really need.

About the Author

Mary Ellen Feron is the maiden name and pen name of Mary Ellen Zablocki, who lives in Buffalo, New York with her husband, Ed. She has two married sons, Francis and Paul. Her writing is done in her 1911 living room on a roll top desk surrounded by over fifty antique family photos spanning three centuries and two continents.

Ms. Feron began writing in high school and has primarily published essays, poetry and spiritual works. She was first published in 1985 in New Covenant Magazine followed by articles and poetry in Franciscan publications The Cord and Tau USA. Her short story, *"Sweet Gloria"* took second place in The Buffalo News first annual short story contest in 2005. Her most recently published poem, *"Night Psalm"*, can be found in Prayers from Franciscan Hearts, by Paula Pearce, SFO (St. Anthony Messenger Press, 2007)

Mary Ellen Feron presents *A Tent for the Sun* as the first novel of a trilogy. Books two and three: *My Tears, My Only Bread* and *White Dawn Rising* will be available in early 2013.

Email the author
maryzablocki@roadrunner.com
Find her on Facebook
http://www.facebook.com/mary.feronzablocki
On the Web
www.maryferonzablocki.com

Glossary of Terms

ACHILL CURRAGH: (SEE CURRAGH) ACHILL CURRAGHS WERE CONSTRUCTED WITH A SPECIFIC REINFORCEMENT IN THE HULL MADE OF OVERLAPPING RATHER THAN SINGLE RIBS. BECAUSE OF THIS, ACHILL CURRAGHS BOASTED GREATER FLEXIBILITY AND SEA-WORTHINESS DURING STORMY WEATHER

AVES: PRAYER HONORING THE VIRGIN MARY, COMMONLY RECITED USING PRAYER BEADS (ROSARY BEADS)

BANSHEE: A FEMALE SPIRIT WHOSE MOURNFUL WAILS ARE BELIEVED TO FOREWARN A FAMILY OF IMPENDING DEATH

BARM BRACK: A TEA BREAD MADE WITH BARM, A YEAST-LIKE LEAVENING MADE FROM OATMEAL JUICE

BAROUCHE: OPEN, FOUR-PASSENGER, FAIR WEATHER VEHICLE WITH HALF HOOD FOR BAD WEATHER

BASTIBLE: A COOKPOT SIMILAR TO A DUTCH OVEN NAMED FOR THE VILLAGE OF ORIGIN: BARNSTABLE, DEVON

BEESTINGS: HIGHLY VALUED YELLOW-COLORED MILK OF A COW RECENTLY CALVED

BELTANE, (FESTIVAL OF): MAY FESTIVAL FROM ANCIENT GAELIC TIMES, SURROUNDED BY SUPERSTITIONS, CELEBRATE THE SURVIVAL OF THE PEOPLE THROUGH THE HARD WINTER AND EARLY SPRING.

BLACKTHORN BROTHERHOOD: FICTIONAL LOCAL BAND OF REFORMERS

BLATHERSKYTE: ONE WHO IS FULL OF TALES, PRIMARILY UNTRUE

BOG FIR ROPES: VERY STRONG HANDMADE ROPES MADE FROM SHREDDED BOG TIMBER

BOG FIR STICKS: SMALL SCRAPS OF BOG TIMBER USED TO IGNITE FIRES

BOG TIMBER: FOSSIL OAK AND PINE OF THE BOGS, USED BY THE IRISH FOR CONSTRUCTION AFTER THE FORESTS WERE STRIPPED IN THE 1600S.

BOOLEY: SMALL STONE OUTBUILDING THAT DOT THE WESTERN IRISH LANDSCAPE BOOLEYS DATE BACK TO ANCIENT TIMES WHEN THEY WERE OFTEN USED TO HOUSE DRUIDS.

BOXTY: RAW, GRATED POTATOES MIXED WITH MILK, FLOUR AND EGGS AND BAKED ON A GRIDDLE. TRADITIONALLY SERVED ON ALL SAINTS DAY

BOYEEN: LITTLE BOY

BREAD PEEL: A WOODEN PADDLE DESIGNED TO PLACE LOAVES OF BREAD IN THE BACK OF AN OVEN

BRIAN BORU: HIGH KING OF IRELAND IN 1002-1014. POPULARLY BELIEVED TO HAVE OVERTHROWN THE VIKINGS IN THE BATTLE OF CLONTARF IN WHICH HE WAS KILLED

BROGUES (BROGANS): HEAVY SHOES WORN BY PEASANTS FOR WORKING

BROUGHAM: ORIGIN, ENGLAND 1837. ELEGANT, BOXLIKE 2 PASSENGER COACH

BUTTER-COOLER: VENTILATED, DOMED CONTAINER USED TO STORE BUTTER UNDERGROUND DURING HOT WEATHER

BYRE: A COVERED MANGER USED TO TETHER COWS AT NIGHT

CAIONE: FUNERAL DIRGE SUNG AT THE GRAVESIDE

CATHOLIC DEFENDERS: 18TH CENTURY IRISH REVOLUTIONARIES, ORIGINATING IN ARMAGH; JOINED WITH THE UNITED IRISHMEN IN A 1796 FAILED ATTACK AGAINST THE BRITISH AT BANTRY BAY

CEAD MILE FAILTE: AN IRISH GREETING LITERALLY MEANING: "A HUNDRED THOUSAND WELCOMES"

CHAMBERSTICK: A CANDLE AND HOLDER DESIGNED TO BE CARRIED TO BED

CHANGELING: A FEEBLE CHILD OF THE FAIRIES BELIEVED TO BE SWITCHED IN THE NIGHT WITH A HEALTHY NEWBORN; USED TO EXPLAIN DEFORMITIES

CHEROOT: A SLENDER CIGAR FAVORED BY THE UPPER CLASSES

CHUCHULAINN: ANCIENT, MYTHICAL IRISH WARRIOR SAID TO HAVE SLAIN "ONE HUNDRED AND THIRTY KINGS"

CLAGHAN: THE CLUSTER OF DWELLINGS BUILT TO HOUSE MEMBERS OF A CLAN IN A SPECIFIC AREA

CLAN: THE EXTENDED MEMBERS OF A FAMILY

CLARENCE CARRIAGE: A DOUBLE BROUGHAM CARRIAGE, LARGE, ELEGANT, WITH A COLLAPSIBLE HOOD, THE CLARENCE, LIKE THE BROUGHAM WAS DRAWN BY FOUR HORSES

CLYDAGH GLYN: FICTIONAL VALLEY BETWEEN THE CLYDAGH RIVER AND DERRYHICK LOUGH

COMPLINE: MONASTIC PRAYER BEFORE RETIRING

COUNTERPANE: LIGHT BEDSPREAD

CRAITHER: VAR. OF CREATURE, REFERRING TO THE DEVIL

CRANE AND HAKE (CRANE AND POT-HOOK): LONG, HINGED, IRON CRANE DESIGNED TO SWING IN AND OUT OF THE HEARTH; HAKE, A NOTCHED ROD THAT OFFERED VARYING HANGING HEIGHTS

CREEL: LARGE UTILITY BASKET, OFTEN WITH A WOVEN STRAP FOR CARRYING ON THE BACK; ALSO CALLED A PARDOG

CREEPIE: THREE LEGGED HEARTH STOOL, KNOWN FOR BEING UNABLE TO BE TIPPED

CROAGH PATRICK: MOUNTAIN WHERE ST. PATRICK IS SAID TO HAVE PRAYED AND FASTED FOR THE CONVERSION OF IRELAND

CROAGHAUN: ANCIENT QUARTZITE MOUNTAINS FORMING MUCH OF THE WESTERN SECTION OF ACHILL ISLAND

CROWBAR BRIGADE: HIRED BY LOCAL BAILIFFS TO TEAR DOWN THE HOMES OF THE EVICTED, THIS MIGRATING BAND OF THUGS WAS MUCH FEARED BY THE POOR IRISH TENANTS

CRUASACH: A DISH MADE UP OF LIMPITS AND VARIOUS SEAWEEDS, COMMONLY FOUND IN FISHING VILLAGES OF THE WEST COAST

CURRAGH: LOW, WIDE FISHING BOAT; RIBBED AND COVERED IN HIDE

DASH CHURN: HAND OPERATED BARREL AND PLUNGER STYLE CHURN

DONNEGAL LONG HOUSE: USUALLY STONE HOUSE WITH A SLOPING FLOOR (FOR EASIER CLEANING) USED TO HOUSE ANIMALS WITH THE FAMILY IN THE WINTER

DRESSER: COMMONLY KNOWN NOW AS A HUTCH; THE MOST IMPORTANT FURNITURE IN THE NINETEENTH CENTURY IRISH KITCHEN

DEMESNE: FROM "DOMAIN", THE LAND OWNED BY THE VERY WEALTHY

DEVIL: CURSE WORD COMMONLY USED INSTEAD OF DAMN

DRUID: A PAGAN PRIEST OF THE ANCIENT CELTIC TRADITION; CONVERTED BY ST. PATRICK TO BECOME THE FIRST BISHOPS OF IRELAND

DULSE: ONE OF SEVERAL KINDS OF SEAWEED HARVESTED FOR HUMAN CONSUMPTION; OTHERS INCLUDE CARRAGEEN, SLOKE, LAVER AND DULAMEN

EAR LOCKS: LONG CURLS OR THIN BRAIDS WORN IN FRONT OF THE EARS LOOSELY LOOPED; SOMETIMES FASTENED AT THE BACK OF THE HEAD.

EEL SPEAR: ANCIENT FLAT TINED, PRONGED SPEAR USED TO IMPALE EELS

FAERIES (FAIRIES): INVISIBLE CREATURES BELIEVED TO HAVE THE POWER TO INFLUENCE DAILY LIFE FOR GOOD OR ILL

FALLING LEAF TABLE: HINGED TABLE, HUNG ON A WALL, UNDER A WINDOW. HUNG FLAT WHEN NOT OPENED FOR MEALS

FARL: ONE QUARTER OF A ROUND, FLAT BREAD BAKED ON A HOT STONE

FARL TOASTERS: WROUGHT IRON RACKS OF VARYING SHAPE USED TO TOAST A SINGLE FARL

FOOD ARK (ALSO MEAL ARK): SINGLE OR DOUBLE COMPARTMENT. USED TO STORE FLOUR AND GRAIN MEAL

GAOL (JAIL): PRISON

GALWAY HEARTH: WITH TWO STONE BENCHES BUILT IN ON EITHER SIDE OF THE FIRE

GARROTE: STRANGLE; NOOSE-LIKE

GROVES KITCHENER STOVE: ONE OF THE EARLIEST CLOSED RANGES KNOWN FOR ITS VERSATILITY

HALF-DOOR: HORIZONTALLY SPLIT DOOR ALLOWING BOTH FRESH AIR AND PRIVACY

HANSOM CAB: A CLASSIC, 2 PASSENGER CAB WITH THE DRIVER'S SEAT HIGH IN THE BACK

HARNEN STAND: WROUGHT IRON STAND FOR TOASTING (HARDENING) A ROUND, FLAT LOAF OF BREAD

HAY BOGEY: HORSE OR DONKEY DRAWN CART USED TO DRAG HAY INTO STORAGE

HAYCOCKS: MOUNDS OF HAY PURPOSELY SHAPED TO WITHSTAND REGIONAL WEATHER

HEDGE SCHOOL: SECRET OUTDOOR SCHOOLS CONDUCTED IN DEFIANCE OF ENGLISH LAW, USUALLY BENEATH THE SHELTER OF HIGH ROADSIDE HEDGES

HEDGEMASTER: HIGHLY REVERED TEACHER, OFTEN RISKING HIS LIFE TO TRADITIONALLY EDUCATE IRISH CHILDREN

HOB-KETTLE: MADE OF CAST IRON OR COPPER, DESIGNED WITH POURING SPOUT

HOOKER: FISHING BOAT

HUNDRED-EYE-LAMP: PRIMITIVE, HANDLED LANTERN WITH HOLES PIERCED ALL OVER TO SHED LIGHT

JENNY LIND: SMALL HARD TOPPED BUGGY COMMONLY USED AS A CAB TO TRANSPORT 1 OR 2; NAMED FOR THE BELOVED SWEDISH SINGER

KEEPING ROOM: SMALL, MULTI-PURPOSE ROOM OFF THE KITCHEN. OFTEN USED TO GIVE BIRTH

KOHL: TRADITIONALLY USED IN THE MIDDLE EAST, EYE PAINT MADE OF SOOT OR ASH

LANDEAU: FOUR WHEELED, SPLIT HOODED CARRIAGE WITH TWO SEATS ACROSS FROM EACH OTHER, DRAWN BY TWO HORSES

LIMPITS: SMALL PLENTIFUL FISH REPUTED TO GIVE GREAT STRENGTH WHEN EATEN

LIMBO: ACCORDING TO ROMAN CATHOLIC TRADITION, PLACE WHERE UNBAPTIZED BABIES WERE ONCE BELIEVED TO GO WHEN THEY DIED

LUCIFER: NAMED FOR THE DEVIL, WOODEN MATCH REPUTED TO LIGHT WHEREVER IT WAS STRUCK

LUMPERS: LUMPY, WATERY, POOR QUALITY POTATOES

MACINTOSH: RAINCOAT

MALARKEY: LOOSE TALK

MAY MORNING: THE FIRST OF MAY; SURROUNDED WITH FOLKLORE AND SUPERSTITION

MEAT-SAFE: WOODEN BOX WITH WIRE-MESH DOOR TO KEEP FLIES OFF OF MEAT AND OTHER PERISHABLES

MICHAELMAS: SEPTEMBER 29, TRADITIONALLY THE FEAST CELEBRATED AROUND THE SLAUGHTER OF THE "BARROW PIG" THE LARGEST OF THE HERD. IT WAS COMMON TO HAVE A GOOSE ON MICHAELMAS FEAST

MOBCAP: SMALL, LACY BONNET WORN AT HOME, OFTEN TO BED

MORGAN LE FAY: POWERFUL SORCERESS OF THE KING ARTHUR LEGEND, AN ADVERSARY OF THE ROUND TABLE DUE TO HER ADULTERY WITH ONE OF THE KNIGHTS

MORNING ROBE: HOUSECOAT, USUALLY WORN BY UPPER CLASS WOMEN DURING MORNING DOMESTIC ROUTINE

MORUADH: A LEGLESS FIN-TAILED WATER NYMPH; A MERMAID

MOSES CRADLE: HOODED, BASKET-WOVEN CRADLE

MUSHA: EXPLETIVE DISMISSING SOMETHING AS NONSENSE

OATCAKE: FLAT HARD CAKES MADE OF OATS, WATER AND BUTTER, AND BAKED AND DRIED

OLLAV: TITLE OF HONOR GIVEN TO A TEACHER

OMETHON: FOOL

PACKAGE BOAT: MAIL BOAT

PALAVER: LOOSE TALK

PANNIE: CAST IRON FRY PAN

PANTECHNETHICA: FORM OF ASSEMBLY LINE MANUFACTURING DESIGNED TO PROVIDE TAILOR MADE GARMENTS IN ONE DAY

PAROXYSM: SEIZURE OF VIOLENT COUGHING

PATTONS: RAISED, OPEN PLATFORM SHOES OFTEN MADE OF IRON AND LEATHER THAT STRAPPED ONTO THE FOOT, ELEVATING THE WALKER ABOVE SLUSH AND MUD

PELISSE: FULL-CUT WOMAN'S ROBE DESIGNED FOR LEISURE WEAR OR IN HEAVIER FABRICS, AS A LIGHT COAT

PHAETON: SPORTY FOUR WHEELED CARRIAGE DRAWN BY ONE OR TWO HORSES, REPUTED TO BE VERY FAST. DRIVEN BY THE OWNER, FAVORED BY PHYSICIANS AND WOMEN

PISEOGS: LOCAL SUPERSTITIONS

POKER OVEN: DEEP BREAD OVEN REQUIRING THE USE OF A POKER TO PLACE AND RETRIEVE LOAVES

POLL COW: A RED COW REPUTED TO PRODUCE EXCEPTIONALLY GOOD MILK AND CREAM

POMATUM: A SETTING LOTION VERY SIMILAR TO MODERN HAIR GEL; MARACHEL POMATUM WAS POMATUM CONTAINING DYE, USUALLY MADE FROM HENNA

POOKA: AN ANIMAL SPIRIT WHOSE UPPER HALF WAS OF A MALE HUMAN AND WHOSE LOWER HALF WAS OF A STEED; THE POOKA IS SAID TO COME AROUND THE FIRST DAY OF NOVEMBER

POTATO BASKET: FLAT ROUND BASKET WITH A WELL IN THE CENTER FOR SALT; USED TO SERVE POTATOES AT THE TABLE

POTEEN: HOMEMADE LIQUOR; MOONSHINE, HOOCH

PRATIES: REGIONAL COLLOQUIALISM FOR POTATOES

QUAY: HARBOR, DOCKSIDE

RACING FOR THE BOTTLE: A WEDDING CUSTOM WHEREBY THE SINGLE MEN FROM BOTH SIDES RACE ON HORSEBACK FROM THE ALEHOUSE TO THE BRIDE'S HOUSE. THE FIRST TO ARRIVE WINS THE BOTTLE WHICH IS FIRST GIVEN TO THE GROOM AND THEN PASSED AROUND THE WHOLE GROUP

REEK SUNDAY: THE LAST SUNDAY IN JULY WHEN PILGRIMS COME FROM ALL OVER IRELAND TO CLIMB CROAGH PATRICK IN HONOR OF THEIR PATRON SAINT.

RETICULE: SMALL PURSE

ST. BRIGET'S CROSS: A TALISMAN MADE FROM RUSHES BELIEVED TO PROTECT A HOUSEHOLD FROM EVIL SPIRITS. ST. BRIGET, WHO WAS A COWHERD, IS AS BELOVED IN IRELAND AS ST. PATRICK. HER FEAST FALLS IN THE SPRING AND IS SURROUNDED WITH SUPERSTITIONS REGARDING LIVESTOCK

ST. DYMPHNA: LEGENDARY SAINT, THE DAUGHTER OF A 7TH. CENTURY IRISH KING, EXILED TO ACHILL FOR REFUSING TO MARRY HIM AFTER HER MOTHER DIED, SHE BUILT THE CHURCH THAT BEARS HER NAME. SHE WAS FORCED TO FLEE TO GEEL, BELGIUM WHERE SHE WAS EVENTUALLY MARTYRED. SHE IS REVERED BY CATHOLICS FOR HER INTERCESSION FOR EMOTIONAL AND MENTAL DISORDERS.

SCULLERY: SMALL AREA ADJACENT TO THE KITCHEN OF WEALTHY HOMES USED EXCLUSIVELY FOR WASHING DISHES

SETTLE BED: WOODEN BENCH BY DAY; OPENED UP TO BECOME A BED AT NIGHT

SHITE: EUPHEMISTIC PRONUNCIATION OF A COMMON EXPLETIVE

SLANE: NARROW SHOVEL USED TO HARVEST TURF

SLIDE-CAR: HORSE OR PONY PULLED CART MADE OF TWO WOODEN POLES CONNECTED BY WOODEN RUNNERS FORMING A PLATFORM FOR BUNDLES

SLIP-BOTTOM CREEL (SLIP-CREEL): BASKET WITH A BOTTOM THAT OPENED FOR DUMPING THE LOAD

SLOKE: A VARIETY OF SEAWEED

SOOT-HOUSE: SMALL HUTS MADE OF SOD AND STONE DESIGNED TO BURN TURF ALL WINTER TO FORM ASH FOR FERTILIZING THE SPRING POTATO CROP

SOUTANE: (FR.) PRIEST'S BLACK CASSOCK

SPALPEEN: MIGRANT WORKERS WHO FOLLOWED THE HARVEST OR HIRED ON TO HERD LIVESTOCK. OFTEN USED AS A DEROGATORY TERM BY THE UPPER CLASSES TO DESCRIBE A YOUNG MAN OF QUESTIONABLE CHARACTER

SPANCEL: ROPE USED TO TIE THE LEGS OF COWS FOR SAFE MILKING

SPONC: POOR MAN'S TOBACCO MADE OF HERBS AND GRASSES

STONE: WEIGHT OR MASS EQUAL TO 14 POUNDS?

STORM LANTERN: CLOSED GLOBED LAMP FOR OUTDOOR USE

STRAW BOBBINS: PEGS USED TO SECURE THATCH ON THE ROOF

SULTANA: DRIED FRUIT COMPARABLE TO A RAISIN

SWISS COTTAGE: FANCIFULLY DESIGNED COTTAGE USED BY THE VERY WEALTHY AS A SUMMER RETREAT. THESE RETREATS WERE FOUND IN IRELAND AS WELL AS CONTINENTAL EUROPE

TATTIES: REGIONAL COLLOQUIALISM FOR POTATOES; SOMETIMES POTATO CAKES

TATTIE-HOKERS: DEROGATORY TERM FOR MIGRANT POTATO PICKERS

TENANTRY: TENANTS

TESTER BED: DESIGNED WITH CANOPY BUT NO SIDES, LOW ENOUGH TO BE COMMONLY USED IN A LOFT

TIN OVEN: A BASIC BOX OVEN MADE OF TIN THAT WAS SET IN THE FRONT OF AN OPEN HEARTH

TINNIE: TIN MILK CAN

TOWNLAND: AREA OF AROUND 325 ACRES OR ½ SQUARE MILE WITH ABOUT 50 INHABITANTS. THE SIZE OF A TOWNLAND IS BASED ON THE FERTILITY OF THE LAND RATHER THAN ACTUAL ACREAGE AND A TOWNLAND NAME IS A LEGAL TITLE CHANGEABLE ONLY BY AN ACT OF PARLIAMENT

TRUCKLE BED: A RAISED BED OFTEN USED IN AREAS OF FLOODING. COMMONLY WHEELED UNDER A CONVENTIONAL BED FOR STORAGE

TURF: FUEL DUG FROM THE BOGS OF IRELAND. CALLED PEAT IN THE NORTHERN COUNTIES

TURF-CREEL: A BASKET USED FOR CARRYING TURF, OFTEN WITH A SLIP BOTTOM FOR EASE OF UNLOADING

TURF-CUTTER: ONE OF THE LOWEST CLASSES OF IRISH PEASANTRY, TURF-CUTTERS LIVED IN THE BOGS THEY HARVESTED, CARVING CAVES IN THE WALLS OF THE BOGS AND LIVING BELOW GROUND

UNDERTAKER: AN ADMINISTRATIVE ASSISTANT TO WEALTHY LANDED GENTRY. AN OVERSEER OF AFFAIRS

WATTLE AND DAUB: BUILDING MATERIALS MOST COMMON IN THE MIDLANDS. WALLS WERE OUTLINED WITH WATTLE, (INTERLACED RODS AND TWIGS) AND COATED WITH DAUB (MUDDY CLAY)

WORKHOUSE: A POORHOUSE WHERE PAUPERS WERE TO BE HOUSED AND FED UNDER THE POOR LAW ACT OF 1838

YELLOW MAN: A HONEYCOMBED, STICKY TOFFEE, SERVED HARD AND BROKEN INTO CHUNKS WITH A HAMMER; POSSIBLY THE ORIGIN OF THE CHOCOLATE COVERED TREAT CALLED SPONGE CANDY

Made in the USA
Charleston, SC
30 August 2013